Still Shot

Still Shot

JERRY KENNEALY

THOMAS DUNNE BOOKS
ST. MARTIN'S MINOTAUR ☙ NEW YORK

This is a work of fiction. All of the characters, organizations, and events portrayed in this novel are either products of the author's imagination or are used fictitiously.

THOMAS DUNNE BOOKS.
An imprint of St. Martin's Press.

www.thomasdunnebooks.com
www.minotaurbooks.com

Library of Congress Cataloging-in-Publication Data

Kennealy, Jerry.
    Still shot / Jerry Kennealy.—1st ed.
        p.   cm.
    ISBN-13: 978-0-312-37091-6
    ISBN-10: 0-312-37091-1
    I. Title.

PS3561.E4246S75   2008
813'.54—dc22

                                                    2007051735

First Edition: April 2008

10   9   8   7   6   5   4   3   2   1

*For the latest addition to the Kennealy clan,
my beautiful granddaughter Natalie*

Acknowledgments

My sincere thanks to my editor,
Ruth Cavin, without whom . . .

Still Shot

One

*S*he wants to see you, Carroll, ten o'clock this morning."

The voice on the phone belonged to Darlene, the receptionist at my place of employment, the *San Francisco Bulletin*. "She" was Katherine "the Great" Parkham, the *Bulletin*'s editor in chief. Parkham had stormed in less than a year ago from the New York City–based conglomerate that owned the paper, with an advertised agenda of either selling or burying the *Bulletin*. So far, neither had happened, but we were all on the edge of our ergonomic swivel chairs, waiting for the other shoe to drop.

"Did the Great say what it was all about, Darlene?" I asked, glancing at the nightstand clock. It was 8:45 A.M.

"No. But she didn't sound to be in the best of moods. I wouldn't be late if I were you, Carroll."

I said "Thanks," rolled out of bed, and jumped into the shower. I work in the paper's entertainment section and have the enviable task of reviewing movies and plays. A job to die for, really. Unfortunately, with the low salary I'm being paid, that's a real possibility. Still, it is a job I love dearly and would hate to lose.

I shaved and dressed in record time and was in the *Bulletin*'s parking lot by 9:45. One of the few perks is a designated parking spot; however, this morning someone had angled their shiny black Jaguar sedan into two spots, leaving no room for even a tiny vehicle like my Mini

Cooper. I had to park in the garage across the street, which charged twelve bucks for four hours.

I walked back to the Jaguar and took a business card from my wallet. I was thinking of writing something nasty, but for all I knew, the car belonged to one of Katherine Parkham's friends, so I just printed a modified line of Bogart's from *Casablanca* on the back of the card: "Of all the spots in all the towns in all the world, why did you have to take mine?"

I slipped the card under the Jag's windshield wiper. When I finally made it to my cubicle, a FedEx deliveryman showed up. He was new to me: stick-thin, with bad posture and a worse attitude.

"I got a package for Carroll Quint," he said in a hostile voice.

"Thanks," I said, reaching out for a box the size of an unabridged dictionary.

He jerked it back. "No. Ms. Quint has to sign for it."

"I'm Carroll Quint," I told him, trying to keep the exasperation out of my voice. This was a situation that happened to me at least once a week, and all because my mother, whom I love dearly despite the fact that she decided to name her one and only child Carroll simply because it means "champion" in Gaelic. What it meant to me was a childhood filled with taunts and teases. Since I'd grown up in the rough-and-tumble Mission District of the city, it also meant a lot of fistfights with local toughs who thought that a skinny little guy who wore glasses and had a girl's name was an easy target.

It hadn't been quite as bad as the Johnny Cash classic song "A Boy Named Sue," but it came close.

"Jeeez," the FedEx guy said, handing me the box. "I read your reviews, and I always thought you were a broad."

I scribbled my name on his electronic order pad and opened the package. It was a press release for a new animated movie about a penguin that somehow ends up in New York City on Christmas day. There was a DVD, a slick twenty-page brochure, three figurines of cute little penguins, a small box of Godiva chocolates, and an invitation to the press-only premiere, which included a premovie supper with champagne

2

and caviar—clever little bribes to woo a favorable review. Since I bribed easily, I marked the date on my calendar with a big red *X*.

Max Maslin, the editor of the entertainment section, leaned into my cubicle and gave me a wide smile and a two-thumbs-up gesture. Max was a short, pudgy guy with a rubicund nose of the type they like to show on Santa Claus when he's home relaxing after his once-a-year gig. Max favored tweed suits and checkered shirts, mostly to hide the small holes caused by the bits of red-hot tobacco that burst from his battered Dunhill pipe.

"Nice piece on the Denzel Washington flick," Max said. His mouth turned down a bit and he coughed into his hand before adding, "The Great wants to see you."

"I know. Is there a problem?"

"Not that I'm aware of. Good luck, Carroll."

Parkham had been remote and even a bit hostile to the paper's staff at first, but she was beginning to thaw, to the point where she had lunch with underlings such as Max and me every few weeks. Still, a summons to her office was something to be concerned about. Just last week, she'd fired two sportswriters and the Washington D.C.–based political reporter.

Her office was on the building's top floor, with a view looking out over the bay. It looked much the same as it had when her genial but slipshod predecessor, Boyd Wilson, ran the paper: oak-paneled walls dotted with oil paintings of majestic sailing ships battling monstrous waves; old, but comfortable cracked-leather chairs, a dark black-and-maroon rug of the type you see in the lobbies of expensive hotels, a massive coffin-shaped walnut desk cluttered with phones, computers, a rosewood humidor, and a crystal ashtray in the shape of a horseshoe.

Her one personal addition was a black-on-white abstract painting, which to me looked like a skid mark on snow. I'd learned recently that it was an original by Franz Kline and was worth a small fortune—to someone with a large fortune.

"Come in," Parkham hollered when I knocked on her door.

She was hunched over a telescope, looking out in the direction of Alcatraz Island.

"Help yourself to coffee," she said without taking her eye from the telescope.

I heaved a silent sigh of relief. If Parkham was going to can me, there would be a poignant little speech along with the coffee: "Sorry, we're letting you go. Good luck" was her blunt way of dismissal, according to those who had received the ax.

I poured myself a cup of coffee from the bullet-shaped thermos on her desk and risked spearing a Danish butter cookie from a small plate of pastries.

"I hear you're a hotshot poker player, Quint," she said, still focusing on the bay. "No one here at the paper will play with you anymore. Do you cheat?"

"No," I replied honestly. To win a few dollars from the likes of Max Maslin and the poker regulars from the sports section, one didn't have to cheat. One simply had to be reasonably sober and know the rules of the game.

Parkham straightened up, put her hands on her hips, and stretched her back. She was a tall, broad-shouldered woman with wedge-cut brown hair sprinkled with gray. Her face was angular, with high cheekbones; her eyes chocolate brown. No one would call her pretty or beautiful, but she was damn good-looking. Think Katharine Hepburn in her prime, six inches taller and with forty more pounds. She was wearing a dark brown pantsuit and a cantaloupe-colored blouse. The single-stone diamond ring on the finger of her right hand had to weigh in at four karats.

"You play poker in the local card houses and on the Web, I'm told," she said.

I wondered who the teller was. "Yes, once in awhile. It's not a problem."

She walked over to her desk and sat down. "It's only a problem when you lose, Quint. Where did you learn to play poker?"

"My uncle is a professional gambler," I told her. Uncle Nick, my mother's younger brother, is more than that. A nice way to describe him would be as my mother does, a "scoundrel." My father is more blunt: "He's a crook." Dad calls Nick "Uncle Crime" because Crime doesn't pay—not for food, lodging, or just about anything else.

When I was a kid, he would come and stay with us for weeks at a time, and I'd pester him to teach me his dazzling array of sleight-of-hand card tricks.

"Could you cheat if you had to?" Parkham asked.

"Why would I want to do that?"

Parkham waved me to a chair. "Sit. This is totally off the record. I'm looking for someone who could spot a cheater in a poker game. Are you up to that?"

I sipped coffee and got comfortable in the old leather chair. "What kind of game are we talking about? Are there professionals at the table? Because if that's the case—"

"No pros, just some successful businesspeople." She leaned back and steepled her fingers in front of her face. "Smart, educated, very successful. I'm one of them."

"Who's the cheat?" I asked.

Parkham pursed her lips and blew a stream of air at the ceiling as if it were smoke from one of her cigars. "I'm not *positive* he's cheating, but he couldn't be that lucky. No one could."

"Are we talking about a lot of money?" I asked, stretching out a hand for another cookie.

"He's walked away with somewhere between ten and twenty thousand dollars from each of the last three games."

It was my turn to blow air through my lips. It came out as a loud whistle. "That's fairly high stakes for an amateur game."

"Everyone at the table can afford the losses." She leaned forward and slammed the heel of her hand on the desk. "But I don't like to lose, Quint. I especially don't like to be cheated out of my money."

"You should really get someone with more expertise than I have, boss. I could ask around—"

"You ask no one, Quint. One word of our conversation leaks out and you're toast. Now, can you help me or not?"

"Tell me more about the game. What kind of poker are we talking about? Stud? Texas hold 'em? Is there a dedicated dealer, or do you all take turns?"

"Dealer's choice," she said. "We take turns with the cards. There are four regular players. Charlie joined the group a couple of months ago. He makes five. Most of us deal Texas hold 'em; he usually calls for seven-card stud."

Finally a name was coming out. "Charlie?"

"Charles Talbot," Parkham said with a grimace.

The name surprised me. Talbot was a true merchant of menace; a Scotsman who ran banks, insurance companies, and, for a time, a movie studio in Hollywood. In fact, as an aspiring young actress, my mother had appeared in a few movies made on his back lot. Back then, there had been rumors about his having been tangled up with the local mob, and throwing orgies at his Beverly Hills mansion. He'd returned to England some thirty years ago, and had been knighted by the queen. He was now back in the States, living in nearby Napa, in the midst of the wine country.

"Sir Charles Talbot?" I said. "Why in the name of—"

"No. Not the old man. His son, Charlie. Most people call him 'Junior.'" She pulled out a drawer, withdrew a pack of playing cards, and slid them across the desk to me. "Can you tell if they're marked?"

I riffed the cards, then spread them across the desk. The deck was a typical Bee brand, with countless tiny red-and-white diamonds all over them. There really aren't that many ways to mark a deck of cards: blocking out one or more of the diamonds with white-on-white ink; shading the red diamonds—daubing, or tinting, them a slight shade darker; shaving the edges; or "sand work," where the cheater uses a small piece of sandpaper to file off a tiny part of the pattern on the card he wants to mark.

You can buy a marked deck of cards at any magic shop, or on the Web, but they're very obvious once you know what to look for, and they are used primarily in magic acts, not serious card games.

"Does Talbot wear glasses?" I asked. Many poker players don sunglasses to conceal "tells" from other players. Movies and novels often come up with plots where one player wears special glasses that allow him to see marks on cards, but I've never heard of it happening in an actual game.

"No glasses, and he plays in his shirtsleeves. I've watched him carefully."

I shuffled the cards a few more times. "These look okay to me. Does Talbot bring the cards to the game?"

"No. The game moves from house to house. The host supplies the cards, always a brand-new deck, and we change the deck every couple of hours."

I dealt out a hand of five cards, facedown, to both of us. "*How* does he win? Steadily throughout the game? Or does he haul in the big pots?"

"A few big pots—really big pots."

"Is he always dealing when he wins?"

Parkham leaned forward and opened the rosewood cigar humidor on the corner of the desk. She paused for a moment, then slammed the lid shut. "No. It doesn't seem to matter who's dealing the cards. Why is he cheating? His family is loaded. Priceless selections from his father's private art collection will be on display at the de Young Museum next week."

I knew about the museum exhibit, and was hoping that Terry Greco, the *Bulletin*'s art critic, would be able to wrangle an invitation for me. She had been working hard on the project for the last couple of weeks, which was one of the reasons I hadn't been seeing much of her lately.

"Maybe Daddy has cut off Junior's allowance."

Parkham twisted her ring around so that the diamond faced inward. "I doubt it."

"Why don't you just come right out and tell him you think he's had more than his share of luck?" I suggested.

She gave me one of the withering stares that she was becoming famous for around the office. "Because I can't. This is not to be repeated to anyone, understood?"

I nodded.

"Sir Charles is thinking of buying the *Bulletin,* and making Junior the editor."

My head snapped back like Sylvester Stallone's after catching a left hook in one of the *Rocky* movies.

Parkham said, "Talbot owns two newspapers—both of them in the United Kingdom. He likes to have a hand on the throat of the press, wherever he lives. He's here now, and he wants a local paper.

"You'd actually sell the *Bulletin* to him?"

"Six months ago, I would have said yes, Quint." She opened the humidor again, this time dragging out a long, thin cigar. There was no smoking allowed in the building, of course, at least *most* of the building—the lone exception being her office. So far, no one had had the guts to challenge her on the subject.

"The paper is turning around," Parkham said. "Advertising is up; circulation is up. I'm starting to like the *Bulletin.* But, if Talbot ups his ante, I'm going to have a difficult time getting my people in New York to turn the deal down."

She turned over the five cards I'd dealt her.

"A pair of fours. What do you have, Quint?"

I flipped my cards over. "Two queens."

Parkham gave a sour smile. "See, I knew you could cheat. Now, help me find out how Junior is cheating, and then I'll suggest to Sir Charles that he lose interest in the publishing business."

I'd have volunteered to do anything short of a felony to keep Talbot from taking over the *Bulletin.*

"How do you suggest I do that, boss?"

"I want you to sit in on the next game, play a few hands, and see if you can figure out what young Talbot is up to."

"It may take more than a few hands," I protested. "And the amount of money involved is a lot more than I—"

"Relax. I'll sponsor you, Quint. Five thousand dollars in chips. Just don't bet foolishly."

"What, if I should win a few hands? And I cash out with more than the five thousand?"

"If it's Talbot's money, you can keep it," Parkham said. She stood up and thrust an arm across the desk. "Deal?"

"Deal," I said, shaking her hand. I was glad neither of us squeezed too hard, because that huge diamond she'd twisted around dug sharply into my palm.

"Won't the other players think it's strange that someone like me, a humble *Bulletin* employee, is playing in a high-stakes poker game?" I asked.

She brushed her hands together as if she had flour on them. "I'll just describe you as an associate, and if anyone asks, I'll tell them that you're gambling with the money you've made on that book of yours, though *we both* know that's not true."

Parkham was talking about my first published work, *Tough Guys and Private Eyes,* a critique of the film noir movies of the forties. It had garnered some excellent reviews and very few sales.

Parkham ran her eyes over me and added, "Dress up a bit, Quint. Presentable slacks and a sport coat will do. I'll let you know where and when to show up."

I gathered the cards together neatly and palmed a cookie in a manner that would have made Uncle Crime proud of me. "Mind if I keep the cards?"

"Help yourself. How's your father doing?" Parkham asked as I was about to head for the door.

Women of all ages were always asking me about my father, John Quint. He's a musician—a singer and jazz pianist of some note—and plays at many of the posher restaurants and social events around town. He's also what used to be described in movies and onstage as a "ladies' man."

"Instant Cary Grant," one longing admirer had dubbed him. He and my mother have been divorced for many years. Dad lives in the flat directly above Mom, and I know that they often share bread and breakfast—whether they share anything else, I don't know, and don't want to know.

"He's fine," I told the Great. "He's in Vegas, a gig in the lounge at the Bellagio."

"Tell him I said hello when he gets back," she said, then picked up the phone and started barking at some poor soul in the paper's business section as I made my way out the door.

Two

I asked myself a series of stomach-churning "What if " questions on the elevator taking me back to my cubicle: What if I can't catch Junior cheating? What if he keeps on winning large pots, and somehow the Great blames me? What if I find out he has been cheating and then *he* finds out that I'm the one who ratted on him? If somehow his father ever did get control of the *Bulletin,* I'd be worse than toast—I'd be unemployed.

Well, there was no sense boo-hooing it now; the deed was done.

Adding to the day's depressions, I found Terry Greco in the coffee alcove, chatting amiably with a slender man in his mid-thirties with neatly trimmed brown hair. He was wearing a shoe-polish brown Italian-style double-breasted suit, a striped shirt with a white collar, and gaudy cuff links—no tie. Just the type to drive a Jaguar and take up two parking spaces.

Terry caught my eye, but she quickly turned her back to me and escorted Gaudy Cuff Links to the elevator.

I poured myself a cup of coffee and waited for her return. I was on my second cup when she strolled back toward me. Terry was the proverbial ten pounds of candy in an eight-pound bag. She was blond, short, firmly packed, and favored snug-fitting skirts and sweaters, following her mother's advice: "If you've got it, flaunt it, because you ain't going to have it forever." Terry was a great flaunter—and a great flirter.

There was no special bond or commitment between the two of us—we just enjoyed each other's company, though I would have been happy to have her to myself alone—she wasn't interested in limiting her choices quite yet.

My mother's first impression of Terry: "What a pair of knockers. It's amazing she doesn't tip over."

Some sexist swine equate the size of a woman's bust with her intelligence—the bigger the boobs, the fewer the gray cells. In addition to her natural charms, Terry had a college degree, and handled the *Bulletin*'s art, book, and restaurant reviews.

"The guy you were talking to," I said. "He looked familiar, but I couldn't place his face."

"That was Ronald Maleuw. He's Sir Charles Talbot's personal curator, and is setting up the art exhibit at the de Young Museum," She smiled sweetly. "I'm still working on getting you on the guest list, Carroll, and believe me, it isn't easy. It's a black-tie affair and the 'donation' for admittance is two thousand dollars."

I nodded, letting her know I understood. Terry and I swapped freebies: I supplied her with tickets to movie premieres, plays, and backstage parties, and she took me along to gallery openings and the restaurants she reviewed—but there were times when it just wasn't possible to take a friend. "What about tonight?" I asked. "Feel like a pizza? We could go to my place and—"

She frowned, sending wrinkles across her smooth forehead. "Sorry. Not tonight. I have a working dinner with Ron. It's really exciting, Carroll—the paintings that Sir Charles is showing from his personal collection: Rembrandt, Monet, Picasso, Utrillo, and some modern artists: Richard Diebenkorn, Helen Frankenthaler, Piet Mondrian. Some of them have never been seen in public before. I helped unpack a Renoir at the museum last night." She held out her hands and flickered her fingers. "*Unpacked* it. I actually handled the frame. It was wonderful."

"What about tomorrow night? We haven't . . . shared a pizza in a more than a week."

"I'm going to be awfully busy until after the exhibit, Carroll."

I'd been afraid she was going to say that. Terry was working on a five-page feature on the Talbot exhibit for the *Bulletin*'s weekend edition, and she had deals in the works with a couple of high-end glossy magazines. She also had hopes that Sir Charles would agree to let her do a book on his entire collection. "What kind of guy is Talbot?"

"Sir Charles?" Her lower lip curled a little. "He's way up there in years. I know he's hard of hearing, and his eyesight isn't very good. I think one of the reasons that he's sponsoring this exhibit is to make amends."

"For what? Being filthy rich?"

"No," Terry said, shaking her head as if I'd asked a particularly stupid question. "Henry Matisse's two sisters. Surely, you've heard of them."

"Talbot was fooling around with Matisse's sisters?"

"Carroll, I hope you're kidding. They were two small oils on canvas, nudes Matisse did of two young sisters. Talbot—this was long before he was knighted—somehow got hold of them, and he had them up for sale to a serious Matisse collector in Paris. Talbot wanted a hundred and fifty thousand for them—a very high price at the time. The buyer refused, said it was a ridiculous amount. Then, right in front of the man's eyes, Talbot took his cigarette lighter and set one of the paintings on fire. Destroyed it! It was unforgivable."

"Why would he do that? I thought Talbot was a smart businessman."

"Oh, he's smart all right. Destructive, vindictive, unscrupulous, and smart. Three months later, he sold the remaining painting to the same man for two hundred and fifty thousand dollars."

I was confused—not for the first time. "Terry, how could he peddle the two of them for a hundred and fifty thousand, and then get more than that for just the one?"

"There was *only* one, Carroll. That's the point—rarity. That's what drives up prices in the art world. One thing's for sure: The museum will earn a good deal of money from exhibiting his paintings, so he can't be all bad."

"What about his son?" I asked. "Charles junior."

She scrunched her face up and folded her arms across her chest. "An obnoxious lounge lizard with wandering eyes, who thinks he's God's gift to us lucky women."

"He made a pass at you?"

"Junior's not exactly suave or sophisticated. 'Hi, Sugar Tits. Fancy a good fuck? I'll get you a role in one of my movies.' That's one of his favorite lines. Luckily, he isn't around that often, and he never tries anything when Ronnie's nearby. There's some kind of tension between the two of them. They definitely don't like each other. Ronnie says to ignore Junior, which I do, but if he keeps pushing me, I'm going to let him have it."

"Good for you. Junior makes movies?"

"I think he tried making films in Europe, but he wasn't very successful."

Terry eased onto her toes and planted a small kiss on my cheek. "I've got to go. We'll get together soon."

I watched her saunter down the hallway and listened to the tattoo of her high heels on the linoleum. "Soon" didn't sound promising. And Mr. Maleuw had gone from Ronald to Ron, and then to Ronnie.

I was barely back in my cubicle when the cell phone on my hip started vibrating.

Not very many people had my cell number, and the way things were going, I opened it up fearing the worst. I was right.

"Carroll dear. You have to come over right now. I was lining the garbage can and I saw that Ulla died. I called and they said it was a suicide. I don't believe it. Hurry."

My mother hadn't had much of a career as an actress in Hollywood, but she'd learned enough to talk on the phone just as they do in the movies: no hellos and no good-byes. Garbage can? Ulla?

The office phone rang. A man's voice, with a refined, upper-crust accent said, "Carroll Quint? This is Ron Maleuw. I found your note on my windshield, and I'm sorry I took your parking spot this morning. If you had to make other arrangements for your car, I'd be glad to reimburse you for the cost."

Maleuw—nice-looking, good dresser, drives an expensive car, has a dandy job, no doubt makes tons of money, and now he has to be polite, too, I thought. No wonder Terry was attracted to him.

"Not a problem, Mr. Maleuw," I assured him. "How's everything going for the museum exhibit?"

"Quite well, thanks. There's really a tremendous amount of work involved, and Terry has been a great help."

"That's nice to know," I said, then followed my mother's lead and hung up without saying good-bye.

The Quint family residence is a pair of Edwardian flats on Liberty Street, in the Dolores Heights section of the city. The building has curved bay windows, a gabled roof, and a circular Tiffany-style stained-glass window in the attic.

The front steps were still glistening from their daily morning scrubbing. My mother was waiting at the door, an anxious look on her beautiful face. She's a shade over five feet in height, with delicate features and bright blue eyes (which she will assure you upon first meeting are bluer than Sinatra's or Paul Newman's), a tipped-up nose, and the fair, clear skin of a woman twenty years her junior. Her once natural blond hair has dissolved into a gleaming silvery gray.

She loves to dress for the occasion, no matter what the occasion is. Unfortunately, when I arrived, she had on a black apron and a puffy white chefs' hat, the kind that looks like a soufflé about to implode— which led me to believe that she was cooking.

"Carroll, thank God you came," she said before hugging me to her chest.

Once inside, I could detect the familiar scents of lemon wax and Windex. My mother goes through Windex like the *Wall Street Journal* goes through ink.

I passed down a hallway whose walls were lined with framed movie posters, advertisements for films in which Mother, under her maiden name, Karen Kaas, had made brief, usually voiceless, appearances. The smiling or snarling faces of the stars—Dean Martin, Richard Burton, Faye Dunaway, Roger Moore, and Steve McQueen—stared back at me from the posters.

There was a new one, from *The Long Goodbye*, with Elliott Gould, a cigarette dangling from his lips, a snub-nose revolver in hand, trying to look like the famed private eye Philip Marlowe. The quotation alongside Gould's face said "Nothing says goodbye like a bullet." Somehow, I didn't think those words had come from Raymond Chandler's typewriter.

"I didn't know you were in this picture," I told my mother.

"My bikini was the only thing briefer than my role, darling. Are you hungry?"

We entered her favorite room, the kitchen. Since leaving Hollywood to marry my father, Mom had gone through a series of "artistic endeavors": oil painting, operating a health-food store and then an upscale boutique, and, finally, home decorating.

She'd spared no expense—mostly Dad's alimony payments—on the kitchen: marble countertops, cherry-wood cabinets, a center island as big as a Buick, featuring a chopping block, a rotisserie, a Viking eight-burner stove, and a copper sink. Overhead hung an array of brightly polished copper pots and pans. Truly beautiful, but wasted, because my mother is one of the worst cooks on the planet.

"Are you hungry, dear?" she asked hopefully. She'd been stuffing vile concoctions containing wheat germ, brewer's yeast, desiccated liver, and tofu down my throat since I was a wee lad.

"No thanks. I already had lunch," I said truthfully, having wisely stopped off at a Burger King before driving over. "A glass of wine would be nice, though."

"Pour me one, too," she said, picking up a wooden spoon and stirring a foul-smelling batch of something green in a large pot.

The stereo was playing one of my father's albums, a collection of Gershwin tunes. The TV was on, showing one of the DVDs from *The Thin Man* collection I'd given her for her last birthday. The sound was muted; William Powell was waving a cocktail shaker at a bartender. "A dry martini you always shake to waltz time," I said aloud as Powell's lips moved silently.

"It's too early for a martini," my mother complained. "Pinot grigio, dear. There's one open in the refrigerator. Though we really should be drinking champagne to honor Ulla. She loved champagne."

"Did she now?" I said, pouring two glasses of wine and handing one to my mother. "Just who is Ulla, Mom? You said she committed suicide in a garbage can?"

"Whatever are you talking about, Carroll? I said that I was lining the garbage can and saw her picture in the obituaries. It's there, over by the jigsaw puzzle."

Another one of Mom's hobbies is assembling jigsaw puzzles taken from famous movie scenes. She'd just started a new one; the puzzle box showed a scene from *Singin' in the Rain*: Gene Kelly, Donald O'Connor, and Debbie Reynolds in yellow slickers, holding umbrellas. Lying alongside was a pair of scissors she used to shape the puzzle pieces that didn't quite fit, a magnifying glass, and a newspaper cutout from the *Bulletin's* obituary page, dated a week ago. "Ulla Kjeldsen," I read. "Passed away peacefully in her sleep on August seven. A native of Denmark, Ulla will be missed by her many friends."

The mortuary was in Sausalito, and the services had been held at a Catholic church there. No listing of family or loved ones. The thumb-size photograph showed the profile of an attractive dark-haired woman.

"Did you know her well?" I asked.

"Yes. We roomed together in Hollywood, Carroll. She was from the same town in Denmark that my family came from, Sandvig. Her father died, and her mother remarried and moved to Italy. Ulla converted, became a Roman Catholic, of all things. She used to tell me God would forgive you for *any* sin, even murder, but not suicide. 'That's the sin of sins, Karen,' she'd say. She really believed all that mumbo jumbo about burning in hell for eternity, with those bearded devils poking you in your roasted fanny with pitchforks. She would *never* have killed herself."

"When did you last see her?"

"In Hollywood. At her beau's wake."

I couldn't remember when the last time was that I'd heard anyone described as a "beau" unless it was in a very old movie. Mom turned from the pot and gave me a mournful look. Tears were forming in the corners of her eyes. "Isn't life strange? If I hadn't been lining the garbage can, I never would have known. I want you to find out who killed her."

I took a big sip of the wine before saying, "Who told you she committed suicide?"

"The man at the funeral parlor. I called and said I was Ulla's sister and that I'd just learned of her death. He said she'd swallowed sleeping pills or something. The police think she took her own life. It's not true. Ulla was murdered."

I went over and patted her gently on the shoulder. "I'm still a bit confused. Why would you think she was murdered, if you haven't seen her in all those years?"

"Because everybody had been looking for her—the police, and some very unsavory characters. She disappeared. They all assumed she was dead. I was *certain* she'd been murdered. Vicky was so beautiful, and she liked to party—more than I did, that's for certain. She used to tell me how much sex there was in the Bible, everyone doing it, saints and sinners, so there was no shame in enjoying sex. As Mel Brooks put it, 'It's good to be the king,' because according to Vicky, King David was quite a cocksman. Imagine living back then, dear—no plays, books, movies, or TV. No wonder they went at it night and day."

That was certainly a perspective of the Bible that I hadn't picked up in school. "Mom, I'm confused. You said Vicky? Is that Ulla?"

"Yes, I'm a bit confused as to what to call her now myself, dear. When she came to America, she had her name legally changed to Anna Borden. That was in New York City. Ulla Kjeldsen is certainly not the name for an actress; you should know that. When she got to Hollywood, her agent suggested she take the name Vicky Vandamn. I was probably the only person she told about her real birth name." She handed me the wooden spoon. "Keep stirring. I'll get the pictures."

I made the mistake of leaning over the pot while I was stirring. The smell was awful.

"What is this?" I asked, when Mom returned.

"Kelp, bladderwort, and alaria. Wonderful sea vegetables, darling. I have to order them by mail from Maine."

I knew what kelp was, but I had somehow blessedly escaped the others.

Mom placed a photo album on the kitchen table and began flicking through the plastic-bound pages. "Here we are, Vicky—I have a hard time thinking of her as Ulla—Jerome, and I. Her hair was a deep honey brown color." She patted her hair. "Not all Danes are blond."

The picture showed a beautiful young blonde in white shorts and a high-collared polka-dot blouse—my mother in all of her youthful glory. The brunette wore shorts, too, and a tight black sweater. They were posing in front of a swimming pool, smiling radiantly at each other. There was a man in one picture, dangling a basketball over Vicky's head.

"Who's he?"

"Jerome Ramsey, Vicky's beau. She moved out shortly after these pictures were taken. It was such a lovely garden-court apartment, but the smog was terrible. Your father used to say he could wake up and hear the birds coughing in the trees.

"Jerome was a frame puller, an assistant cameraman, which back then meant he went for coffee and swept floors, too. But he was very talented, and took beautiful still shots. He was murdered, but the police called it suicide. When I saw Vicky at his wake, she was devastated—and frightened. 'They killed him, Karen, and if you ever hear that I committed suicide, you'll know they killed me, too.' "

"Who is 'they,' Mom?"

"Vicky never told me. The mob, I suppose. Or one of her lovers. Jerome's older brother, a nice man, but not nearly as good-looking as Jerome, came to the funeral. He was very comforting to Vicky."

I flicked the pages over. There were several eight-by-ten glossies, studio still shots of Mom, and two of Ulla/Anna/Vicky—both showing her in profile, wearing a low-cut dress and gloves. The cameraman had obviously known what he was doing: The lighting was perfect. At the bottom right-hand corner of the pictures was the notation "Talbot Studios."

Mom picked up her wineglass and stared at the contents. "All of the usual wolves were after her: Warren, Burt, Jack, Marlon. She had a crush on your father, of course. They all did. I think he may have crushed back, before he met me. Unfortunately, Vicky got involved with a bad crowd, Carroll. Do you know what they called the gangsters in Hollywood back then? 'The Mickey Mouse Mafia.' There was no Tony Soprano, just Tony Silvain. 'Tony Silk,' they called him—a small, mean-faced man who slowly but surely took over all of the clubs on the Strip and started peddling those awful drugs."

I ran my finger across Vicky's Talbot Studios still shot. "Did you know Charles Talbot, Mom?"

"Know him?" She put her glass on the table and raised the hem of her skirt and apron to show off her dancer's legs. "I kept in shape just running away from that man. He was a despot. A real casting-couch producer. Fifty-Buck Chuck was one of the reasons I left Hollywood. I wouldn't get within ten yards of him." She tilted her head at the ceiling. "Your father was the other reason."

"Fifty-Buck Chuck?"

"Yes." She sighed, picking up her glass and taking a sip of the wine. "The pig would promise the girls parts in movies, and after the poor dear had dropped to her knees and performed *avalerla la fumée,* he'd hand her a fifty-dollar bill and a Kleenex. The movie roles never happened, of course. Talbot told Vicky he loved her, and she believed him. She believed everything men told her."

Mom topped off my glass with more wine. "I always thought that the two of them, Tony Silk and Charles Talbot, had something to do with her disappearance. Freeze did, too. But he could never prove anything."

I dived into the wine before asking the obvious question. "Who is Freeze?"

"Detective Willie Chanan, of the Los Angeles Police Department,

Carroll. Everyone called him 'Freeze.' He claimed that he was the one who originated the line, the one where the cop pulls out his gun and tells everyone, 'Freeze!' He was a crook, of course, but a charming and likable one. He was a real specimen—a weight lifter and bodybuilder. He liked to strut his stuff for the girls down at Muscle Beach. All of the studios called Freeze when one of their stars was in trouble. He had connections with the newspapers and television people. I was certain Vicky had been murdered and buried in the desert. That's where they dumped all the bodies."

"What made you think that, Mom?"

"Freeze told me, dear." She went back to stirring her pot of sea vegetables. "Now *please* find out about Vicky. I have to know what happened to her—I just have to."

I slid out one of the studio still shots from the album and studied Ulla's profiled features. Pouty lips, a bit of an overbite, arched eyebrows. "I don't remember ever seeing her in a movie."

"You'd have to look awfully hard, dear—a crowd scene, just a body to fill up screen space—I don't believe she ever had a spoken line. She had a rather unusual accent, the mix of Danish and Italian, I suppose. We were so very close; it was almost like she was my little sister. She was only seventeen when she came to Hollywood. She'd lied about her age, saying she was older. That was unique—everyone else claimed they were younger. I wonder why she didn't contact me when she moved to Sausalito?"

I'd been wondering about that, too. "I don't think there's much I can really do."

She placed a hand on my shoulder. Tears were forming at the corners of her eyes again. "I'm sure you'll think of something, dear. Pretend you're one of those private eyes in that book of yours. Maybe you should write a new book, Carroll. About Vicky, the Hollywood gangsters, and her disappearance. I'm sure people would love reading about her."

If this had been a comic strip, the panel would have shown a frontal view of my bewildered face underneath a large lightbulb. An idea was born. From my mother, of all people. My literary agent had hinted strongly that if I wanted to continue to be a published author, I should think about doing something serious about the crime and corruption in Hollywood: "Sex, drugs, orgies, incest, murder, all that stuff the stars were involved in, Quint. That's what the public wants—not reviews of old movies."

I could see that my mother was really upset about her Hollywood friend's death. "Mom, maybe Vicky didn't call because she didn't know you were living here in the city. Had you seen her after you married Dad? Did she know you two had tied the knot?"

Her lips molded into a half smile. "I thought everyone knew about our marriage, but you could be right. Vicky disappeared before John and I were married in Las Vegas."

I kissed her on the check. "I'll check it out, I promise."

"How's that little cutie pie Terry? I haven't seen her in awhile. Bring her over soon. I'll make a tofu and kale quiche."

"I'll tell her," I fibbed. I was having trouble enough seeing Terry without threatening her with Mom's cooking. "I'll let you know what I find out about your friend."

Three

I drove back to the *Bulletin* and spoke to Danny Byrne, the paper's "keeper of the tombs." Danny was a florid-faced guy with bulldog jowls. He'd handled the obituaries for the paper for more than thirty years.

I gave him the death notice my mother had cut from the paper. "Danny, I want to know who called the ad in, and who paid for it."

He scowled at me and scratched his bulging stomach with thick ink-smudged fingers. "And what would be your interest in all of this, if I may ask?" he said with a strong touch of the Blarney in his voice.

Danny protected the obit files as if they contained military secrets. It was his turf, and he would defend it at all costs.

"I'm just an errand boy for the Great, and she's in a hurry."

Danny reacted like a marine recruit who'd been given an order by his drill sergeant, and within a few minutes I had all the paperwork on Ulla Kjeldsen.

The information on her death had been called in by a Della Rugerio. Residence: Harbor Point, Sausalito. Rugerio had also paid for the notice.

I carried the papers back to my cubicle and did some sleuthing. I checked the *Bulletin*'s data bank, but there had been nothing in the paper regarding Ulla Kjeldsen's death, other than the obituary.

I turned to a reporter's best friend: Google. Nothing on Ulla, but to my surprise, there were several hits on Vicky Vandamn—cuts from Los Angeles newspapers and *Variety*. One story linked her to Tony Silvain "who," the article stated, "prefers to be called Tony Silk, a bone-breaking gangster who paid his dues as a Chicago Mafia hired gun and now runs the local mob."

Another story had famous Hollywood cop Willie "Freeze" Chanan stating that starlet Vicky Vandamn "is either under the Nevada desert or is fish food. The kid knew too much about a certain local big shot. Methinks she's a goner."

There were dozens of hits on Silvain/Silk. One had a picture of him as a slim young man in the ring, boxing gloves cocked and ready for action. The picture taken weeks before he'd been sent to jail for five years on income tax evasion charges showed him as a short, fat, balding guy with a pockmarked face. In jail, Silvain had been involved in a fight with a fellow prisoner, suffered a brain hemorrhage, and died after serving barely one year of his sentence.

Along with gambling, drugs, and extortion, he allegedly was involved in blackmailing movie stars, arranging for them to spend a night in a swank hotel, and then recording and filming their lovemaking. Then he would threaten the stars—either pay up or he'd release the smut. Apparently, most paid, but Yves Montand, the great French entertainer, reportedly ordered extra copies to pass around to his friends.

I drew a blank on Jerome Ramsey, Ulla's "beau," according to my mother.

Willie "Freeze" Chanan had made Google in a big way: four pages of hits reporting his exploits helping unnamed stars out of jams, and putting away so-called mob figures.

There was a photo of him in a dark overcoat at Silvain's funeral. He looked handsome enough to be in the movies: a thick Brad Pitt–style crew cut, deep-set eyes, and a dashing mustache. " 'Silky thought he was Robin Hood, but he was Rotten Hood,' says famed L.A. copper at hoodlum's funeral."

The final story was a piece on Chanan retiring from the

department because of a disability. A fellow cop claimed Freeze had become disabled "from packing around his wallet."

What was it my mother had said about him? "He was crook, of course, but a charming and likable one." If I had asked her what she'd meant by that, I'd still be trapped in her kitchen.

The hits on Sir Charles Talbot took up dozens of pages of Google's unlimited space. I skimmed through them, learning little that I didn't already know. He was rich, ruthless, and randy: five wives and liaisons with untold numbers of young women. The last photograph had been taken eleven years ago and showed Talbot standing tall in a tuxedo, accepting some type of an award from a middle-aged woman in a white dress and turban. Talbot had the look of an aging athlete: sloping shoulders, thick chest. His facial features projected strength and a touch of arrogance.

There was nothing on the story Terry had told me about Talbot putting the flame to a Matisse.

I pecked in Talbot junior's name. He was apparently a chip off the old blockbuster. There were numerous stories about his exploits in Paris and London, always involving a young woman—two of whom had filed suits claiming that Junior had roughed them up. One photo showed him in a restaurant, his face hardened in anger, pointing a threatening finger at the photographer.

Terry had said that Junior claimed to be involved in the movie industry in Europe, but there was no mention of that in the Google hits.

I dialed the number Della Rugerio had provided when she called in the obituary.

The phone was answered by a soft, caressing voice. "Hello. How may I help you?"

"Ms. Rugerio, this is Carroll Quint of the *San Francisco Bulletin*. I was wondering if you could spare me a few minutes of your time. I'd like to talk to you about Ulla Kjeldsen."

"For what purpose?" she responded cautiously.

"I'd like to know more about her."

"I'm sorry, but I—"

"Ulla was a good friend of my mother. They roomed together in Hollywood."

There was a pause; then she said, "How interesting. Come in the morning. Before eleven. My first client doesn't arrive until eleven."

"I'll be there," I promised. "Did Ulla live with you? Or nearby?"

"Very nearby. She was murdered, you know. *Arrivederla*."

I ran Rugerio's address on Google Earth and the satellite zeroed in on a pier. She lived on a houseboat.

The trip to Sausalito from San Francisco isn't a long or difficult drive—it's only about eight miles. Since the Ferry Building is only a few blocks from my condo, I decided to take the scenic route—the ferry.

I sat on the stern of a 140-foot three-deck catamaran commuter yacht and enjoyed the view through my prescription sunglasses: Alcatraz, the lion-colored hills of Marin County, a flotilla of powerboats, paper-hat sailboats, and, of course, the Golden Gate Bridge.

The bridge opened in May 1937, and the toll at that time was a nickel, with promises that that fee would be dropped and use would be free once the thing was paid for. Then came the politicians. Someone much brighter than I am once said that providing politicians with money is like giving teenage boys kegs of beer and the keys to the car.

The pols decided that to discourage cars and lessen traffic, they would build a fleet of buses and ferrys to help get those commuters to and from San Francisco. The idea looked good on paper, the problem being that the paper soon turned out to be paper dollars—millions and millions of them. The buses were the most modern, comfortable, and costly the Bridge District could find, but somehow they always seemed to be breaking down. The ferryboats were big, beautiful, powerful, and capable of thirty-six knots—when they weren't in dry dock for repair, which was quite often.

So politicians, being who they are, found a solution to the problem: Throw more money around. Our money—there's talk about a ten-dollar toll in the not too distant future.

The big boat slowed down and churned up root beer–colored mud as it pulled to the dock. Sausalito was once considered the hot-tub, kinky-sex, and designer-drug center of the West Coast. The chamber of commerce likes to describe it as a "quaint Mediterranean-like village." Maybe it was at one time, but it's gone commercial: upscale restaurants, art galleries that only those with a pinch of Sir Charles Talbot's money can afford, no parking spaces, and steely-eyed locals who stare at the tourists as if they're visiting from another planet. Of course, that's probably exactly how all those quaint little Mediterranean villages on the Riviera are now.

I bought an espresso for six bucks and strolled down the main street until I came to the entrance of Harbor Point.

Della Rugerio's houseboat was listed at G-7 on the address post. There was one of those "You are here" maps shielded by a sheet of heavy Plexiglas. I traced the route to Rugerio's place and started off on the path leading to her slip.

The pier was some twelve feet wide, but it narrowed down quite a bit thanks to flowerpots of all shapes and sizes containing cactus, succulents, dwarf fruit trees, and rosebushes that somehow managed to survive the struggle against wind, sea air, and neglect. The houseboats were more house than boat, all set on concrete barges. Everything from cozy cottages to elaborate two- and three-story structures in a variety of styles, a few christened with too-cute names: *XTESEA, Nora's Ark, Wet Dream, Aquaholic.* Many had wraparound decks and windows sporting pots of flowering geraniums; some looked to be brand-new, others like they'd been there for years, cobbled together with raw lumber and bits of driftwood. There were a few actual boats stuck in between the houseboats: old tugboats and flat-bottom craft that listed dangerously to one side. There were several house trailers set on barges, as well as a few exotics: one made up like a Chinese junk, another like a Pullman train car. The pier ended in a dogleg left turn. The final three houseboats were facing south, and had no neighbors on the opposite side. The planks wobbled under my feet as I stepped over coiled hoses and the occasional dog dropping before coming to the last boat on the pier, a purple-and-red shingle affair with a high-pitched roof. G-7 was neatly painted on a post near the entrance. A stained-glass window featuring a white-on-red hexagon dominated the front of the structure.

A curious wide-eyed harbor seal popped his head out of the water and wiggled his whiskers at me.

Before I could knock on the weathered redwood door, it was snapped open and a somber-faced woman greeted me.

"You must be the newspaperman," she said.

She looked to be in her early fifties and had ivory-colored skin. She had a full figure and down-slanted gray eyes. Her dark hair had jagged lighting bolt–like streaks at the sides. She was wearing a short-sleeved white blouse and white slacks.

"Come in, please," she said. "I can give you twenty-six minutes. No more." She smiled and added, "I do not keep my clients waiting."

There was the heavy scent of incense. Candles of all shapes, sizes, and descriptions were burning all over the place. The walls were all painted in bright colors: red, yellow, green, and deep blue. A round table with a purple felt top and two chairs with wooden backs were the only pieces of furniture.

"Sit, sit," Della Rugerio urged me. "Tell me about your mother and Ulla."

"It was before I was born, but I know they were very good friends at one time. My mother never knew that Ulla had moved back to the Bay Area. She's saddened that Ulla never contacted her. The last time she saw her, they were in Hollywood, struggling to get into the movies."

"Ulla often talked of Hollywood. What is your mother's name?"

"Karen Kaas."

"Yes, Ulla did mention her. She said Karen was one of the few people in Hollywood she considered a friend."

I shifted uncomfortably in the chair. One or two of the legs were uneven. "Did you know Ulla's Hollywood name? Vicky Vandamn?"

Rugerio waved her hand slowly back and forth in front of her face as if chasing away a fly. Each of her fleshy fingers had at least one ring, and there were several gold chains on her wrist. "I knew her long enough to love her, but not long enough for her to confide *all* her secrets to me." She brought her hands together, interlocking the fingers. "She was murdered. I could have prevented it, if she had confided in me."

"There was nothing in the papers about the police investigating her death."

Two deep clefts formed between her dark eyebrows. "The police. Complete fools. They are fat, lazy, corrupt."

A piebald cat strolled into the room and stopped to stare at me. His tail flicked back and forth like the tongue of a grandfather clock. He took a few steps toward me and arched his back.

"I don't think your cat likes me," I told Rugerio.

"Caribbean Joe? Pay no attention to him. Are you going to write a story about Ulla?"

"I'd like to," I said. "Who told you she was murdered?"

"She did." Rugerio whisked a deck of cards from out of nowhere and began slapping them onto the felt. "She spoke to me last night. I am a psychic." She stabbed herself in the chest with one of the cards, then tapped it against her temple. "In my heart and in my brain, I know. Would you like me to do a reading? You look like a troubled man."

I got a good look at the backs of the cards: cartoonish drawings of a man hanged upside down, dogs barking at the sun, a naked woman under a bright star, a horned devil. Tarot cards.

"You're a fortune-teller?"

She pursed her mouth in a gesture of contempt. "Fortune-tellers are crooks, charlatans. I am a psychic, I do not use cheap tricks and theatrics."

"When you spoke to Ulla last night, did she tell you who killed her?"

"It is a misconception that once a soul reaches the other side they disclose all their secrets. It will take time, but eventually she will reveal all to me." She went through the card to the heart and to the temple thing again, then said, "I am gifted. I can help you, young man."

I almost said it was too bad she couldn't help Ulla. "Where did Ulla live?"

"Next door. She was a wonderful neighbor. She took such good care of Joe after the accident."

"Ulla's accident, or yours?" I asked her.

She snapped her fingers and the cat came to her. "My Joe, he was bitten by a dog, a cowardly Doberman, but I made sure he paid a price for what he did. Joe almost died. The veterinarian charged me a fortune. I had to cancel my vacation to the Caribbean—that's how he got his new name. Ulla loved him."

"How long had she been here in Sausalito?"

"Oh, nine months, I think. Not a year. Before that, she was in Canada."

"Where in Canada?"

"If she told me, I've forgotten. The past wasn't important—it was the future that Ulla was interested in."

"How did she die, Della?"

"She was poisoned. Someone put something into her drink. One of her men did it."

"*One* of her men? Did she know a lot of men?"

Rugerio studied my face for several seconds before responding. "Ulla had a weakness for men. She was afraid, Mr. Newspaperman. That's why she didn't call her friends, like your mother."

"Afraid of what? Of who?"

She gave me a sly smile, then slowly shuffled her tarot deck. "The man who killed her, of course. I'd been worried for Ulla. I hadn't seen her in two days. If she went away, she always told me. I found her. She was in her bed. Ulla always kept herself so clean, and wore nothing but the best perfumes. It was obvious she was dead. Her color. The smell. It was awful."

"Did she work? How did she make a living?"

"Work," Rugerio scoffed, snapping a card showing a knight on horseback down on the felt table. "Ulla had no need to work. Every month she would go to the bank and pick up cash—all that she needed—and she told me that there would be more, much more, coming in. She was writing a book, her memoirs. She was always click-ing away on her computer—she took it with her everywhere, even on the bay in her kayak when the weather was right—but she never let me see any of it. 'Not till it's finished, Della,' she would say, teasing me. Maybe the murderer was someone in the book. She did tell me she was 'naming names' and that there were going to be some very upset people—some would certainly go to jail, she said. Their lives would be ruined, but Ulla didn't care. She said they deserved it. Whoever killed her took the computer. I checked the houseboat thoroughly. It was gone."

"The computer was a laptop?"

"Oh, yes. An expensive one."

"Who were the people she was naming?"

"She didn't tell me."

"Did she have a publisher? An agent?"

Rugerio gave a one-shoulder shrug. "These things, she did not discuss with me. But she did tell me the title. *Payback*. Interesting, no?"

Interesting yes. "My mother mentioned that Ulla was a devout Catholic. Was she still practicing her religion?"

"Mass every Sunday, confession more often than that. Sins of the flesh didn't seem to bother her. She had a crush on the priest. 'Father Hunk,' she called him. I saw him at the funeral, of course. He is very good-looking. I didn't hold it against her."

She reached under the table and came out with a sheet of orange paper. She handed it to me carefully, as if it were fragile. "I have many talents. I can help you with life's problems."

It was a flyer. In bold type it said: "Madam Della, Physical and Spir-itual Healing. Specializing in Tarot Readings, Hypnosis, Tea-Leaf Readings, Healing Herbs, and Clark Cleansing—Special Discounts for Seniors."

I had to ask. "Clark cleansing?"

"A natural colon and bowel cleanser. You cannot have a clear mind if you do not have a clean body."

I'd had enough of the seasickness-inducing chair. I stood up and dug a card out of my wallet. "If you can think of anything that would be of help, give me a call."

"You will talk to the police? The detective who spoke to me was a young woman. Kay Manners. She is a Pisces, on the dark side. Secretive, vague, weak-willed, and easily led—hardly attributes for a detective. You're a Gemini. Communicative and witty, cunning and inquisitive. *You* would make a good detective."

She was right about my birth sign. A lucky guess?

"The policewoman told me that Ulla had taken sleeping pills," Della said. "That is not correct. She had no need for sleeping pills. Even after her surgery, she did not need those. She preferred champagne and ganja to pills. She smoked nothing but the finest sinsemilla, made from the flowering tips of a female marijuana plant that has been isolated from the male. She believed that champagne wasn't fattening, and called it her 'Jesus water.' "

"Surgery. She was ill?"

Della placed her two index fingers along the outside of her eyes and pulled them taught. "Cosmetic surgery. Ulla was addicted to it. She had a real fear of getting old, or at least looking old. She gulped down vitamins, health-food supplements, Chinese herbs, diet pills. Did you like the picture I put in the paper? It was my favorite of her. I took it here, on the dock. She did not allow me to take many pictures. A shame, because she was so beautiful."

"Yes, she certainly was. Did she have any special friends? Any family? Children? The obituary mentioned her many friends."

"Many *acquaintances,* but no family, no real friends. Just me, and Caribbean Joe."

"I'd like to see her place," I said on the way to the door.

"Yes. I knew you would. It's the big white one right next to mine. I left the back door unlocked." She waggled a finger at me. "Do not take anything of hers. I will know if you do."

A bell chimed. "My eleven o'clock," she said. "Would you mind leaving by the back way? Sometimes my clients are nervous about being seen."

Four

*D*ella Rugerio led me through a small kitchen and out to the back deck, which had a terrific view of the bay and the beautiful skyline of San Francisco. She hurried back inside after once again warning me not to take anything from Ulla's houseboat. I moved cautiously past an upturned bright red kayak and across a two-foot watery divide to the neighboring houseboat, a two-story white cottage-style structure with a stone fireplace stretching up past the roof.

The rear was all windows and a sliding glass door. I slid the door open and stepped in. There was a neat kitchen with modern appliances and a teak dining table. An empty wine bottle with a label featuring an abstract yellow painting sat alone on the marble countertop. A tingling sensation crawled up and down my spine. I was in someone's home, without their permission. Or was I? Della said she had been talking to Ulla through her psychic powers, so, I reasoned with myself, in a way I did have the owner's permission. As if afraid to wake the dead, I tiptoed into a combination living room/dining room. The walls were white, but each wall was a slightly different shade. The carpeting was pale gray, as were the leather L-shaped couch and two matching club chairs. The dining room table was a large rectangle of polished glass, surrounded by eight black-lacquered chairs, and a clear Lucite crucifix was positioned on the wall next to a big-screen television. The cross blended in so well with the wall that it was nearly invisible. Black-and-white photographs in silver frames were scattered around the room. I wrapped my right hand in a handkerchief and picked one up, a profile shot of Ulla Kjeldsen's lovely face. All of the photographs were of Ulla: sitting on a swing, standing on a dock, her hands in the back pockets of her slacks, leaning against the mainsail of a yacht, staring out to sea with her hands clasped behind her back.

She held the same pose in every photo: chin up, neck stretched, head tilted back. Eight photographs, and not one with a smile.

The only touch of color in the room was a large oil hanging over the couch: Ulla, dressed in a low-cut black dress, her matching elbow-length glove holding a single yellow rose.

Shutter doors concealed a well-stocked wine collection, which included a variety of champagne: Dom Pérignon, Cristal, Mumm, Moët, and some that I'd never heard of. There were special bins for French reds, German whites, and California varieties, but most of the space was taken up by the champagne.

There was an ebony desk under a shuttered window. The desktop was neatly laid out with a telephone, stapler, a silver mug filled with pens and pencils. There were two books stacked at one end: a dictionary and a thesaurus. Writer's tools. A Hewlett-Packard laser printer was anchored on the opposite end of the desk—the hookup cable dangling from its back.

There was a cable modem box but no computer.

I punched the play button on the answering machine and a mechanical voice informed me that there were no messages. Then I pushed the phone's memory dial button and after three rings was connected to another recorded voice—that woman at the phone company who provides you with the exact time.

Believing in the theory that a clean desktop usually means messy desk drawers, I went through the desk. Again, everything was neat—too neat: reams of paper, envelopes, boxes of paper clips, staples, scissors, folder labels, but not a single CD, floppy disk, or anything relating to a computer, nor any notes on *Payback,* the book she supposedly had been working on.

A black wrought-iron circular staircase led to the upper floor. The bedroom was massive—the full width of the houseboat and thirty feet deep. Again, the floors were gray, the walls white, the furniture black, and there were more framed photos of Ulla. They could have been taken the same day, or at least the same week, because she looked identical in each one. Another painting of her hung on one wall. Here, she was wrapped up in a white fur coat, one long leg sticking out mischievously, her gloved right hand now holding a red rose. Even in the paintings she didn't smile, as if she was afraid flashing her teeth might cause a wrinkle to appear.

A large makeup vanity featured a round mirror surrounded by lightbulbs. There were literally dozens of jars, bottles, hairbrushes, and tubes of makeup, along with a few handheld magnifying mirrors.

The bed was of a size to match the room and was covered in a white fur that I assumed was faux, but which felt awfully soft and real when I brushed my hand against it. This was the bed where Della Rugerio had found Ulla's dead body.

I slid open one of the bedside dresser drawers, only to slam it shut quickly when I spotted an array of penis-shaped vibrators.

The all-white bathroom was bathed in morning sunlight, which filtered through filmy lace curtains. The doors of the medicine cabinet were open, revealing bars of soap, more makeup and skin cleansers, hair-coloring products in a color called "velvet brown," and a variety of vitamins, minerals, and food supplements that rivaled those in my mom's pantry. There were no prescription medicines that I could see.

There were numerous closets, which I didn't invade. The adjoining room was nearly as big as the bedroom, with gray rubber mats covering the floor, mirrored walls, and a collection of gym equipment: treadmill, rowing machine, exercise bike, padded benches, and a variety of barbells and weights.

I was starting to feel a little creepy, and like a creep. What was I doing prying in a woman's home? What had I expected to find that the police hadn't?

Something brushed across my ankle, and I let out a yelp.

Caribbean Joe looked up at me with his sneering face. Maybe he had a right to sneer. I stepped over the cat and let myself out the same way I'd come in, leaving the door open a few inches so Joe could leave when he was good and ready.

I hiked toward the ferry dock, thinking that maybe I'd been watching too many old private eye movies. Then again, maybe I hadn't seen enough of them. How had Rugerio known I was a Gemini? And why hadn't there been some trace of Ulla's *Payback* manuscript?

The Sausalito police station was within a block of the ferry dock. I stopped in, hoping to have a talk with Detective Kay Manners, the Pisces who, according to Della Rugerio, had pegged Ulla's death as a suicide. If nothing else, it might get my mother off my back.

The sergeant sitting behind the glass enclosure had a face that looked as if it had argued with a heavy wooden door and lost.

I introduced myself as a being with the *Bulletin* and asked to speak to the detective handling the death of Ulla Kjeldsen.

He flipped through a thick journal, then informed me that Detective Kay Manners was in charge of the case. "Not much of a case—suicide, the book says. Manners is unavailable. Call between nine and nine-thirty in the morning to make an appointment."

A half-hour window to talk to a cop. They were getting to be more exclusive than some of the Hollywood actors I had to gab with. And I really wanted to gab with Manners, because either the police had taken Ulla's computer or someone else had. Maybe my mother and Rugerio were right, and the woman had been murdered.

I got back to the *Bulletin* in time to file a story about the concern in Hollywood over the downward spiral in box-office attendance. The great unwashed out there were staying away from the picture palaces in record numbers and the studios couldn't figure out why. Somehow the concept of making better pictures, with interesting new stories, rather than remakes and sequels of sequels that were much the same as the original, hadn't penetrated the moguls' heads. It was penetrating their bank accounts, so perhaps there was hope.

My phone rang as I was spell-checking the story.

"You're not doing anything Saturday," Katherine the Great said.

She was not asking—there was no question mark on the end of that sentence. Maybe she was a psychic, like Della Rugerio. Parkham was right, though. Terry Greco had broken our Saturday-night date.

"I do have some plans, boss, but if there's something you need help with, I'd be glad to—"

"The poker game is on for Saturday, at Sir Charles Talbot's place in Napa. I'll get you a map. Dinner, then the game. It may last well into the night, so bring a change of clothes. I'm sure Junior can find you a room."

I caught Max Maslin as he was getting ready to leave the building. Max had worked for the *Los Angeles Times* entertainment section before landing at the *Bulletin*.

"How about a drink, Max?"

He patted his abundant belly and winced. "I don't know. I'm trying to lose a few pounds. Do I look heavy?"

"No. You're just a little short for your weight," I assured him. "Come on, I'm buying."

Max was what I'd describe as a "cheap date" drinker. Two glasses of his favorite foul liquor, Cherry Heering, and he'd get the giggles and tell you everything you wanted to know.

I took him to MoMo's, a trendy pub across from the Giants' stadium, because it was within walking distance of my condo, and had an outdoor patio where he could smoke his smelly pipe without starting a fight.

The best time to go to MoMo's is when the Giants are out of town, which was the case on this particular evening. We sat, drank, watched the antics of young men making moves on young women, or vice versa, and talked of Hollywood.

"Freeze Chanan. You're going back a bit, Carroll. By the time I got to the *Los Angeles Times*, he was out of the police department. Pushed out was the way I heard it. They caught him putting the squeeze on a visiting United States senator from Rhode Island or some damn place.

The good senator had come west to jump into bed with a bevy of young wanna-be actors, and Freeze had suggested that he could keep the story out of the papers if a certain number of gold coins crossed over into his hands. The senator wanted him fired, but from what my sources said, Freeze knew where more bones were buried in Hollywood than the grave diggers at Forest Lawn, so he skated with a full pension. He worked as a private eye for a while, then supposedly retired to Palm Springs, but he came back to help the Clinton team when they were chasing down all of those alleged floozies. One of Clinton's investigators went to prison, if memory serves me right, but not Freeze. He was too slick for that. He's got to be pushing seventy from one side or the other."

"What about Sir Charles Talbot?" I asked, signaling the waitress for another Cherry Heering for Max.

"What about him? That man's life could fill more than one book. We're talking library when we're talking Talbot."

"When he ran the studio down in Hollywood, Max."

"Before my time," he said after tapping his pipe stem against his teeth. "He was supposed to be a holy terror on producers, writers, actors, and especially actresses."

"Does the name Vicky Vandamn ring a bell?" I asked him.

"Not even a tiny chime." The waitress came with his drink, bending her head out of the way of his pipe as she placed it on the table. "What's your interest in all of this, Carroll?"

"I'm thinking of doing a book on Hollywood during that era. Rumor has it that Talbot had some connections with the local mob. Vandamn worked at Talbot's studio, then vanished. She turned up in Sausalito. Supposedly committed suicide about a week ago."

Max sampled his fresh drink and smacked his lips. "When I was working Hollywood, the mob was known as 'the geriatric gang.' Old toothless tigers who were no match for the East L.A. hoodlums." He puffed on his pipe to get the embers going, then said, "I watch the Irish scratch sheet pretty closely, Carroll. I didn't see an obituary on Vicky Vandamn."

"She went back to using her birth name, Ulla Kjeldsen. She'd changed it to Vandamn for the movies."

"No one could blame her for that," Max said with a chuckle.

"My mother knew her in Hollywood. They roomed together for a while."

"Ohhh," Max said, as if that cleared things up in his mind. "Your mom wants you to stick your nose into this, huh? Watch yourself, Carroll. Talbot still swings a lot of weight. He's living among us now. You wouldn't want to make an enemy of him."

No. I didn't. Or of his son, who could possibly become the next editor of the *Bulletin.*

Five

The next couple of days passed in a reasonably quiet fashion. I worked at the paper, and at home, trying to sketch out ideas for a new book on old Hollywood, possibly involving Vicky Vandamn/Ulla Kjeldsen. I tried calling Sausalito detective Kay Manners, but she was still "unavailable." I left my office and cell phone numbers, then contacted the Marin County coroner's office and ordered a copy of Kjeldsen's death certificate, at the *Bulletin*'s expense.

On Saturday, I woke up late and spent the morning playing poker with myself and practicing card tricks. Then I drove to my parents' place, hoping to sneak into my dad's flat unseen, but Mom was out front, armed and dangerous: a weed-killer spray bottle in one hand and a can of ant and roach spray in the other. She was wearing a khaki shirt and one of those pith helmets you see in the old British war movies, with an attached veil of mosquito netting to shield her face. I did mention that she dresses for every occasion, didn't I?

"Carroll dear. Have you learned anything about Vicky?" she asked, swiveling around to squirt an unsuspecting spider that had picked the wrong time to climb the front steps.

"Vicky hadn't been living in Sausalito very long. Her neighbor, who knew her only as Ulla, told me that she had been writing a book about her days in Hollywood. A tell-all book, titled *Payback*. I guess she was planning to get even with some old enemies."

"*Payback*? Didn't Mel Gibson make a movie by that name? Back when he had all his hair and was reasonably sober. I wonder if Vicky mentioned me in the book?"

"I don't know. I'm going to play in a poker game at Charles Talbot's place in Napa tonight. I'll drop Vicky's name on him."

"Drop anything that's heavy and pointed on his miserable head, dear. The book. I suppose that's why the poor dear was murdered. Have you seen it?"

"No. I couldn't find the manuscript, and the computer she was using is missing. I've been trying to talk with the detective handling the case, but she's been busy. Sorry, but I can't stay, Mom. I just need to borrow one of Dad's watches."

"Really? And whom are we trying to impress?"

"My boss, that's whom. She invited me to the poker game."

She flipped her veil back and gave me a kiss. "Do you know the Groucho Marx story regarding when to say *whom*?"

"No, that's one you haven't told me yet."

She grabbed my elbow and escorted me up the steps. "Groucho was invited to some boring dinner party, and one of the guests was a pompous professor who was lecturing everyone on and on as to when it was proper to say *who* or *whom*. Groucho suddenly jumped to his feet and said, "Whom farted?"

I laughed dutifully, kissed her good-bye, and ducked into my father's flat, heading directly for his bedroom. My father and I are pretty much the same size, and he gives me free rein to plunder his wardrobe, as well as passing along to me whatever clothes he no longer wears. Since he's a clotheshorse (*GQ* magazine once did a story on him) and is always updating his wardrobe, it works out great for me. I sifted through his collection of expensive wristwatches and chose a gold Cartier tank watch. There was an inscription on the back: *Siempre, Francesca.*

I hoped Francesca wouldn't mind my wearing the watch. I selected one of Dad's cashmere sport coats and then slipped out quietly to avoid running into my mother. I headed for Napa, the famed California wine region.

I followed the map Katherine Parkham had provided, which took me across the Bay Bridge, past Berkeley and Vallejo, and eventually onto the Silverado Trail, which once actually led to a silver mine where the likes of Black Bart hid in the trees, waiting to ambush stagecoaches carrying the mining payrolls.

The silver ran out pretty quickly, but the land itself turned into gold—the greatest premium wine acreage in the United States. I stopped to check the map again, and had to backtrack half a mile. There were no signs to mark the entrance to Talbot's place, just a small opening in a clump of flowering pink rosebushes. After a short, bumpy journey over a dirt road, I closed in on a small log cabin–style gate-house, complete with a mechanical barrier of the type seen at railroad crossings, and a welcoming sign that said STOP OR ELSE!

I came to a rolling stop as a husky, bald-headed man with a neck nearly the width of his shoulders strolled up to me. He was wearing faded jeans and one of those shirts with shoulder straps and loops to hold shotgun shells. The loops were filled with bright red shells and he carried a double-barreled shotgun in one clawlike hand. He tilted his head to one side, studied the Mini Cooper for a second, then said, "What the hell do you want, buddy?"

"Eternal life and enough money to buy a plasma TV. That and for you to raise the gate. I'm expected. Quint. Carroll Quint."

I knew it was coming, and it came. "Carroll? You kidding me?"

I leaned my head out the window and said, "Do you speak to all of Sir Charles's guests like this?"

He stiffened and backed off a step. "Sorry about that, Mr. Quint. I saw your name on the invite list. Your car kind of threw me. We get a lot of nosy people trying to sneak in here." He rested the shotgun against his hip, leaned down, and told me to drive up the mountain for a mile or so. "You'll come to a fork in the road. Turn left and it'll take you to the winery, so veer right and keep drivin'. You'll see the house. Can't miss it. Don't stop to get out of the car. Some of the dogs can get kinda mean. Hope y'all enjoy your stay."

The road was bordered on both sides by grapevines—seemingly

miles and miles of them. There was no sign of any dogs. My cell phone went off just as I hit the top of a steep cup-shaped hill.

"Is this Carroll Quint of the *Bulletin*?" The voice was a woman's, and it was soft, flat, and completely devoid of expression.

"Guilty," I said.

"This is Detective Manners. What can I do for you?"

"It's about Ulla Kjeldsen, Detective. I know you have the case listed as a suicide, but I have some questions—"

"I read the *Bulletin*, Mr. Quint. You handle movies and plays, not real-life situations. What's your interest in Ms. Kjeldsen?"

"Several people have contacted me and claim she was not the type to commit suicide," I said, feeling rather foolish. "Her neighbor let me into the houseboat, and I noticed that her computer was missing. She was writing a memoir about her life in Hollywood, *Payback*, and I wondered if you still had the computer, because—"

"Hollywood? Computer? Memoirs?" There was definitely some expression in her voice now. "This is all news to me. Who let you into the boat? Rugerio, the so-called physic?"

"Yes. I didn't see any crime tape across the door, so I took a look. Ulla had been an actress years ago; she'd used the name Vicky Vandamn. Rugerio told me that Ulla had lived in Canada before coming to Sausalito. Have you looked into that?"

"Why would I? It looks like an open-and-shut case of suicide. Are you telling me that she was murdered?"

"Well, I don't have enough information for that yet, but—"

"Do you know how many murder cases we had in Sausalito last year? Zip. And the year before? Same thing. No murders, one rape, and fewer than half a dozen aggravated assaults. Compared to the rest of the country, we're damn near crime-free, so if there's a chance there was something fishy about Kjeldsen's death, I want to look into it. Where are you, sir? We'd better have a sit-down on this."

"I'm in Napa, and I won't be back to the city until sometime tomorrow."

"I'm off till Monday morning, and I've got a full schedule. Could you meet me at the station, say eight o'clock Monday morning? We can have coffee and discuss this."

I agreed to the meeting, then, after hanging up, wondered what kept Manners so busy if the town was damn near crime-free.

The Talbot house was something to behold. It wasn't the kind of place for people who liked to throw rocks, but it was an exhibitionist's dream come true. The main building was huge: towering angular sandstone walls dominated by large slashes of glass. There were a half dozen or more smaller structures of the same modern design flanking the big house. It was built to startle and dazzle the onlooker, and that it did.

Well off to the right was a large black helicopter resting on a concrete pad. From this distance, it looked like a praying mantis ready to strike.

I parked the Mini amid a cluster of Mercedes, BMWs, two Rolls-Royces, a Cadillac Escalade, a racy-looking red convertible I couldn't ID, and one shiny black Jaguar sedan. I grabbed my overnight bag and exited the car, doing a few leg squats to get the driving kinks out of my legs.

A golden-colored horse—a palomino, I guessed—trotted into view. The rider was a woman, and she sat astride the horse as if she were sitting on a throne: back erect, shoulders straight, neck stretched. She looked to be in her mid-thirties. Her long blond hair was pushed through the adjustable band of her white baseball cap. She wore lavender-tinted sunglasses, a white silk shirt, and faded jeans, which were tucked into her polished leather boots.

"Are you the piano player?" she asked. I backed away as the horse got too close to me. I like horses, but my main interest in them is whether they win, place, or show.

"No. I'm a guest. Carroll Quint."

"Oh," she said, as if that didn't exactly please her. "One of Junior's friends. You'll probably find him in the pool." She prodded the horse by digging silver-wheeled spurs into its flank.

An arched stone bridge crossed a sparkling pool that seemed to stretch around the house like a moat. When I was halfway across the bridge, someone called out to me. "Hey there. You must be the fresh meat."

I looked down into the pool. A narrow sunburned face smiled up at me. "You're Quint, right? I'm Charlie Talbot. Welcome aboard. The poker game will start after dinner. Fancy a swim? George will show you to your cabana. You'll find trunks there." He gave a friendly wave, then swam away with a powerful, graceful stroke.

While I was watching Talbot, water splashed up onto my shoes. I looked down. There were two faces in the water now. One belonged to Terry Greco, the other to Ronald Maleuw, the Jaguar's owner.

Terry was on her back, treading water. She was wearing a yellow bikini, which I remembered only too well.

"I didn't know you were coming," she said.

"Life is full of surprises, isn't it?"

"This is Ron Maleuw," Terry said, kicking her feet to stay afloat.

"Pleased to meet you in person," Maleuw said without meaning it.

"Get a suit and join us," Terry said. "The water's wonderful."

"I'll do just that," I promised, without meaning a word of it.

A man who looked to be a well-maintained sixty or so, with a deep tan and a lopsided nose, came out to greet me. His hair was cut so close to his scalp that it was difficult to determine its color. He wore white tennis shorts and a red T-shirt with the sleeves rolled up to show off his well-muscled arms. There was a fading tattoo—capital letters *RM* on his left bicep.

"I'm George, Mr. Quint. I'll show you to your cabana. Want the Cook's tour first?"

He had some kind of a British accent, the one used by actors portraying soldiers or gangsters in the movies. Cockney? Definitely not Oxford.

"Why not?"

George sort of shuffled along, his feet barely raising themselves above the ground, like a prizefighter moving in against his opponent. He escorted me into the house. The interior was even more impressive than the outside: soaring walls in desert browns and tans, most of them displaying very large canvases of modern abstract works. I wasn't paying much attention to George's spiel until he took me into a triangle-shaped room dominated by a massive canvas that looked like two soft-edged bars of yellow floating on a paler yellow background. The painting was the same as the one on the wine label I'd seen on Ulla Kjeldsen's kitchen counter.

"Who is this painting by?" I asked George.

"Some gent named Mark Rothko. Doesn't do much for me. I like the ones where you can see that the trees are trees and ocean waves are ocean waves, but the boss, he likes a lot of this modern stuff."

"I think I've seen it on a wine label."

"You bet," George said enthusiastically. "Sir Charles features a different painting from his collection on his labels. The blanc de noirs one is a Rothko."

"What's it worth, George?"

He shrugged his shoulders. "Two million, four, something like that. Sir Charles bought it thirty years ago for almost nothing. He's got the touch. Anything he touches turns to gold, you know what I mean?"

Eventually, George led me to my "cabana," a stand-alone cubist structure that was twice the size of my condo. He showed me where the liquor was kept, which button to push on the phone if I wanted food, a massage, or clean sheets; then he flicked a wall switch and the re-tractable glass wall opened up to a small patio complete with a bubbling hot tub big enough to hold four or five people.

"There're plenty of swimsuits and robes in the closet, and anything else you want, you just call me, Mr. Quint. *Anything,* you know what I mean? Dinner is casual tonight, buffet on the patio. Cocktails at seven, dinner at eight. The man likes everybody to dress—nothing fancy, but wear a coat. That one looks fine."

After he left, I fished a beer out of the refrigerator in the small kitchen, then contemplated my next move. Swimming with Terry and the gang? Both Junior and Ron Maleuw had lifeguard suntans, and my pink shell-like body hadn't seen the sun in six months.

I stripped, picked out another beer, and carried them both out to the hot tub, where I intended to sit and sulk until the cocktail gong gonged.

I was dozing peacefully, face in the sun, bubbles tickling my skin, when someone slipped into the tub next to me. It was Terry. She put her lips next to my ear and whispered, "Fancy a kiss, handsome?"

I fancied. When we broke for air, she said, "What are you doing here? Who invited you?"

"The Great. There's a poker game tonight."

"Parkham's coming?"

"Yes," I said, surprised that she was surprised. "You didn't know?"

Terry arched her back and stuck out her legs so that the tub's jets could massage her toes. "No. But I'm glad there's a poker game tonight. Anything to keep that disgusting Junior occupied."

"What about Jaguar Ron? Isn't he defending your honor?"

"When he's around, but he's so busy with the upcoming museum exhibit. I get the feeling that this may be his last big project for Sir Charles. Ron wants to open his own gallery in London."

"That sounds like it would be expensive."

"Ronnie is a very talented painter. He did a lot of restoration work on very valuable paintings before going to work for Sir Charles. He'll be very successful. He's fed up with Erica and Junior, and I think he'll be glad when the exhibition is over. So will I. It's a once-in-a-lifetime opportunity for me, but there's so much tension around here, it just gets on my nerves."

"Erica? Is she a gorgeous blonde who rides horses?"

"You met her, huh? She's Sir Charles latest wife, and, as he so charmingly puts it, 'The latest is the greatest.' A lady not to be messed with." She arched an eyebrow at me. "If she invites you out for a ride, be careful. There's a quaint little bungalow a couple of miles down the road, and I've heard she takes her special friends there for a little saddle-up time."

"Does Sir Charles know about this?"

Terry undid the top of her bikini and tossed it casually over her shoulder. "There are only so many Viagra pills a man of his age can take, so my feeling is that he doesn't want to know. But when Sir Charles gets angry with someone, he sics George on them. George is an ex–Royal Marine."

"I've met George. Does Talbot ever mention the old days in Hollywood?"

"Don't get him started on that," Terry said, splashing her bare breasts with water. "He goes on and on forever about all of the actresses he's bedded."

"My mother said his nickname was 'Fifty-Buck Chuck.' He'd promise the girls a role in a move for a blow job, then pass them a fifty on the way out the door."

"That sounds like him. Why are you so interested in Sir Charles?"

"One of his former starlets, Vicky Vandamn, was a good friend of my mother. She disappeared from Hollywood. It was a big mystery at the time; the rumors were that she'd been murdered. She turned up in Sausalito, living on a houseboat, until she died last week. The police say it was suicide."

"Is there any reason to believe it wasn't?"

"Two reasons: my mother and the psychic who lives next to Vandamn. They believe she was murdered. Vandamn was writing a tell-all book about her Hollywood days, and I'm going to drop her name at dinner tonight and see what happens."

Terry cupped some water in her hand and poured it on my forehead. "You've been in the sun too long, Carroll. Let's go inside and rest up before dinner."

Six

*A*fter I'd dressed in fresh slacks, shirt, and my dad's sport coat, we stopped at Terry's cabana, and I pretended to watch TV while I observed her slipping into a skintight red metalliclike mesh dress.

Cocktails were served on the patio, a half-moon-shaped affair that abutted a rectangular Olympic-size swimming pool. There was a grotto at the far end of the pool, with large slabs of cantilevered stone steps climbing up some twenty feet. A couple of the stones jutted out far enough that they could be used as diving platforms.

We were the first to arrive, and George was there to greet us with a tray of drinks. Knowing I was going to be playing high-stakes poker in a short time, I stuck to club soda.

The others began showing up, and they all were unknowns to both Terry and me. Some of the men were dressed in suits and ties, the women in formal gowns, others in casual dress, and a few as if they'd just put the horse in the barn and hadn't had time to brush all the hay from their Levi's. There was a lot of talk about vineyard pests and diseases, the rising price of horse feed, and the upcoming museum exhibition.

A longhaired young man in a white shawl-collar tuxedo was playing Broadway show tunes on a Bösendorfer imperial ninety-seven-key grand piano, and doing a fine job of it.

Terry was powdering her nose and I was polishing my glasses with a cocktail napkin when Katherine Parkham appeared with her significant other, Harry Crane, the owner of a chain of upscale jewelry stores. The Great was all in black: slacks, sweater, and jacket. The diamond necklace gracing her throat would have paid my salary for the next few years.

"Are you ready?" she asked when she sidled over to me.

"As ready as I'll ever be," I told her.

She passed me a plain white envelope. "Five thousand dollars, Quint. Bet it wisely."

"I will," I assured her. "If I do spot Junior cheating, I'll give you a signal. I'll tug my right earlobe. Then maybe you can call for a break for a drink or whatever, and we can discuss it."

"Be *certain* that's he cheating, Quint. I can't afford to embarrass the Talbots unless we're damn sure about this."

Sir Charles Talbot and his wife, Erica, made an entrance just before 7:30. She was decked out in rust-colored suede paints and a matching vest. It was obvious that under the vest, there was nothing but Erica. She was holding on to her husband's arm with a tight grip, as if she were afraid he'd fall once she let go.

Sir Charles wore a faded denim shirt with snap buttons, one of those suede fringed jackets, and jeans with the cuffs rolled up at least three inches. His belt buckle, the size of a dessert plate, was studded with turquoise. He looked pretty good for his age. His shoulders were still broad, and he stood tall. His face had molded into a perpetual scowl. He wore a pair of black plastic-frame glasses. One eye was milky with cataracts, the other was moss green, clear and steady, and there was still a sign of toughness in the set of his oversized jaw. What was left of his hair was pure white.

"Hello everyone," he bellowed in an accent that sounded a bit like Sean Connery's. "Eat, drink, be merry, for tomorrow *you* may die. I'm not allowed to, myself."

There was a chorus of polite laughter. Erica left her husband's side and hooked an arm around Ron Maleuw's shoulder. She was talking rapidly, and Maleuw seemed to be very interested in what she was saying.

I ended my alcohol fast with a glass of wine, Talbot blanc de noirs. It was a beautiful light copper color. Serious wine enthusiasts—a testy bunch—get all worked up if you call California bottled wine champagne—sparkling wine is the correct terminology if it's not from France. Whatever, it was damn good.

As I turned around, I nearly bumped into Sir Charles himself. I raised up my glass and said, "This is excellent."

"Indeed. Who are you, might I ask?"

"Carroll Quint." When that didn't seem to excite him, I added, "I'm with Katherine Parkham."

"Ah, Kate." He smiled. "She's a dab hand. I'd like to have her on my payroll."

He gave me a brief nod, and was about to walk away, when I said, "I ran into someone from your past, Sir Charles."

"Who might that be?"

"Vicky Vandamn. Do you remember her?"

Talbot's shoulders gave a quick little jerk, as if he'd gotten a chill. "What are you talking about? She's deader than Elvis."

"Yes, but only recently. She reportedly committed suicide last week, on a houseboat in Sausalito. She had switched back to her given name, Ulla Kjeldsen. She was writing her memoirs, a tell-all book, *Payback*, about her Hollywood days. She told a friend that it might result in some people going to jail."

Talbot's glasses slipped lower on his nose. "I don't like barmcakes pulling my wick. Vandamn's been in the ground thirty years."

"You're mistaken, Sir Charles. I thought you might have been in touch with her." I raised the wineglass. "She had a bottle of your wine in her kitchen."

For a moment, I thought he was going to rear back and take a punch at me, but then his wife joined us.

"Is there anything wrong, Charles?" She patted her husband's arm gently. "Remember what the doctor said. You've got to watch your blood pressure."

"You bloody watch it," Talbot said, giving me a fierce look before he walked away.

"What have you been telling my husband?" Erica asked. "I don't like to see him upset like that."

She was a real beauty up close and personal. She had smooth, lightly tanned skin, lavender-tinted eyes, and a wide, sensual mouth. Her long blond hair fell around her face, and she had a habit of hurling it back with a brief shake of her head. "We were just discussing his wonderful wines," I told her.

She put her hand on my shoulder and slowly let it graze along the length of my arm, then caressed her own arm. She was the touchy-feely type, hands always in motion, stroking something, if only herself.

"I have to apologize to you, Mr. . . ."

"Quint. Carroll Quint."

"This afternoon, I mistook you for the piano player. That was silly of me. What do you do?"

Her right hand was back in action, fiddling with the buttons holding her vest together. I tore my eyes away from her fingers and spotted Sir Charles over by the bar, talking to George and Maleuw.

"I'm with the *San Francisco Bulletin*, Mrs. Talbot."

"Erica. Call me Erica. Ah, the press." Her fingers were toying with the vest's top button. "Tell me, Carroll, are you staying over tonight?"

"It looks that way, Erica. I'm playing poker with your son, and I understand the games last well into the night."

"Stepson," she said, quick to correct me. "I take an early-morning ride. I'd like to get the chance to talk to you alone and hear just what it was that upset Charles. It's really not good for his health. Shall we say nine o'clock? The stables are out back. George will be happy to drive you to the stables and fit you up."

George was staring daggers at me now, looking as if he wanted to do more than just fit me up.

"I'll do my best to be there."

She ran her fingernails across the back of my hand. "I'm sure you will."

Someone else was in a touchy-feely mood.

"Getting hungry?" Terry Greco asked, clinking my glass with hers.

"Starving."

She noticed me staring at the wall just behind her. There were two large paintings, both geometrical squares within squares of bright colors. In between was a subject I was more familiar with—a silkscreen of Marlon Brando in a torn T-shirt, standing at the bottom of a staircase.

"Like it, Carroll?"

"I'm not sure," I said truthfully. "Why the Brando thing? It's from *A Streetcar Named Desire*."

"Right. He's calling to his wife. Remember her name?"

"No one who saw the movie will ever forget Brando screaming his wife's name: 'Stella! Stella!' "

"It was Ronnie's idea to put Brando there in the middle. The two paintings are by a famous American minimalist painter, Frank *Stella*. Kind of clever, huh? What was Erica stroking you about? She looked to be in full sexual-attack mode."

"I rattled her husband when I mentioned Vicky Vandamn. Erica wants to know what got him riled up. I'm invited for a morning gallop with her to discuss it."

"What did Sir Charles say?"

"That Vicky has been in the ground for a long time. Which is just what the Hollywood gossip was at the time of her disappearance. He called me a 'barmcake.' Do you have any idea what that means?"

"No, but I'm pretty certain it wasn't a compliment. Let's eat," Terry suggested. "Some of the people who live in this house are creepy, but the food is fantastic."

Apart from being christened Carroll, I always figured that I'd had a lucky childhood. My mother submerged me in Hollywood lore and gossip; we spent a lot of time at the movies, and watching old films on TV. After just two lessons, my father knew I was not destined to be any kind of a piano player, but he taught me how to use my fists, and he got me into a serious reading habit: mostly classic mystery and crime novels, especially those chronicling Nero Wolfe and Sherlock Holmes.

It took a little more than an hour to prove to myself that Charles Talbot, Jr., was cheating. I had to give some credit to an old Sherlock quote, from the *Sign of Four*: ". . . when you have eliminated the impossible, whatever remains, however improbable, must be the truth."

The cards were not marked—a new deck had been chosen from a stack of six or seven. They were cleaner than the Pope's rap sheet, to use one of the bon mots that my mother picked up from the Web or off a bumper sticker. That left just one possibility. I spotted Junior culling a card from the deck, palming it, and putting it into a pants pocket or under his fanny until the chosen moment.

"Elementary," to quote from Holmes again.

There were five of us at the poker table. Joel Baxter was a slim gentleman in his late sixties and had an exceptionally wide mouth. He had made his money as a currency trader. Evan "Call Me Buddy" Albright was a sandy-haired man about the same age as Baxter. Albright was a likable guy, well over six feet in height, and he had to push the bathroom scale up to 270 pounds. He was a Silicon Valley venture capitalist. Katherine Parkham, Charles Talbot, Jr., and I made up the rest of the group.

Talbot was quite a specimen: a lean six-footer with lank dark hair and his father's moss green eyes and broad shoulders. His nose had a slight flat spot about midway down and his lips were chapped and cracked. I had managed to get the seat directly to his left, which gave me a good view of the way he handled the cards.

"Call me Charlie," Talbot told me after we'd been introduced properly by the Great. She'd described me as an "associate," and no one had pressed the issue, which I was grateful for, until it dawned on me that that meant they had never bothered to read any of my reviews.

The rich have subtle ways of letting one another know that they are members of an oh-so-exclusive society. Women have it the easiest: diamonds, pearls, rubies, designer clothes. With men, it's a little different. An expensive Swiss watch, of course, but then it gets tricky. I leaned out to reach for some peanuts, flashing my dad's Cartier watch, and also the cuffs on the sport coat, which featured working buttonholes. One of the most useless items in the male wardrobe, yet they add a couple of hundred dollars to the price tag. I mean, who ever unbuttons the damn things? Or rolls up the sleeves? No one. But Joel Baxter's blue blazer had the damn things, and so did Evan Albright's chalk-stripe jacket. Talbot was wearing a white V-necked sweater with a red cowboy-style bandanna knotted around his neck.

We were in the game room, which featured walls decorated with all kinds of fencing swords and ancient battleaxes. There was a pool table, billiards table, as well as the emerald green felt-covered circular table we were using for the poker game. There was a drinks cart positioned nearby; it featured Polish vodkas, English gin, Kentucky whiskey, single-malt scotch from tiny villages hidden in valleys of heather, cognacs, and a variety of Talbot Estates wines. Parkham and I stuck to coffee, while the others sipped slowly at the liquor.

After an hour or so, the coats were off, sleeves rolled up, and the air thick with smoke. The Great, Baxter, and Albright were puffing on cigars of various lengths, thickness, and aromas, and Junior was chain-smoking his way through a pack of unfiltered Camels. A plump, dark-skinned woman in her forties, whom I'd seen serving lobster at the buffet dinner, stopped in every twenty minutes or so to empty the ashtrays and pour fresh drinks.

Junior called her Carla, as in "Carla, clean up this stuff."

All poker players, including the professionals you see in those TV tournaments, have "tells"—those body-language tip-offs that often make the difference between winning and losing. Baxter was a cautious player. He kept his chips in tight stacks and stiffened his back and edged closer to the table when he had a good hand. Albright, perhaps because of his size, liked to stare his opponent down, usually a sign of a bluff. And sure enough, every time Albright tried it, he was bluffing.

The Great was the best of the three of them, but she had a habit of fiddling with her necklace when she had good cards.

Talbot was in a class all his own. He had a variety of nervous tics and he constantly toyed with his chips—he had even perfected the "finger roll," where the player rolls a single chip across the back of his knuckles. He had a pianist's long fingers, except for the two pinkies, which curved decidedly inward. If he had a real tell, it was glancing at the strongest player's chips after looking at his hole cards to see just how much he should bet.

Just as the Great had said, whenever it was Talbot's turn to deal, he chose seven-card stud, which required more handling of the cards, since each player can draw up to seven cards. Junior was culling a card from the deck, an ace. Just one card, but it made a world of difference. A single ace-high is sometimes good enough to win a hand, and if the player draws another ace in a five-player game, he has an over 60 percent chance of winning the hand. Talbot would never have gotten away with this in a casino or a game with professionals, but he had very fast hands and was good enough to fool most amateurs.

Everyone else, including me, chose Texas hold 'em. This game has turned into a major sports event on TV. Simple enough, really. Each player is dealt two cards, facedown, and bets are made. Then the dealer turns up three cards in the middle of the table; this is called the flop. All of the players can use those cards with their hole cards. The players bet, and then another card, the turn card, is dealt faceup on the table. Another round of betting ensues; then comes the seventh and final card, the river. Of course, a player can choose to drop out at any time after he's given his hole cards.

I was glad I was playing with the Great's money, because the size of the pots was a lot more than I was used to. Baxter was the banker, and for five thousand dollars I was given a stack of red, white, and blue chips. The reds were twenty-five bucks, the whites fifty, and the blues a hundred.

After Talbot had raked in a pot worth some four thousand dollars, I looked over at the Great and tugged on my right earlobe. She nodded and rose to her feet.

"Rest room time, boys. How about a ten-minute break?"

I stood up and stretched, then wandered over to the window to enjoy the view while the "boys" hit the bar. In a few minutes, Parkham walked over to me and said one simple word: "How?"

"He's culling cards. He hides an ace either in his pants pocket or under his butt until it's needed. Didn't you notice that when he wins a hand, it's almost always because he has an ace or two, or three?"

"A lot of winning hands involve aces," she said before turning away from me and looking out the window. "Can you prove it?"

"No. But I might be able to embarrass him, let him know that I know he's cheating. There's a risk, of course."

Her head snapped around. "What risk?"

"I could lose all of your money."

A smile stretched her cheeks. "That's a risk I'll take. Break the bastard."

"I might need a little help. If you drop out of a hand, and you happen to have an ace, let me know."

"And just how am I supposed to do that?"

"Take off one of your earrings. The right one."

Before she walked away, I asked a question. "Do you know what *barmcake* means? Sir Charles called me that."

"You must have annoyed him, Quint. That's Brit slang for *idiot*. He was calling you an asshole."

That was bad news. I figured that if the Talbots ever did take control of the *Bulletin,* barmcakes would be booted out the door pretty damn fast.

Seven

I poured myself a large glass of wine before retaking my seat. The game resumed slowly, as if the break in the action caused all of us to play cautiously for a while. I had a couple of options. I could embarrass Charlie Talbot—say something about the deck feeling light, then count out the cards and show everyone that an ace was missing. Or I could wait for an opportunity where I could expose him *and* make some money for myself. I was on my second glass of wine and acting a little tipsy by the time the golden opportunity came a-knocking.

There was only one way to pull it off—by cheating: the old "It takes a cheat to catch a cheat" theory. I had no qualms about going after young Mr. Talbot; he was, in fact, stealing from everyone at the table, and he'd apparently been doing so for some time. Like Katherine Parkham, I couldn't imagine why someone with his wealth would cheat, but doing it he was.

Junior had added to his chip count at the expense of both Joel Baxter and Evan Albright. The Great was down to a couple of thousand dollars, and I was about even.

Poker at any level can be boring and monotonous for long stretches of time—no one gets good cards, or one player has an obvious winner and can't draw his opponents into the pot—but the charm of the game is that sooner or later there comes a hand where fireworks are guaranteed.

"Hold 'em," I said when I scooped up the cards after Junior's last deal, palming the ace of spades and slipping it under my butt before shuffling the deck, just as I'd seen Junior do moments before. I dealt out the hole cards, then took a peek at mine: the five of clubs and the five of spades. Not bad. Parkham opened the betting with a hundred-dollar bet, and everyone at the table followed suit. The flop was terrific, at least for me: the jack of diamonds, the eight of clubs, and a lovely five of diamonds.

Parkham bet five hundred dollars. Baxter hesitated for a moment before calling the bet. Albright wisely folded. Junior went through his twitching routine before upping the ante to a thousand. I looked at my hole cards a couple of times before tossing in ten one-hundred-dollar blue chips, and Parkham and Baxter both called the raise by pushing in five hundred dollars in chips.

The next card was the king of spades. The Great decided she'd had enough. She took off her right earring and sighed loudly before folding her hand. The king seemed to please Baxter. He tossed in a thousand dollars' worth of chips, which signaled to me, and Junior no doubt, that he had a pair of kings. Junior called and raised another thousand. I took a long swig from the wineglass and called the bet after a polite burp. Junior gave me a pitying glance, figuring I was bluffing or drunk, than settled his eyes on Baxter, who pushed in his chips after saying, "You're not going to bluff me out of this one, young man."

I threw out the river card, the ace of diamonds. The Great let out a loud groan and drummed her empty glass on the table. Joel Baxter's face went through a series of contortions. The upturned ace was bad news for him, too. He stared at his cards while Junior performed his chip across the knuckles trick, then said, "Damn it," and threw in his cards.

Junior casually shoved a stack of blue chips into the middle of the table. "Another two thousand dollars, chummy. Fancy a chance at that big pot?"

Indeed I did. I knew that Talbot had a pair of aces, the one on the table and the one he'd culled from the deck. The Great had signaled me by taking off her earring that she had discarded an ace—the third ace—and the fourth was tucked safely under my fanny.

I figured Junior's other hole card to be a jack or an eight, to match the flop cards—so, the best he could hold would be two pairs. There was no way he could beat me, unless I folded.

I drained what was left in my glass and said, "I'm all in. Three thousand, six hundred."

"Call," he said gleefully, then stood up and turned over his cards. "Two pairs, aces and jacks, fancy that."

The Great gave me a look that could have frosted a martini pitcher.

"Nice hand," I said, congratulating Talbot, then casually turned my hole cards over. "Three fives, Charlie. Fancy *that.*"

"I'll be damned," Albright said, ironic applause in his voice. "I figured Charlie for three aces, and you come up with three lowly fives."

"Yeah, I had a hunch he was going to pull another ace out of his pocket, or from under his butt," I said. "It's amazing how lucky you are with aces, but some things just never last, do they?"

There was a cold silence for several moments; then Junior locked his eyes on mine and said, "Are you accusing me of cheating, old cock?"

I raked in my chips and began arranging them in neat stacks. "I wouldn't think of it. I'm just saying that you're a lucky guy." I paused a few beats, then added, "Or you used to be."

Junior leaped to his feet. His face reddened, and for a moment I thought he might yank one of the swords off the wall and challenge me to a duel.

Evan Albright hurried over and got his bulk between the two of us. "The game is over, gentlemen. Joel, dole out the winnings. I think we could all use a drink."

Talbot wasn't having it. He tried to edge around Albright, but he was no match for the older man's size.

"I'll see you later," he threatened, pointing a finger at me before turning on his heel and exiting the room.

The Great was busy dealing out the deck of cards we'd been playing with, arranging them in neat order by suit, from deuce to ace.

"There's one card missing, boys," she grumbled nastily. "The ace of spades."

"Missing?" Joel Baxter was confused. "How the hell can that be?"

I pushed my chair back, and in doing so, I knocked over the empty wineglass, which gave me all the cover I needed to flip to the floor the ace I'd culled. "There's your answer, Mr. Baxter. The ace of spades, on the carpet, by Talbot's seat. It must have fallen there sometime during the game."

Albright's eyes moved from mine to Parkham's. "Katherine, I think we'll have to rethink the makeup of the game from now on. Do you expect Mr. Quint to play with us again?"

"No," the Great replied firmly.

"How about your friend Harry Crane?" Baxter asked. "Would he be interested in joining us?"

The Great looked up at me and said, "I'll ask him, Evan. Quint, I'll settle things here, and give you your winnings in the morning."

I said good night to all, then went looking for Terry Greco. As I passed the big pool by the patio, I saw a dark figure swimming underwater. He touched one side of the pool, then pushed off, staying under for a long time before coming up for air. It was George. He dived under again without noticing me.

Sir Charles Talbot wasn't happy with me. His son was mightily pissed off at me. I had the feeling that George, the former Royal Marine, was ready to do me harm on the orders of either of them, and now Erica Talbot was going to be upset because I'd missed our morning horse ride.

I took full responsibility for the men being after my hide, but Erica being angry with me was Terry Greco's fault. We had spent the night at her cabana, and I had halfheartedly tried to get myself out of bed at the appointed time to go riding, but Terry had locked her legs around mine and mumbled, "Go back to sleep," and I'd followed orders.

The big house was strangely silent when we went prowling for breakfast a little before eleven o'clock; even the ever-present George was nowhere to be seen.

Terry was wearing low-riding jeans and a yellow midriff blouse that exposed her smooth, freshly tanned stomach.

We had fruit, cinnamon rolls, and coffee in the same room where the dinner banquet had been held the night before.

"What is it with all of these swimming pools?" I asked. "The moat around the house, this big pool, the diving grotto. A bit overdone, isn't it?"

"Sports are part of the Talbot lifestyle. Erica is crazy for horses. There's a driving range and putting green, as well as an archery and pistol range just down the road. Sir Charles was quite a swimmer in his time," Terry said. "Marathon stuff, the English Channel thing. He swims every day for half an hour or more to keep fit. He likes to take his dip when there's no one around to watch."

I remembered a story about George Abbott, a major figure in the Broadway theater, whose productions included *Call Me Madam, The Pajama Game,* and *Damn Yankees.* He lived to the very ripe old age of 107, and worked right up to the end. He had outlived his tennis partners, and gotten too old for golf, so his wife had a swimming pool put in at their country estate, Mr. Abbott reportedly had been quite a swimmer in his youth. The first time he went in, he sank to the bottom. When rescued, he told his wife, "Send the pool back. It doesn't work."

I finished my cinnamon roll, and then told Terry I had to get going. She insisted on showing me Talbot's art collection.

I followed her out of the house, around the big swimming pool, and over to an adobe building the size of adjoining rest rooms in a public park.

Inside were two steel-fronted elevators. There was an ivory-colored phone on the wall. Terry picked it up and after a moment or two said, "Ron? It's Terry. Can I come down?"

She hung up and the elevator doors pinged open, then whooshed shut after us. She pushed a button and we descended very fast.

"Fifteen feet," Terry said, anticipating my question. The door opened and we stepped out onto a polished variegated-marble floor. Ronald Maleuw was there, a smile on his face, until he saw me.

"Good morning," he said formally. He was wearing a white smock with specks of paint on the sleeves.

Terry grabbed his arm and dimpled her cheeks. "Is it all right if I show Carroll around?"

Maleuw pinched his lower lip between his thumb and forefinger and frowned. "Sir Charles doesn't like just anyone down here, Terry. I thought I made that clear to you."

"We'll only be a few minutes. Carroll has to get back to the city." She did the dimples thing again. "I hope we have a chance to use the pool again before I leave this afternoon."

Maleuw surrendered gallantly. "Oh, all right."

He took us on a tour, first describing the humidity-control features and warning me not to touch *anything*. The walls were vanilla-colored rough stucco and the doors and archways were rounded, which enhanced the fact that we were in an underground cave.

"Originally, Sir Charles intended to use this as a wine cellar," Maleuw said, "but later he decided it would be a perfect spot for storing his paintings."

Terry enthusiastically sang out the names of the artists whose magnificent works hung on the walls. Gauguin, Cézanne, Renoir, Manet, Degas, those names I was familiar with, but there were many I did not know. We moved from long room to long room, going from French Impressionist paintings to a whole room of Picassos, then into a room with several paintings by Georgia O'Keeffe and a huge number of abstract canvases, including a few more Rothkos, similar in style to the one Talbot used as a wine label, but in different colors.

It was, in a word, overwhelming.

Maleuw glanced at his watch pointedly and said, "I'm afraid I have to get back to work, Terry, or we'll never make that swim date."

I thanked him sincerely, and when we were back up on terra firma and inhaling fresh air, I said, "That's incredible, Terry, damn near obscene. How did one man obtain that amount of great art? Does anyone besides the chosen few ever get to see them?"

"Sir Charles regularly loans a few of the paintings to various museums around the world. You didn't see everything, Carroll. There are rooms stocked with canvases by well-known painters—some that haven't been seen by anyone but Sir Charles and Ronnie. As to how Talbot got them, he did it the old-fashioned way—by lying, cheating, stealing, just like the robber barons of old. Talbot, for all his faults, has a great eye for talent. He purchased a lot of the works directly from the artists. You see all of these extraordinary prices paid for paintings at auction, but the actual painters may have sold them for peanuts—to someone like Talbot, for cash, at a fraction of the auction price. Otherwise, their agents and the galleries would have taken most of the money. Do you know how many paintings van Gogh sold in his lifetime? One, just one. He didn't make enough money to pay for his paint. But Picasso was just the opposite. As a young man, he'd turn out a painting every morning, then work on stone, ceramics, or metal in the afternoon. The known number of his creations is more than thirty thousand, but that's not a complete list. He was a multimillionaire by the time he died. It's the way the art world works."

"I've never been able to get into that line of work, damn it."

"Talbot brags about how he picked up some wonderful abstract paintings when he was running his Hollywood studio, simply by offering the artist the favors of one of his starlets. No wonder his son is such a jerk. The apple doesn't fall far from the tree."

"True, but the same boiling water that softens the carrot hardens the egg."

She came to an abrupt halt, stuck her chin out at me, and said, "What?"

"One of my mother's favorite sayings," I explained. Mom used it whenever Dad kidded her about her family genes, especially when it came to her brother, Uncle Crime. "How did Maleuw end up with the choice job of caretaking Talbot's art collection?"

"Ron describes himself as a 'lucky orphan.' He was adopted by Philip and Cynthia Maleuw. His father was a successful set designer, his mother a first-class artist and teacher."

"Set designer? You mean Hollywood? Did he work for Talbot?"

"Among others," Terry said. "Talbot remained a family friend, and when he went looking for a curator, he contacted Ronnie. Ron told me his family moved to England when he was about three years old. He was educated there, and in Paris at the Ecole des Beaux-Arts."

"I wonder if his parents knew Vicky Vandamn in Hollywood?"

"We'll never know," Terry said. "They've both passed away. I'm sure he wouldn't have any memories of Hollywood."

Maybe, but it wouldn't hurt to bring the subject up the next time I had a chance to talk to Maleuw.

We stopped at my cabana to pick up my overnight bag. Terry gasped out loud when I opened the door. The room was a mess: the bed ripped apart, liquor bottles from the refrigerator broken and scattered around the rug, my overnight bag turned inside out, shorts and T-shirts torn apart.

"This is awful, Carroll. I don't understand. There are alarms and dogs prowling outside at night. Who would do this?"

I had an idea, but I just said, "I'm glad I slept at your cabana last night." I picked up the phone by the bed, punched the button listed for room service, and explained the circumstances to the Spanish-accented voice on the other end of the line.

"I'll go find George," Terry volunteered. "He'll know what to do."

"I'm sure he will, Ter. You explain. I've got to get going."

She walked me out to the car. There were long, wavy scratches on both sides of my Mini—the kind inflicted with a knife blade, or the teeth of a key.

"This is terrible," Terry said, stamping a sandal-sheathed foot in anger. "We should call the police."

I unlocked the car door gingerly, actually considering that there might be a bomb somewhere. They do teach things like bomb making in the Royal Marines. But I told myself Sir Charles wouldn't want anyone killed on his property.

I used my cell phone camera to the take photos of the damage. Terry went back to the house to report the incident.

The clip-clop of hooves announced the arrival of Erica Talbot.

"You didn't show up," she said from high in the saddle.

"Overslept," I explained. I pointed out the damage to the Mini. "Someone keyed my car last night, or early this morning."

"It must have been the gardeners, with their wheelbarrows. Tell George about it. He'll see that you're reimbursed for the damage. I still want to have that conversation with you, Mr. Quint. My husband was very upset with you; he had a terrible night. We have to talk. Do you have a card?"

I took a *Bulletin* business card from my wallet, jotted down my cell phone number, and handed it to her.

"I'll call you," Erica said. "I have some business in the city in the next couple of days. Don't disappoint me this time."

She dug those silver spurs into old paint and galloped off. Sharp silver spurs. They could have done a good job on the Mini's paint.

Eight

Walking into the newspaper office on Sunday afternoon was like walking into a ballpark when there was no game scheduled—it was deserted. No noise, no excitement. The only sound was the clicking of my own heels as I walked by the area where the paper's crime reporters worked. Before he left the *Bulletin*, Carl Dillon, a bright young reporter, had taught me a few tricks on tracking people. How bright was Dillon? He quit the paper, leaving behind his meager salary, and joined the San Francisco Police Department, where, as a rookie, he was making more than ninety thousand dollars a year, in addition to a great pension, overtime, sick leave, and a full month's vacation every year. I should be so bright.

I set my coffee cup down on my desk, booted up the computer, and went to work on Ulla Kjeldsen. For the princely sum of fifteen dollars, a data-search firm checked her name and Sausalito address—and came up with a hit that included her Social Security number, which was the key to Pandora's box, according to Dillon. With a Social Security number, all things were possible.

I entered the Social Security number into another database firm—this one was costing the *Bulletin* an additional twenty-five dollars. Because of the expense, and the possibility of claims of invading someone's privacy, the paper preferred its reporters not use the databases, but since I was in the Great's good graces at the moment, I didn't think there would be a problem.

Bingo. Ulla/Vicky showed up with yet another name, Vicky Ramsey, and an address in James Bay, Victoria, British Columbia. Spouse's name: Arnold Ramsey. According to my mother, Ulla had had a beau in Hollywood named Jerome Ramsey, who had allegedly committed suicide, and Jerome's brother had attended his funeral.

I ran Arnold Ramsey through the database and came up with the same home address in James Bay, as well as a business address: Baum and Ramsey Realty, also in Victoria.

I entered the business's name in Google and was rewarded with the firm's Web page, which featured photos of the two principals. The two men were standing side by side. Harry Baum was the taller of the two, a craggy-faced man with a shock of steel gray hair that flopped boyishly over his forehead. Arnold Ramsey was balding and had a long nose and close-set eyes.

I dialed the number listed on the Web site and was lucky to find someone in the office, Mr. Baum himself.

I told him that I was interested in speaking with Ramsey.

"Arnie? He died, sir. Over a year ago. Is there something I can help you with?"

"I'm calling from San Francisco. Did you know Arnie's wife, Vicky?"

"Yes. Very well. Is she living down there now?"

"She was living in Sausalito, just across the bay. I'm afraid I have some bad news. She passed away several days ago. Did she have any family? Children?"

"No. Nobody. Maybe you'd better tell me just who you are, mister," Baum wisely said.

I told him the truth—or some of it: that I was a reporter and that there were some suspicions regarding the circumstances of her death.

"Poor Vicky," Baum said. "She was—she really enjoyed life. Damn, she was a good-looking woman."

"How did her husband die?"

"An accident. Arnie wasn't in good health; he was an epileptic, and he had diabetes. He loved to fish. We were fishing on Lake Cowichan, which is not far from Victoria. Best fly-fishing in the world. We had split up, and Arnie must have had a seizure. He went over a cliff and landed on some rocks. By the time I found him, he was dead."

"Did he have a brother? Jerome Ramsey?"

"Holy Christ." Baum laughed. "You're going back a hell of a long way. Yeah, Jerome. He died years ago. He was a Hollywood writer, or producer, something like that."

"Vicky knew him in Hollywood. They'd dated."

Harry Baum was getting agitated. "How do you know this stuff? And how do I know you're who you say you are? What's your telephone number?"

"My mother was Vicky's roommate in Hollywood." I gave him the *Bulletin*'s switchboard number and my extension, and Baum said he'd call right back.

I sipped at my cooling coffee and waited.

"Okay, you're legit," Baum said when we were back on the line. "Vicky told me she'd had a brief fling in Hollywood, but she didn't go into many details. I knew Jerome when we were kids, and she never told me they were an item, either."

"You sound like you knew her pretty well," I said.

There was a long, cold silence; then Baum said, "I'm not telling tales out of school. You could ask anyone in town who knew Vicky and they'd tell you the same thing. She liked to . . . socialize. After Arnie died, we became pretty good friends."

There was something in Baum's voice that gave me the impression that they'd been pretty good friends before her husband died. "Was Vicky in good financial shape, Mr. Baum? She was living on a houseboat in Sausalito, and her neighbor said she seemed to have all the money she needed."

"Arnie was in the real estate racket with me for a long time. He wasn't hurting. As soon as the probate went through, Vicky put most of the properties up for sale; a local bank is managing the rest. She skated out of town with a healthy bankroll, that's for sure. Enough to keep her in champagne for the rest of her life. You said that there were suspicions regarding her death. Are you telling me she was murdered?"

"The police think it was suicide, but her neighbor believes differently. Do you know anything about a book she was writing about her Hollywood days?"

"Vicky? A book? I never saw her *read* a book, much less try writing one. She liked to sail, dance, and have a good time. Was there anyone . . . special she was seeing down there?"

"Not that I know of. Apparently, she did have a few men friends."

Baum let out a grunt that could have been a sob or a laugh. "Yeah, she always had men friends."

"Didn't her husband object?" I asked.

"Did you ever see Vicky, Mr. Quint?"

"Just her pictures."

"Well, she was one of those women who look better than their pictures. She wasn't just beautiful; she was special, you know what I mean? She never seemed to age. And Arnie, he was a nice, decent guy, but nothing to look at."

"I saw his picture on your Web site."

"Yeah? I forgot about that. I'll have to update the site. Arnie was a lifelong bachelor; all he liked to do was hunt and fish. I couldn't believe it when she came up here and married him. Arnie was grateful, I guess you could say. Grateful he had what he had of her. What he didn't know didn't hurt him, you know what I mean?"

I knew exactly what he meant. "How long had she been living in Victoria?"

"Oh, she came to town about ten or eleven years ago, I guess. It didn't take long for Arnie to hook up with her."

Ten or eleven years. That still left quite a gap between Hollywood and Victoria. "Do you know where she lived prior to that?"

"She said something about Mexico, or South America, I think."

"Did you ever hear the name Ulla Kjeldsen?"

"Ulla who? No, and it's not a name you'd be likely to forget. Who is she? One of Vicky's old friends?"

"Yeah, I guess she was. Thanks for your time, Mr. Baum. I'll let you know if anything turns up on the investigation."

I went back to the databases. There was nothing regarding Ulla's address prior to Victoria.

I leaned back in my swivel chair and tried to put the puzzle together. The problem was, I didn't have enough pieces yet. Ulla was certainly turning out to be a mystery woman. Maybe there *was* a book in all of this for me.

Back to the computer. Dillon, the crime reporter, had told me that now private eyes spent most of their time in front of computers. I tried to imagine how that would have worked for Sherlock, Nero Wolfe, Philip Marlowe, Mike Hammer, et al. One thing was for certain: It would have made for boring reading.

Willie Chanan popped up on a database with an address on Dinah Shore Drive in Palm Springs. Telephone information had a number for W. Chanan, no address.

I dialed and was connected to a rough-sounding voice on the answering machine. "Leave a message, pally."

"My name is Carroll Quint, I work for the *San Francisco Bulletin,* and I'm calling about Vicky Vandamn. If you can—"

"Who the hell are you?" the same rough voice said. The guy must have been sitting by the phone when it rang.

I went through my spiel again, then said, "Are you Willie 'Freeze' Chanan?"

"That depends on just what you want, pally. What's this crap about Vicky?"

"She died in Sausalito last week, and I was wondering—"

"Get real, punk. What is this, a gag? Vicky entered Forever City a long time ago; she kicked the oxygen habit, pally. Get it?"

"Incorrect," I told him. Great word, *incorrect.* For some reason, it really ticks people off a lot more than simply saying "You're wrong."

"Yeah, well, you ever bother me with this crap again, you'll be sleeping the in the Motel Deep Six, get it?"

I laughed out loud. "Those are terrible lines, Freeze. Who gave them to you, one of Chuck Talbot's writers?"

"Hold on a minute," Chanan shouted. I could hear the receiver being dropped to a desk or table, then the clicking of a keyboard. My guess was he was checking me out on his computer. Why not? He supposedly became a private investigator after being asked to retire from the LAPD.

"What the hell kind of a name is Carroll for a man?" he said when he got back on the line. "You're a movie critic. You wrote one lousy book about old flicks, sold about three copies. And now you're talking to me like you're some tough guy. I used to use punks like you for ashtrays, pally."

"Talk slower. I'm trying to write all of these lines down, Freeze. You missed your calling. You should have worked for Talbot. Or maybe you did. I understand you helped out the studios when their stars were caught with their whatevers down around their ankles. How well did you know Vicky Vandamn? Were she and Talbot an item? What about Jerome Ramsey? Did you investigate his death? Was it really a suicide? Or was Tony Silk involved?"

"You're a regular question man, pally. Let's see. You're in Frisco. Tell you what we're going to do. I'll meet you halfway. The Caffe Roma in Beverly Hills. Just off Rodeo Drive. Tomorrow night, eight o'clock."

"I can't make it, Freeze."

"Then it's your loss, pally. And don't bother me again, get it?"

He slammed down the receiver so hard that I had to jerk the phone from my ear.

I shut down the computer and decided I'd worked hard enough for one Sunday afternoon. I wondered if Freeze Chanan would dig deeper into my background—deep enough to realize that he once knew my mother, the former Karen Kaas, and that my father was a fairly famous jazz pianist—and whether or not that would make any difference to him.

As old and full of corny clichés as he was, Freeze Chanan would be an excellent source, both on Ulla's death and for the Hollywood book that was now forming in my little gray cells.

I drove to Sausalito the next morning for the meeting with Detective Kay Manners. She was waiting for me at the entrance to the police station. A woman of medium height, she had shoulder-length reddish brown hair. Her heart-shaped face was dotted with freckles. She was wearing gray slacks and a blue blazer with an emblem of the Sausalito Police Department on the breast.

"Mr. Quint," she said enthusiastically. "I'm Detective Manners. Had breakfast yet?"

She seemed delighted when I said no. She ushered me into her unmarked car and we chatted about the weather and traffic while she drove to the Lighthouse Café, a historical landmark dating back to the 1920s. A miniature lighthouse on the deck above the entrance looked as if it hadn't been painted since it was put in place.

Manners did what cops love to do—parked right in front of a fire hydrant. The café was small—about twenty seats. The young woman acting as hostess led us to an empty booth in the back.

Once we were seated and given cups of steaming black coffee, Manners said, "Try Gabriel's corned beef hash. It's terrific."

I studied Manners while she spoke to a skinny waitress with a ponytail that reached below her waist. Under that blue blazer was a body that was a little heavy in the hips and bust. Her hands were red and rough and she wore no nail polish or rings. Her watch was a black plastic digital sports model, the kind you can you use to time your laps and monitor your heartbeat. The black leather purse hanging from a strap around her shoulder was big enough to store a gun, handcuffs, and all the other paraphernalia gendarmes have at their disposal.

"So, Carroll, tell me what you know about my ten-fifty-six?"

I don't know why, but cops like to talk to the general public as if we know all of their response and scanner codes. I just frowned and cocked my head to one side.

"Suicide," Manners explained. "Ulla Kjeldsen. I went over my notes and the coroner's report, and I couldn't find anything that would make me think it was anything else."

"What about Ulla's missing computer, and her manuscript? Ulla told Della Rugerio that the book, *Payback*, would be sensational and that some people might end up in jail because of what was in it."

Manners rolled her eyes. "Rugerio. A phony psychic is hardly what my captain would call a reliable source. She does more than read palms in that pad of hers. She applied for a massage license and was turned down, but we believe she's giving her customers a 'happy ending' massage, if you know what I mean, so you'll have to do better than that, Carroll. And how do you know the computer wasn't there? Did you look everywhere in the houseboat?"

"I couldn't find a computer. Rugerio said she'd looked for it and it was gone."

The waitress brought our breakfast: two huge platters loaded with corned beef, eggs, hash browns, and toast. Whoever the Gabriel was they'd named the dish after must have had an enormous appetite. Manners attacked hers with gusto as I told her a bit about Ulla Kjeldsen's background. I held back the information about contacting Freeze Chanan and Harry Baum, figuring I could use that later as a bargaining chip.

By the time I was finished talking, Manner's plate was clean and she was signaling for more coffee.

"I can see your interest, Carroll. It all sounds like a made-for-TV movie—Hollywood starlets, suicides, gangsters, phony physics—but it doesn't add up to anything for me. And I just know you're going to ask me why there was no note. Well, I checked the figures. In suicides involving women over fifty, only forty-two percent leave notes."

"What did the autopsy show?" I asked, scooping up a forkful of the hash.

"Kjeldsen had ingested Nembutal, a prescription barbiturate that is primarily used as a sleeping pill and is readily available on the streets. 'Yellow jackets,' they're called. It's the preferred way of committing suicide. Many elderly folks buy them from dealers, then hide them away until the time comes when they'll be needed. You'll appreciate this, Carroll. I did some research on the drug and learned it was used by Marilyn Monroe, Judy Garland, and Jimi Hendrix when they ended their lives. Kjeldsen had been drinking, and smoking dope. Her alcohol level was quite high, which would have enhanced the effect of the Nembutal. I found a stash of marijuana in her dresser drawer." She waved her cup of coffee in my direction. "Did you happen to look around in her dresser drawers when you were there?"

I had no intention of confessing to finding Ulla's vibrators. "No. The bathroom medicine cabinet was wide open, but I didn't take an inventory."

"There were no prescription medicines, if that's what you're thinking. We found a stash of dope lying alongside an assortment of sexual toys in a drawer by her bed. Apparently, Ms. Kjeldsen had an active libido. In addition to vibrators, there were contraceptives, and she had a closet full of Victoria Secret–type lingerie."

"Despite her strong sexual appetite, she was a practicing Catholic, according to Rugerio—Mass, confession, the whole banana. My mother said she was quite religious when they were in Hollywood— lots of boyfriends, but she made time for church, too."

"Then apparently she did a lot of confessing," Manners said, brushing her hair away from her face. "I spoke to the parish priest. He wasn't a lot of help—that 'sanctity of the confessional' stuff. He was genuinely surprised at her suicide, though."

"Rugerio referred to the priest as 'Father Hunk.' "

Manners smiled widely. "Father James Carmody. Yeah, he's one of those 'what a waste' priests all right. Did you notice the Lucite crucifix on the downstairs wall in Kjeldsen's place? I almost missed it. It was the only one in the house, and barely visible. If there was a shrine there, it was to Ulla—all those photographs and the paintings. All of herself."

The waitress came by, picked up my half-filled plate, topped up our coffee, and dropped the check in front of me. The bill came to more than twenty-six bucks.

"I'll take care of the tip," Manners said, unzipping her purse.

John Leary, an Irish kid who had lived next to me when I was growing up, had a family full of uncles and brothers who were either cops or firemen, and he'd explained the difference to me: "A fireman always wants a discount; a cop wants it for free." I was lucky Manners volunteered for the tip.

As she peeled off three one-dollar bills from a small roll, she said, "Carroll, I would *really* dig into this case if I thought there was a reason to do so. But the body's been cremated, at Ms. Kjeldsen's request. She appeared to be one of those women who can't face getting old. You saw her home gym. The coroner's report listed numerous cosmetic surgeries: a face-lift, a nose job, breast enhancement, liposuction—the works. There was evidence that she'd had a cesarean section, and that she'd had her tubes tied years ago. I couldn't find a record of a living relative. The child may have died. Perhaps she was lonely, unhappy—it happens."

"The missing computer and manuscript worry me," I said, digging my money clip out of my pocket. "How could they just disappear like that? And I didn't find any backup or floppy disks. The answering machine was unplugged, and the last phone call she made was to get the correct time—hardly the thing someone contemplating suicide would do. The book she was writing, that could have been a motive for murder."

Manners pushed her chair back and stood up. "Maybe she was embarrassed about something on the computer—this *supposed* book, some incriminating letters, who knows. Ulla could have just tossed it in the bay." She held out a hand like a traffic cop. "And don't suggest that I have divers search for it. The captain wouldn't okay that, and even if they looked, the tides could have taken it out to deeper water. Or she could have dumped it from her kayak."

"The only kayak I saw was a red one on Rugerio's deck."

Manners took a final sip from her coffee cup, then said, "That belonged to Ulla. She probably told Rugerio to take it during one of their nightly séance chats. I'll tell you one thing, Carroll. If somehow it's proved that Kjeldsen didn't commit suicide, Rugerio would be my prime suspect."

Nine

I turned down Detective Manners's offer of a ride back to the police station, telling her that I wanted to walk off breakfast. As soon as her unmarked car had disappeared from sight, I went back into the restaurant and asked the waitress who had served us if she knew where I could find Father Carmody.

Her face broke out into a broad smile reminiscent of Manners's when I'd brought up the priest's name.

"Ohhh, Father Jim. He's at St. Agnes Church. It's just a couple of blocks from here."

I followed her directions, walking up a long, winding road until I came to the church. It was done in the old Spanish style: white adobe walls covered with blooming purple bougainvillea, and a heavy red tile roof.

A neatly trimmed privet hedge bordered a brick path leading to the back of the church. A young kid, twelve or so, in dark blue corduroys and a red sweater was running full speed down the path.

"I'm looking for Father Carmody," I yelled as he whizzed by.

He slowed down long enough to tilt his head and yell back, "In the gym. The building in the back."

The building looked new: concrete block walls and a flat roof. I could hear the pounding of a basketball on a hardwood floor.

A slender young girl in white nylon shorts and a red sweatshirt was shooting hoops. She stood at the free-throw line, dribbled the ball three times, and then took her shot. The ball swished through the net. She made six shots in a row before she noticed me.

"Can I help you?" she asked politely.

"Father Carmody?"

She made a gesture with her thumb over her shoulder. "The weight room over there."

I inhaled the familiar gymnasium smells as I walked across the basketball court: stale sweat, Ben-Gay, moldy leather, dead socks.

The weight room had an impressive array of equipment, almost as well appointed as Ulla Kjeldsen's home gym. There was just one person in the room, and he was pounding away at a heavy punching bag, grunting each time his gloved fists made contact. He was wearing baggy gray pants and a sweat-drenched T-shirt. There was a locker-room gray towel wrapped around his neck.

"Father Carmody?" I said as I approached him.

He swiveled around, gave me a quick look, then went back to his punching.

"I'd like to talk to you about Ulla Kjeldsen, Father."

He said, "In a minute," and continued his assault on the bag. It was obvious he knew what he was doing. He moved gracefully on the balls of his feet, shifting and shuffling, bobbing from side to side. It brought back memories. My father used to tell me that watching a boxer with good footwork was like watching a graceful dancer, "except he's a dancer who wants to beat the hell out of his dance partner."

Carmody gave the bag a final whack, then used his teeth to help pull off his right glove. "What's your business with Ulla, Mr. . . ."

"Quint. Carroll Quint. I'm with the *San Francisco Bulletin.*"

He pulled off the other glove and tossed it with some force against the wall. "I can't help you. The poor woman is dead. Let her rest in peace."

I could see why the ladies were attracted to Carmody—he was of medium height, with a muscular build that showed he'd spent a lot of time working out. His hair was a mass of black curls, and he had denim blue eyes under broad, arched eyebrows and a deep cleft in his chin. He was saved from being outright pretty by a crescent-shaped scar on his right cheek. Think a pint-size version of Tom Selleck when he was doing his *Magnum* series.

"Father, there are some people who are saying that Ulla might not have committed suicide. That she was murdered."

He stood with his palms planted on his hips and glared at me. "You newspaper jerks never give up, do you? Just who is spreading this junk about Ulla being murdered?"

"My mother, for one. She roomed with Ulla in Hollywood years ago, when Ulla was using the name Vicky Vandamn."

Carmody walked over to a weight bench and sat down. "Hollywood. She told me she'd been in the movies, but I thought she was just making it up." He composed his handsome features into a frown. "Did you know Ulla?"

"No. My mother hadn't seen her in years. It bothered her that Ulla had lived so close to San Francisco but never contacted her."

"What makes your mother so sure that Ulla didn't commit suicide?"

"A man who Ulla loved died in Hollywood; the police said it was suicide, Ulla told my mother it was murder. She admitted to a lot of sins, Father, but said that she'd never commit suicide, that it was the 'sin of sins' and that God would forgive anything, but not that."

Carmody whipped the towel from his neck and blotted his face with it before saying, "For what it's worth, I never thought of Ulla as the type to take her own life." He snapped the towel out. "Are we off the record?"

"Certainly. I'm not a crime reporter; I cover movies and plays. I'm just looking into this because of my mother."

"Ulla was a generous woman. Most of the equipment in this room she donated to the church. She was intelligent, full of life, and an out-and-out prick teaser. I was one of her targets."

"I know you can't go into anything she said in confession, but when you saw her outside of the confessional, did she ever mention she was writing a book about her experiences in Hollywood?"

Carmody raised one ankle to his knee and began massaging it. It took awhile, but he finally said, "Yeah, she did mention something about a book. Ulla liked to say things that she hoped would shock you, it was like she was acting, playing the part of a naughty girl. She was too old for the role."

"Did she go into any specifics about her book? Mention any names?"

"Not that I can remember," he said with a slow shake of his head.

"Charles Talbot? Willie 'Freeze' Chanan? Jerome Ramsey? Tony Silk?"

Another shake of the head. "I wasn't paying much attention to what she said. I figured it was just another fantasy, like . . ."

I gave him a few seconds then said, "Like what, Father?"

Carmody stood up and did some shadowboxing in front of a full-length mirror. "Ulla had a vivid imagination. I'm sorry I can't be of more help. I liked Ulla, and if you, or someone else, can prove that she didn't take her own life, it would be a good thing."

"I didn't know the Church allowed services for Catholics who kill themselves."

"Things change," Carmody said, strolling back to the heavy bag. "My father thought he'd go to hell for eating meat on Friday. Today, we offer Masses and say funerals for those who have taken their own lives. We trust that God can understand what was going on in a mind tortured by depression."

"Ulla's computer is missing, Father. If she was murdered, it's possible the killer took the computer, that there was something on it that could identify him."

"I remember seeing her with a laptop. She would sit in the park by the school yard sometimes and work on it—flashing her legs at boys." He laughed lightly, then added, "She was a prime-time prick teaser, believe me. Age didn't matter."

I thanked him for his time and, before leaving, said, "I was raised a Catholic, but I drifted away, Father. I can't seem to find the motivation to come back."

Carmody took a deep breath before responding. "The Church isn't perfect, so if your not happy with it, leave, find another church, one that you think is perfect, but remember, once *you* join, it will no longer be perfect, either."

I stopped at a body shop on the way back to work. After examining the scratches on my Mini, the coveralled estimator looked me right in the eye and with a straight face told me, "I can fit you in in about ten days. It'll run you fourteen hundred and sixty-three dollars."

I almost upchucked my breakfast of corned beef hash. "How much?"

"Shop around," he advised me. "You ain't gonna get it cheaper."

On the advice of my insurance broker, I had a policy with a thousand dollars deductible, so the most they would pay was the four hundred plus, and then they'd probably raise my rates by at least that amount when I renewed.

I was in a foul mood when I got back to the *Bulletin.* As soon as I sat at my desk, the phone rang. I snarled, "What?"

Katherine Parkham's edgy voice: "You want to see me." Again, there was no question mark at the end of the sentence. "I have something belonging to you," she added before hanging up.

It dawned on me in the elevator on the way to her penthouse office why she wanted to see me. My poker winnings. Parkham had said that any money I won from Talbot was mine to keep but that she was going to return the losses to Buddy Albright and Joel Baxter, which seemed fair to me.

Parkham's secretary, Rosie, a sharp-faced woman with hair the color of melted butter, had come along with the Great from New York City. She greeted me with a smile.

"She's waiting." The smile faded a bit. "She's been waiting since nine this morning, Carroll."

Parkham was ensconced behind her desk. I tried to get a read on her mood, but her face was as blank as a robot's.

"Hi, boss," I said cheerfully, while trying to look cheerful.

She hefted a bulging white envelope in one hand, as if she was assessing its weight.

"I understand your room was trashed after the poker game."

"Yep. Luckily I wasn't in it. Junior is a sore loser."

Parkham dropped the envelope onto the middle of her desk, glanced at her wristwatch, then waved her hand toward the cupboard on the far side of the room. "It's lunchtime. Fix us a drink. I'll have a small scotch."

And so would I. The liquor cabinet held a fine array of upscale booze. I settled on a bottle of Bowmore twenty-five-year-old single malt.

"No ice," Parkham told me unnecessarily. Adding ice or water to twenty-five year-old single malt would be a sin much worse than eating meat on Friday.

We raised our glasses in a silent toast; then the Great said, "So you weren't in your room. You left after the poker game?"

"No."

She sampled more of the scotch, then said, "It's none of my business where you were, but I can guess. I just want to be certain it wasn't you who wrecked the room."

"It wasn't."

"I believe you. Junior is claiming that you not only cheated at the game but also tore up the room. He's demanding that I fire you. One of the Talbot family attorneys called my people in New York and raised a stink. Junior is a nasty piece of work, isn't he?"

"I can't argue with that," I told her. "Someone keyed my car pretty good at Talbot's place."

Parkham slid the envelope over to me. "Five thousand, Quint. That was Junior's original stake in the game, and it should take care of your car bills."

"What about Sir Charles? Is he still interested in buying the *Bulletin*?"

"I haven't heard anything lately. Look, Quint. I'm the one who got you into that poker game, and I have no problem in how you handled things. In fact, I think you did damn well, but it might be better if you avoided Charlie Talbot, Junior, from now on."

That was fine with me, but I was going to have to tell Parkham about Sir Charles's connection to Ulla Kjeldsen. "I can avoid Junior, but I'm not so sure about the old man. Let me tell you what I've been working on."

I gave Parkham a brief, concise version of the life and death of Ulla Kjeldsen, aka Vicky Vandamn. She asked a lot of questions along the way, and her secretary, Rosie, came in about the halfway mark with a pot of coffee and platter of smoked ham and cheddar cheese sandwiches that were too hard to resist, even with a lump of corn beef hash wedged in my stomach.

When Parkham had finished digesting my story and one of the sandwiches, she said, "That's all very interesting, Quint, but what's in it for me, and the *Bulletin*? Talbot may be a miserable old bugger, and his son a useless sniveler, but I am not going to allow you to write something about him and an actress he happened to be banging who committed suicide decades later. He'd have his attorneys all over me. When you pick a fight with someone who has the money Talbot has, you better have the referee and judges in your pocket; otherwise, you're going to get killed. For all we know, Talbot hadn't seen Vicky Vandamn in years. She may have done exactly what the police say she did— committed suicide. And that wouldn't make much of a story. This *Payback* book of hers may have been just a fantasy."

"I know," I assured her. "I wasn't thinking of submitting anything until I investigated it thoroughly and ran it by you."

Parkham let out a light, tinselly laugh. "Yeah, sure. Don't think you're putting this over on me, Quint. You see a book in this, don't you?"

"It's possible, but my first loyalty is to the paper, boss. I'd work on this on my own time, and it wouldn't interfere with my regular work. I just wanted you to know about it."

"And if I tell you to drop it right now and forget about it? What then?"

"You'd disappoint me. If Talbot was somehow involved, this could be big, and a signature story for the paper, just like the Hitchcock murders were."

She leaned back in her chair and eased her feet onto the desk. "I wondered if you'd bring that up."

The previous year, a man by the name of Jules Moneta had committed four murders, all as a cover-up to get to his real target, his partner and San Francisco's premiere patron of the arts, Gineen Rosenberry. Moneta had used me as a sounding board, sending me E-mail messages with clues from old Alfred Hitchcock movies. Eventually, with the help of the police, I'd nailed the guy. The Great had made sure that the *Bulletin* got full credit for figuring it out. The story had gone national, and it helped change her opinion of the paper, and those of us who worked for it. It had also helped to keep her New York associates from selling the paper—so far.

"I think it's worth looking into, boss. I'll be careful."

Parkham poured herself a fresh cup of coffee. "Fifty-Buck Chuck. What a pig. Okay, Quint. Look into it, but it's for my eyes only. Try to find out about *her* book. If it's for real, it could be dynamite."

"Sir Charles's eyes almost popped out of his head when I mentioned it to him."

"Find out if she had an agent, a publisher. You know the drill. And don't let anyone, including Max Maslin, or your friend Terry Greco, see one word of copy. Understood?"

I nodded. Max wasn't going to be a problem, but Terry had a way of wheedling things out of me. There are rumors that I talk in my sleep.

Ten

*M*onday was Terry Greco's day off at the *Bulletin*. I called her apartment, got her answering machine, and left a brief message. I was anxious to know how things had gone at Sir Charles Talbot's place after I took off on Sunday. I should have asked the Great how she'd found out about my room there being trashed, since she and her friend Harry Crane had left right after the poker game. I had visions of Terry paddling around the swimming pool with Ronald Maleuw, and perhaps Junior accidentally drowning. Why had Junior bothered to cheat at cards? There didn't seem to be a compelling reason, so all I could come up with was that he did it because he could. Maybe it made him feel important, and cleverer than everyone else. Maybe he couldn't handle living in the overpowering shadow of his father. Ah, the superrich—they do have their burdens to bear.

I spent the afternoon and early-evening hours hard at work, watching movies in a comfortable chair in a small private theater in the lobby of the Hobart Building on Market Street. There was a select audience: myself, the movie reviewers for three other local newspapers, and the studio flacks hawking the films. One of the movies, about a woman who ran a home for abused hookers in Houston, wasn't scheduled for release for two weeks; the other, an Indiana Jones rip-off where the hero uncovers a lost pyramid in an Egyptian jungle, was scheduled to open the following day. The rule of thumb in my line of work is, the worse the picture, the less time they give you to review it. The rule worked again. Thumbs way up for the Houston angel of mercy, two thumbs in the eyes for the pyramid hunter.

I exchanged pleasantries with my fellow reviewers, told enough white lies to the studio flacks to frost a cake, stuffed some of the left-over buffet canapés into a manila envelope, and headed for home—a pleasant eight- or nine-block walk.

I was approaching the condo lobby when someone grabbed me roughly by the shoulder and shoved me up against a brick wall. Something cold and round, the size of a gun barrel, was stuck into the base of my skull, and a rough voice said, "Freeze!"

I froze.

"Now hug the wall like it was your mother."

As I was edging up to the wall, the voice said, "And your mother was worth hugging, pally. Though I never had the chance myself. She had a lot of class."

I turned around with my hands in the air and saw a man in a white trench coat. He was holding a silver pen in one hand and smiling.

"Willie 'Freeze' Chanan," I said.

"In the flesh, pally."

His flesh wasn't holding up too well. He still wore his hair in a crew cut, but most of the crew had bailed out. His face was seamed, weath-ered, and dotted with moles—the face of a man who'd seen too much sun. He was six feet or more and had a thick, stocky build.

"Had you worried, didn't I?" Chanan boasted. "Come on, let's eat. I'm starving, and I'm in the mood for Chink. Don't let anyone kid you—you can get any kind of grub you want in the desert, but for Chink, you've got to come to Frisco."

A chauffeured Lincoln limousine was purring at the curb.

"I think I'll pass," I told him.

Chanan flexed his arm and consulted his watch. "I gotta be back at the airport by eleven o'clock, or my charter will kick into overtime."

"You chartered a jet to come here from Palm Springs?"

"Sure. I've got a time-share in a Learjet. It's the only way to fly. I always pack heat, and even though I've got a permit, I don't like to go through that airport security crap. Come on, Quint," he urged. "I'll tell you some stories about Hollywood that I bet you've never heard before, including what really happened to Jerome Ramsey."

Chanan gave the driver explicit directions and told sordid stories about Marilyn Monroe's love life on the way to the restaurant, including one where he claimed to have solid evidence that the last person to have sex with Marilyn was "an actor's wife, someone with political connections. They were a kinky bunch, that gang."

"Give me a break, Chanan. If that were true, it would have surfaced by now. You couldn't keep something like that buried all these years."

"Wanna bet?" He rubbed his thumb and forefinger together. "A lot of money changed hands that night. I've got a million of those stories. I should write a book."

Though I was born and raised in San Francisco, I'd never heard of the place Chanan took me to. It was in a small alley in Chinatown, barely wide enough for the Lincoln to navigate. There was a line of elderly Asian men and women waiting to gain entrance to a grimy brick building. There was no sign to indicate it was a restaurant.

Chanan charged up the stairs, mumbling "Excuse me" and "Out of the way, pally" as we climbed up two flights and entered a low-ceilinged room filled with diners who were busy eating and pointing their chopsticks at one another. The walls were painted prison gray; the ceiling was smoke-coated plaster, and sickly yellow fluorescent lights were affixed to it. There wasn't another Caucasian in sight.

A big-bellied Chinese man in his sixties with a flattened nose saw Chanan and smiled. He gave a slight bow, then waved us over to an empty table.

"Hey, Wiley, you old cat burglar, how are you?" Chanan said, embracing the man to his chest. "Quint, this is Wiley Lee, the best god-damn Chink cook in the world."

Mr. Lee accepted this politically incorrect compliment with a wide smile, which showed an expanse of gold teeth.

"Good to see you again, Mr. Freeze. You and your friend sit, enjoy. The food begins."

A waiter in a soiled white jacket began slamming plates on the table. I sat down in a rickety folding chair and watched as Chanan slipped out of his trench coat. He rolled his shoulders and twisted his neck. He was in good shape for his age—no longer Muscle Beach material, but he must have kept to his regimen of lifting weights. He was wearing a light blue shirt with three-button cuffs and little puffs at the shoulders. His shoes were black suede loafers with gold tiger-head buckles.

"Dig in, pally," he said as he spooned portions of food from small plates onto the large one in front of him.

Wiley Lee, still smiling, brought over a cracked red carafe and poured clear liquid from it into three cracked red teacups. He picked up one of the cups, said, *"Gan bei,"* then tilted his head back and swallowed.

"Gan bei. It means 'Empty the glass,'" Chanan said. "Try it. It's Maotai *baijiu,* the best booze the Chinks make."

He gulped his down and wiped his chin with a napkin. "Drink, man. You don't want to insult Wiley. He can be an ornery bastard."

I picked up the cup, took a sniff, which was a mistake, then pinched my nostrils and gave it a try. "Not bad," I said in a voice that I didn't recognize.

Wiley filled up our glasses again, then turned on his heel and began barking out something in Chinese.

"We'll have to have a few of these just to be social," Chanan said, throwing back another cup of the clear liquor. "Sixty proof, this stuff is, so be warned."

Chanan kept up a steady patter as he expertly flashed his chopsticks while explaining the dishes as they came to the table: dumpling purses bursting with minced shrimp; banana leaves stuffed with chicken and pork and doused with fiery mustard sauce; shredded filet mignon in crisp bird-nest baskets; and a variety of pork and duck dishes. I blessed the waiter for having brought cold bottles of beer.

Wiley Lee came by to see if everything was all right, and he and Chanan had what sounded like a warm conversation in Chinese. As soon as Lee departed for the kitchen, Chanan let out a loud burp and said, "I saved one of his sons from some heavy time in the crossbar hotel. Dumb kid was peddling cocaine on the Strip. He dumped the stuff down a sewer before the cops got him, but he didn't realize that LAPD stands for the Los Angeles Perjury Department. Now the little coolie owes me big-time."

"If I wanted to hear cop stories, I'd watch TV, Freeze. You were going to tell me what really happened to Jerome Ramsey."

"Was I?" he said, reaching for his beer.

"Thanks for dinner," I said, getting to my feet.

"Sit, pally, sit. Okay, but if you say I told you, I'll deny it. I could never prove that it wasn't a suicide, but the guy I figured gave Ramsey an eternal hangover was the Sandman."

"The sandman? Is this a joke?"

"It wasn't to Ramsey. Johnny Sands, real name Sandini, a Mafia hit man. They're not happy if they don't have a nickname, so he was the Sandman, because he put people to sleep—forever. Get it?"

"Why kill Ramsey? Who ordered the hit? Tony Silk?"

"Johnny worked freelance—anyone could have hired him."

"Did you ever ask him? I assume you were a cop at the time, and that it was your duty to put killers behind bars, right?"

"Yeah, yeah. No way I, or anyone else, could prove it. I just got the word on the street that the Sandman did the hit. Ramsey was found on his bed, a gun in his hand, and the crime lab was certain that he'd pulled the trigger—one bullet right to the temple. It was messy—the pillow looked like a Salvador Dalí landscape. But before he died, his body was worked over real good—it looked like someone had beaten him with a sackful of marbles."

"What about the gun? Was it Ramsey's?"

"An old Colt forty-five semiautomatic. It belonged to Talbot Studios—they had dozens of them that were used by the security guards, so Ramsey could have easily picked one up and taken it home."

"Where's this Johnny Sands now?"

"I've been giving you a lot of goodies for free, Quint. That's not the way I work. You want more, you've got to pay."

I started to get to my feet again, but he waved me down.

"Stop being so antsy, pally. I need something. Not a lot. It's a matter of principle, not the dough. Duke me a twenty."

"Twenty dollars?"

"Yeah. For starters."

I thought about it a few moments, then took out my money clip and dropped a twenty-dollar bill on the table.

Chanan's chopsticks flashed out, picked up the bill, and deposited it into the pocket of his shirt. "Sands is dead. Shot to death by person or persons unknown. That's the problem with being a hit man. A guy hires you to kill someone—say his wife. You do the job; then the guy hires another hit man to kill you because you know too much."

"That wasn't worth twenty bucks," I said. "Why would Sands kill Ramsey? Because Ramsey was dating Vicky Vandamn?"

"Dating? I wouldn't call it *dating*, pally. Ramsey was a puff, and a beard. Girls liked him because he wore silk undies like they did, and guys used him to escort the broads around so they didn't have to. You get the picture?" Chanan barked out a laugh. "Hell, who knows. Maybe one of his butt-pirate friends beat up Ramsey with his purse before he blew himself to Maggot Munchkinland. I tell ya, when those fags get mad at each other, they do nasty things."

"Ramsey was gay? Then he wasn't the father of her child. Who was?"

"Child? What child? She had a kid?"

"The autopsy showed that she did."

Chanan stroked the bristles on the edge of his jaw with the edge of a chopstick, making a rasping sound. "That's news to me, pally."

"A lot of this is news to you, isn't it?" I said, challenging him. "You told my mother that Vicky was dead, buried in the desert, yet she turns up alive years later, living in Sausalito."

He shrugged his shoulders indifferently. "That was the rumor at the time. I looked into it, couldn't find out anything different. I didn't look hard enough, I guess. I'll tell you something. Her Ulla Kjeldsen name—I never knew that. I thought her given name was Borden. That's what Vicky told me anyway. Who tipped you? Your mother? Were Karen and Vicky talking to each other all these years?"

"No, my mother saw her picture in the obituaries. She hadn't seen Vicky since they'd roomed together. I didn't get a chance to tell you this on the phone, but Vicky was writing a book—her memoirs. She called it *Payback*."

Chanan was speechless for all of twenty seconds. He cleared his throat like a man with a cold coming on. "A book. I'd like to get a gander at that. Where is it?"

"It disappeared, Freeze. Along with her computer. Maybe that's why she was murdered. The killer took them."

His eyes narrowed, adding more wrinkles to his crow's feet. "You don't know Vicky was murdered, pally. Neither do the cops—I checked. And what the hell could she put in a book that would get someone to torpedo her? She was nothing to the heavy hitters in Hollywood, a bit player, a hot-looking broad with great legs that she didn't mind parting if she thought it would do her any good."

"When I told Sir Charles Talbot that Vicky had recently committed suicide, it shook him up, Freeze. He thought that she'd died years ago. The L.A. newspapers quoted you on it; you said something about her either being under the Nevada desert or fish food, that she knew too much about a certain local big shot. Was Talbot the big shot?"

"Chuck Talbot," Chanan scoffed. "How did *you* get within fifty yards of him?

"I was a guest at his place in Napa the other night. We shared a bottle of his champagne. When's the last time you saw Talbot?"

"We do a little business once in awhile."

"What kind of business? Talbot's been out of the movies for a long time."

"I found him a few paintings over the years. Is he still married to the lovely Erica?"

"You know Mrs. Talbot?"

"She did a little dancing in New York and Vegas. She's a lot of woman. Maybe too much for Talbot right now. What about Talbot's flunky, George Mandan, the Brit marine? Is he still in the picture? If he is, be careful. He's a tough little monkey."

"What about Talbot's son, Junior? Do you know him?"

"Nah, but from what I hear, he's bad news. You look like a bright guy, Quint. In L.A., and the desert, I know my way around, but here, I might need a little help. Vicky was an okay broad. If she was killed, I want to know who did it."

"I've got a job working for the *Bulletin*. If I do find out anything about Vicky's death, the information goes to the paper, not to you."

Chanan dug a business card out of his wallet and handed it to me. "Come on, pally. We scratch each other's backs. You give me, I give you. That's the way these things work."

"So far, I've given you a lot, and all you gave me was some story about a dead hit man named Johnny Sands, who doesn't have anything to do with Vicky."

Chanan smiled, crumpling his face further. "Don't be too sure about that. The word on the street was that Johnny took Vicky for a ride. Maybe he did, and maybe he let her out of the car instead of killing her. Vicky could be very persuasive with guys like Johnny."

I chewed that around for a moment, then said, "If that's true, then find out who paid Johnny Sands to take her for that ride. Give me that, and then I'll give you something."

"You're out of your league, Quint. These are tough people. My kind of people, the kind *you* only see in the movies."

I pushed my chair back and stood up. "You can reach me at the paper, Freeze. Thanks for dinner."

"Say hello to your mother for me. And your father. Now *he* was a tough guy. You—I got my doubts."

Eleven

I spent a long, restless night in bed, partly because I had so many questions rattling around in my brain regarding Ulla/Vicky, and I was worried about Junior trying to get me fired, or perhaps worse. Junior was a rich, spoiled brat with violent tendencies—a lethal combination—there was no telling what his next move against me might be.

Thoughts of Freeze Chanan kept me awake for a while, too. He wouldn't have flown up to San Francisco on the chance to meet me just because he thought Vicky was a "good broad." He wanted to know if she'd been murdered, and he was interested in her recent past, really interested, especially in Vicky's alleged tell-all book. There must have been enough skeletons in Chanan's closet to throw a hell of a Halloween party. Detective Manners said the autopsy report showed she'd had a child. Had it survived? If so, whose was it? Where was it? Vicky hangs with Jerome Ramsey, who is allegedly gay, then ends up wedding his brother years later in Vancouver. And what about those long unaccounted-for years?

Chanan's offer that we work together rang hollow. He had admitted that the Ulla Kjeldsen name had been news to him. I had to assume he had much better databases than the ones I had accessed through the *Bulletin*. When I'd called Chanan in Palm Springs, I'd mentioned that Vicky Vandamn had died, not Ulla. He could have easily accessed the *Bulletin*'s online obituary filings—seen her picture, realized it was the same person.

Then he would no doubt have done deep background check on Ulla/ Vicky—and found out about her Vancouver address and her marriage to Ramsey's brother. How much more might he have dug up? Apparently, not much, or he wouldn't have wasted his time flying up to see me.

It was a relief when the alarm clock went off. I shaved, showered, had an Alka-Seltzer for breakfast, and drove to the *Bulletin*.

Terry Greco was waiting for me in my cubicle. She looked as delicious as ever in a tight emerald green sweater and skirt outfit. She had a determined look on her face, and before I could say hello and sneak a kiss, she said, "I kneed him in the balls."

"Anyone I know?"

"Junior. I'd finally had it with him. The creep claimed that you'd trashed your room, and when I told him that you couldn't have, that you were with me all that night, he went ballistic, called me all kinds of names and put his hands on me, so I kneed him. Real good."

"Congratulations," I said. "You did the right thing, Terry."

"He threatened to have me fired, Carroll. He said that he'd call Mrs. Parkham and tell her . . . well, tell her all kinds of lies."

"I wouldn't worry, Terry. He tried to get me fired, too. The Great is no fan of Junior. She wouldn't believe anything he told her. Trust me. But I'd get it on the record with Parkham; tell her just how Junior was harassing you."

Terry heaved a massive sigh of relief. It was a sigh well worth watching.

"You're sure of this, Carroll?"

"Positive."

She gave me a toothpasty kiss full on the lips. "I was really worried," she said when we broke for air.

"Where was Ronnie Maleuw during all of this?" I asked, hoping to bury Maleuw once and for all.

She gave a nervous brush to a lock of hair that had fallen over her forehead. "I didn't mention it to Ron. The de Young Museum exhibit is on Thursday, just two nights away. I've put a lot of effort into this, and I don't want to miss it. Junior will probably try to throw me out if he sees me."

"I'll be there to protect you," I said gallantly.

"Carroll, I tried, but I couldn't get you a ticket. There's no way they'll let you in."

"Where there's a will, there's a way. I'll be there."

She reached out and ran her hand down my arm. "You're sweet. My place tonight? Bring a pizza."

Ah, things were looking up. Junior was walking around with blue balls, I had a date with Terry, and the mention of a pizza hadn't sent my stomach tumbling around. Now all I had to do was figure out how to get into the de Young Museum.

I cranked out reviews on the two movies I'd seen the night before, answered E-mails from movie fanatics who seemed to delight in bringing up questions that they were certain I couldn't answer. I was using Google to field a question about Harrison Ford's earring—was it on the left earlobe or the right? A steady E-mail correspondent wanted to know. While I was searching Google, I dropped in the name Johnny Sands, and was rewarded with several stories about Sands being arrested in Los Angeles on suspicion of homicide charges, but there was no indication that he'd ever been convicted. The last article had a picture of Sands, or what was left of him, lying on a sidewalk, legs spread out as if he'd been running. Someone had covered his head with a jacket. THE SANDMAN GETS HIT! read the headline, which was dated some twelve years ago. "Notorious hit man Johnny Sands was shot to death by persons unknown on the Strip last night. The colorful gangster, also known as the Sandman, had been rumored to be a hit man for the Mafia, though his only conviction dates back to his days as a young tough in Chicago." The reporter's name was Jack Dornay.

Interesting, but what did it tell me? Oh, and if you're curious, Ford wears the earring in his left earlobe, and, according to the Web, left ear is for straight, right for gay.

The desk phone and my cell phone started chirping at the same time. I picked up the office line and a sultry voice said, "I'm in town. We *must* talk."

It took me a moment to put the voice to a beautiful face—Erica Talbot.

"One second, Erica. My other phone. I'll be right with you."

The voice on the cell phone was dripping icicles. "Remember me?" Dramatic icicles.

"Mom, I'm on the other line. I'll call you right back. Promise."

I half-expected Erica to have ended the call. She didn't appear to be the kind who would put up with being placed on hold. I was wrong; her voice was all sugary sex.

"I came to the city especially to see you, Carroll. Please don't disappoint me."

"I wouldn't think of it," I said. "What did you have in mind?"

"We keep a small pied-à-terre on Russian Hill for when I have to shop or go to the theater. The Carlton Arms, at Filbert and Larkin. Suite ten-B. Shall we say four o'clock?"

"Yes, that's fine with me," I assured her. The Carlton *Arms.* I never understood how the word *arms* got attached to buildings. I asked Google, and got an answer: It dates back to the old English inns, which were frequently named after a local duke or earl and often displayed the nobleman's coat of arms over the door. All well and good, but I doubted if there'd ever been a Lord Carlton in San Francisco. More likely, Carlton was a Realtor who thought he could jack the rent up a few notches with a classy name.

I called my mother. She was playing the role of wounded mommy.

"I hope the other call was important, Carroll. I wouldn't want you to waste your time with the person who brought you into the world."

"Mom, it was important. I was talking to a woman who may be able to help me learn what happened to your friend Vicky. Erica Talbot, Sir Charles's latest wife."

That caught her interest, and when I told her that I'd had dinner with Freeze Chanan the night before, she started outright purring.

"Really? Did he ask about me? How does he look?"

The conversation took some fifteen minutes and would bore the hell out of you. I gave Mom a brief, sanitized version of what had taken place so far: my visit to Ulla Kjeldsen's houseboat and Talbot's Napa mansion, as well as the dinner with Chanan. She was very pleased that

Freeze remembered her so well, that he thought she was a "classy broad," and that he looked like a dried apricot.

"The sun," she moaned. "I tell everyone to stay out of the sun, but they don't listen. You should have called me, Carroll. I probably could have gotten Freeze to open up to you."

"Next time he's in town, we'll make it a threesome, Mom. Chanan did tell me something interesting. He said that Jerome Ramsey was gay."

A pause. "You mean a homosexual?"

"That's just what I mean. Didn't you know?"

"He was very handsome, Carroll. They always said that about handsome people: Tyrone Power, Caesar Romero, Troy Donahue. It was the kiss of death back in my day; now it's all the rage. Gay cowboys, dear. Can you imagine John Wayne and Robert Mitchum making a movie where they pretended they were gay in the saddle?"

It wasn't a pretty picture, I had to admit, but I pressed her on Jerome Ramsey. "Freeze is certain Ramsey was gay, which, for one thing, means he probably wasn't the father or her child."

"Child? Vicky had a child? When? With whom?"

"I don't know, Mom. I'm just going by what the autopsy revealed."

I could hear her shudder over the phone. "Autopsy? Don't you dare allow that to happen to me, not under any circumstances. Is that understood?"

"Perfectly. Did you ever run into a character by the name of Johnny Sands in Hollywood? His nickname was 'the Sandman.'"

"I remember a Johnny Sands. He had a bad reputation, but he was very nice-looking."

Good looks swayed my mother's estimation of people. "According to Chanan, he was a mob hit man, Mom."

"Well, that is interesting, isn't it? Maybe he had something to do with Jerome Ramsey's murder. I'd so like to see Vicky's houseboat, Carroll. I knew her so well. Maybe there's something there, a clue of some kind, that I can spot."

"I don't know, Mom. The police may have it locked down. I'll call you as soon as I learn anything new."

"Calls are nice, dear, but I miss seeing you. What about dinner on Saturday? Bring your friend Terry. I'm making tofu tamales and soybean cake with salsa."

When I didn't have the guts to answer quickly, she added, "And margaritas, of course. You bring the tequila, dear." Then she hung up.

Trapped. And I had to bring the booze. I looked at the computer screen, wondering if I should check Amazon.com and see if there was a book with instructions on how to say no to your mother. If not, there should be. It would be an automatic best seller.

I stopped at a few body shops, getting more estimates for the scratches on the Mini. They were all higher than the first estimate I'd gotten, but at least I had the printed forms that I could wave in front of Erica Talbot. There was no sense spending that hard-earned poker cash in my pocket on the car if I didn't have to.

I snuggled the Mini in between two Mercedes sedans three blocks from Talbot's little pied-à-terre. The French do have a way with words like that, don't they? It sounds so much more sophisticated and sexy than a small apartment or vacation cottage.

The building was a redbrick one with limestone cornices, lacy wrought-iron balconies, and an arched maroon awning over the front entrance. A short, bearded man in a jacket and coat that matched the awning perfectly gave me a glassy smile and asked, "Your business here, sir?"

"Carroll Quint. Mrs. Talbot is expecting me," I told him.

He tipped his cap in a semisalute and opened the door for me. "Tenth floor, apartment B, sir. Enjoy yourself."

Was it my imagination, or was there a lewd twist to those last two words?

The lobby walls were hung with bronze-colored mirrors that gave me a healthy tan look.

The elevator was nearly as big as my bedroom. They could move a piano in without any difficulty.

There were just two units to a floor. I tapped lightly on the door marked with a big brass *B*, wondering if Erica would be dressed in anything exotic.

The door swung open and I was looking into the squinty eyes of George Mandan, Talbot's flunky and "tough little monkey," according to Freeze Chanan.

"He's here," George called over his shoulder. He backed away a bit, but I nearly had to brush against him to gain entrance to the place. He had thirty years, and probably thirty pounds, of muscle I didn't, and he looked like he was itching to exhibit his old Royal Marine combat techniques on me.

I tapped him on the shoulder with the body-shop estimates. "Mrs. Talbot suggested I give these to you. My car was keyed the night I stayed in Napa."

George examined the estimates, then glared at me. "That's a lot of brass for that tin can you drive. And it's a lot less than what it will take to fix up the room you trashed."

"You and I both know I had nothing to do with that."

He held my eyes and waited for me to blink. It gave me time to study him. There was a slight smear of pink at the corner of his lower lip.

We both stared at each other in a juvenile way, and I had the satisfaction of seeing his head twist away first when Erica hurried up to us.

"Oh, Mr. Quint. So good of you to come. George was just leaving, weren't you, George? What are those?"

She took the estimates from George and gave them a cursory glance. "I'll write you a check, Carroll." She flicked her eyelashes at George. "Drive carefully. I'll see you tomorrow."

George seemed reluctant to leave. He hesitated at the door, then exited quickly, without saying a word.

"Alone at last," Erica said with a wide grin. She was wearing a short pleated lavender skirt and a matching V-necked sweater that displayed a generous décolletage. Her hair was worn in a tightly coiled chignon. She wore gold hoop earrings the size of curtain rings. Her lipstick was a light pink color, obviously the same pink that George had had on his lower lip.

Too obvious? George didn't seem to be the kind of guy to make a mistake like that. Then why do it? To let me know that he and Erica had something going on? Or just to show that he was more than just Sir Charles's flunky, as Freeze Chanan had described him. Or was it Erica's idea? Her way of showing that *she* was in charge of George, not her husband.

Erica twirled around in a circle, sending her skirt flying up and revealing her long shapely legs and the straps of a garter belt connected to her nylons. Garter belts—visions of Frederick's of Hollywood catalogs flashed in my mind. I, like every horny American male, consider Allen Gant Senior a traitor to his gender. Who is Senior? The guy who invented pantyhose and made a bloody fortune from it. Sure, sure, the hose are more comfortable, more convenient, but absolutely nothing in the female wardrobe can produce an instant *boing* in the male anatomy as fast as a garter belt.

She nonchalantly crossed the room to the floor-to-ceiling window that looked out over the jagged skyline of downtown San Francisco.

The room was sparsely decorated. The walls were pale lavender, and a cream-colored carpet covered the floor. There was a long eggplant-colored upholstered couch, two of those great-looking but terribly uncomfortable black leather Barcelona chairs, and a glass-topped table set with a silver tray holding an ice bucket in the shape of a top hat, a silver cocktail shaker, a bottle of Bombay Sapphire gin, two glasses, and a tray of lemon twists. Soft classical music was coming from speakers set into the wall.

Erica did her twirling thing before settling onto the couch.

"I hope you're not rigid," she said.

I dipped my head toward my shoes, wondering if I was that obvious.

"About drinks before five o'clock," she said. "Charles has this boring rule that no cocktails can be poured before five. I'm dying for a martini. Would you mind?"

I didn't mind at all. I went through the motions of mixing the drinks—there was no vermouth, so the martinis were pure icy-cold gin in a tall-stemmed glass that held up to three shots of the potent liquor—while Erica took a checkbook and fountain pen from a royal blue crocodile Hermès purse.

How did your sharp-eyed reporter know it was a Hermès purse? Because the *Bulletin*'s fashion reporter had done a full-page article on such purses a week earlier. A crocodile-skin purse with palladium hardware that retailed for forty thousand dollars! My first thought was of a purse snatcher grabbing the thing from a woman's arm and tossing the contents as he ran away. The purse was the prize target.

Erica ripped the check free and handed it to me.

"There, that's out of the way. Now we're free to talk."

I passed her a martini and sat down on the couch, keeping a yard or so away from her.

"Cheers," she said raising her glass and downing about a third of the drink. It was beginning to dawn on me that Erica might have had a drink or two with George before I arrived. She was fidgeting all over and slurring her words slightly.

I kept up with her on the first drink, then made us another as she scattershot small talk about how she loved Napa, hated London, loved martinis, thought wine was overrated, and that horses were better than men in *almost* every way. I knew this was all a setup, that her purpose was to ply me with booze, pump me for whatever information she wanted, then kick me out or have George return unexpectedly. A setup for sure, but I had to admit it was a hell of a set. We were working on our second martinis when she began inching closer to me.

"Now, Carroll. Tell me what got Charles so upset the other night? He was beastly to me for talking to you, and he wouldn't tell me what it was all about."

"I mentioned an actress he knew in Hollywood. Vicky Vandamn. She died not long ago."

Erica waved her free hand in the air and said, "I'm so bored hearing about all of his show business conquests. Was there something special about this one?"

"I don't know. She more or less disappeared from sight, and ended up in Sausalito. She was using her given name, Ulla Kjeldsen. The police think she committed suicide."

"*Think?*" Erica said sliding closer to me. "They're not sure? Are you telling me the woman was murdered?"

"There's some speculation about that."

She drained her second martini. "Drink up, Carroll, and fix me one more."

While I fixed the drinks, she crossed her legs, exposing those garter belt snaps.

"Charles can be a difficult man, Carroll. It's dangerous to cross him. I hope you know that."

"I wasn't planning on crossing your husband," I assured her.

"Still, if he's involved in something sordid, like this woman's death, it can't just be swept away, can it?"

"I didn't say he was involved in Kjeldsen's death, and I—"

The couch made squeaky sounds as she slid over next to me. "I was thinking that we could work together on this." She clinked her glass against mine and again said, "Cheers."

"There must be some reason for Charles being so upset. Tell me more about the woman. She must have been quite old."

"She took good care of herself. She was still very beautiful."

"Ah, so you saw her. Before she was found dead in her houseboat."

I had told Sir Charles about Vicky's houseboat, so Erica must have given her husband a grilling over the whole subject. Or maybe Charles had told George and he'd passed it on to Erica. "No. But I've seen recent pictures of her. She kept in shape and had some help from a plastic surgeon or two, according to the autopsy."

Erica dived back into her martini while I stared at her legs. They were long, slender, tanned, shapely, and apparently hollow, because I was noticing that the more we drank, the more my speech slurred and hers became crisp and precise.

"Charles is very wealthy, Carroll. Very. But he is cautious with his money. He doesn't throw it around, if you know what I mean."

My eyes flicked over to the forty-thousand-dollar purse. "Is that right?"

"He's been married five times. Did you know that?"

"Someone mentioned it."

"And not one of his former wives was . . . happy with the financial arrangements when they separated."

Ah, light was beginning to show at the end of the gin bottle. "They all signed prenuptials, did they? And you, too?"

"Charles insisted. Diana, his first, got hardly a dime. Luvina, Junior's mother, died. Then there was Rakel, an icy blonde from Sweden, whose brain most have become frozen during one of those long winters. I don't know what ever became of her. And there was Serena, a Peruvian bombshell, whose charms started sagging, so dear Charles dumped her. 'When the looks go, so do the wives,' some wiseass told me at our wedding reception."

"You seem to know a lot about your predecessors, Erica."

"I made it a point to find out everything about them." She leaned down, pressing her elbows against her sides, causing her breasts to surge up from her sweater. "Charles is not in the best of health. He sees doctors all of the time. I'm worried about him."

"He looks like he keeps himself in pretty good shape."

"It's his heart. All those years of hard living have clogged up his arteries."

"This may be an indelicate question, Erica. But what about his will? Are you . . . well provided for?"

"Charles has suddenly gotten religion. He plans on leaving the majority of his wealth to churches, synagogues, you name it. He's writing them checks every day. If there is a heaven, he plans to buy his way in. He's become obsessed with his own death, and the cruel thing is, that's not really good for his health. I'm afraid he's getting senile. That's why I'd like you to help me. To tell me everything you can about this woman's death. So I can keep it from upsetting Charles." Her tongue darted out and took a long, slow lap around her lips. "I'd be very grateful for anything you could tell me about her."

She leaned over and brushed her lips against my ear. "Charles told me she was writing a book. Do you know anything about that?"

"It was mentioned. *Payback.* A tell-all book about her life. Supposedly it reveals all the dark secrets about her days in Hollywood. Vicky told someone that people might go to jail once it was published. But her computer disappeared, and there's no hard copy that I know of."

"If you could find it, I would *very* grateful. There could be something in the book that would upset Charles." The hand she was holding her drink with was steady as a rock; the other was running up and down my pant leg.

"What about George? Has he been looking into this for you? Or your husband?"

"George is . . . loyal, and discreet. He's tough, too, but he's not very clever. I need someone like you to help me, Carroll. You strike me as a very clever young man."

George: loyal, discreet, tough, and quite possibly waiting outside the door or in the next room ready to catch me with my pants down. It took a physical and moral feat of great magnitude for me to lower my glass to the table without spilling it and push myself to my feet.

"Erica. You've got a deal. I'll try to find out what I can about Vicky's book. Meanwhile, you let me know what your husband and George are up to."

She cocked her head and looked up at me with a quizzical expression on her face.

"You're not thinking of leaving?"

"Yep. I have to. I have a date."

"Break it."

"I can't. It's with my mother," I said, lying gracefully.

She arched her back and pushed her chin up. "Your *mother*? You're leaving me to see your mother?"

"Sometimes blood is thicker than martinis. I'll be in touch."

I walked in what I thought was a swaggering manner to the door, but I probably looked like a duck skidding across ice. I made it to the elevator. The doorman gave me a skeptical look before saying, "May I make a suggestion, sir? A taxi."

Twelve

*W*hat's that old theory about martinis? One is all right, two is too many, and three's not enough. Or something like that. I figured I must have downed the equivalent of five or six of the damn things with Erica. When I arrived at Terry Greco's place on wobbly legs, with a warm Neapolitan pizza in hand, she greeted me with a cold look and an even colder shoulder. And even after a cold shower, I was not the best of company.

A dinner of hot coffee and the pizza helped to bring me around, but not fast enough to do me much good with Terry. She quizzed me about my afternoon tête-à-tête with Mrs. Talbot.

"What did she really want from you, Carroll?"

"Some dope on her husband, and Vicky Vandam's book. Everyone is interested in the damn thing. Erica's afraid old Chuck will kick the bucket and leave her with an empty shopping basket."

"The man's worth millions."

"No doubt, but Talbot's gone through four previous wives without losing a nickel, according to Erica. She'd like to have something to hold over his head, and I guess she thinks that Vicky's death may be it."

"You don't think that Talbot had anything to do with her death?"

I dunked a piece of the pizza in the coffee and took a bite. It wasn't bad. "Who knows. Maybe there is something in *Payback* that casts

Talbot in a less than flattering light. He played things fast and loose when he ran his Hollywood studio."

"Do you think you'll ever find the book?"

"I don't know. I'm not certain there was a book, or much of one. No one has seen it."

"Carroll, your book, *Tough Guys and Private Eyes*. Remember how many times you had me check the manuscript? And you showed it to your mother, and to Max Maslin, before you sent it to your agent. When someone is writing a book, they show it off, get feedback from other people. Vicky must have shown it to someone."

Terry had a point. Writers crave feedback. I told her about my meeting with Willie "Freeze" Chanan.

"He sounds like someone in a very corny detective novel," she said, grabbing the last slice of pizza before I could get my hands on it.

"He *is* a corny old detective," I told her. "But my mother spoke somewhat highly of him."

"How is your mother?" Terry asked.

"Funny you should ask." I told her about the dinner invitation for Saturday. It didn't go over well. Terry likes my mother a lot, but not her cooking. Hell, who does?

"We'll eat light at Mom's, then hit Esperento's for some of those Spanish tapas you love. She'd like to see you, Terr. Her old friend's death really has her depressed."

To my surprise and delight, she agreed—to dinner at my mother's, but not to me staying the night. "I better take you to your car before they tow it away."

On the drive over to my car, I bounced something off Terry that had been rattling around in my brain. "It's interesting that Freeze Chanan claims he didn't know Vicky's birth name—Ulla Kjeldsen. If he had been looking for her when she disappeared from Hollywood, it shouldn't have been too hard for a cop to find that out. Have you ever heard of a restaurant in Chinatown run by a guy by the name of Wiley Lee?"

"No. Should I have?"

"It's a strange place, located in a dead-end alley, and there's no sign to indicate it's there. Chanan claims he's hardly ever been to San Francisco, yet he gave the limo driver directions to the place and seemed to be right at home."

"Meaning what?" she asked, pulling to the curb behind the Mercedes nudging my Mini's back bumper.

"Meaning that if he's been to San Francisco, maybe he's also been to Sausalito."

Terry leaned over and gave me one of those tongue in your tonsils kisses that make saying good-bye hard indeed.

"Be careful, Carroll," she said as I opened the door. "If Vandamn was murdered, the killer is still out there. Don't get in his way."

I got to work early the next morning, answered E-mails, then wrote a column on the sad fact that local movie theaters were hurting due to the way the studios marketed the pictures on DVDs within a few months of the original release date.

I handed the copy to Max Maslin, who treated it with a yawn.

"Max, when you worked in Los Angeles, did you ever come across a crime reporter by the name of Jack Dornay?"

"Black Jack Dornay? Sure. What's your interest?"

"He wrote an article about a Mafia hit man—Johnny Sands, aka the Sandman. It might tie in with something I'm looking into—Vicky Vandamn, the friend of my mother's who died."

Max scratched his temple with the stem of his pipe. "Dornay was a good reporter, when he was sober. If anyone could fill you in on the dark underbelly of Hollywood, it'd be Jack. I don't think he's working anymore. I can find out, if it's important."

"It could be, Max. See what you can do."

He ran his pipe stem down his cheek hard enough to leave a red mark. "Ah, Carroll. Does the Great know that you're looking into this? I wouldn't want her to—"

"She knows," I assured him. "But I wouldn't bring it up if you don't have to."

I contacted my literary agent and asked him about Ulla/Vicky's book. "Did you ever hear of it, or her, Bob?"

"No. Jesus, Quint. Do you have any idea of how many unsolicited manuscripts I get in the mail every day? Dozens, and I'm just an agent. The publishers get hundreds of the damn things. Everyone in America thinks they can write a book. The writer, she was never published before?"

"No."

"You might try the self-publishing outfits, vanity presses—they'll print anything, as long as the author pays them enough."

I wasted a couple of hours calling local publishers and agents, telling them my name, that I was a reporter for the *San Francisco Bulletin*, and that I was trying to trace down a manuscript submitted by an Ulla Kjeldsen, or a Vicky Vandamn. "I'll make sure that you get maximum publicity in the article," I promised.

None of them had heard of Ulla or Vicky, or Carroll Quint of the *Bulletin*, for that matter.

I ran all of Ulla's names through several freebie directories that list E-mail addresses, but I had no luck, which wasn't surprising. Unless they're insurance salesmen, people don't want their E-mail addresses made available. If I *could* get her E-mail address, I might be able to access her account via an Internet mail site. There was a tech geek in the *Bulletin*'s business section who wrote articles now and then about how to protect one's computer secrets. He bragged about how he could crack anyone's E-mail password in a matter of minutes. Vicky's E-mail might lead me to her editor or publisher, or someone who would know more about the book.

I'd had enough of my office for the day. I deposited the check that Erica Talbot had given me, then dropped my car off at the body shop. The work would take at least five days. I was able to rent another Mini Cooper, this one bright red. While I was emptying my trunk and glove compartment, it suddenly dawned on me that Ulla Kjeldsen must have had a car. And a car trunk would be a good place to keep a laptop computer.

I called my mother and asked her to go with me to Sausalito. What she'd said about her seeing things in Vicky's place that I might have missed could be true. Besides, it would be interesting to see her tangle with Della Rugerio.

When I picked her up at her flat, she was all decked out, as if I were taking her on a yacht, rather than to a houseboat. She had on a top with blue-and-white vertical stripes, a white cashmere sweater tied over her shoulders, tight cigarette-legged white slacks, one of those black Greek fishing hats, and huge black-rimmed glasses with lenses the size of teacup saucers. She called them her Audrey Hepburn, *Breakfast at Tiffany's* sunglasses.

I filled Mom in on Della—her alleged physic skills, the tarot cards, and the fact that the police and her neighbor thought she was giving "happy ending" massages to horny middle-aged men. "I'm hoping we can find a floppy disk hidden somewhere in Ulla's houseboat, Mom."

I considered calling Rugerio and advising her I was on my way. If Ulla had wanted someone to look at *Payback,* Rugerio would seem to be a good bet. The more I thought about it, the less chance I figured there was that the computer would be in her car. Still, you never knew. I decided to surprise Rugerio—there were a slew of questions that I should have asked her about Ulla's postal mail, where she banked, whether she had a cell phone. Ulla must have kept her phone bills and banking records. Where were they? Had they gone missing along with the laptop?

I had to park several blocks away from the harbor. Mom seemed to be enjoying herself. It was a bright sunny day, several men gave her the once-over, and two women stopped to say, "I love your glasses."

I knocked loudly on Rugerio's door. It was opened immediately, as if she'd been expecting me. She was wearing a nurse's uniform: a short white dress with a zipper front and one of those crisp white hats. The zipper was halfway down, exposing a black bra and a lot of flesh.

"You're not my next appointment," she said angrily.

"I was in the neighborhood, Della. This is my mother, Karen. She was a friend of Ulla."

"I'm so pleased to meet you," Mom said. "I imagine you gave Ulla a lot of comfort while she was here."

Rugerio softened a bit. "I tried. She spoke of you fondly."

"Carroll tells me you're a psychic. I would love to arrange a session with you. Have you been in contact with Ulla?"

"Yes. I'm busy right now, but I would be delighted to meet with you, Karen." Della turned her attention to me, grabbed the zipper on her dress, and pulled it up toward her neck. "What is it you want?"

"To see Ulla's place again. And I was wondering about her car? Where did she keep it?"

"What is your interest in the car?"

"Maybe she left the computer in the trunk, or a floppy disk."

"There's nothing in the car. I told that to the men who were by yesterday."

That got my attention. "What men?"

"A grumpy old man, bald, with glasses. He had the nerve to shout at me. He had a Scottish accent. I couldn't understand much of what he was saying. He was obstinate—a Leo, on the dark side—rude, pompous, bossy."

"What did he want?" I asked.

"He asked questions about Ulla. He wanted to get into her houseboat."

The old man had to have been Sir Charles Talbot. "Who was the other man? A short guy with muscles?"

"No. A tall, handsome man with dark hair. He didn't say a word. The old one did all the talking."

Tall, dark, handsome. Maleuw?

"Did you let them into Ulla's houseboat?"

"Of course not." She walked past me and peered down the deck. "These people make appointments, then don't show up! It wastes my time."

"Della. What about Ulla's E-mail address? She must have had one."

"I know nothing of such things."

"What about her regular mail? Is it still being delivered?"

"It goes to the post office." She peeked back down the dock. Her eyes lighted up a bit. "My appointment's coming. Wait."

She ran back into her houseboat and came back with a set of keys. "Go check the car out. It's parked in space G-seven, under a green tarp. The key for the boat is on the ring also. Just leave them in the flowerpot by the door. Karen, if you really want to talk to me, make an appointment. My time is valuable."

As we reached the dock, a nervous-looking middle-aged man wearing an olive-colored suit and dark sunglasses passed us and turned in toward Della's place. He kept his eyes down and didn't respond when I said, "Nice day."

I opened the door to Ulla's houseboat, and, after making sure the place was empty, told my mother I'd see her shortly.

"Take your time, dear," Mom said, closing her eyes and inhaling deeply. "I can feel Ulla's spirit here." She opened up her purse and took out a pair of rubber gloves. "Don't worry, I won't leave any fingerprints."

"Did you just *happen* to have the gloves in your purse, Mom?"

"Yes. I use them when I get gas for the car, dear. God, how I miss full service."

Ulla's car was well worth keeping under a tarp. It was a vintage steel blue Sunbeam Alpine two-seater convertible with a long, louvered hood, raked windscreen, and smoothly tapered tail. This baby had to date back to the 1950s. It was a real head turner, and, when I thought about it, just the kind of car the Ulla/Vicky I was learning about would have wanted to drive. I went through the glove compartment and trunk and found nothing of interest, not even old mail, credit-card tags, or matchbooks. Remember those old movies where the private eye or cop always solves the case by finding a matchbook identifying the bar or restaurant the victim frequented? Ah, the good old days. Now if you even ask for a matchbook, the waiter looks at you as if you're an arsonist about to burn the building down.

Della was no doubt in the middle of her "appointment" and not to be disturbed, and Mom would stay all day in the houseboat if I let her, so I decided to interview Ulla's other neighbors, figuring she must have talked to someone besides Rugerio.

I'd found that there were two ways I could approach people. The first was to tell them that I was with the *Bulletin* and working on an article. I often got a mixed reaction—the person either wanted to tell me anything I wanted to hear just to get his or her name in the paper or wanted to inflict bodily harm because of some grudge he or she had against the mainstream media. The other approach was to say I was working on a book and could use their help. The response was usually positive, because, as my agent had pointed out, everyone thinks that they have a fascinating book germinating inside their head, just waiting to emerge. The danger was that the wanna-be author would pester me to read his stuff and introduce him to my agent and editor.

The houseboat on the west side of Ulla's place was at least as large as Ulla's: two stories with a rusty metal roof. Dozens of animal-shaped whirligigs topped the fence protecting the front of the property: ducks, rabbits, dolphins, squirrels, and birds. I opened the gate and crossed an arched bridge leading to the front door. A hand-printed sign attached to a small wooden tiger said PULL MY TAIL. I followed instructions. The motion set off a chorus of chimes.

The front door was opened by a heavyset woman with a cloud of bleached-blond hair. She was wearing denim shorts and a Rolling Stones T-shirt, the one with the big tongue sticking out of oversize lips. She had chubby cheeks that turned her eyes into slits when she smiled, and she looked like she smiled a lot.

"Hi y'all," she said in a sweet southern accent. "I'm Mary Tucker. Y'all here to see Bert?"

"I'd like to talk to you, Mary. My name's Carroll Quint, and I'm with the *San Francisco Bulletin*. It's about your neighbor next door, Ulla Kjeldsen."

"She's dead, ya know. Bert said she was murdered."

"Maybe I should talk to Bert, then."

"You bet. Come on in." She pushed the door wide open, then

turned and called over her shoulder. "Bert. You get down here. A newspaperman wants to talk to you."

When Bert didn't answer right away, she crossed the room and planted a flip-flop-clad foot on the steps leading topside. There was a tattoo of a golden butterfly creeping out of her belt line. "Damn it, Bert. He's from a *newspaper!*"

She turned toward me and gave me one of her slit-eye smiles. "That husband of mine. When he's working, he doesn't hear nothin'. Be right back."

"What kind of work does Bert do, Mary?"

"He's writin' a book," she said before disappearing up the stairs.

I took a look around. The place was cluttered, but somehow it looked clean.

A pyramid of mahogany boxes, each ascending one a foot or so smaller than the one below it, with highly polished brass locks and hinges climbed up one wall.

Heavy feet began pounding down the stairs. A slump-shouldered man wearing cargo-pocketed khakis and a light blue shirt speckled with catsup stains came into view. He had a lion's mane of iron gray hair and the flowing white beard of a biblical prophet. He walked over close to me. His eyes were dulled by something he had smoked or drunk.

"You want to write about my book? Who told you about it?" He had a deep-chested voice that went well with his beard.

"I didn't know about your book, Bert. I'm looking into Ulla Kjeldsen's death. Mary tells me you think she was murdered."

He snapped his head around, looking for his wife, who was still upstairs.

"Mary talks too much, damn it. To anyone she sees. Always has. You got some kinda identification? How do I know who I'm talking to?"

I took out my wallet, showed him my press card, and gave him a business card.

"Tell me about Ulla," I urged him.

"Damn fine-lookin' woman, she was. Full of life. A crime to kill her like that."

Mary suddenly appeared from the back of the houseboat, carrying a tray with three bottles of beer. There must have been an outside staircase.

"Tell him who you saw do it, Bertie."

Her husband's face turned into a gargoyle of rage. "Damn it, Mary. Shut your trap. I got to think about this."

Mary gave me a beer, then settled herself onto one of the four red vinyl-topped stools that were clustered around a bamboo-fronted home bar.

"Have you spoken to the police about this, Bert? You actually saw the person who killed Ulla?"

Mary said, "He saw him go into her place just before she died, right, Bert?"

Bert stomped his foot down in anger and swore, but it didn't seem to faze Mary. My guess was that she had seen all he had to give over the years, and it didn't bother her anymore.

A low growl rumbled in Bert's chest. "I ain't talkin' no more."

"It was the priest," Mary said with one of her smiles. "The good-lookin' one. What's a man like that want to be a priest for? Show the man your spy room, Bert."

Thirteen

I followed Bert up the stairs. Mary was behind me, nipping at my heels. The hallway was narrow, the walls were eggshell-colored, and the areas above the doorknobs bore fingerprint smudges.

Bert kicked open the door to a large L-shaped room. The windows looked out at Alcatraz, Angel Island, Tiburon, and Ulla Kjeldsen's houseboat. A ceiling fan big enough to lift a helicopter whirled around on slow speed. Stacks of books made hip-high corridors in irregular patterns. There was an oak table against one wall, scarred with cigarette burns and circles from years of forgotten coffee cups and beer bottles. An old IBM Selectric typewriter sat in the middle of it, surrounded by black leather binders and reams of paper. A heavy enamel ashtray from Caesar's Las Vegas had been wiped clean, but there was still the distinctive sweet, skunky smell of high-quality marijuana in the air.

Then there were the telescopes: long, narrow ones, short, fat ones, all on sturdy tripods. Six of them, spread out along the windows. If that wasn't enough, there were three pairs of binoculars perched on the window casings and another pair on the oak desk.

"Bert likes to watch people and things," Mary explained.

I walked over to the window and looked into Ulla Kjeldsen's bedroom and exercise room. The drapes were closed, thankfully; otherwise, we might have spotted my mother searching the place. I wondered how often Bert had peeped in on Ulla when they were open.

Mary must have been reading my mind.

"She used to open them drapes when she was pumpin' iron and stuff. She was half-naked most of the time. Got old Bert all hot and bothered, right, Bert?"

Her husband mumbled something I couldn't hear, then tore a half-typed page from the typewriter. He opened a drawer in the oak table and pulled out a pair of glasses. One of the bows was missing and he had to hold the frames to his eyes to read. He scanned the paper from the typewriter before handing it to me.

"There it is. Where I'm at in my book. Just about finished."

The left-hand margin showed the book's title: *The Michelangelo Cipher*. The page number was 1408. The two paragraphs detailed the adventures of someone named Devlin chasing someone else through the Sistine Chapel.

Mary piped in with, "It's gonna be a lot better than that Da Vinci thing."

I handed the paper back to Bert and wished him good luck.

"Luck ain't got nothing to do with it. Hard work. That's all it takes."

"Tell me about Ulla, Bert. Did you talk to her often? See her—"

"He saw a lot of her," Mary said with one of her smiles. "He was always looking at her, and she knew it. She kept those drapes open just to tease him, didn't she, Bert?"

"Did you see the men she was with?" I asked after taking my first sip from the bottle of beer Mary had given me.

Bert dropped his glasses to the table and stroked his beard as if it were a pet cat.

"I did see her with men, when she wanted me to. She knew I was watching. But there were times when she didn't want me to see. So she closed the drapes."

"What about the priest you saw. Exactly when was that?"

"A few days before her body was found. He was the last one I saw in her house."

"Were they . . ."

Bert clamped his lips tight together and stroked his beard some more.

"Fuckin'," Mary said. "He wants to know if you saw them fuckin', Bert."

"No. I never saw her do that with him."

I picked up a pair of binoculars and focused in on Ulla's place. They were almost too powerful—I could make out the cracks in the wood siding. If the drapes had been open when he was watering, it would have been like being in the room with Ulla. "Did you recognize any of the men you did see her with, Bert?"

"I figured I was protecting her in a way. If someone got rough, or out of hand, or . . ." He paused and looked up at the ceiling fan. "Well, you know what I mean. I could have maybe done something."

Mary had already stabbed her husband in the back with a knife, so now she decided to twist the blade in deeper. "Oh, sure, darlin'. You were just dying to *help* Ulla."

The two of them stared at each other for a long time. It was Bert who turned his head away first.

"You and Ulla had something in common," I said to Bert. "She was writing a book, too. *Payback.* Did she ever tell you about it? Show it to you?" I turned to Mary. "Or you?"

"Ulla didn't show me nothin'," Mary said, wiping her hands on her hips. "It wasn't women she showed things to. I got to go down and fix lunch. I'll let you two boys get down to some dirty talking. Nice meetin' ya, Mr. Quint."

Bert waited until he'd heard her feet going down the stairs before taking a deep breath and blowing it through his lips as it if were smoke.

"I love that woman, but there's times when she's a walking, talking migraine."

"If you need a smoke, Bert, go ahead. Grass doesn't bother me."

He gave me a roguish look, then opened the drawer again and took out a half-smoked cigar—a blunt, a regular cigar with some of the tobacco removed and replaced with marijuana. It was easier than rolling a joint, and you could extinguish it and relight it a number of times. When I was twelve or so, I had watched my Uncle Crime carefully drill a hole in a thick Havana, then pack it with grass. He'd wink at me when my mother would lecture him about the dangers of smoking.

Bert used a black Zippo to get his blunt going. I let him inhale a few lungfuls before saying, "Did you and Ulla get your dope from the same source? Della Rugerio told me that she used nothing but high-grade stuff."

"Della's a whore. Claims she gives massages that restore life and energy." His right hand made obscene pumping motions. "A jack-off queen. You can't take anything she says for real."

"Ulla was smoking dope when she died, Bert. And drinking champagne, and taking sleeping pills—Nembutal. Where did she get the pills? And the grass?"

Smoke leaked out of his mouth slowly and he waved it away with the flat of his hand. "Not from me. She . . . gave me some of her stash when I worked for her, but I never gave her none."

"Worked? What kind of work?"

"Fixing things. She wasn't very handy. I put in a garbage disposal, took care of her plumbing problems, worked on her car. Little things like that. I didn't charge her nothing."

"Tell me about her book," I said, fixing the binoculars on the man in the olive suit walking past Ulla's place. He had some pep in his step and looked more relaxed then he had when I'd seen him heading for Della Rugerio's houseboat.

Bert took another hit on the blunt, holding the smoke in for a long time before blowing it out in a long stream. "She used to joke with me, say that her book would be finished before mine—but she never let me get a peek at it."

"Did she tell you what it was about?"

The grass and the fact that his wife wasn't there was relaxing Bert, loosening his tongue. "About two hundred pages." He laughed at his own joke and then sucked on the cigar again.

"The book may be the reason Ulla was killed, Bert. What happened to it? And her computer is missing. Where is it?"

He teetered on his heels for a moment, hesitating. I jumped in quickly. "You help me and I'll help you, Bert. The woman who does book reviews for the *Bulletin* is a good friend of mine. I can guarantee that she'll give your book a review, maybe write an article about you. A good review can do a lot for a book. Who was Ulla's agent? Her publisher? The two of you must have talked about things like that."

His sucked in some more smoke before saying, "Would she look at my stuff? This reviewer of yours? What's her name?"

"Her name is Terry Greco, and absolutely she'll look at it. You've got my word on it." I figured I couldn't get in trouble volunteering Terry's services. Publishers look at first-time novelists' fourteen-hundred-page manuscripts about as often as big oil companies voluntarily drop the price on gas.

"Ulla told me it was going to blow the lid off a case, one where the police didn't think a guy was murdered, but he was. She wouldn't go into any details, wouldn't let me see any of her work."

"Did she mention any names? Someone from Hollywood?"

"Hollywood? You mean she really was an actress? I thought she was just making that stuff up."

"She had some small parts, and worked as an extra. Then she disappeared. A lot of people thought that she was dead—that someone had her killed."

"And you're telling me that her computer is gone? What about the manuscript itself?" He tapped one of the binders on the table. "She had it when I last saw her."

"When was this, Bert?"

"Oh, I'm not sure. A week or so before she died maybe."

I questioned him for another ten minutes, asking about Ulla's agent or publisher, her men friends, but he answered everything with a negative shake of the head or a "Don't know nothing about that."

I looked around the room again—the clutter, the telescopes, the binoculars. Mary had called it his "spy room." Something obvious was missing.

"Where are the photos, Bert? Where's the camera?"

He took several hard, fast drags on his blunt before responding. "Whatcha talking about?"

"You took pictures of her, Bert. I know that. Where are they?"

He held up his hands in protest. "I ain't no pervert. I didn't take pictures." He gave a twitch of a smile. "Mary didn't mind me watching, but she'd a had a fit if I took pictures."

Like most men when they talk about sex, he was a lousy liar. He was damn near blushing. He had photographed Ulla, and maybe the men in her life, but if I pressed him, he'd wait until I'd left, then destroy the pictures.

"Tell me the truth, Bert," I said in a man-to-man voice. "You did see her with men, didn't you? When they were making love, right?"

He walked over to the door and peered out. When he turned around, there was a nasty smirk on his face.

"She did 'em in bed, on the floor, even in the exercise room. Right on the workout bench. These guys would be banging away for all they were worth and she'd be looking over her shoulder, smiling—at me. Damnedest thing I ever did see. She was a free spirit, Ulla was. She just didn't give a damn about anything."

"The men, Bert. If I brought some photographs over, do you think you could recognize their faces?"

He was high as a kite now, giggling like a schoolboy. "I wasn't much paying attention to their faces."

"Come and get it, Bert," Mary yelled from the floor below. "While it's hot!"

Bert gave me a lewd wink. "She talking about lunch, you know."

I left, declining Mary's invitation to stay for "ham hocks and beans, my special recipe."

I went back to Della Rugerio's houseboat. She didn't respond to my knocks on the door, so I left Ulla's houseboat and car keys in the flowerpot. Rugerio was obviously doing more than giving tarot readings, but that didn't mean much. Great neighbors—Della providing "happy ending" massages to middle-aged men, living next door to an aging nymphomaniac exhibitionist, who lived next to a dope-smoking Peeping Tom.

A few more puffs on his blunt and Bert might have shown me those photographs he'd taken of Ulla. He'd hidden them somewhere, a place where he thought Mary wouldn't find them.

My mother was waiting for me with a chilled bottle of Schramsberg sparkling brut from the refrigerator.

"Let's open it and have a final toast for Ulla," she suggested.

We did just that; then she said, "I couldn't find any computer disks, dear. The houseboat is *too* clean in some places. The bedroom and the living room are spotless, but the rest of the place could have used some work."

"Meaning that the killer tidied up after himself but didn't worry about the rest."

Mom picked up the champagne bottle, then said, "Yes. Come on upstairs. I want to show you something."

In the bedroom, she opened the shuttered door to a closet that was about the size of my condo bedroom. There were neat racks of dresses and coats. My mother had left the built-in bureau drawers open, revealing neatly arranged garments of lace, suede, silk, and cashmere. On one wall were angled shoe racks with what appeared to be more than a hundred pair of shoes: high heels, boots, sandals, in every imaginable color.

My mother gave me a knowing look, then swiveled one of the racks away from the wall. A little niche held two large polished wooden jewelry chests. She opened them up, and there in the silk-lined drawers was a pirate's treasure of earrings, bracelets, necklaces of pearl, and colored stones.

"Most of this is just costume jewelry, Carroll. Did you notice the rings on Della Rugerio's fingers? They were the real thing."

I fingered one of the necklaces. "So the psychic has been helping herself to the goodies."

"Psychic my tight little butt. Those streaks in her hair are a terrible dye job, and that outfit she was wearing was more suited to a naughty boy/bad nursie sex session than a reading of tarot cards. The perfume she was wearing was Yves St. Laurent's Opium, which goes for a hundred and fifty dollars a half ounce at Nordstroms. I know because I sneak a sample dab on my wrist when I'm shopping there."

Jewelry, expensive perfume—what else was Della poaching from the houseboat?

My mother topped off our glasses with more of the bubbly. "All this detective work is making me hungry, dear. Do you want to go back to my place, or shall we find a decent restaurant around here?"

Even an indecent restaurant would be better than her home cooking. I took her to the Lighthouse, and planned my next move, which was trying to figure out how to get into the Talbot exhibition at the de Young Museum the following night.

Fourteen

"You can gain access anywhere as long as you have the proper attire, and a clipboard," my Uncle Crime had lectured me in my youth. And we had the pictures to back that up. My mother would clip newspaper photos of Crime sitting ringside at champion boxing matches, dancing at Hollywood after-Oscar parties, standing alongside the owners of a newly crowned Super Bowl championship team. Since one of his other self-commandments was "If you have to pay, it's not worth going," we knew he'd somehow wiggled his way into these prestigious affairs.

So there I was in chilly, fog-swept Golden Gate Park, decked out in one of my father's tuxedos, holding a clipboard and pencil and striding toward an army of catering trucks parked in the rear of the new de Young Museum, the largest copper-clad building in the world, complete with a twisting nine-story tower. The museum had reopened in the fall of 2005, replacing a venerated old building that was torn down due to earthquake damage. It had drawn a lot of criticism from locals, who'd christened it the "Howard Johnson's of the future."

A uniformed rent-a-cop was positioned alongside the ramp leading to the rear entrance of the museum. A portly, hook-nosed man in a full-fledged chef's outfit, clutching a clipboard much like mine, was standing alongside troops of white-jacketed waiters and waitresses carrying aluminum foil–covered trays into the museum. He spoke briefly with each one before making a notation on the clipboard and waving the person on his way.

I heard one of the waiters call him "Claude."

"Claude," I said in a voice loud enough to reach the rent-a-cop, "the director wanted me to check with you to be sure things are running smoothly." I lowered my voice a notch. "We know that some of our regular kitchen staff can get a little huffy when someone with your reputation takes charge of an event like this. So, if anyone dares give you any trouble, just let me know and it will be taken care of immediately."

He bowed his chef's hat in acknowledgment and said something in French. It sounded like a compliment. Of course, everything *sounds* like a compliment in French, even when they're surrendering.

I scratched a sloppy X on the clipboard paper as I marched hurriedly toward the double doors leading into the museum. The rent-a-cop was a potbellied middle-aged guy with a dirty-brown walrus mustache and large bags under his eyes.

"Sergeant," I said, before he could challenge me. "I've spoken to Claude, the caterer, and I made it clear that there is to be plenty of food for you and the rest of your crew. If he gives you any trouble, just let me know."

"Yeah, thanks," he said as I hurriedly strode past him, then went through the doors and into an industrial-size kitchen. I followed the back of a waiter carrying a full tray of steaming hors d'oeuvres down a narrow corridor, then into a large room filled with men in tuxedos and women in evening gowns. I'd made it. Uncle Crime would have been proud of me.

I ditched the clipboard and picked up a glass of wine from a passing waiter's tray. It was copper-colored, no doubt Talbot's vintage.

Everyone seemed to be in a good mood: chatting, drinking, nibbling, and listening to a string quartet playing a tango.

I said a few hellos to people who had no idea who I was but who nodded back nevertheless, until I finally spotted a familiar face—that of Katherine Parkham, elegant in a ruby-colored velvet off-the-shoulder dress.

"How did *you* get in?" she greeted me. "I tried getting a pass from Terry Greco and she told me no way. I had to pay retail, Quint. Two thousand dollars."

"An old family secret, boss. There's always an open door somewhere at these functions."

Before she could fire back at me, Harry Crane, her steady Eddie, came over, whispered something in her ear, nodded at me, and then guided her toward a cluster of well-dressed gentlemen huddled at the bar. Each and every one of them looked rich enough to buy a newspaper.

I nibbled, sipped, and wandered until spotting another familiar face—that of Erica Talbot. She was nearly falling out of a well-cut, double-breasted indeed, satin tuxedo jacket that reached down to mid-thigh. She was wearing a glittering diamond necklace, matching bracelets on both wrists, and diamond earrings the size of dimes on her ears.

She bumped her hip against mine and said, "How's your mother?"

"Fine thanks. I'm working on what we talked about. I could use a little help on your end. Is there any way you could find out if your husband had been in contact with Vicky Vandamn before she died? Telephone calls? E-mails?"

She arched an eyebrow and gave me a "You've got to be kidding" look.

"What about pillow talk?" I suggested.

Her other eyebrow arched up and she said, "We have separate bedrooms, Carroll, and when we are together in bed, Charles doesn't waste what breath he has left on idle chitchat."

Erica looked over my shoulder and frowned. "Here he comes. You'd better leave." Her hand snaked out and a finger dipped into my cummerbund. "I'll call you. We have to talk. And make sure your mother has a knitting class or something that night."

I took off in search of Terry and found her looking nervous and upset. I had tried to contact her the night before, and when she finally answered the phone, she'd told me she had been at the museum, and would be there most of the following day, with Ron Maleuw, helping to put the final touches on the exhibit. She was dressed conservatively—for her: a floor-length black dress with a mock turtle collar. She was still the sexiest woman in the room.

"I made it," I told her.

"I'm so glad, Carroll. But I'm worried. Ron hasn't shown up. He and Sir Charles had an argument this morning and he took off without saying anything to me. He's just disappeared. No one can find him."

"What was the argument about?"

She glanced nervously at her watch. "Sir Charles wanted him to bring a Picasso oil to the exhibit. It was a last-minute decision by Talbot, and Ron wasn't very happy about it. No one has seen it in years; some doubted it even existed. Apparently, Talbot bought it from a dealer years ago for a bargain price, and he wanted to wave it in the man's face."

I snatched a glass of wine for Terry from a passing waiter.

"Sir Charles almost bit my head off," she said. "He flat out accused Ron and me of stealing it."

I craned my neck around and spotted Charles Talbot, Jr., smiling into the eyes of one of the waitresses. She wasn't smiling back. Sir Charles had disappeared, and Erica had her arm latched around that of a bulky gray-haired man whose profile I recognized—Buddy Albright, one of the men who'd been in the poker game at Talbot's house.

Junior was saying something to the retreating back of the waitress when his eyes met mine. It didn't take a professional lip reader to know that he was saying nasty four-letter words.

He started swimming through the crowd in my direction. Terry pinched my hand to remind me she was there.

"I'm going to check with security and see if Ron's turned up, Carroll."

I stood my ground and waited for Junior. He bore in on me, the tips of our shoes almost touching.

"How the hell did you get in here, Quint?"

First the Great, and now Junior. "I paid for the ticket with my poker winnings, Charlie. Fancy another game soon?"

"I'm going to knock those glasses into your ugly skull, you bastard." He made a fist of his right hand and pulled it back, ready to throw a punch.

"Look out for the woman behind you," I warned him.

Talbot jerked his head around, giving me time to plant the toe of my patent-leather shoe in the middle of his right shin. He swore and grabbed his leg with both hands, hopping around like a one-legged rabbit, bumping into a waiter, then falling to the floor, causing the waiter to send a tray of wineglasses flying.

I melted into the crowd, hoping that the Great hadn't witnessed the altercation. I was looking for her when my cell phone began vibrating.

"Carroll Quint. Is that you?"

It was Kay Manners. The Sausalito detective. "Yes. What's up?"

"It looks like I may have finally gotten a one-eighty-two, Quint. A homicide victim."

"Congratulations. Ulla's officially a homicide?"

"It's a man by the name of Ronald Maleuw. He had one of your cards in his wallet. There's a somewhat threatening note printed on the back: 'Of all the spots in all the towns in all the world, why did you have to take mine?' Did you write that?"

"Yes. Maleuw had parked in my spot at the newspaper. I put the card on his windshield. I didn't even know who he was. That was days ago."

"I don't get it, Quint. What's it mean?"

"It's parody of one of Bogart's famous lines from *Casablanca*."

There was a pause, then Manners said, "The movie? I've never seen it."

The phone trembled in my hand. Never seen *Casablanca*?

"Where are you, Detective?"

"Near Harbor Point. Maleuw's body was found washed up on the shoreline. About a quarter mile from Ulla Kjeldsen's houseboat."

"I'm on my way."

I found Katherine Parkham upstairs at the bar, deep in conversation with Mark Selden, the *Bulletin*'s chief in-house legal counsel.

Selden was a small terrierlike guy who looked like he was ready to bite at any moment. He had mud-colored hair and a face that narrowed to a tapered chin. You know the old joke about attorneys? How can you tell when one is lying? Their lips move. Selden had solved that problem. His lips never moved—he could have been the world's greatest ventriloquist if he had decided to take up an honest profession.

I coughed loudly to get Parkham's attention. She swiveled to face me. "What?"

Just the one word, but it carried a lot of weight.

"Problems, boss. There's been another possible murder."

"Who?"

"Ronald Maleuw, Sir Charles's curator."

"What are the details?"

"I'm not sure yet. I just received the news from Sausalito detective Kay Manners."

"Exactly where was the body found, Quint?"

"All she would tell me is that it was near Harbor Point, not far from Ulla Kjeldsen's houseboat. Kjeldsen was the woman I—"

"I know who she was," Parkham replied testily. "Does Manners have any idea who killed Maleuw?"

"She didn't say. I'm on my way over there now."

"Did Manners ask you to meet her, or is this just your idea of a good move? And why did she call you in the first place? Have you got something going with this cop?"

"Manners found one of my business cards in Maleuw's wallet. I met with her Monday morning to talk about Ulla's death. She's never handled a homicide before. She's like a kid who found the keys to a candy store."

"Never handled a homicide? Don't they have any cops with street smarts over there?"

"There hasn't been a homicide in Sausalito in years, boss."

"Christ, that's impossible. Even Disneyland has homicides. What do you have on this Maleuw?"

"He was supposed to bring one of Talbot's paintings, a Picasso, to the museum today. He never showed up. Talbot thinks that Maleuw might have stolen it. Terry Greco knows more about that than I do."

"Okay. Get over to Sausalito, Quint. See what you can pick up. Do you have a camera?"

"Yes, I can use my cell phone camera, though I'm not sure the cops will allow pictures."

"You're a newsman, Quint. Get some pics. Pump this cop—don't let her pump you. We've got first bite at this baby; we don't want to let it get away from us. What the hell was Maleuw doing in Sausalito?"

"I'm not sure, but it's too much of a coincidence, Maleuw being found so close to Ulla's place."

"If you ever start believing in coincidences, Quint, you're fired. Call me as soon as you've talked to this cop. I want this in the morning edition. Manners is going to find out about the missing painting soon enough—so pass the information on to her, but make it sound like you're doing her a favor. And make sure she returns the favor."

"Sir Charles Talbot was over at Ulla's houseboat the day before yesterday, boss. He was with a young man, tall and handsome. That description could fit Maleuw. They were run off by the next-door neighbor. Do I give that to the police?"

A long silence, then Parkham said, "I think we have to. But get something for it, and call me in an hour."

"Ah, boss, there's something else. Young Charlie Talbot has had a sort of accident."

Parkham expelled her breath slowly. "What sort of accident?"

"Someone kicked him in the shin and he sort of fell to the ground."

Selden knocked back the remains of his wine before saying, "Let me take a wild guess, Quint. You attacked the son of Sir Charles Talbot. At a museum. In front of dozens of witnesses." He turned his beady eyes on Parkham. "Katherine. I told you to fire this man last year. You should have listened to me."

"I didn't say it was me," I said before the Great could get started. "And if it was, there were no witnesses. Junior is drunk and was getting ready to throw a punch. It would be Junior's word against mine, and I don't think he would make an issue of it. Maleuw's death and the missing Picasso could be a hell of a story."

"Has Sir Charles or his son called the police?" Selden asked, disgust obvious on his rigid lips.

"Give me the kicker, Quint," Parkham said tersely.

Kicker. The first two or three lines of a story, what sets up the rest of the copy.

"Sir Charles Talbot's curator found dead. Priceless masterpiece vanishes, never arrives at the de Young Museum gala."

I could see the wheels turning inside Parkham's brain, calculating how long she had to get the story into the morning edition, and if it was worth sparring with the Talbots again.

She held her whiskey glass up to the ceiling and looked through the bottom of it. "For two thousand dollars a ticket, they sure pour some awful scotch. Mark, find Terry Greco. Get her out of here. I'll meet the two of you back at the paper."

Selden opened his lips an eighth of an inch or so and it seemed as if he was going to argue with Parkham, but he quickly strode off in search of Terry.

Parkham turned her venom on me. "Quint, you better get your ass out of here, too. If Junior stirs up a fuss over the kick to his shin, you're on your own."

I followed orders, skirting around the crowd and going out the same kitchen doors I'd entered through.

The potbellied security guard was still on duty. He rubbed his amble stomach and said, "When's the grub coming?"

"Any minute," I assured him. I'd parked under a dew-dripping cypress tree in a dark, deserted area of Golden Gate Park. By the time I reached my car, the air was suddenly filled with the ululating sound of police sirens.

Fifteen

/pointed the rented Mini's nose in the direction of Sausalito, a myriad of ideas ricocheting around my head: Who killed Maleuw? Why was he killed? What's the involvement of the ruthless Talbot family in all of this? Did I somehow put myself in the middle of it, and am I next in line? And Ulla, always Ulla, and her missing book, *Payback*. How in the world could that have anything to do with Ron Maleuw?

When I arrived, there were police and fire trucks parked helter-skelter, searchlights in place, and a group of uniformed policemen keeping a gathering crowd from getting too close to the edge of the bay.

The sky was clear, sprinkled with stars, and it was balmy—at least twenty degrees warmer than it had been in Golden Gate Park. The air stank of diesel from the fire rigs and portable searchlights.

I wriggled my way into the crowd. A white ambulance had backed down to the water's edge. Kay Manners was having a heated argument with a tall man in a dark blue windbreaker and rubber boots. There was a lot of arm waving. I couldn't hear what they were saying, but it was easy to see Manner's lips were forming the word *bullshit* quite often.

Someone tugged at my sleeve. It was Bert Tucker, Ulla's neighbor, a fat, half-smoked cigar stuck in his mouth. He sucked on it, even though it wasn't lighted.

"Hey, fella. A tux. Fancy duds. The paper must be paying you a lot of money."

"Hi, Bert. What's going on?"

He took the cigar from his mouth and pointed it at the nearby black-and-white police car. "Jeannie Kasin found a stiff when she was out jogging."

An attractive young woman in an orange running suit was talking to two policemen. Her arms were wrapped tightly around her chest and she was shivering in the warm night air.

"Jeannie's an airline flight attendant," Bert told me. "She likes to run at night." He jabbed the cigar in the direction of a neighboring pier. "She lives over yonder."

Yonder was certainly within range of Bert's telescopes and binoculars.

"Have the police spoken to you, Bert?"

"Nope. Don't see no reason why they should, do you?"

"Ulla dies of an overdose; then a dead body floats right up on the shore. What is it—about a quarter of a mile from here to her houseboat and your place? That might make them want to talk to you."

Bert frowned and stroked his beard. "I never thought of that. Who's the stiff?"

"I won't mention your spy room to the cops, Bert, if you show me the pictures you've taken of Ulla and her visitors."

"I told you, there ain't no pictures," he said heatedly.

I borrowed a word from Detective Manners's vocabulary. "Bullshit. Think about it, Bert. You and Mary wouldn't want the police searching through your boat."

I left him sucking on his dead cigar. Someone familiar had joined Manners and the man she was arguing with—Father James Carmody.

They spoke briefly; then Carmody walked over to the ambulance and disappeared from sight. I dug my press card from my wallet and flashed it at the nearest uniformed policeman, a slump-shouldered man in his fifties.

"Detective Kay Manners called me. I know the victim."

"I'd wait until she and Lieutenant Candella are finished discussing the matter," he said with a cold grin.

"What are they arguing about?"

He cocked his head and eyed my tuxedo suspiciously. "What paper are you with?"

"The *Bulletin*. Anything you tell me is off the record," I said. I'd been waiting years to use that line.

"Jurisdiction. Candella is a Marin County homicide dick. He wants to take charge. Manners doesn't see it that way."

I caught up with Father Carmody as he was climbing up onto the pier.

"Hi, Father."

His handsome face took on a scowl; then he recognized me. "The newspaperman. You look like you're dressed for a wedding, not a funeral."

"I knew the victim, Father. Or at least met him. Ronald Maleuw. He worked for Sir Charles Talbot. Did you ever hear Ulla Kjeldsen mention his name?"

"I don't believe I did. Do you know if he was a Catholic?"

"I don't, but I may be able to find out for you."

"Thanks." He started to walk away, then made an abrupt about-face. "I was thinking of calling you. I remembered that Ulla did tell me something of a rather personal nature, but it wasn't in the confessional. She said that she'd had a child a long time ago, that the baby died shortly after birth. It upset her that he was never baptized."

"He? She said the baby was a male?"

"Yes. I asked about the father, but she wouldn't go there."

I thanked Carmody and headed for Detective Manners. Lieutenant Candella was striding in my direction, his hands in his jacket pockets, his face twisted in anger.

He looked to be in his forties. He was tall, gaunt, and had wavy gray hair. His eyes were on high beam.

"Who the hell let you down here?" he snarled as we got within talking range.

My instincts warned me that if I told him I was a reporter, he'd aim one of his rubber boots at my backside.

"Detective Manners sent for me," I told him. "I knew the deceased."

"Bully for you," he growled, walking away.

Manners was talking with two men in rubber diving suits. I wandered toward the ambulance. The rear doors were open and what looked like a body on a stretcher, covered with blankets, was lying on the floor.

"Hey, Quint," Manners called out. "Can you positively identify the subject for me?"

"Yes, I could do that."

She came over and shook my hand. Hers was icy-cold. She was still wearing her police blazer and slacks. The ends of her trousers were wet and her shoes were crusted with sand.

"What can you tell me about the victim?" she asked.

"Ronald Maleuw was the personal curator for Sir Charles Talbot. There was a showing of Talbot's paintings tonight at the de Young Museum."

"Really? Well, let's make sure we've got the right man."

She climbed into the ambulance and motioned for me to follow. She then bent down and gently lifted the blanket from the corpse.

"That's him," I said after taking a few hard swallows. Ronald Maleuw's face was scraped and bloated. His eyes protruded from his face, as if he had strained mightily to get one last look at the world before he left it.

"Are those injuries from before he died or after he was in the water?" I managed to say.

Manners covered Maleuw with the blanket, then said, "I don't know yet. I'll have to wait for the coroner's report."

"You must have some idea of how he died," I said, pressing her. "Was he shot? Hit over the head? Drowned? What?"

Manners voice took on a "Me cop, you not," tone. "You and the rest of the press will get that information when I decide it's time for it to be released."

"Detective, I've got some information that could be of help to you. What I need is a little something in trade."

"Withholding information from a—"

"Yeah, I know. I watch TV, too. What I have may or may not be relevant to Maleuw's death, which, as far as I know, could have been accidental. But it would make a good page in your murder book."

She stepped over the corpse and pushed me outside. We walked down toward the water's edge. The tide was out. The smell was something that people who lived in houseboats had to learn to endure—a mixture of sewage, dead fish, and salty air. Thank God for the salty air, I thought.

"All right," Manners said finally. "What have you got for me?"

"How did Maleuw die?" I countered.

She turned to face the shoreline. There was still a crowd of rubberneckers milling around.

"We're not sure. There are plenty of cuts, bruises, and contusions on his person, so it could have been a suicide, or it could be something else. There's a wound on the back of his head that looks suspicious, but we'll have to wait for the autopsy."

"I'm betting he was murdered, Detective. Maleuw was supposed to deliver one of Sir Charles Talbot's paintings, a Picasso, to the museum today. He never showed up."

Manners bit down on her lower lip and made mewing sounds. "That's interesting. Sir Charles Talbot. I bet he's going to love talking to me. I'll probably have to go through a wall of lawyers to get to him."

"I wouldn't think so, Detective. He's anxious to get his painting back, and there's a link between Talbot and Ulla Kjeldsen."

Her eyes widened and her chin jutted out at me. "Kjeldsen? What?"

"She worked for Talbot, at his Hollywood studio years ago, under the name Vicky Vandamn. Rumors are that they were romantically involved. Talbot was nosing around Ulla's houseboat just two days ago. He talked to Della Rugerio, who told him to bug off. There was a man with Talbot, and the way Rugerio described him, it could have been Maleuw."

"You don't say. We could be talking about *two* homicides." Her eyes glazed over. She was probably thinking about the possibility of there being a serial killer roaming the streets of crime-free Sausalito. "What else have you got?"

"Maleuw drove a black Jaguar sedan."

A uniformed cop yelled out to Manners—something about her captain wanting to see her.

"Detective, I've given you quite a bit. I want to take a picture of the deceased."

"I couldn't allow that," she said, then added, "Of course, I have to go see my captain, so I can't monitor everything you do. Stick around. I may have some more questions for you."

I watched her trudge up the beach, then I ducked over to the ambulance. I pulled back the sheet covering the remains of Ronald Maleuw and snapped off a few quick shots. I tugged the sheet down farther, and saw that Maleuw was dressed in a tuxedo. The bow tie had disappeared, but there were still studs in the shirt buttonholes. One jacket sleeve was pushed up to his elbow, revealing a large gold coin cuff link. Maleuw had been dressed for the museum gala.

I took a few more pictures, then melted into the crowd, and making it to the Mini without Detective Manners spotting me.

Sixteen

*T*he phone was ringing, but when I groped out for it, all I grabbed was a throw pillow. That wasn't right. I was in my condo, the phone was right alongside the bed, and it kept ringing.

I sat up, remembered I'd fallen asleep on the couch, and stumbled over to the phone sitting next to my computer. The answering machine had kicked on and my voice was telling whoever was on the line to leave a message.

Max Maslin was saying, "Quint, you're a lousy photographer. Give me a call as soon as—"

"I'm here, Max." I yawned into the phone. "What's up?"

"Not what, *who*. The Great. She hasn't gone home yet, just took a nap in her office after you and Terry left. Have you seen the morning edition?"

"No. How's it look?"

"Your picture of the late Ronald Maleuw is above the fold on the front page. It's not exactly Pulitzer Prize quality—grainy and a bit out of focus—but Parkham was delighted with it, and she was impressed with your reporting, too. We beat everybody in town on this one. She now wants you to concentrate on Maleuw's murder and—"

"We're not sure he was murdered, Max."

"Of course he was murdered. Concentrate on that and the missing Picasso. 'Have Quint feed the beast' was the way Parkham put it. She wants more and she wants it now. I'll be taking over your reviews until further notice. How's Terry doing? She didn't look so hot when the two of you left the paper."

Max was right. Terry had been down in the proverbial dumps. Finding out that someone you knew and liked has possibly—in fact, likely—been murdered can do that to you. She hadn't wanted to go back to her place, so she came to my condo. We had one drink together; then she went straight to bed, and I went straight to the couch.

"She'll be fine, Max. Any developments on Maleuw's death, or the missing painting?"

"If there is, no one is telling me. I'm just an entertainment editor, Carroll; you're the ace crime reporter. Parkham wants Terry in her office at two o'clock for another meeting with Mark Selden. What's your next move, Sherlock?"

"Damned if I know, Max. I have a feeling that the Talbots, senior and junior, would be happy if I disappeared—permanently."

"There's always Mrs. Talbot," Max suggested. "And by the way, I found that reporter you wanted to talk to, Black Jack Dornay. He's living up in Lincoln, just past Sacramento, in one of those Sun City senior citizen communities. Jack was a pretty wild guy. Last place I thought he'd end up. I gave him a call, and he said he'd be happy to talk to you. Here's his phone number."

After Max gave me the number, I said, "Why the 'Black Jack' handle? Is he a gambler?"

"Oh, yeah, and there's a casino near his house, but he got the name because of his fondness for Mr. Daniel's bourbon. If you end up meeting with him, it might be a good idea to take a bottle with you. Let me know how you two get along," he said before hanging up.

I tiptoed past Terry and got into the shower. When I came out, she was still sound asleep. I grabbed some clothes, closed the bedroom door, made coffee, booted up the computer, and went through the morning ritual of checking E-mails. There were the usual forty or more from readers who either agreed or disagreed with my last review. I sent back short, polite replies to all—a reader who disagrees with you still counts as a reader.

While I was doing that, an E-mail came in from Detective Kay Manners. Simple and direct: "Call me."

I got right through to her. It sounded like she was on a cell phone.

"You disappeared on me last night, Quint."

"I've got a job, Detective."

"I saw the paper—the photo, and the story," she said with an edge to her voice.

"I spelled your name right, didn't I?"

"Yes. We located Mr. Maleuw's Jaguar. It was parked on Cypress Street, about three blocks from where we found his body."

"No Picasso in the trunk?"

"No. Nothing of interest . . ."

Her voice was fading away.

"Where are you?" I asked.

"En route to the Talbot's house in Napa."

"Are the autopsy results in?"

Her voice was still fading out, but I heard her say something about "later in the afternoon," and that it "wasn't for publication yet."

"You know, Detective, I'm handling the story for the *Bulletin* now, and I was thinking that a picture of you—say, sitting at your desk, typing something, or talking on the phone—would look good in the paper."

"I'll be back in my office by three o'clock, Quint. I could fit you in."

"I'll send a professional photographer, so we get it right. But I can't do the story without the autopsy results."

Her voice became quite clear and precise. "You're sort of a prick, aren't you, Quint? I can't give you the complete autopsy, but I'll tell you what you need to know."

"Good luck with the Talbots," I said before breaking the connection.

I dialed the number that Max had provided for Black Jack Dornay. A voice full of gravel said, "This better be good. I'm entertaining the Dallas Cowboys Cheerleaders, and they get grouchy when we're interrupted."

"Carroll Quint, Mr. Dornay."

"Drop the pom-poms, girls," he shouted, then in a whispered voice asked, "What can we do for each other, Quint?"

"I'd like to talk to you about the old days in Hollywood. The Johnny Sands, Tony Silk, Vicky Vandamn days."

"Dose was da days," he said, the gravel back in his voice. "I've got an opening in my calendar tomorrow morning, early. It gets too damn hot after ten. I'm at sixty-two Arnold Drive. Bring love. See ya."

I took another peek at Terry. She was all tangled up in the bed-sheets, one lovely arm hanging over the side of the mattress. As I was about to close the door, one of her eyes opened and she said, "Any word about Ron?"

"No, other than that they found his Jaguar in Sausalito." I remembered Father Carmody asking if Maleuw was a Catholic. "Was Ron religious, Terry? A Catholic?"

"No. He was a card-carrying atheist, from the way he talked."

"Parkham wants you in her office at two o'clock. I've got a meeting with Detective Manners this afternoon. Maybe she'll know something by then."

She elbowed herself up into a sitting position and combed her hands through her hair.

"Anything good in the refrigerator?"

"Not really."

She leaned over and looked at the clock on the nightstand.

"Do you think it's too early for a pizza? I haven't had a bite of food since Parkham hustled me out of the museum."

"I'll call for a pizza. Maybe I'll make it two. Don't forget, we're dining at my mother's tomorrow tonight."

Terry groaned, lay back, and buried her head under the pillow. Not an uncommon reaction when people are reminded of dinner dates with Mom.

I called the *Bulletin* and arranged to have a photographer meet me at the Sausalito Police Department at three o'clock.

Terry's appetite deserted her. She barely touched the pizza. I dropped her off at her place. She didn't mention anything about seeing me later in the day or that night, and I didn't press it—there are times when you just want to be alone. She knew all she had to do was call and I'd be there.

I had several hours to kill before meeting with Detective Manners. Since I was in my reporter/private eye mode, I decided to return to the scene of the crime. I bought a copy of the *Bulletin* en route to the bridge. Max was right: It wasn't a very good picture of the late Ronald Maleuw.

It was a beautiful afternoon in Sausalito: sunny skies, flotillas of seagulls bobbing in the blue-green water of the bay.

I parked the Mini on Cypress Street, where Detective Manners said Maleuw's Jaguar had been found, then walked down to Harbor Point. I passed small apartment houses, a few single-family residences, a dry cleaner's, and a coffee shop before arriving at the pier. There was no way that anyone could have carried Maleuw from his car to the pier without being noticed.

The small beach where his body had been found was deserted, except for a few stray dogs and a guy in a sombrero-style straw hat waving a metal detector across the slushy gray sand. The tide was in, covering the area where the ambulance had been parked the night before.

I ducked as a huge shadow crossed my path. A brown pelican had skimmed by just a few feet over my head before swooping into the bay, where it scooped up lunch, then arched gracefully up into the sky, showing off like an old World War I bi-plane after a bout with the Red Baron.

Della Rugerio's door was open a crack. I leaned closer and listened to the voice of Dr. Laura Schlessinger on the radio. She was advising a sweet-voiced young woman on her upcoming choice of a husband: a man twenty years her senior who had three children, each from a different woman, none of whom he'd married.

"Stop shacking up and dump the loser," the good doctor ordered.

I knocked loudly on the door. The volume faded and Rugerio came and yanked the door wide open.

"You!" she said in disgust. She was all in white again, tight slacks and a thin V-necked shirt molded to a 1950s-style pointed-cup bra. Her streaked hair looked like it had been attacked by robins searching for nesting materials.

"The police were here." She waved two fingers at my nose. "Twice. Scaring away my clients. I cannot make a living like this. It's your fault!"

"Della, the police now believe there's a possibility that Ulla was murdered. I thought you'd be happy about that. Did they tell you about the body found on the beach last night?"

"Yes. That fat woman cop. She woke me up. For nothing."

I showed her the newspaper photograph. "Does this man look familiar to you?"

She snatched the paper from my hand and studied it before handing it back to me.

"Della, the young man in the photograph is the one who died. Ronald Maleuw. He worked for Sir Charles Talbot. Was he one of the men who came—"

"Yes, the police showed me his picture. He was here. I'd never seen or heard of him before. But Sir Charles Talbot," she scoffed. "Ulla told me all about *him*."

"Did you mention this to the police?"

"Why should I? They are costing me my livelihood." She curled her fingers around the edge of the door. "And I'm not making any money wasting my time talking to you."

I waved the paper at her. "I've been assigned to Ulla's murder. I'll be writing about it every day. I could drop your name, mention your psychic skills. That could bring in some customers."

Her eyes narrowed as she gave that some thought.

"Have you had lunch?" I added hastily. "There's a great place called the Lighthouse not far from here. Let me buy you lunch."

"I'm not dressed for lunch. Come in. I'll fix tea."

She sat me in that wobbly-legged chair and in a few minutes came back with two white Styrofoam cups filled with hot water and tea bags.

"What did Ulla tell you about Charles Talbot, Della?"

She took her tarot cards out and began shuffling them. "I sometimes think better when I'm working."

I sighed, pulled out my money clip, and freed two twenty-dollar bills, dropping them on the table. What the hell, lunch for two at the Lighthouse would have cost more than that.

She picked the bills up and tucked them into the V neck of her shirt.

"The vault," she said after they disappeared between her breasts. "Though this doesn't buy you much of my time. My clients donate two hundred dollars for an hour of my services."

I had a sudden vision of Della and Freeze Chanan fighting over money with sharpened chopsticks.

"Ulla told me that this Talbot was a nasty man. Uncouth. 'A corrupter,' she called him. He turned lovely young women into harlots by promising them roles in his films."

"I know about that. What else did she say?"

Della turned a card faceup, showing a color drawing of a man holding a candlelike object over his head.

"The cards know him as the Magician: totally committed, able to apply his force of will on people, full of vitality. The Magician is very powerful, he believes in himself, and he's not afraid to act."

"Is that how Ulla spoke of Talbot?" I asked, sipping at the tea.

"She said he was a jerk most of the time but that he could be a charmer. I think he was in love with Ulla once."

"Talbot's been in love with a lot of women—five wives and a string of movie starlets like Ulla."

She flicked another card onto the table so that it faced me: a young woman in an elaborate robe sitting in a gilded chair.

"The Empress," Della said. "That was Ulla—giving and receiving pleasure, being earthy, experiencing *all* of the senses."

"Ulla told Father Carmody that she'd had a son who died at birth. Did she mention the father's name to you?"

She responded by turning over yet another card. I'd had enough of them. I covered it with my hand. "What did she tell you, Della? Was the child Talbot's?"

She bobbed her tea bag and watched the water darken. "I'm losing my powers of concentration. Perhaps you should come back later."

"The story I'm writing in the paper—I *could* mention your other skills. Detective Manners said you gave 'happy ending' massages to your customers. Your neighbor Bert Tucker was a little more graphic."

"Tucker! That pervert. He probably killed Ulla. He was always drooling over her, watching her, taking her picture."

That got my attention. "How do you know he took her picture?"

She waved a meaty arm over her head in a circle. "Ulla told me. She thought he was a pig."

"But Bert worked for Ulla, fixed her appliances, and her car."

"Even a pig has uses," she said in a self-satisfied voice.

"Does Tucker have a key to Ulla's place?"

"How would I know?"

"Who would have a key besides you? Did Ulla have a house-keeper?"

"She was a very clean person. She took care of everything herself, newspaperman."

"Della, I want to know what Ulla told you about her child."

She tapped her wristwatch with a fingernail. "I have a client, a paying client, coming any minute. We will have to continue this conversation later."

I wobbled out of the rickety chair and headed toward the door. "I wasn't kidding about that newspaper article, Della."

She snapped her fingers together and a card appeared magically in her hands: an armored knight on a strong, rearing horse.

"This is you, Mr. Newspaperman. The Knight of Wands: superficially charming, cocky, daring, adventurous, often acts without thinking, presumptuous. You would make a serious mistake in slandering me in your paper."

"It's not slander if it's true, Della. You better have some answers for me when I come back."

"The Knight of Wands also is reckless and rash and doesn't give danger its due respect," she said to my already-retreating back.

I turned around and walked back to the table.

"I'd like to take another look at Ulla's houseboat."

"Perhaps tomorrow. My client is due any moment." She flicked her fingers at me. "Leave."

"Ulla's book might be worth a lot of money, Della. More than you could make with your tarot cards in a lifetime. And she must have made a will. Who has it?"

She shuffled the deck of cards so they made a sound like a burst of fire from an automatic weapon.

"I have no idea. I didn't pry into her affairs."

"You pried into her houseboat." I made sniffing noises with my nose. "That's an expensive perfume you're wearing." Della stood up abruptly, bumping the table. She strode over to a shelf full of candles, scooped up an object, and tossed it at me.

"There is the key to her houseboat, newspaperman. Look for the book, the will, for whatever you want, but leave me alone."

"Why didn't the police take the key from you, Della?"

"Ask them. I told you that fat woman cop isn't very bright. I should have—"

The doorbell chimed and she made shushing sounds. "Out. The back way. And if you come back tomorrow, be prepared to pay for my time."

Seventeen

I noticed the red kayak was missing from Della Rugerio's back deck as I hopped over to Ulla's property.

According to Harry Baum, the Canadian Realtor, Ulla had left town a year or so ago with a bundle of dough, and she still had some real estate holdings in British Columbia. I hadn't found any record of them, nor anything relating to bank accounts, brokerage accounts, or insurance policies. And no cash. No purse with ID, for that matter.

Her estate would attract the usual suspects: Distant relatives would make their love of Ulla known—their attorneys would pop out of the woodwork, demanding a piece of the action; old friends, churches, and charitable foundations would remember Ulla had promised them money—*their* lawyers would crawl out of freshly dug ground, petitioning for a percentage of the loot; tax collectors would wade in and demand their unfair share—federal and state authorities would descend like locusts.

The key slipped into the lock and the door slid back. I had no idea what I was doing there again, other than killing time before seeing Detective Manners. I just couldn't believe that there wasn't something that the police had missed, and that neither my mother nor I could find.

There was something different about Ulla's place this time—it had been searched by someone without my mother's gentle touch: kitchen drawers ajar, the couch cushions thrown around the floor, paintings taken from the walls.

The upstairs bedroom was in even worse shape.

My cell phone vibrated against my hip. When I opened it up, the seductive voice of Erica Talbot purred into my ear: "Carroll, tonight at my pied-à-terre for dinner. Eight o'clock, and tell your mother she shouldn't wait up to tuck you in. Understood?"

"I'll be there," I promised. "I imagine you're still thinking about Ron Maleuw's death."

"Yes. We'll discuss it tonight. Come hungry," she said before breaking the connection.

I used the cell phone to call the *Bulletin*. Katherine Parkham was unavailable, so I spoke to her secretary, Rosie, and asked her to have someone check with the local county offices to see if Ulla had filed a will, or any civil documents that might be of interest.

"You're a little late, Carroll. Kate had me working on that the minute I came in this morning. Nothing much so far, except for the fact that she owned the houseboat free and clear. Mr. Maleuw was also negative in Marin County civil files. Kate wants something for tomorrow's edition. I wouldn't disappoint her if I were you." Rosie was the only person who worked on the paper who could get away with calling the Great by her first name.

"I'll have it for her," I promised.

I checked the door locks and windows but didn't see any scratches or marks of forced entry; then I locked up the houseboat. I was about to leave the key in a flowerpot next to Rugerio's front door but then decided to keep the key, make a spare, then return the original.

Maybe it was my imagination, but I thought I heard low groaning sounds coming from inside the sorceress's lair. It reminded me of the time I'd been tapped for jury duty—a criminal case involving a police raid on a house of prostitution. The lady in question's attorney had asked the arresting policeman what had caused him to force his way into the premises.

"I heard the sounds of intercourse," the cop, a fatherly-looking guy in his fifties with reddish hair and thick glasses, had replied politely.

The attorney had jumped on the cop with both of his crocodile-skin boots. "Sounds of intercourse? Are you an expert on those? How interesting. Please describe to the jury just what you consider those sounds to be, Sergeant."

The sergeant had gone through a series of loud groans and moans that made Meg Ryan's orgasmic sounds in the restaurant scene in *When Harry Met Sally* sound positively chaste.

The lady of the evening's attorney had protested vigorously, but the judge then asked the cop how many prostitution arrests he'd made under similar circumstances.

"Over twelve hundred, Your Honor."

The judge had then said that that number certainly qualified him as an "expert in the sounds of intercourse," and he gaveled out a judgment of guilty as charged.

Detective Kay Manners was behind her desk, phone in hand, steely eyes looking right into the camera held by Al Doyle, the *Bulletin*'s top photographer, a frisky seventy-year-old with a nose that could slice cheese. Manners's office was a standard-size room filled with dented metal filing cabinets. The rug was battleship gray and the walls were painted that light slimy green color that city planner's love.

"Good, good," Al said, "let's try a profile shot."

"My left side is my best," Manners said, tilting her head upward to stretch out her double chin.

Al took a few more snaps, then put his camera away. Before he left, he wrapped an arm around my shoulder and said, "Keep your day job, Carroll. The shots of the stiff were awful. What the hell did you use?"

"My cell phone, Al. It was all I had."

"You should have called me."

"I didn't have the time," I told him truthfully.

"Carroll. The guy wasn't going anywhere, was he? See you back at the paper."

Once Al and his camera were gone, Detective Manners's mood turned sour.

"That was a wasted trip up to Sir Charles Talbot's place," she complained. "He was 'unavailable,' according to his wife. A minor stroke, she said. She also said that she was suffering from depression and fatigue. Imagine that. The woman looked like she was suffering from a hangover to me."

"Did you speak to George Mandan, Talbot's valet/bodyguard?"

"The charmer with a heavy tan and shaved head? Oh yeah. He was a bundle of information. He said he knew nothing, and that if he did know anything, he'd have to clear it with Sir Charles, or the family attorney, before talking to the likes of me."

She reached over her desk, opened her purse, and rooted around for something.

"He did show me Maleuw's cabana." She took a Kleenex from the purse and wiped off her lipstick. "The frame from the alleged missing painting was right there in the middle of his bed. Wasn't that convenient of Maleuw, leaving it right there where we couldn't miss it?"

Manners leaned back in her chair and held her fingertips to her temples, as if contemplating her thoughts. "According to George, only Maleuw and Sir Charles had access to the records relating to the art collection. He also said that your fellow reporter Terry Greco and Maleuw were 'doin' a bunk-up,' meaning they were sleeping together."

"George has a dirty mind. What about the son, Charles junior? What did he have to say for himself?"

"He was also 'unavailable.' Some important business meeting."

"Talbot keeps a boat at the Corinthian Yacht Club in Tiburon, Detective. That's just a few miles from here by car and a very short voyage by boat. A strong swimmer could probably make the trip in under an hour."

She dropped her hands to her lap. "Do you have any influence with George, Talbot junior, or Lady Talbot?"

Lady Talbot. That was the first time I'd heard Erica addressed by her British title.

"I may be meeting with her soon. What's the word on Maleuw's autopsy?"

She ruffled through some papers on her desk. "Nothing specific yet."

"How far have you gotten on Maleuw's background?"

"He had a California driver's license. The listed address is the Talbot's place in Napa. Lady Talbot did say that his parents had predeceased him, and that he had no living next of kin."

"I stopped by Ulla's houseboat on the way to your office. It's been ransacked—a sloppy job, from what I could see through the window, and her red kayak is gone, too."

"Maybe Rugerio sold the kayak. The houseboat has been vacant for a while; that's an engraved invitation to a burglar."

"Here's something you might not know. Maleuw was adopted when he was a baby. In Los Angeles. His father was a set designer, his mother an artist. The father worked for Talbot. They moved to Europe when Ron was a small child. Sir Charles hired Maleuw to be his curator several years ago. He was well qualified for the job, from what Terry Greco told me; however, he was thinking of opening his own gallery in London."

"Thanks. Here, I have something for you. A copy of Ulla Kjeldsen's autopsy."

She handed me a thick sheaf of papers stapled at the edge. The copy I'd ordered from the Marin medical examiner's office days ago still hadn't arrived at the *Bulletin*.

"You must know something about Maleuw's death," I said. "I need it for the for the story, with your picture, in tomorrow's *Bulletin*, Detective."

"Just go with 'appearances of foul play' for now, Quint. You'll get the info right after I do."

She was holding something back, and I couldn't budge her. I switched gears and asked about Ulla's bank accounts, her missing ID, purse, and personal papers.

"I'm working on that. And as soon as I—"

"Sure, sure. I know. You'll pass it right on to me." I didn't believe that, so I didn't pass along the information regarding Ulla's real estate holdings in Victoria, British Columbia.

"Someone went through a great deal of trouble to make sure Maleuw's body was found on that beach. What about dragging the bay around her place? Now that you have two suspicious deaths, maybe your captain will okay a couple of divers. Who knows what you might find."

"Thanks for telling me how to do my job, Quint."

"Ulla had a baby years ago, a son, who died at birth. Father Carmody told me that she mentioned the child, but he wasn't specific as to who the father was. What if the baby didn't die? Ronald Maleuw would have been about the same age as that child now."

"So would you, Quint."

"My mother wouldn't like that crack, Detective. What about a DNA check? It would either confirm or eliminate the possibility that Maleuw was Talbot's son."

She walked her fingertips across the desk and picked up a pencil. "Talbot would never agree to that."

"A strand of his hair, a glass he's drunk from—that's all you need, right?"

"So what's your theory, Quint? Someone kills Ulla, and then Ronald Maleuw, because that person thinks he's her son? Or she commits suicide and Maleuw does a copycat job?" She tossed the pencil into a red coffee cup filled with a dozen of the things. "There's nothing to connect Mr. Maleuw to Ms. Kjeldsen."

"Except that they're both dead and their bodies were found a few football fields' distance apart."

"Touché," she groaned. "Listen, Quint, I have a meeting with the captain in a few minutes, so we'll have to call it quits for now. If you meet with Lady Talbot—"

"I'll keep you posted."

We shook hands and she slumped back into her seat as I went out the door. I had the distinct feeling that Manners was starting to regret her wish to handle a real-live homicide case.

Terry Greco's meeting with Katherine Parkham had gone well. The Great was in no mood to let someone the likes of Junior push around one of her employees.

Her knee to Junior's groin was greeted with great glee, but my nudging his shin with my shoe was considered a no-no.

I had a fifteen-minute legal lecture from *Bulletin* attorney Mark Selden on the dangers of a newspaper reporter accosting a civilian, no matter how uncivil he'd been.

I took advantage of Selden's time by asking him about the legal implications of the death of Ulla Kjeldsen.

"She either committed suicide or was murdered. So far, a will hasn't surfaced. What happens now, Mark?"

Selden thrust his hands into his pant pockets, no doubt counting small change before responding. "When a person dies intestate—that's without a will—there is an order of priority among her surviving relatives as to who gets what. Typically, the surviving spouse takes the whole estate. If no spouse, then the children. If no children, then the deceased's parents, or, if they are dead, then the surviving siblings of the deceased."

"As far as I know, Ulla's husband and parents are dead. There was a son, who reportedly died at birth, and there's no ID on who the father was."

"Well," Selden continued in his best professional tone, "if none of these people exist, the property escheats—reverts—to the state the person died in. Whatever bank or agency holds the property would *probably* notify the state, and the state officials would petition the probate court to allow the property to revert to the state. Are we talking about a lot of money here, Carroll?"

"Her husband was well-off, and he had no other living relatives, nor did she, as far as I know. Ulla went by two other names, so things could get complicated."

"Indeed. If the lady was murdered, then the person responsible can never partake of the estate. Of course, the longer it takes for a probate to be filed, the more opportunity there is for unknowns to plunder the deceased's soft assets—cash, jewelry, gold coins, et cetera, et cetera. Even where there is real property—a house, an apartment, insurance policies, stocks, mutual funds and the like—the estate might be worth nothing by the time it gets to court. And if what you tell me is true, it may well be that there will be quite a time gap before the wheels of legal justice begin turning."

Selden bowed his head and pinched his nose. "Who was that fat old drunken comedian with the bulbous nose?"

"W. C. Fields? The man was a comedic genius, Selden."

"Perhaps, but he wasn't very smart. He allegedly socked away huge sums of money in banks all over the country under assumed names. His heirs missed out on a fortune." Selden's sealed lips twisted in an evil smile. "The banks loved him, though. They got to keep the money."

While Selden was in what for him was a good mood, I asked, "How hard would it be for a woman to have a prenuptial agreement nullified, or at least modified, if, say, the husband was getting old, and was ill, perhaps a little senile."

"Unlikely, if the original agreement was drawn up properly. Whom are we talking about?"

"Sir Charles Talbot."

"Forget about it, then," Selden said sharply. "Talbot would have had the document drawn up by a well-qualified attorney." His voice dropped into a conspiratorial whisper. "Of course, if Mrs. Talbot wanted *me* to represent her, I wouldn't discourage her, and you and I could perhaps work something out, Carroll. If you get my meaning."

I got his meaning; then I got out of his office as fast as possible. I had figured out why most people took an instant dislike to Selden—it saved time.

Eighteen

Katherine Parkham slashed through the printout of my story for the paper's morning edition with a red marking pen. When she was finished, she looked me straight in the eye and said, "Not bad, Quint. But it could be better. This Sausalito cop knows a lot more than she's telling you."

"I know, but if I push too hard, Manners will just cut me off."

That produced a long "Hmmmmm"; then she picked up the photograph Al Doyle had taken of Detective Manners sitting at her desk. "She's too young to be a detective. She looks like she just graduated from Stanford or *some* goddamn college out here—little Miss Prim and Proper. I like old fat-guy cops with baggy suits and lousy haircuts, who look like they've been around the block a few times."

"If I said that, it would be considered a sexist remark," I told her.

"Then don't say it. Did you confirm what Manners told you about Sir Charles? Did he suffer a minor stroke, or is he just stalling the investigation?"

"I'll find out tonight. I'm meeting with Erica Talbot."

Parkham's neatly plucked eyebrows rose toward her forehead. "Really? In Napa, or at her Filbert Street pad here in the city?"

"Filbert Street," I said, wondering how she knew about Erica's pied-à-terre.

"Good going, Quint. Use your boyish charm on her, but stay away from Junior. I'll have someone from the crime beat handle him. According to Terry Greco, who is one sharp cookie, Picasso, in addition to being a manipulative, slimy son of a bitch, was amazingly prolific. So see if you can get Mrs. Talbot to identify the exact painting that's gone missing. Have you come up with anything that will connect Ulla Kjeldsen to Ronald Maleuw?"

"Nothing solid—yet," I told her. "But I'm working on it."

"If you pick up anything interesting from Mrs. Talbot, call me on my cell, and we'll squeeze it into the morning edition."

"Will do, boss."

I pushed myself to my feet and headed for the door.

"Quint. Watch yourself. I hear that Erica is a real man-eater. Don't go kicking her in the shin, or other vulnerable places. Understood?"

The same maroon-hatted doorman who had loaded me into a cab on my last visit to the Carlton Arms was on duty. He tipped his hat in a mock salute and held the lobby door open for me.

"Nice to see you back, sir. I believe you know the way."

"Indeed I do," I assured him. I checked my image in the bronze-colored mirrors as I waited for the elevator: gray slacks, blue button-down shirt, one of my dad's dark blue blazers. Boring, but practical. I had that early-morning appointment with retired reporter Black Jack Dornay, so I hoped to be out of Erica's place and home in my own bed before midnight.

I rode the elevator up to the tenth floor, going over the questions I was going to ask Erica, and wondering if she'd be alone—or if George would be lurking in a closet, waiting to do me bodily harm.

There was no reason for me to be nervous. I was single. Terry dated other men; I saw other women. Erica was an adult, a married woman, who fooled around a lot, possibly with her elderly husband's consent. Consent or not, I vowed to have nothing physical to do with her—just ask the questions, get the answers, and skedaddle.

All those good intentions vanished like smoke in the wind when

Erica opened the door to her pad. She was dressed in lavender again. The material was soap bubble–thin, and the dress was cut low in front, with two thin rhinestone shoulder straps and crisscrossed lacing at about six-inch intervals that held the front and back together. Her hair was parted in the middle, drawn back behind her ears, and anchored by two lavender jade butterfly-shaped clips.

"Come in, come in," she said, waving me into the room.

A circular dining table with a snow-white cloth and silver place settings was positioned in front of the window. The smell of chicken and rosemary permeated the room.

The cocktail table held a blue bottle of Bombay Sapphire gin and the same top-hat ice bucket that had been there on my last visit.

Someone coughed behind me, and I swiveled around. A small, neatly dressed man with a waxed mustache was standing there.

"Everything is ready, madam." He gave a curt bow. "You will no longer be needing me?"

"No, Maurice. Thank you, just send the bill to this address."

While Maurice bowed his way out of the room, Erica went to work on the gin.

When she handed me my drink, she said, "I trust that your mother will not be bothering us tonight."

"I think we're safe. What about your husband? Does Sir Charles pop in here now and then?"

"No. Never. When he comes to the city, he always stays at the Bohemian Club, where he can drink and play poker with his fossil friends."

"What about Junior?"

"Seldom, and certainly not tonight. He had one of his trollops in the pool when I left Napa."

"That leaves George," I said.

"He is under specific orders not to disturb me here, and if George is good at anything, it's following orders."

We clinked glasses. "What shall we toast, Carroll?"

"How about Ron Maleuw. May he rest in peace."

It wasn't what she had in mind, but she took a deep, lip-smacking swallow of the gin before saying, "Poor Ronnie. I was worried that he'd do something like that."

"Like what?" I asked, settling onto the eggplant-colored couch.

"Kill himself. He was so depressed."

"Why was that? He looked healthy, and he had a great job."

"Oh, he was healthy all right," she said with a wicked grin. "But he was . . . What's the right word? Unfulfilled. He was an excellent artist, but there was no way he could make a living on his own by painting. He gave it up completely when he came to work for Charles. Handling all of those masterpieces day after day probably didn't help. They just reminded Ronnie that he was not up to the task. Drink up, Carroll. We're here to enjoy ourselves."

I sampled the gin as she wiggled close to me. "How is Sir Charles? I heard he had a stroke."

She crossed her legs, causing the hem of her dress to ride up toward her thighs. "Where did you hear that? From that dumpy police-woman?" She put a finger to her lips and made a shushing sound. "Just between us, I told her that so she wouldn't bother Charles. He's so up-set about Ronnie's death, and that damn missing painting."

"Which one of Picasso's paintings is it that's missing?"

"I have no idea. Charles has so many of them." She swallowed more gin and motioned for me to do the same. "Apparently, the man Charles bought the Picasso from years ago, for nearly nothing, was going to be at the exhibit, and my husband wanted to flaunt it at him."

"What was the man's name?" I asked.

"I have no idea. Drink up."

"Didn't George drive Sir Charles to the museum for the exhibit?"

"Oh, yes. He had to be there early that day to supervise things. George dropped Charles off, then came back for me."

"I didn't see George at the museum that night."

She dived back into the gin, then said, "Why would you have wanted to? He was there, and he drove both of us home."

We chatted about Sir Charles's paintings for a few minutes, but I didn't get any more information about the missing Picasso.

She leaned over, bumping her bare shoulder into mine and asking for a refill.

"You look so warm in that jacket. Take if off. Relax."

I freshened our drinks and took off the jacket. Her one free hand began playing with my shirt buttons.

"Your husband's paintings must be insured," I managed to get in while her tongue flicked at my ear.

"No. The premiums would be prohibitive." She leaned back, kicked her shoes off, and swung her legs up onto the couch. "What else did the police tell you, Carroll? Do they think that Ronnie committed suicide?"

"They're waiting for the autopsy. Erica, it's too much of a coincidence. The missing Picasso. Maleuw dying, and then his body turning up very near the houseboat of a former actress who years earlier worked for your husband, disappeared mysteriously, and supposedly committed suicide."

"You could be right," she said, squirming her hard round butt into the couch. "Charles is so upset. He hates to have *anything* taken from him."

"Who would buy the Picasso? You just don't pick a painting like that up on eBay."

Her hand went back to picking my buttons. "Collectors are a curious lot, Carroll. Between you and me, Charles's collection has paintings that have dubious provenances, to say the least. If he were to show them, there could be quite a scandal. But he doesn't care—it's *having* them, and someone else *not* having them; that's all that matters." Her hand dropped to my lap. "You know the old saying, Boys and their toys. Whoever ends up with the most toys wins." She drained her glass and handed it to me. "Let's have one more, then really relax."

"What about that actress, Ulla Kjeldsen? Your husband was sniffing around her place the other day."

"Yes. That was your fault. You brought up her name to Charles at the party. He's obsessed with finding this book of hers. What was her acting name?"

"Vicky Vandamn."

She wrinkled her nose and waved her glass at me. "That sounds *so* old Hollywood. Charles actually named one of his bimbos Lorna Lovely, can you believe it? How did you learn that Charles was 'sniffing around'?"

"Someone in a neighboring houseboat spoke to him. And Ron Maleuw was with him. The police find that very interesting."

Erica made a tut-tutting sound, then said, "Ronnie often drove my husband places. Charles shouldn't drive himself, and I insist that he doesn't drive at night, but he's a very stubborn man. Sometimes he'll take off and disappear for hours on end. I'm getting quite concerned. He's become so forgetful. I think it's the start of dementia."

"What do you suppose the connection is between Maleuw and Vicky Vandamn?"

"I don't know that there is one," Erica said. "The woman must have been old enough to be his mother."

"Could she have been his mother?"

"That would be weird, wouldn't it? But you never know. Ron *was* adopted."

"You and your husband have a boat in Belvedere, don't you? Did Maleuw ever use it? Take it out by himself?"

"The *Sir Charles*? I haven't been on it in months. It's not really my thing, a forty-eight-foot catamaran. I remember Ronnie being with us one day when Charles was in the mood to go sailing. Junior is about the only one who makes use of the boat now. It has so many gadgets, one man can operate it by himself. Charles used to take it out a lot when it was docked in the Caribbean, but it's just too cold for him here. I don't know why he doesn't get rid of the thing."

"How's Junior taking all of this?" I asked while reaching for the gin bottle.

"He's such a suck-up. He thinks if he's nice to Charles, he'll be forgiven for past sins and will get back into Charles's will. He's dreaming."

"What were his past sins?"

Erica put her glass to my lips and poured a stream of gin into my mouth.

"Junior lost a great deal of my husband's money on those dreadful movies of his. *No one* actually saw them, thank goodness."

"I couldn't find a listing for any of them on the Web."

"The London producers took Junior for a ride. He financed the pictures, and they used some old, has-been actors. Everything on the cheap: filmed right on the streets, no studio work. They were complete rip-offs of old Hollywood movies, total flops. The video people wouldn't buy them, and they buy everything. Charles insisted that the name Talbot not be used in any way."

"What did Junior call his company?"

"Shields Productions."

She watched me intently while I puzzled that out. It rang a distant bell, but I couldn't quite place it.

"Remember Kirk Douglas in *The Bad and the Beautiful*? He played a ruthless movie producer by the name of Jonathan Shields." Erica gave a tinkly laugh. "Charles once told me that the movie gave him the idea to go to Hollywood and get into the picture business."

I should have remembered. It was a wonderful movie, circa the mid-fifties, Douglas in his prime, a prime his son Michael never reached; Lana Turner and a host of big-name actors were in the cast. The haunting theme song was one of my father's favorite pieces, and he was one of the few musicians who would tangle with it solo on the piano.

"Surely Junior must be mentioned in his father's will."

"Oh, yes. Charles will take care of his *son*, but Junior won't end up with as much as he's hoping for. Not at the rate Charles is writing checks and donating his paintings to all those churches. Luvina, Junior's mother, was an English snob with a small pile of her own money. It was through her family's connections that Charles received his knighthood.

When she died, she left all her money in a trust fund for Junior. He was a child at the time, and he only gets so much a year. I don't know the dollar figure, but he's always complaining that he needs more."

Maybe that explained why he'd cheated at poker. "Luvina must have been a young woman. How did she die?"

"Luvina had health problems—self-inflicted. Cocaine—'Devil's dandruff,' Charles calls it—and other naughty drugs. She spent a lot of time in bed, but not for recreation. I think they had to strap her in to keep her away from the stuff. She died at sea, on the *Queen Mary,* en route to England."

"Where was Junior born? In England?"

"No. In Stamford, Connecticut. Charles had a beautiful estate there. Acres and acres of rolling hills. Great horse country. He sold it a few years back. Luvina hated it, apparently. She thought that anything west of Manhattan was filled with cowboys and Indians. Charles told me that she went out to Hollywood once and stayed about an hour before flying back home."

"You're certain Charlie was born in Connecticut?"

"Oh, yes. I checked out my husband's ex-wives and trollops very thoroughly. I didn't want anyone coming out of the woodpile, claiming to be a member of the family, after Charles is gone. Junior is, for better or worse, his one and only."

"I met with Detective Manners this afternoon. She referred to you as Lady Talbot. Maybe I should call you that, too."

She slipped my glasses off and put them next to the gin bottle. "Don't bother. I used the title when we were first married, until my charming husband started humming 'The Lady Is a Tramp' whenever I was so addressed. I may use it again, once he's no longer here."

Erica had finished with my shirt buttons. She drained what was left of her drink, then used both hands on my belt.

I had always thought of myself as a pretty good athlete: too short for basketball, too small for football. In baseball, I was all field and no hit. My three best sports were track, boxing, and sex.

You don't consider sex an athletic endeavor? You would if you saw Erica Talbot in action. Those long, hollow legs were very strong from all that horseback riding. Erica was not shy about shouting out encouragements and letting me know what pleased her. I wouldn't have been surprised if the doorman had heard her down in the lobby. In equestrian parlance, I was rode hard and put away wet. Twice!

In between bouts, there were much-needed bites of delicious rosemary chicken, cubed potatoes the size of dice, roasted asparagus, and goblets of champagne.

I managed to ask a few more questions about the Talbot family. Junior was making noise about trying his hand at the movie business again, but his father wasn't keen on the idea. There was talk of buying a magazine or newspaper, possibly the *Bulletin,* to give Junior something to do with his spare time.

"I wish he'd just go back to Europe and stay there," Erica said. "He upsets Charles something awful."

She leaned over me with a platter of chicken and said, "Breast or thigh?"

They were both delicious.

Around 1:00 A.M., I slipped out of bed—easy to do with satin sheets—scooped up my pants, shirt, shoes, and socks, and slinked out of the room, closing the door quietly behind me.

My sport coat was on the floor, the pockets turned inside out. I didn't remember Erica or me doing that. Had George made a visit while Erica and I were hashing around in the bedroom? Luckily, I always kept my wallet and money clip in my pants pocket. The jacket was a hand-stitched Brioni, and had cost my father, or one of his admirers, a goodly amount of money. The pockets held nothing but notepads, old ticket stubs, and breath mints.

I spent several minutes looking for my glasses and finally found them floating in the top-hat ice bucket.

I checked Erica's bedroom. She was dead to the world, her legs wrapped around a pillow, a light snore fluttering her lips.

There was no sense waking her to tell her that someone had searched my coat and tried to drown my glasses. Who? George? Junior? Or maybe old man Talbot had decided to check the place out.

There had been a changing of the guard in the lobby. The door-man, a young man with razor-thin pointy sideburns, was at his desk, hunched over a thick book.

He got up from behind his desk when I exited the elevator, hurrying over to open the front door.

"Wait," I said. "Has anyone come in, in the last hour or so?"

"Ah, I don't know if—"

"I'm a guest of the Talbots. On the tenth floor. We thought we heard someone trying to get in, but when we opened the door, no one was there."

He gripped his forehead as if trying to squeeze the memory out. "No one came in during the last couple of hours, mister. Of course, if someone drove into the garage and took the elevator from the base-ment, I wouldn't have seen them."

"Did anyone *leave* in the last couple of hours?"

"No. It's been real quiet." He jerked his head toward the desk. "That's how I like it. I'm studying for the state bar."

I thanked him for his time and then exited out onto Filbert Street. It was cold, and the icy wind whipped the building's canvas awning. I had taken about five steps when something whizzed just behind me and exploded on the cement.

I yelled something and ran back toward the Carlton Arms door-way. The soon-to-be-lawyer doorman stuck his head out and said, "What the hell was that?"

That turned out to be a watermelon-size clay flowerpot—or what was left of it. Shards of clay, clumps of dirt, and a couple dozen yellow mums were splashed on the sidewalk. If the damn thing had landed a couple of seconds sooner, I'd have been among the splashings.

I ran into the middle of the street and looked up toward the building's upper floors. There was no sign of anyone on any of the balconies.

"You think the wind could have done that, mister?" the doorman asked.

"No."

"Maybe a cat, huh? A cat bumped into it and knocked it over."

"How do I get to the garage?"

He took me back into the lobby. "You can take the elevators, or the stairs over there."

I chose the stairs, taking them two at a time. I heard the squeal of breaks before I could reach the garage door. By the time I'd opened it, the squealing had stopped and all I saw was the rear end of a bright red sports car zooming up the outgoing ramp. I gave futile chase, but when I ran up the ramp to the street, there was no sign of the vehicle.

The doorman gave me a friendly smile when I returned to the lobby.

"You want me to call the police, mister?"

"No. I don't think that would do much good."

He twisted the end of one of his pointed sideburns between his fingers. "You know, you could have been badly injured by that flowerpot. You may be suffering mental stress right now. You might think of filing a negligence claim against the owners of the building, and the tenant involved."

God, what a night. Ravished by Erica, almost killed by a wayward flowerpot, and now I was witnessing the birth of another Mark Selden.

Nineteen

Billboards lined the freeway with pictures of youthful-looking senior citizens smiling widely while holding tennis rackets or golf clubs. The men all had suntans and full heads of wavy gray hair; the women were trim and attractive. Their happiness was all because of the fact that they were living in a wonderful active adult community in Lincoln, "only two hours from San Francisco." Two hours if there was no traffic on the Bay Bridge, which happened about as often as a congressman takes a pay cut. If you tried the trip during rush hour, it was an aggravating four-hour-plus excursion.

I'd been up and on the road by 7:00 A.M., mainlining a Starbucks double cappuccino, so when I glided to a stop in front of the gates leading to Black Jack Dornay's gated community, the Mini's dashboard clock showed it was 9:36.

The guard sitting in the neat flagstone gatehouse was a weary-faced gent wearing a starched tan shirt and a uniform cap that rested on ears shaped like a catcher's mitt.

He leaned forward and said in a dry, lifeless voice, "What are you here for?"

"To rape, loot, and plunder," I said, in hopes of cheering him up.

He was uncheerable. "The golf course, real estate office, or visiting a resident?"

I gave him Jack Dornay's name. "He's expecting me."

He wheeled around in his chair, clicked a few keys on a computer, muttered something to himself, then handed me a map of the community.

"You go down to the first palm tree, take a right, cross over the bridge, take another right, and you're on Palmer Drive. Dornay's house number is sixteen."

I followed directions. The bridge was a graceful flagstone and wooden beam beauty that crossed over a stone creek. The traffic consisted of mostly golf carts driven by people with smiling faces much like those on the billboards.

The houses I drove by were all large, sprawling ranchers or two-story McMansions done in a style that Realtors like to described as having "a Tuscany feel": tile roofs, sun-bleached adobe walls, two-car garages, and carports sporting one or two golf carts. The lawns were all emerald green, and flowering orange marigolds seemed to be the plant to have. The homes probably sold for somewhere in the $600,000 to $800,000 range. If you could plop one down on a lot in San Francisco, it would be worth at least a million dollars more.

The garage door at Dornay's place was wide open. Inside were a candy-apple red Corvette and an old yellow Cadillac convertible, the model with huge shark fins.

I rang the doorbell a couple of times before it was opened by a thin, leather-skinned man. He was wearing baggy khakis, a Hawaiian shirt featuring pink hibiscus blooms, and sandals. He had a long, narrow skeletal head topped by thin strands of black hair, which was carefully brushed from one side to the other. He sported a pair of wraparound sunglasses, with a pair of half-lens reading glasses balanced in front of them on the tip of his nose.

"You must be Quint," he said, shooting out a hand. His grip was strong and dry. Then he spotted the paper bag under my arm and smiled. "Ah, I see you came well armed. Come on in."

The floors were polished hardwood, the walls warm beige tones. The air-conditioning was on, and a radio was tuned to a country and western station, Johnny Cash in the middle of giving out good advice: "Don't take your guns to town."

"Drink or coffee, Quint?" He reached for the paper bag. "Or both?"

"Just coffee, thanks."

A copper-haired woman came into the room and smiled at me. Maybe Dornay hadn't been bragging when I'd called him the day before. The lady could have been a Dallas Cowboys Cheerleader—thirty years ago. She had kept her figure, and kept her face out of the sun. She was wearing white shorts and a red tank top with WRITERS DO IT DAILY printed across the front.

"Hi, I'm Connie," she said, then turned her attention to Dornay. "I'm going to the casino with Doris. See you for lunch, Jack."

"Nice lady," Dornay said when Connie had left. "A widow. This place is loaded with them." He patted his toast-rack chest. "A homely old widower like me makes out like a bandit. They sell Viagra by the bucket up here."

The kitchen was filled with up-to-date stainless-steel appliances. The cabinets were walnut, the counters a dark-veined marble. Dornay clicked off the radio, poured us both a cup of coffee, and led me to a table in a small alcove with a view of the golf course, where plaid-clad men and women were gouging out divots in the lush fairways.

"Nice place, Jack."

"Yeah." He curled a pair of knobby hands around the cup and frowned. "Real nice. Everything a man could ask for, but to tell you the truth, I miss the action, the sleaze of old Hollywood—all those phonies trying to cover up their sins, and, man, there were a lot of them: murders, rapes, blackmail, extortion. Yeah, I miss the action. Reporting it anyway. Watcha' need from me, Quint? Max Maslin was kinda vague."

I gave him a five-minute rundown on Vicky Vandamn's death.

"Vicky was a walking wet dream, though if a man could get her a job in a movie, she might stop walking for him."

"How well did you know her?"

"Not as well as I would have liked. She was a nice kid, but she knew which sides of the sheets were buttered. Believe it or not, I wasn't a bad-looking guy in those days. That's the trouble with living life in the fast lane. You get to the end of the road too damn soon. I couldn't do Vicky's career any good, and that's what she was interested in—being a movie star." He took a pull on his coffee and then walked over to the counter where he'd placed the Jack Daniel's I'd brought, cracked the cap, and brought the bottle over to the table. "Want some?"

"Not right now."

He dribbled bourbon into his cup and sat down. "There were so many of them, gorgeous young creatures who would do anything to get a film role."

"I know that Vicky had a thing with Charles Talbot, but it didn't seem to do her much good as far as movie roles went."

"Talbot," Dornay scoffed. "He had the pick of the litter all right. Talbot would use some flunky director, order him to put one of his 'starlets' in a scene, have them say a line or two, only the cameraman was instructed not to bother to put film in the camera. When the dolly asked what happened to her big moment on the silver screen, Talbot would tell her that she was great, but because of the director, it ended up on the cutting room floor."

"Vicky had a child who died shortly after it was born. Any chance that Talbot was the father?"

"Damn good chance, I'd say. Every once in awhile, I'd be invited to the parties at his mansion. Talbot liked to keep the press, even us lowly crime reporters, happy. I caught him and Vicky together. In the flesh. I opened a door upstairs, thinking it was a bathroom. It was what Talbot called a 'playroom'—silk pillows, mirrors on the walls and ceiling, some leather stuff scattered all over: whips, dog collars, harnesses."

"Talbot was into bondage?" I said, taking my first sip of the coffee.

"We're talking Hollywood, Quint. Bondage, coke, it was the start of the 'If it feels good, do it' times. All those designer drugs: ecstasy, China White, which was a sort of synthetic heroin, and methyfentany speed bombs."

"What about Freeze Chanan? Was he a regular at Talbot's parties?"

"Freeze. Jesus, no one has a higher opinion of Chanan than I have, and I think he's an asshole." Dornay stood up, leaned his head out into the hall, then opened up a kitchen drawer, rooted around for a bit, and came out with a pack of Marlboro cigarettes and a book of matches.

"Connie doesn't like me smoking," he explained as he lighted up. His cheeks hollowed as he devoured the smoke.

"Chanan was pretty friendly with Talbot, wasn't he?" I asked.

"Freeze was friendly with anyone he thought he could screw out of a nickel."

"What about Tony Silk?"

"He was plain bad news. No one shed too many tears when he went to jail, or when he died there."

"Did that include Johnny Sands? I saw your story about him on the Web."

Dornay exhaled streams of smoke from his nostrils. "Johnny Sands. He was a good-looking guy—curly dark hair, that gangster aura that women love. Talbot used him a lot."

"For what?" I asked. "Why would a rich man who ran a movie studio need a hit man?"

"Johnny was a lot more than a hit man. You remember that great scene in *The Godfather* where the movie producer wakes up in bed with a horse's head? Well, things like that really happened. Tony Silk, and the big boys from back east, they all wanted a piece of the studios. But if you had a guy like Sands on your payroll, they kept their distance. He came in handy when the unions or the Actors Guild made trouble for the producers. Johnny wasn't just a killer; he was a bone breaker. People used him to collect debts, and I know that that one movie bigwig hired him to break up an affair between his wife and some hotshot actor. Johnny messed the guy's face up pretty bad. He didn't work again for a long time."

"Were Sands and Vicky Vandamn ever an item?"

Dornay took several hard, fast drags on his cigarette before tapping the ashes into a cactus plant on the windowsill.

"Where are you going with this, Quint? Why all the interest?"

"Vicky was a good friend of my mother, Karen Kaas."

"Karen Kaas?" Dornay shook his free hand as if he'd just touched a hot stove. "Wow, there was a cutie. And no one could get anywhere close to her except—" He slapped his palm across his forehead. "John Quint. Christ, he's your father, isn't he? Kid, you come from a hell of a gene pool."

"Vicky and my mother roomed together for a while. Then Vicky moved in with Jerome Ramsey. Remember him?"

"Yeah, sure. Ramsey, a closet queen. Talbot used him as a beard for the girls. So did a few other guys."

"Vicky claimed that Ramsey had been murdered."

"I thought so, too, but I could never prove it."

"What about the police?"

"You'd have to ask Chanan. It was his case."

"He told me that he knew Sands killed Ramsey, but he couldn't prove it. Ramsey was beaten up pretty bad before his head was blown off."

"You talked to Chanan? In person?"

"He came to San Francisco. He's interested in Vicky's death."

"Yeah, I bet he is. Chanan was known to work guys over—beat a confession out of them. He used a pair of sap gloves, heavy leather gloves with buckshot sewn into the knuckles."

"What about Johnny Sands's murder? There was no doubt that was a professional hit, was there?"

"Johnny Sands was one tough piece of meat. He had the biggest hands I've ever seen on a man. I gave him a ride once, from some party—it might have been at Talbot's place—to a joint on the Strip. He was always bumming rides. He didn't like driving a car. He told me that that's the easiest way to get rubbed out, when both of your hands are on a steering wheel. I was doing him a favor, and I was scared he'd knock a few of my teeth loose if I ran over a bump in the road. Whoever killed Johnny was either someone he trusted—and there weren't too many people in that tribe—or someone who could get up close to him, probably from behind, like maybe a cop."

I leaned back in the chair and watched Dornay puff away until the cigarette was down near the filter.

"Jack, are you telling me that Freeze Chanan killed Johnny Sands?"

"I never tell anybody anything that I can't back up with enough proof to print in the paper. I do know that Chanan and Sands hated each other's guts. They both used to frequent the Villa Capri. So did I. You'd see Chanan at one end of the bar, the Sandman at the other— and the manager was careful never to sit them near each other in the dining room. I was there one night when Chanan came in, a warm summer night, but he was wearing a raincoat, and he had his hands in his pockets. If you knew Freeze, you knew that meant he had his mitt on a gun in one of those pockets. He strolled over to Johnny Sands at the bar, and everyone backed away, just like in the old Westerns when the two gunfighters are going to go at it.

"Chanan said, 'Let's go, Johnny,' and I was looking for a table to dive under, but the Sandman acted real casual, told the bartender to get him a pen, which the man did, slid it down from the other end of the bar. Johnny scribbled something on a cocktail napkin and tossed it to Chanan. Freeze picked it up with one hand, the other one still in his raincoat pocket, gave it the once-over, then rolled it up into a ball, put it in his pocket, turned on his heel, and walked out of there real slow."

"What was on the napkin?"

"I don't know for sure, but another wise guy told me that it was the name and telephone number of a police captain. There were rumors that Johnny had removed a certain thorn in the side of one of LAPD's finest, the copper having been caught with his hand in the wrong cookie jar."

"By wise guy, you mean someone from the Mafia?"

"Yeah, the Villa Capri was quite a joint. Sinatra was a co-owner with Patsy D'Amore, so all the mob guys loved it, and Dino, Sammy, Joe DiMaggio, Monroe, they were regulars. James Dean had his last Hollywood meal there. He took that damn Porsche Spyder there to show it off to his buddies. Legend has it that Dean bumped into Alec Guinness, of all people, that night, and Guinness warned him, 'Never get in that car, or you'll be dead in a week.' Guinness was right on; Dean died in the car exactly one week later. The Villa lost a lot of its luster when the movie stars stopped coming in. You know what changed it all?"

Dornay didn't wait for an answer. "When Sinatra's son was kidnapped. That really rocked the whole community. If they could touch Frank, they could touch anyone. Suddenly, the stars were all vulnerable, so they stopped going out in public, unless they were surrounded by bodyguards."

"Why would Chanan have wanted to get rid of Sands?"

Dornay took a last drag on his cigarette, then ground it out in the cactus plant container.

"I wish I knew. If I did, I could probably write a book about the whole thing."

"Vicky was writing a book that she titled *Payback*, about her Hollywood days. The manuscript and her computer are missing."

Dornay gulped down half of the coffee, then loaded it with more bourbon. I wished I could have seen his eyes behind those glasses. His feet were tapping on the floor, and his lips had developed a twitch.

"What about a man by the name of Philip Maleuw," I asked. "He was a Hollywood set designer. Worked for Talbot, among others. He adopted a baby son, then moved to England about the time Talbot did."

"Never heard of him. Any reason I should have?"

"His son, Ron, went to work for Talbot as his personal curator. His body was found on a beach in Sausalito, not far from Vicky's place. The police haven't come up with a cause of death yet."

"This has got my juices flowing, Quint."

"I'd like to find out just what happened to the Vicky Vandamn of Hollywood. People thought she was dead, but she turned up in Canada ten or eleven years ago, not too long after Sands was rubbed out. Where was she before she went to Canada? Someone up there said she'd mentioned something about Mexico or South America."

"I've still got some connections down in La-La Land. If I come up with something, can you get my story into your paper? Under my byline?"

"I don't know, but if you come up with anything and pass it on to me, I'll make sure you get credit for it. I don't think there'll be any money, though. The *Bulletin* is awfully tight with a buck."

Dornay rubbed his hands together and smiled. "Money isn't a problem for me. You know those bonbon candies you buy at the movies? Connie's dearly departed owned the company. She calls herself 'the bonbon queen.' Give me a day or two and I'll let you know if I'm still any good at this reporter thing. You'd better leave me a number where I can reach you, day or night. The people I know work mostly at night. And they don't work for free, so your paper might have to spend some dough."

Twenty

I was feeling pretty happy about my meeting with Jack Dornay. He was obviously missing the excitement of his reporter days and was anxious to dig into Vicky's Vandamn's past.

I decided to do a little gambling at the nearby Thunder Valley Casino; not on the slot machines, but on the restaurant's menu. The vast parking lot was less than half-full. I parked and had just started toward the casino, when my cell phone began vibrating. It was Katherine Parkham.

"Quint. Where are you?"

"A couple of hours away, boss. I'll get in as soon as I can."

"Don't bother," she said. "As of now, you are officially on vacation."

That stopped me in my tracks. I sat on the Mini's warm hood and croaked, "What?"

"It's the best I could do at the moment, Quint. The powers that be in New York wanted me to fire you. There's going to be a meeting on the sale of the paper. Apparently, Talbot's attorneys are out for blood and are applying a lot of pressure. Junior is going to be there. You haven't done anything foolish regarding Junior since we last spoke, have you?"

"No. Not at all." I thought of telling the Great about the flowerpot aimed at my head from Erica's balcony, but that would lead to questions about why I'd been out in front of the building sometime after 1:00 A.M.

Parkham said, "I'm off to New York City. I'm going to try to squash Talbot's bid for the *Bulletin* once and for all."

"Do you think you can do that?" I asked hopefully.

"I don't know, but don't worry. If worse comes to worst, there's an opening for an entertainment editor at the *Des Moines Chronicle*. I'm sure I can get you in there."

"Des Moines, as in Iowa?"

"Yes. I want to cover all bases, so you are not to come into the *Bulletin* until you hear from me. If you need something from your desk or computer, get it from Max or Terry Greco."

"What about the murders of Ulla Kjeldsen and Ron Maleuw? The missing painting?"

"You're on vacation, Quint. I can't stop you from working on the story, but nothing goes in the paper under your name. If you come up with anything, give it to Max. Or if it's really hot, like you've solved the murders and found the painting, call me in Manhattan. I'll be at the Algonquin Hotel. Watch yourself, and don't do anything foolish."

I disobeyed orders right away, walking into the casino and heading straight for the bar. The first two Bloody Mary's did nothing to take away the pain. Des Moines? I was sure it was a fine city, full of fine, noble citizens, but as Sergeant Smith said on the way to the Little Bighorn, "Please, General Custer, I don't want to go."

I fueled up on pancakes and bacon, then went directly back to the car. The way my luck was running, I figured there was no sense in stopping to play the slots or blackjack.

Before turning over the engine, I checked my answering machine. Two calls. One from George Mandan, Sir Charles Talbot's flunky.

"The boss wants to see you, Quint. Today. I wouldn't keep him waiting if I was you." He gave me a number to call. I called. George answered.

"I can be there in about an hour," I told him. "What's up, George?"

"Just be here."

George didn't worry me. Sir Charles did. What was his sudden interest in me? Had George tattled about my visits to Erica's pad? Was Talbot mad that George, or his miserable son, who had missed me with that flowerpot?

The second call was from Father James Carmody.

"Mr. Quint. I wonder if you could stop by for a few minutes. There's something I'd like to show you."

I made good time from Sacramento over to Napa. The same bull-necked guard was waiting for me, shotgun in hand. No conversation this time; he just waved me through.

There was a big black Caddy SUV and a Mercedes sedan situated in front of the entrance to Talbot's house. No fiery red convertible, but then, Junior was supposedly in New York City for the meeting with the Great and the *Bulletin*'s money people.

George opened the door for me. He was wearing a small black nylon Speedo swimsuit, the type that no man his age, no matter what kind of shape he was in, should wiggle into. He was pounding his right fist into his left palm, as if practicing to take a punch at someone.

I tapped my lip with a finger. "No lipstick on your mouth this time, George. I'm glad you're being careful."

"Fuck you," he said eloquently.

He led me through the house and out to the Olympic-size swimming pool. A table with a bright green umbrella held a variety of glasses and a thermos bottle. A black robe was draped over one of the chairs, and a small pile of thick white towels was stacked on another.

Sir Charles was in the pool. He spotted me, ducked under the water, and swam over to the side. As he got close, I could see he was naked. His face looked like a blowfish. He surfaced, spit out air, said, "Step into my office," then went under again.

George nudged me with an elbow. "If you want to talk to him, you'd better get in the pool."

"I didn't bring trunks."

He hooked his thumbs into the top of his Speedo suit. "You don't need any. We're a friendly bunch around here."

I debated for a long time. All the while, Talbot paddled steadily around the pool. He looked like a different man in the water—strong, fluid, not the unsteady old man in need of a cane.

"Come on, come on," Talbot shouted. "I haven't got all day."

I took off my clothes, folded them neatly, and put them on the chair with the robe. I thought about leaving my boxers on for a moment, but they went, too, along with my glasses.

The city of San Francisco has provided the world with a number of world-class athletes—baseball, football, and tennis players, boxers, but not many swimmers. The reason for that is simple enough: The weather isn't conducive to it. There are very few public swimming pools and only a handful of private ones. There's the ocean and the bay, but the waters are icy-cold, there are sharks, the tides are strong, and you'd better be a damn good swimmer before you stick a toe in there.

My swimming history had consisted of splashing around the nearby Russian River during summer vacations, and my best dive was a cannonball. I sat on the side of the pool and eased myself into the water. It was warm and had an almost oily feel. It came up to my belly button, which was deep enough for me.

Talbot dived under again and popped up alongside me. The hair on his head might have thinned, but his body more than made up for it. Thick coils of dark hair covered his chest and arms.

"Have you had any information about the missing painting, Sir Charles?"

"No. But that's not why you're here. What do you know about the book Vicky Vandamn was writing, Quint?" He spoke softly, almost in a whisper, and I had to move closer to him to hear what he was saying.

"Just that she was writing one, and she called it *Payback*. Whoever killed her took the manuscript and everything associated with it."

"You sound like you're certain she was killed. That's not what I hear."

"Who have you been listening to, Sir Charles?"

He ignored the question and said, "I want that book. And I want it damn quick."

"What's in it that's got you worried?"

He began moving around, throwing punches under the waterline.

"Are you too young to know who Rocky Marciano was?"

The water had moved up toward my chest. Talbot was leading me into deeper waters, in more ways than one.

"Marciano, a great heavyweight champion."

"The *only* undefeated heavyweight champ. He held the title from 1952 to 1956. He used to like to work out in a swimming pool. You can't pull a muscle that way."

That was interesting, but it didn't have anything to do with Vicky's book.

Talbot threw some more punches, than said, "I'll pay you a hundred thousand for the book."

"If I had it, I'd certainly sell it to you."

"Someone told me you do have it, Quint."

"Someone told you wrong, Sir Charles. If I had found the book, I'd have gone to Katherine Parkham with it right away."

Talbot shook water from his head, then wiped his eyes. "Kate is a smart woman, and they're as rare as rocking horse shit. If I buy the *Bulletin,* I'll keep her. But you, Quint, you'll go out with the trash, along with that tart Ronnie was getting a leg over. He turned out to be a great disappointment to me."

"Is that why he's dead? His body being found so close to Vicky's houseboat is suspicious, don't you think?"

He kept edging away from me. The water was now up to my neck.

"Forget about Ron. Find the book, laddie," Talbot said. "You'll get the money, and you'll keep your job."

"What do you think is in *Payback*? Long-buried secrets? Maybe something about Tony Silk. Or Freeze Chanan. Didn't he cover up the dirt for a lot of the stars? Or Johnny Sands. He was a hit man; they called him 'the Sandman.' Some people think he may have killed a man who worked for you at the studio—Jerome Ramsey. He and Vicky were friends, weren't they?"

There was a splashing sound, and I turned around and saw that George had dived into the pool. He was behind me, in the shallow water.

"Ramsey was an airy-fairy guy," Talbot said. "One of his powder puffs killed him," he added angrily.

"Vicky had a child. A boy." I began dog-paddling toward the side of the pool. "The child died. I wonder who the father was."

Talbot waved an arm toward George. I was trapped between them.

"Lunch is ready, Sir Charles," a voice called.

It was Carla, the attractive Latin woman who had served drinks during the card game.

"A cup of coffee for me, please," I shouted as I lurched to the side of the pool. She turned her back to me as I crawled up onto the tiles. Being sandwiched between Talbot and George in deep water was something I wasn't going to let happen. I grabbed a towel, dried off quickly, and put on my clothes.

"Get me that damn book," Talbot bellowed.

"I'll do my best, Sir Charles."

Carla came back with a cup of coffee as George pulled himself up from the pool in one graceful athletic move.

"I'll be in touch," I said, grabbing Carla's elbow. "Would you mind showing me to the door?"

George followed us to the door, leaving wet footprints on the tile and carpet. He waited until I was at the car before yelling what sounded like "Foad!"

I didn't bother calling Father Carmody; I decided just to drop in. I had all the time in the world. I was on vacation.

I headed south, taking the Richmond–San Rafael Bridge over to Marin County. Unless you live in the area, you've never heard of the Richmond Bridge. It takes you from the East Bay and deposits you in Marin County, right alongside San Quentin Prison in San Rafael. It's a nice enough bridge, and does its job handling tons of traffic, but it just doesn't have the star quality of its sister bridges. It's never used in commercials or movies. I have a friend who writes thrillers, and on almost every one of his books the cover depicts a bomb exploding on either the Bay Bridge or the Golden Gate Bridge, though neither of them ever appears in the novels.

I found the priest in his living quarters, a small house situated behind the gymnasium, with the same stucco walls and red tile roof featured on the church.

I knocked on the front door and Carmody shouted, "Come on in."

The first thing I noticed was one of those change machines you see hanging on Laundromat walls, the kind that turns five- , ten- , and twenty-dollar bills into piles of quarters. Alongside that was a life-size carved wooden figure of a masked cowboy with a slot-machine chest. One shirtsleeve was tucked under to indicate a missing arm; the other hand held a gun and served as the handle on the machine. A true one-armed bandit.

Carmody walked over. He was wearing jeans and a dark green hooded Notre Dame Fighting Irish sweatshirt.

"Thanks for stopping by," he said.

I rapped a knuckle against the cowboy statue's head. "Does this thing work?"

"Oh, sure. And all of the profits go to a worthy cause."

"Which worthy cause is that, Father?"

"The care and feeding of impoverished priests," he said with a smile. "Give it a try."

I slipped a five-dollar bill into the change machine and transferred the quarters, one by one, into the cowboy, then began pulling his gun hand.

When my last quarter clanked into the machine's stomach, Carmody said, "Too bad you didn't win. Roy Rogers sings 'Happy Trails to You' when you hit a jackpot."

I had a hunch old Roy hadn't warbled a note in a long time.

"You mentioned you had something to show me, Father. I hope it wasn't just this one-armed bandit."

"No. Come on back here."

"Back here" was a living room with a comfortable-looking coffee-colored sofa, a battered rolltop desk, and a big-screen TV. The walls were decorated with framed blow-ups of old boxing champions: Muhammad Ali dancing around Joe Frazier; Joe Louis standing over a prone Max Baer; and Sugar Ray Robinson hammering on a bloody-faced Jake LaMotta.

Carmody opened a drawer in the desk and extracted a small piece of paper. He handed it to me. It was a bank check—Sir Charles Talbot's check. The amount was for a $100,000. The *pay to the order of* line was blank. Talbot's signature was on the bottom line.

"Did Talbot give this to you, Father?"

"Yes. Yesterday." He flopped down on the couch and lazily crossed his legs. "Sir Charles came by unannounced. He asked a lot a questions about Ulla Kjeldsen, though he told me he never knew her by that name."

"What kind of questions?" I asked.

"What happened to her, how she looked, whether she had married, had any more children, and—"

"*More* children. He actually stated it that way?"

"Yeah." Carmody sat up straight and coughed into his hand. "Talbot is an elderly man, but he seemed to be in charge of his senses—not dottering or senile in any way. He told me that Vicky—he called her Vicky, not Ulla—had been 'a mackerel snapper' in Hollywood, meaning a Catholic who never eats meat on Friday. And he said she used to 'sneak out and go to church all the time.' He said this as if it had been a dumb thing to do."

Carmody massaged his knees with his palms before adding, "Then Talbot said he wanted to become a Catholic, and he wanted to make his confession—right then and there."

"What did you say?"

"I told him that it wasn't quite that easy, that there was an extended period of instruction before he could be baptized and become a member of the Church. That didn't sit too well with Sir Charles. He asked me how much money it would take to 'bypass all the bullshit.' "

I waved the check at him. "Is that when he gave you this?"

"No. That was a little later." Carmody shifted around on the couch as if he'd gotten a cramp. "What I'm telling you is not for publication, Mr. Quint."

"You've got my word on that, Father. But if it has something to with the death of Ulla or Ron Maleuw, I'd have to pass it on to the police."

"Talbot wanted to know if someone could get into heaven—in other words, if God would forgive him—even if he'd had someone killed."

"Did he mention a name?" I asked quickly.

Carmody took a few seconds to respond. "No. He did say this took place a long time ago. I feel a great conflict here, Mr. Quint. Sir Charles was talking candidly to me. This was nothing covered by the bonds of confession, but still . . . I'm uncomfortable about discussing it."

"Did he give any hints as to where this took place?"

"No. He did seem genuinely sorry about Ulla's passing; he said he was told that she had died in an accident years ago."

"Who told him that?"

"He didn't say. He then wrote out the check, and told me he wanted a daily Mass 'and all that candle stuff' for Vicky. And he said that there would be more checks in the future."

"Talbot's wife told me that her husband is giving away money and parts of his art collection to several churches and different religious organizations, in hopes of buying his way into heaven."

"From everything I've studied, Saint Peter's a tough guy to bribe."

"Did you tell Talbot that, Father?"

Carmody pushed himself to his feet. "I told him that God would welcome him into the kingdom of heaven, no matter what his past sins, if he repented."

That must have made Talbot unhappy. He had a lot of repenting to do. "Was anyone with him when he was here?"

"No. I walked him out to his car, a big Cadillac SUV."

I waved the check at him. "What are you going to do with this?"

"Somehow, I think God would have a hard time forgiving me if I made that out to myself. I'll turn it over to my bishop and let him decide what's best."

"Thanks for telling me this, Father. I'll see you in church."

I was halfway to the door when Carmody let out a whistle that could have been heard by a cabbie two blocks away.

"The check, Mr. Quint. I wouldn't want it to fall into the wrong hands."

I put my wrong hands on the Mini's steering wheel and headed for the Sausalito Police Department. Detective Manners was in her office, sitting behind her desk, which was piled with loose papers and manila folders. She didn't seem pleased to see me.

"What do you want, Quint? I'm busy. Three juveniles spray-painted obscene words on a public rest room in the city park."

"I was wondering if there've been any developments on Maleuw's murder."

"Murder? What gives you the idea he was murdered?" She rummaged through the papers on her desk, found the one she was looking for, and began reading.

"This is the Marin County medical examiner's report on Ronald Maleuw. The official cause of death is suffocation due to immersion of the nostrils and mouth in a liquid—salt water. Terminal pulmonary edema. In words that you can understand: He drowned."

Manners's face had turned a deep red color. She was mad at someone, and I just happened to be in the room.

"Mr. Maleuw's blood indicated that he had taken Valium and that he had a rather high blood-alcohol level, point zero nine, which would have gotten him arrested for drunk driving. He weighed one hundred and eighty-three pounds, so he would have consumed at least seven or eight drinks."

"Booze and drugs? Doesn't that ring a little bell, Detective? Ulla Kjeldsen supposedly overdosed on drugs, grass, and alcohol."

"We found a prescription bottle of Valium in Maleuw's car. His prescription. No pot in the car, or in his system, so there is a difference between the two victims."

"Where was Maleuw drinking?" I asked. "Was any booze found in his car?"

"No. He also suffered from hypothermia before death. The water temperature in Richardson Bay that night was fifty-two degrees, Quint. Damn cold. The scrapings, cuts, and bruises are consistent with someone who had been in the water for several hours and whose body had hit bottom."

"Where did he go into the water, Detective?"

"Beats me," she said, dropping the report back onto her desk.

"It doesn't make sense. Yet you're telling me he drives from Napa to Sausalito, after popping a tranquilizer, is drunk to the gills, and then calmly walks down to a pier and jumps into the bay? Someone would have seen him. He was wearing a tuxedo, which suggests he was planning to go to the exhibit at the de Young."

"You would think so, wouldn't you? Nice talking to you, Quint, but I've got work to do."

"Could Maleuw have been drowned in a swimming pool, say, then dumped into the bay?"

She thought for a moment, one finger brushing her lips. "You're suggesting those pools at Sir Charles Talbot's place, aren't you? The same possibility crossed my mind. They're freshwater pools. I checked with the coroner. Freshwater dilutes the victim's blood. Salt water extracts water from the blood and increases chloride concentration. Maleuw drowned in salt water. Period."

"What about Ulla Kjeldsen?" I asked, pressing her. "You can't tell me that you're going to let this go. Two *alleged* suicides, and both of the deceased associated with Sir Charles Talbot, who also happens to have had a valuable painting stolen from—"

"The painting is not my concern, Quint," she said belligerently. She waited for her voice to steady, then added, "Captain Bennett has advised me to discontinue my investigation into the two suicides. The painting was allegedly stolen in Napa County; that's out of my jurisdiction. If you have any further contact with our department regarding the death of Ms. Kjeldsen or that of Mr. Maleuw, I suggest you go directly to Captain Bennett."

"So Sausalito remains damn near crime-free, huh, Detective? Another year without a homicide."

I felt sorry for Manners. She'd been tied up in civil service knots, ordered to be a good cop and keep her nose out of the case. I almost told her she was lucky the captain hadn't insisted that she go on vacation.

I was in a gloomy mood by the time I got back to the car, and then I remembered that I was having dinner at my mother's that night. The gloom deepened, my stomach rumbled in protest, and I went looking for a Burger King.

Twenty-one

The cat was out of the bag about the Great's trip to New York City; everyone at the *Bulletin* knew, and when I told Terry Greco about my forced vacation, she took the news nearly as badly as I had, rightly figuring that if the Talbots took control of the *Bulletin*, both of us would get booted out.

"This is terrible, Carroll. Can Parkham do something about it?"

"I hope so," I said as I pulled the Mini into my mother's driveway.

"You don't look well," Terry said as we climbed up the stairs to my mother's place."

"I'll be fine," I lied. "And ixnay on my vacation, with Mom, okay?"

" 'Ixnay'? What in the world does than mean?"

"It means no, don't mention it. Didn't you ever watch the Three Stooges?"

"The three who? Who are they?"

God, the world was crumbling around me. First, Detective Manners never seeing *Casablanca,* and now Terry totally ignorant of Larry, Moe, and Curly.

As soon as my mother opened the door, I knew something was wrong. Gone were the scents of Windex, lemon wax, Febreze, and her foul cooking. They'd been overpowered by something wonderful, spicy, and fragrant: garlic, ginger, onions.

"Guess who stopped by for dinner?" Mom said brightly as we stepped aside.

"Hey, pally. How ya doin'?" a rough voice called out from down the hallway.

Mom kissed Terry on both cheeks and told her how beautiful she looked. Terry was dressed in a short white skirt and a red stretch silk body blouse that accented all of her positives. Mom grabbed my elbow and said, "Freeze Chanan stopped by earlier, and I asked him to stay for dinner. He gallantly insisted that I stop cooking. He sent out for some food, dear. There's enough for an army." She tapped the bag under my arm. "You did bring the mixings?"

"Oh, yes." There was a quart of tequila, margarita mix, and four limes in the bag.

Willie "Freeze" Chanan had his wrinkled rump planted in one of the kitchen chairs. He was outfitted in his lounge-lizard mode: a black silk shirt with an oversize collar, striped gray slacks, and black suede loafers with buckles and crepe soles. A man in search of a disco.

He stood, took Terry's hand in his, and planted a kiss on it. "Pleased to meet you, gorgeous."

I made the introductions and Chanan turned on his charm button. "You work for a newspaper? You could be in the movies, no kidding. I know some people you should talk to."

"Please," my mother said sweetly. "One actress at dinner is more than enough. Carroll, our drinks are empty. Would you do the honors?"

There were dozens of little white take-out cartons on the kitchen-cooking island, along with an empty bottle of Chardonnay.

"I had Wiley Lee send over some Chink stuff," Chanan said. "You seemed to like it last time."

I didn't know if margaritas were the right thing to serve with Chinese food, but anything with alcohol seemed like a good idea at the time.

Chanan wandered over and held out his empty glass as soon as I had the first batch under way.

"Those are real, kid. I can tell."

I was holding a lime in my hand. "Real what? Limes?"

"No," he said shaking his head. "Your lady friend's rack. I've seen more boob jobs than the all the plastic surgeons in Beverly Hills—good ones, bad ones, and really bad ones. They only last for about ten to fifteen years, give or take a leak or two. But those are the real Mc-Coy."

"Thanks for that information," I said, topping off his glass, then pouring drinks for the rest of us.

"Your mother looks terrific. She ages like fine wine. Where's your father hanging his hat these days?"

I tilted my head to the ceiling. "In the flat directly above us."

Chanan sniffed his glass, took a sip, then said, "We gotta talk. Something big has come up."

"After dinner, Freeze. The girls are hungry."

Chanan entertained Mom and Terry with more of his Hollywood tales, including an implausible story about the Charles Manson murders of actress Sharon Tate, the wife of director Roman Polanski, and her friends. According to Chanan, certain members of the LAPD homicide detail had found a batch of amateur porn videotapes in Polanski's basement that showed Tate with Steve McQueen, Dean Martin, and an assortment of showbiz types. "The cops sold the tapes for a lot of dough."

As usual with Chanan's stories, it was hard to challenge him, because all of the people he talked about were dead.

After we had demolished the food, Mom brought out a bottle of cognac. Chanan picked up his snifter and asked if there was somewhere we could talk alone.

I led him out to Mom's redwood patio, with its view of her beautiful "enchanted garden," which she'd filled with dozens of rosebushes, mums, and clay pots with herbs of every kind, which somehow never managed to spice up her meals. Water spouted from the mouth of a bronze frog into a small pond.

The Mission District has about the best weather in the city, and it was a warm and cozy night. San Francisco warm and cozy. In Palm Springs, it would have been considered chilly, and Chanan had slipped on his black leather sport coat.

"Any fish in that pond?" he asked after he had settled into a cushioned chaise lounge. His pant leg crept up, and I could see his ankle holster.

"Fantail goldfish. You said that something big had turned up."

"You bet. But it's going to cost you."

"Quit acting like a crooked cop and tell me what you've got."

Chanan folded his arms across his chest and gave me a patronizing smile. "Don't push it, kid. You stick your nose in the wrong place, you could end up in a skeleton slumber party."

"Please," I groaned, "no more corny death lines."

He made clucking sounds with his tongue, then shifted in the chaise and brought a paper from his jacket pocket.

"Take a look at this, tough guy." He pulled another paper from his jacket and dropped it in my lap. It was Ulla Kjeldsen's cell phone bill.

"Where'd you get this?" I asked. I'd searched Ulla's houseboat thoroughly, and there was no sign of a cell phone or any bills.

"In my line of work, you gotta have contacts. Any private eye who can't pull a credit record or a phone bill is in the wrong line of work. I've got a contact that can get anyone's phone records, pally, including yours. Vicky's residence phone number was a waste of money— nothing interesting there—but the cell phone was a different story, pally."

There were sixteen calls on the bill. Chanan had printed out the names and addresses alongside the numbers Ulla had called.

There were five to Della Rugerio, two to Bert and Mary Tucker's houseboat, four to St. Agnes Church, two to a Sausalito liquor store, another to a beauty salon, one to the Mercantile Security Bank, in Victoria, British Columbia, and one to the Irene Jansen Publishing Company, in Los Angeles, three weeks ago. The last call Ulla had made was to St. Agnes Church, on August 6, the day before she died.

"Did you contact the publishing company?" I asked Freeze.

"Yeah. It's one of those, 'You send in the pages and we'll print it' outfits. Vanity press. The sucker spends thousands of dollars for a few hundred books, which mostly stay in the boxes they're shipped in."

"What did they say? Did they receive a manuscript? Did you get to see it?"

"They didn't get the manuscript. Just a letter from Vicky that she was working on a project—*Payback*—'that sounded quite interesting,' according to Irene Jensen herself. 'Murders and naughty doings.' But no specifics. Jensen sent Vicky a contract, and Vicky sent her a check for fifteen hundred clams, 'to get the ball rolling.'"

I took a deep breath and held it as long as I could. That removed all doubts about Ulla writing a book. She could have been just been pretending with Rugerio and Father Carmody, and Bert Tucker, boasting about her writing project. But now it was a sure thing.

"*Payback* was going to be a tell-all book, Freeze. And her killer obviously took it from her houseboat."

"Yeah. He tombstoned Vicky, and got the book, but maybe there's a copy, or a floppy disk around somewhere. It could be worth a lot of dough to the right party, if you get my drift," Chanan said.

"Sir Charles Talbot thinks that I have the manuscript, or that I know where it is."

"Do you?"

"No. But someone told me that it was going to blow the lid off a case, one where the police didn't think a guy was murdered, but he was."

"Who told you that?" Chanan asked sharply.

I wasn't about to give him Bert Tucker's name. "Just someone Vicky spoke to. My source never actually saw the manuscript. She had a child, the kid supposedly died, and I'm betting that Charles Talbot was the father."

"I know about the kid. I saw the autopsy report, but there's no way you can prove that Talbot was the father, unless we come up with the book."

"I learned something else about Talbot. He had someone killed when he was running his studio. Who was the victim, Freeze? Jerome

Ramsey? Johnny Sands? Sands was one tough cookie. He could handle himself. Knuckles the size of walnuts, I hear. Not the kind of guy to let just anyone sneak up behind him with a gun. Someone told me you and Sands almost had a shoot-out at the Villa Capri but that he bluffed you out of it with a cocktail napkin."

I had really hit a nerve. Chanan put his snifter on the floor, made a gun out of his hand and forefinger, and said, "Who you been talking to?"

"You're not the only guy with contacts in Hollywood. You may have made a lot of money there, but you also made some enemies. One cop was quoted as saying you got a disability from carrying around a heavy wallet."

"That was Dick Bianco, a dumb homicide cop, and he was sorry he said it, believe me." He bulged his lower lip with his tongue, then said, "No. You didn't talk to any cops. There's not many still alive who remember those days, pally. Who was it? Some newshawk? Those guys were the scum of the earth. They took more bribes than we ever thought about."

Behind that wrinkled kisser was a sharp brain. I didn't want Chanan to figure out that Jack Dornay had been my source. I had a hunch it was Chanan who had searched Kjeldsen's houseboat, so I said something that I thought would throw him off balance.

"How did you like Sausalito? Vicky's houseboat. You were seen, Freeze."

"Bullshit," he responded quickly—too quickly. He picked up his snifter, took a sip, then said, "You know, they say that history repeats itself."

"I've heard that said."

"That story I told at dinner, about that punk Charlie Manson killing Sharon Tate and her friends, that was legit. And so were the videos. History repeats. Get it, pally?"

I didn't get it, not at first. It took me a minute or two, and Chanan sat there with a Cheshire cat grin on his face while I did my pondering.

"Jerome Ramsey," I finally said. "He was a cameraman, and you're telling me that he took some porno flicks? Of who? Where? At the studio, or at Talbot's mansion?"

"That's what we've got to find out, pally." Chanan snatched the phone bill from my hands and pocketed it. "What I haven't been able to find out is where Vicky took off to after she left L.A., where she lived before she ended up with Jerome Ramsey's brother in Canada. I wonder if the brother was a fag, too. Funny how many hot-looking broads migrate to these cockaholics. I just gave you a lot of info for free, Quint. You owe me."

"Tell you what I'll do, Freeze. I won't tell Detective Manners of the Sausalito Police Department that you were seen in Vicky's houseboat. Is that breaking and entering? Or burglary? Or both?"

"You should try the turtle thing, pally. Pull your neck in, instead of sticking it out where it can get whacked off. Tell me what you know about this missing Picasso, and maybe we can do business."

"What's your interest in the painting?"

"Let's just say I'm an admirer of fine art. Did that Maleuw guy swipe it?"

"I honestly don't know."

"Maleuw's body washing up at Vicky's back door is just not kosher. Tell me more about this character, Quint. He's new to me."

"He was about my age, good-looking, worked for Talbot as his personal curator."

"For how long?"

"I'm not sure. Several years, I think. He was the adopted child of Philip Maleuw, a set designer who worked for several studios, including Talbot's. From what Terry told me, Maleuw was very good at what he did."

"What he did was get killed, pally. You don't waste a guy who stole a valuable painting before you get the painting back, you know what I mean?"

"A painting like that would be hard to sell, Chanan."

He snapped his fingers sharply. "I could find a home for it in ten minutes. For a hell of a lot of dough. I've put Talbot onto some choice paintings several times. Worse comes to worse, we could peddle it to the insurance company."

"Sir Charles doesn't have his collection insured. It costs too much, even for Talbot."

"I'm sure old Chuck would ante up a nice finder's fee if we come across it."

We seemed to be creeping into Chanan's vocabulary quite a bit.

"Okay," I said. "So how are we going to find out where Vicky disappeared to after losing her child?"

"I'm working on it. Why the hell she went to Canada, beats me." He shivered lightly. "Cold goddamn place, the men are all wimps, and the food stinks. I've got copies of Vicky's credit-card bills, but they don't tell us much—other than that she spent a lot of dough on booze, beauty salons, and clothes at Nordstrom."

"You obtained her credit-card bills?"

"Sure. This is the big leagues, and I'm a major player. You, you're still in Little League, pally. I was hoping that there would be some travel charges, hotels, that kind of stuff."

"You told me that Jerome Ramsey had been roughed up before he died, 'like someone had beaten him with a sackful of marbles' was the way you put it, Freeze. Maybe the person who worked him over wanted those porno flicks you say Ramsey filmed, and maybe the guy was wearing sap gloves."

Chanan drained his snifter and struggled to his feet. "Jesus, you keep pecking away, don't you? I come here, bring you food, I'm nice to your mama, I show you the phone records, and you jump on me like I'm dog meat. I don't appreciate it, so back off."

"George, Sir Charles's man, called me a 'foad.' It must be an acronym for something. Ever hear of it?"

"You've led a sheltered life, kid. F.O.A.D. Fuck off and die. It's a Brit thing. They're good at that stuff." He smiled widely, then did a quick about-face and disappeared into the kitchen.

Twenty-two

I laid back in the chaise lounge and closed my eyes. My little gray cells were whirling around like atoms in a nuclear physics experiment. Freeze Chanan had actually given me some interesting material. The phone bill and credit-card information had to have cost him quite a bit of money. Maybe that's what it all boiled down to—follow the money. Chanan was after Vicky's manuscript because it was worth a lot of money to someone. An old actor or producer who didn't want his dirty lingerie washed in public? Talbot was willing to pay me a $100,000 for it. Who else? Chanan himself? He must have had a cellarful of dirty deeds that he didn't want to see the light of day. All of those years in Hollywood had rubbed off on Chanan. He was a pretty good actor himself.

What had happened to Vicky's cell phone? It disappeared along with her purse and ID.

Chanan was right about Ronald Maleuw's death not being "kosher." His body washing ashore on a Sausalito Beach. Why there?

Something nibbled on my ears. Terry Greco's sharp little teeth.

"Are you sleeping here tonight, Carroll?"

"Not a chance," I said, hopping to my feet.

Mom was in the kitchen, placing the leftover food cartons into paper bags.

"You children take this with you," she said. "It was good, but a little too rich for me."

I gave her a kiss on the cheek and promised to see her soon.

"John called earlier, Carroll. He wants to talk to you." She used a pencil to write out a phone number on one of the paper bags. "It's his room at the Bellagio. He doesn't get to bed, at least to sleep, until seven or eight in the morning in Las Vegas."

My father was in the habit of checking with Mom every few days while he was away, but he seldom called me.

"Did he say what he wanted?"

Her face broke into a wide smile. "Possibly to borrow some money. He has a hard time balancing his gross habits with his net income when he works Vegas. Whatever they pay him, he usually loses at the roulette table."

"What did you think of Freeze Chanan after all these years?"

She pursed her lips before saying, "I was rather disappointed in Freeze. Not just his appearance, though he looks like he's been pickled in vinegar. He just isn't as *nice* as I remembered him."

"Are you telling me he made a move on you?"

"Of course," she said innocently, batting her eyes. "He's still a man. But I made it clear to him that I had no interest. He backed off right away." She sighed theatrically—1920 silent movies theatrically—with the back of her hand to her forehead. "I think he's a little frightened of your father. For *all* his faults, John is a protective devil. Let me know if *he* answers the phone, would you, dear? Your father is getting to an age when he should start *acting* his age."

Terry elbowed me at a little after 2:00 A.M. We were in my bed, at my condo. She had thought ahead and brought along an overnight bag so that she could go directly to the *Bulletin* in the morning.

"I'm a little hungry, aren't you?" she asked in her "Be nice to me and I'll be nice to you" voice.

"I'm stuffed. I couldn't eat a thing."

"Maybe I'll just just fix a small tray, Carroll."

I fumbled for my glasses as she strode barefoot into the kitchen. I heard the ping of the microwave a few minutes later and she came back carrying a tray filled with small dishes and two cans of Coke.

She slipped into bed, propped up the pillows behind her back, and began digging into the Wiley Lee leftovers. It is truly one of life's great wonders that she can eat the way she does and keep that luscious figure, I thought.

"I spoke to the Sausalito detective handling Ulla's and Ron Maleuw's cases, Terr. They are both considered to be suicides."

"That's ridiculous," she said, plopping a kung pao shrimp into her mouth. "Ron wasn't the suicidal type," she mumbled between bites.

That was the same thing Father Carmody had said about Ulla. I took a hit on a Coke, then said, "His blood test showed a high amount of alcohol and some Valium."

"I know Ron used Valium. I saw his prescription bottle."

I was tempted to ask where this vision had taken place, but I didn't want to break my own heart.

She gobbled down a spoonful of sautéed mushrooms, wiped her chin, and said, "He liked a martini or two, and he'd have a few glasses of wine during dinner."

"A blood-alcohol count of point zero nine means six or seven drinks, Terry."

"He wouldn't have drunk that much before the exhibit. I think he was murdered. Your mother does, too."

Well, that settled that. What were a police investigation and an autopsy report compared to the thoughts of my mother and Terry? She had a few bites of deep-fried sesame beef, downed half the Coke, then got up and carried the tray to the kitchen.

"I'm full now," she said when she returned. "Good night."

She jumped into bed and pulled the sheet up over her shoulders.

I was wide-awake. I snuggled close. "There's a rumor that Chinese food makes you horny," I whispered in her ear.

"There's enough left over for dinner tomorrow, Carroll. We can test out your rumor then. I need some sleep. I have to get up early. I'm a working girl, remember? It's you who's on vacation."

Wide-awake, horny, and in bed with a gorgeous woman who wanted to do nothing but sleep. What a way to spend a vacation.

Terry was in the shower early the next morning. Even though it was Sunday, she wanted to get to the paper and work on her museum piece. Ron Maleuw's death had certainly turned that upside down. I made a pot of coffee and decided to give my father a call in Vegas.

He sounded tired when he answered the phone.

"Hi, son. Thanks for calling back. I'm worried about your mother. What's all this jazz about Vicky Vandamn?"

I told him everything, from the beginning, which took about fifteen minutes.

"I never figured Vicky for an author, son, but she was involved with some pretty wild characters in Hollywood, so I guess she would know a thing or two."

Terry had bounced into the kitchen, raided the fridge for more Chinese food, then disappeared into the bedroom.

The thing that seemed to concern my father the most was Freeze Chanan's visit to Mom's place the previous night.

"I don't want Chanan anywhere near Karen. He was a crooked, no-good bastard back when I knew him, and I doubt if he'll ever change."

"I'll make sure Chanan doesn't see her again," I promised. "Just how bad a cop was he?"

"He was a shakedown artist, and went after everyone—the stars, the studios, even those goddamn drug dealers that ruined the town. That's why I took your mother out of there. It was turning into a cesspool."

"Did you know a character by the name of Johnny Sands? They called him—"

"The Sandman. Sure, I knew Johnny. He used to hang around the clubs. A stone-cold killer. His only endearing quality was that he was a lousy gin rummy player."

"How about a man by the name of Philip Maleuw? He was a set director, and worked for Talbot, among others. His son, Ron, was Talbot's personal curator."

"No, never heard of them, until you mother told me about that man being found dead near Vicky's houseboat."

"Did you know Jerome Ramsey? He was an assistant cameraman at Talbot's studio."

"Yeah, I remember Jerome. He liked good music. He hung around the Hotel Bel Air when I played there."

"Mom described Jerome as Vicky's beau, though he was gay."

"Yes and no. He was a switch-hitter—bisexual. He was dating a cocktail waitress at the Bel Air. Angela. I forget her last name. Nice kid. She assured me that Jerome knew what to do in bed. In fact, he got her pregnant, and when she told him she didn't want the kid, he paid for an abortion. There was no morning-after pill back then, and some of the abortionists were real back-alley butchers, but Angela said that Ramsey took her to a first-class clinic and a real doctor performed the operation."

"Did he take her to Tijuana?"

"I never asked."

Terry came back to top off her coffee, wiggled her fingers at me, said, "Dinner, here, tonight," then headed for the front door.

"Listen, son. I never mentioned this to your mother, and this is just between you and me. I ran into Vicky awhile back. Oh hell, it must have been fifteen years ago. In Venice. I was working a cruise ship that hit all the major Mediterranean ports. We stopped in Venice, and I had the day off. So I wandered around, playing tourist. I made a mandatory stop at Harry's Bar, the place Hemingway made famous in *Across the River and into the Trees*. I was at the bar, having a drink, and I spotted a beautiful woman sitting between two gentlemen at a table. I didn't recognize her at first, but it was Vicky all right. Older than when I'd last seen her, but, if anything, more beautiful.

"Her eyes went wide when she saw me. It was obvious she didn't want me to come to the table. I had another drink, and she stopped to talk to me on the way to the rest room. She was nervous as hell. 'Please don't tell anyone you saw me, John,' she said. I tried to find out where she was living, but all she would say was that she had a new life now and didn't want anything to do with the past. She went back to her table and ignored me."

"Did you get a good look at the men she was with, Dad?"

"Yeah. They were what I thought was old back then—in their sixties. Both well dressed, one with a beard, the other clean-shaven. Vicky was holding the hand of the bearded guy. I never saw them or Vicky again, and I honored her wishes about not telling anyone, including your mother. You know how Karen is. She probably would have flown over to Venice to look for Vicky."

He had a point there. Venice. Mom had said that Vicky's mother remarried and moved to Italy from Denmark. So the two men could have been people Vicky's mother knew.

"I can cancel out of this gig here and be back home by this afternoon."

"I don't think that's necessary, Dad. I've got things under control." That *might* have been an exaggeration. "But if I need help, I'll call."

"Do that. And take care of your mother."

I called the *Bulletin,* and wasn't surprised to find Rosie, the Great's secretary, manning her post, even though it was Sunday.

"Any news out of New York?"

"Yes. None of it very good, Carroll. Have you come up with anything Kate can use to keep the wolves at bay?"

"Not yet, but I'm getting close."

"Call me as soon as you have something. And you'd better make the call soon. Kate didn't sound very hopeful this morning."

Despite the threat of impending doom for the paper and my job, I was hungry, but the refrigerator held nothing except the leftover Chinese food, and that was going to be dinner, so I decided to follow my father's Venice experience and act like a tourist.

Some bright thinker at city hall had purchased a string of vintage streetcars gathered from all over the world—Australia, Japan, Moscow, London, New Orleans—and restored them to service on several of the city's trolley lines. I took a bright orange trolley that had originated in Milan, Italy, in the 1930s and now traveled the city's Embarcadero. It dropped me off at Fisherman's Wharf and I walked a couple of blocks to one of the city's prime watering holes, the Buena Vista, whose famed Irish coffee was introduced to America by Pulitzer Prize–winning humorist Stanton Delaplane.

I had a mandatory Irish at the bar, then ordered a cheese omelette while I thought about my conversation with my father. Vicky in Venice. Could I trace her actual whereabouts? Find out where she'd been living and under what name? Possibly, but what good would it do me? She wasn't writing a novel about death in some Venetian lagoon. Of more interest to me was why she'd moved to British Columbia and married Jerome Ramsey's brother, Arnold. Venice might explain her choice of a houseboat in the European-like setting of Sausalito. All of this was interesting, but not very rewarding. Where was the manuscript of *Payback*? That's what I had to concentrate on.

I concentrated halfway through the omelette, without results, then chewed over what Dad had said about Jerome Ramsey being a bisexual, which meant *he* could have been the father of Vicky's child. I had already pegged Charles Talbot into that hole, and I didn't like Ramsey unpegging things.

One of the charms of eating and drinking at the BV is that the place is usually filled with foreign tourists. Families and couples around me were chatting away in French, Italian, and some tongues I couldn't decipher. I was trying to tell a big-bellied man with a heavy German accent, who was sitting next to me, that there were *no* good fish restaurants on Fisherman's Wharf, when my cell phone began vibrating.

"Hey, Quint. Is this you? Jack Dornay here. What are you doing for dinner?"

One thing I wasn't going to do was drive back up to Lincoln again. "Have you found out anything, Jack?"

"There's a guy you should meet. Vinnie Renzo. He was a wheelman for a lot of people, including Charles Talbot and Johnny Sands."

"Wheelman?"

"Driver. They didn't call them chauffeurs in those days. Listen to this. He took Vicky down to a medical clinic in Tijuana, more than once."

The big German guy dug an elbow into my side and said, "Vere es good *Hackepeter* for lunch?"

"Meet us at Musso & Frank Grill, at seven o'clock. That should give you plenty of time."

"For what?"

"To get to the restaurant. It's in Hollywood, Quint. Come on down. It'll be worth the trip. Vinnie said he read your book, and liked it. He's a fan."

The distance between San Francisco and Hollywood suddenly shrank.

"Vinnie has the goods. I want him to tell you all about it personally. And, Quint, he has expenses, so if you come, bring money."

"How much money?"

"He started out asking for ten grand, but I explained the facts of life to him about how cheap newspapers are. I got him down to three grand. Believe me, you'll think it's worth it. See ya."

Three thousand dollars? I had my poker winnings, and if Renzo's information was good, Katherine Parkham should reimburse me. If she was still in charge of the paper, that is.

My German friend was holding a catsup bottle in one hand and making munching sounds with this mouth. "*Hackepeter*, eh? *Nein* Big Mac, okay?"

"Ah, hamburger." I wrote the name and directions to the Balboa Cafe on a napkin for him, then called Terry at the *Bulletin*.

"There's a change of plans for dinner," I told her. "We're going out. I'll pick you up in an hour."

"Why so early?" she asked.

"It's a long drive. Or a short flight. Maybe you should bring an overnight bag."

Twenty-three

For once, Terry Greco turned down a chance for a dinner out, so I flew down to Los Angeles alone.

Jack Dornay and a small man with thick gray hair parted in the middle and combed through with Brylcreem were waiting for me in a high-sided booth with red leather upholstery at Musso & Frank Grill.

Jack introduced the man as Vinnie Renzo. He rose from his seat and bobbed his head at me. Renzo was an interesting-looking character: He had a bulging forehead, deep-socketed, shifty licorice-colored eyes, and a chin with a prominent cleft. He was wearing a black mohair suit, a starched white shirt, and a narrow black tie. He looked like the kind of guy who could get you anything, anytime, including three crosses and nine long nails. My guess was that he was in his mid-seventies.

He shook my hand and said, "Wonderful book you wrote, Mr. Quint. *Tough Guys and Private Eyes.* I thoroughly enjoyed it. I hope there is a sequel in the making."

"I'm thinking of one, Mr. Renzo."

"Vinnie, please call me Vinnie." He flapped a hand in the air, and within moments a waiter appeared wearing a bright red jacket that matched the leather in the booth. He looked to be of an age that could have made him Vinnie's older brother.

"I highly recommend the martinis, Mr. Quint."

Dornay seconded the recommendation.

We made small talk until the drinks came, discussing my flight from the city, traffic, and whether I was staying the night.

We all had a sip of our drinks; then Renzo laid his cards right down on the table.

"Jack has told me of your interest in Vicky Vandamn. I believe I can help you; however, I expect a little help from you in return, Mr. Quint."

"What kind of help, Vinnie?"

He smiled, showing off a set of teeth too white to be true.

"If we're off the record, I'll give you a lot of information. Information that could not be used in print, for it would surely point back in my direction, but I do think it will lead you to your quest. I was a driver for many of the stars and producers, Mr. Quint. For a time, I worked exclusively for Charles Talbot, driving him and anyone else he assigned me to. I'm reliable, and know how to keep my mouth shut." He paused and grinned. "Until now of course. I would pick up Miss Vandamn and take her to the studio or to Mr. Talbot's house, anywhere he wanted her to go. There will be a small fee for the information, of course."

"How small?"

"Three thousand dollars sounds like a reasonable sum."

I looked over at Dornay, thinking that even if he was living with a bonbon queen, he was probably getting a piece of the action.

"You're getting your money's worth," Dornay said. "I guarantee it."

"You accept cash?" I asked.

He showed me his teeth again. "Always."

The waiter came back with another round of drinks. He didn't bat an eyelash as I peeled off hundred-dollar bills from my roll and slid them over to Vinnie Renzo.

Vinnie raked the bills in like a croupier at the roulette table, stashed them in his jacket, and took me down memory lane.

"One day, Mr. Talbot told me to take Miss Vicky to Tijuana. She was accompanied by a young man from the studio, a cameraman—"

"Jerome Ramsey," Jack Dornay piped in, just to show he was part of the game.

"Yes," Renzo continued. "I took Miss Vicky and her escort to a clinic run by Dr. Walter Foley. Charming place, really. It looked more like a resort motel than a clinic, but it was well known as an abortion mill. I had previously driven other young women there. Miss Vicky was very nervous on the trip. She was crying and carrying on.

"We were there only an hour or so, when Miss Vicky came out of the clinic. It was obvious she was upset. Mr. Ramsey was very comforting to her. Vicky sobbed all the way home. She kept saying that she couldn't go through with it. She became sick, and vomited in the backseat." More teeth. "I was wheeling a Cadillac Fleetwood then. Beautiful machine."

The waiter came back and Renzo insisted on ordering for us: sand dabs, salad, and a bottle of white wine.

"What happened next?" I asked.

"I took her to the studio, and Mr. Ramsey to his apartment."

"And when did you see Vicky again?"

"Oh, the next day, I think it was. She and Mr. Talbot took a trip to Lake Arrowhead. It's only ninety miles east of Los Angeles, but it was a different world. They both seemed happy. Talbot had a beautiful place there, right on the water, and he had several speedboats, those jazzy wooden Chris-Crafts. I took the two of them there numerous times. When it became obvious Miss Vicky was pregnant, she stayed at Lake Arrowhead for several months. On occasion, I would stay over, and drive Mr. Talbot back to Los Angeles."

"Tell him about Ramsey," Dornay said, lapping up the last of his second martini.

"I never saw the man again after that trip to Tijuana. A few days later, I learned that he had committed suicide. That surprised me, since he seemed like a man who enjoyed life."

Dornay got the ball rolling again. "Tell him about the other trips, Vinnie."

Renzo rubbed his hands together like someone moving closer to a fire. "It was six or seven months later that Mr. Talbot had me drive Vicky back to Tijuana. She was accompanied by Johnny Sands. Sands was—"

"We know all about Sands," Dornay said.

Renzo gave him a look that made it clear he didn't like being interrupted. "I drove the two of them to Dr. Foley's clinic. I thought she might have the child in the backseat. She checked into the clinic, with Sands. I left them there, then came back to Los Angeles."

"Do you think Sands was the father?"

The waiter came with the food, and Renzo suggested he finish his story after we ate. Dornay and I wolfed our chow down, but Renzo cut his food into small pieces and chewed each morsel thoroughly. In between bites, he told stories about the restaurant.

"Orson Welles threw a party in that booth over there to celebrate winding up filming *The Lady from Shanghai,* with his then-wife, Rita Hayworth, and the production staff. I drove Rita home. She was wonderful, but Welles was drunk and belligerent. Bogart, Jack Warner, David Niven, they all ate here. Even the Rolling Stones come in when they're in town."

I was in no mood for ancient Hollywood gossip. "Tell me about Johnny Sands, Vinnie. Was he the father?"

"I would think not. Both Sands and Miss Vicky spoke excellent Italian, as do I. It's funny, Mr. Quint. When you're a wheelman, the first day or two with a client, they say very little. But after awhile, they treat you as part of the furniture, as if you're not really there at all. Two days after driving Sands and Miss Vicky to Tijuana, Mr. Talbot had me drive him to the clinic."

Like any good storyteller who knew he had his audience on the hook, Vinnie let me dangle. He wiped his lips with a neat white napkin and ordered cheesecake for dessert.

"This is all interesting, Vinnie, but for three thousand dollars, I was hoping for a little more."

He pushed his dessert plate away and said, "Where was I?"

"In Tijuana with old man Talbot," Dornay said, draining the remains of the wine in his glass.

"I stayed in Tijuana, not at the clinic, but at a nearby motel. The next morning, Mr. Sands called me, told me that the baby had died, and that I should return home."

"What about Talbot?" I asked. "Did you drive him back? How did he take the death of the baby?"

"I don't know. I never saw Mr. T. again. I don't know how he returned to Los Angeles. Perhaps Johnny Sands rented a car and drove him, or he may have flown directly to his home back east—in Connecticut, I believe. It was a real shame."

Dornay circled his spoon in his coffee. "What was a real shame, Vinnie?"

"Losing a client like Mr. Talbot. He sold the studio. I did run into Johnny Sands some months later. I asked him what had happened to Miss Vicky and he told me that she had died as a result of an auto accident. He told me never to repeat this to anyone, or I'd be 'taking a long dirt nap.' That's exactly how he phrased it."

It sounded like one of Freeze Chanan's lines.

"Truth be told," Vinnie said, waving a hand for the waiter, "if Johnny were still alive, I wouldn't be telling you this now, Mr. Quint. He was a very intimidating man."

"Did Sands say where this accident took place?"

"He did not, and I certainly wasn't going to ask."

Dornay said, "I had a buddy at the *San Diego Union-Tribune* check Baja Canternia public records, Quint. There was nothing on the birth or death of the baby, and zip on Vicky Vandamn."

"What can you tell me about a cop by the name of Willie 'Freeze' Chanan?" I asked Vinnie.

"Mr. Dornay and I have talked quite a bit about Chanan. He was an unpleasant man, and he was a frequent visitor to Mr. Talbot's studio and his mansion, but I never had any dealings with him."

He ordered brandies all around and asked the waiter for the check, which I paid when it came. As we left the restaurant, he pointed out the booth where George Clooney and Brad Pitt had filmed a scene for *Oceans 11.*

Jack Dornay was going to stay in Los Angeles for another day to "do some more digging." For my three thousand dollars, plus the dinner tab, Vinnie offered to drive me back to the airport in his gleaming black Lincoln Town Car.

Renzo told me more about his days as a wheelman to the stars on the way to the airport. When he parked in front of the terminal, he said, "Anything about my story seem strange to you, Mr. Quint?"

"Yes. Why would Talbot have sent Vicky to an abortion mill in Tijuana to give birth to a child? And why did Sands claim that Vicky had died? She was alive and well up until a short time ago."

Out of habit, Vinnie got out of the car, came around to the curb, and opened the door for me. He shook my hand formally, then said, "Tijuana. I didn't much enjoy my time down there. It was a wild, dangerous place. You could get *anything* you wanted, if you had the money. Have a nice flight home, Mr. Quint."

The flight wasn't bad, but it was the usual hassle going through security before boarding the plane. Ah, the romance of travel. It's less than an hour in the air from L.A. to SFX, but all the hassle of going through security to get to the plane doubled that time.

I arrived home a little after 2:00 A.M. It was one of those good news/bad news deals. The good news was that Terry Greco was waiting for me in bed. The bad news was that she told me that it looked like the *Bulletin* had been sold.

"Parkham is flying back, and she's going to make an announcement to the entire staff. It's not final, but everything we hear points to it being a done deal. How was dinner in Hollywood?"

I filled her in on my conversation with Vinnie Renzo, and while I was brushing my teeth, Terry told me that there was a strange message from my mother on the answering machine.

I pushed the play button.

"Carroll dear, I forgot to tell you I found some more pictures of Vicky in the attic. You must see them. Freeze called again, but I told him I was busy. I think he got the message. I didn't mention the pictures. Oh, and I think I know why that young man's body was found near Vicky's houseboat. Clifton Webb, darling. Remember him? Call me soonest. Come for breakfast if you can."

"Who is Clifton Webb?" Terry asked after I crawled into bed.

"A long-dead actor. He was gay, and flaunted it, except when he was on-screen. He was the bad guy in *Laura,* one of the greatest film noir movies of all time."

"Why would your mother think he would have something to do with Ron's death? It must be another Clifton Webb."

"We're talking about my mother, Terr. Anything's possible."

She snuggled close and scraped her toenails down my leg.

"What are we going to do, Carroll?"

I twisted around and snuggled back.

"About our jobs, I mean," she said. "Did you learn anything helpful from that man in Hollywood?"

"Could be. Talbot sent Vicky to have an abortion in Tijuana. She went there with Jerome Ramsey, but she balked, couldn't go through with it. And a short time after that, Ramsey supposedly committed suicide. Several months later, Talbot sent Vicky back there, with Johnny Sands as a chaperone, to have the baby. The kid died, and later, according to Sands, so did Vicky. There's no public record of Vicky's death, or the birth and death of her baby. That's why Talbot picked an abortion mill in Tijuana. No matter what took place, it couldn't be traced back to him. He shut down the studio. Vicky vanished until after Sands was murdered; then she popped up in Canada and married Jerome's brother. When I told Talbot that Vicky had been alive and living in Sausalito, he jumped all over me, said that she was deader than Elvis. Either he believed that Vicky died in an accident or he paid Sands to kill her. For whatever reason, Sands made up the accident story, and let her get away."

Terry's right index finger began making circles on my chest. "So what does it all mean?"

"I wish I knew. Something I didn't get to tell you was that I spoke to my father. He saw Vicky briefly in Venice, a long time ago. She begged him not to tell anyone that he'd seen her, and that she was alive and living in Italy. He also told me that Jerome Ramsey was bisexual. That he'd gotten a cocktail waitress in a family way, and the lady had an abortion."

"In Tijuana?"

"Dad didn't know for sure."

"Then Ramsey could have been the one who got Vicky pregnant."

"Everyone seemed to think Jerome was a homosexual, so they trusted him around their women. But Sir Charles Talbot isn't the kind of man to have sent Vicky to have an abortion if he wasn't sure the baby was his. So let's assume Talbot was the father, and let's further assume that the child, like Vicky, didn't die in Tijuana. Say Talbot took off with the baby. Vicky was certain that the child had died. She told a priest that she was sorry it hadn't been baptized."

"So Junior is actually Vicky Vandamn's child?"

"According to Erica, Junior's mother was an English aristocrat with a drug problem, and the kid was definitely born in Stamford, Connecticut, where Talbot had a big estate. Your friend Ron Maleuw was an orphan, adopted by friends of Talbot, and when the adopted parents died, Talbot took Maleuw into the house, gave him a great job, and treated him like one of the family. So Talbot and Vicky's child could have been Ron Maleuw."

Her finger stopped and the nail began digging into my stomach. "Ron and Junior brothers? I don't know about that."

"Half brothers. Talbot wouldn't have wanted people to know he had *two* sons, both born around the same time. His wife wouldn't have liked it, either, and she could have made a lot of trouble for him. So he passed the baby off to some people he knew—Philip and Cynthia Maleuw. That way, he could keep an eye on the kid. It fits. Talbot sent Vicky down for an abortion, she balked, came home, and they drove up to his place in Lake Arrowhead. I guess Talbot couldn't talk her into having an abortion, so he decided to let her have the baby, but he kept her up at the lake, out of sight, once it was obvious she was pregnant. That's why the birth took place in Tijuana, so Talbot could pay off the doctor, and make sure there was no record of the birth."

"If it fits, then who killed Ron?"

"I don't know, but think about it. If Ron was a Talbot, then he'd have been in line for a windfall when the old man died. Erica said

Talbot is giving away a ton of his holdings to various churches. Junior wouldn't have wanted to split any part of his father's estate with Maleuw. Or we can go with my mother's theory, that the killer is an old gay actor who died forty years ago."

Terry took a deep breath and blew the air onto my shoulder. "What do we do now?"

I grabbed her finger and whispered, "Make a bigger circle."

Twenty-four

I hurried over to my mother's early in the morning. I wasn't that interested in seeing more pictures of Vicky, and I didn't think Clifton Webb had done Ron Maleuw in, but I was worried about her saying that Freeze Chanan had telephoned her. I'd promised my father that Chanan wouldn't get next to Mom again, and that was a promise I didn't want to break.

"My God, it's not nine o'clock yet," Mom said when she answered the door. "When I said you should come for breakfast, dear, I was thinking more like tenish."

She was wearing one of those superthick white terry-cloth robes that usually hang in the closets of the suites in upscale gambling casinos and resorts. Mom considers them, along with an ashtray or two, as part of the price of a room. When management tries to bill her for them, she puts on her "Who me?" act, and somehow gets away with it.

She raked her hands through her hair as I followed her to the kitchen.

"You should have called, Carroll. I don't like you seeing me like this, with no makeup, and the place is a mess. Put on some water for tea."

I told her she looked beautiful, which was true, then put on the teakettle. Within a couple of minutes, she was back, wearing a tangerine-colored turban and her Audrey Hepburn glasses. She was carrying a legal-size manila envelope.

"Has Freeze Chanan called again?" I asked her.

"No. And he won't. I made it crystal clear I didn't want to see him." She dropped the envelope on the table.

"If he comes to the door, don't answer and don't let him in."

She placed her hands on her hips and tilted her chin out. "I can handle myself, thank you."

I pecked her cheek with my lips. "Let's see the pictures."

"I found them in a box in the corner of the attic where you used to hide your *Playboys* and other smutty magazines."

She took out packets of small snaps held together by rubber bands. She rummaged through them and came up with a group of colored photos that had faded to a dull orange.

"Those were taken at a picnic at a beach in Santa Monica."

It was easy to recognize my mother in a polka-dot bikini, running down toward the surf.

"Vicky's hair was much lighter back then," she told me.

Indeed it was. Vicky was sitting with her arms wrapped around her knees as a well-muscled young man smiled at her.

"Who's the hunk?" I asked.

"Oh, just someone I knew before I met your father." She opened the manila envelope wider and slid out a dozen or so eight-by-ten black-and-white glossy still shots.

"These are by Jerome Ramsey, dear. I told you he was talented, didn't I?"

Mom looked spectacular, and so did Vicky, with her dark, haunted eyes. Again, no smiles. In one scene, she was leaning forward, hands under her chin à la Rodin's *The Thinker*. In all the others, she was wearing dark silk dresses and gloves.

"What was it with Vicky and gloves? In almost every picture I've seen, she was wearing them."

"She had Fred Astaire hands, Carroll," Mom said, as if that explained everything.

"Astaire's hands?"

"Yes. Haven't you noticed? Watch his movies closely and you'll see. He always curled his fingers inward like this." She held out her hands and folded her fingers into her palms. "Mr. Astaire had absolutely huge hands and fingers, and he thought them ugly, so he disguised them when filming. Poor Vicky's were worse. She'd had her pinkies operated on, and told me it had been ever so painful."

"What was wrong with her pinkies?" I asked, closely examining the still shot with her hands under her chin.

"They both curved inward. Very predominantly. There's a name for it, but I can't think of it. A family trait. She told me her father's fingers were exactly the same."

"Jesus Christ," I said, flopping down into a chair like a runner whose legs had gone out on him.

"They weren't *that* bad, dear. Would you like a muffin with your tea?"

While my mind whirled, Mom prattled on about Vicky. I thought about Vicky's fingers. Charles Talbot, Jr., had the same big hands, a pianist's long fingers, and his two pinkies definitely curved inward.

"I've got to use your computer, Mom."

While the machine booted up, I checked in at the *Bulletin* with Rosie, the Great's secretary.

"Is the boss back?"

"Not yet, Carroll. But I'm afraid you won't be happy to hear what she's going to say. The deal is done. All that is necessary is for the papers to be signed by Sir Charles. He's going to be here around lunchtime."

"Tell her I've found the silver bullet. Talbot will *not* buy the paper. Make sure nothing's signed until I talk to her."

"I'm not sure if Kate will—"

"Tell her to call me on my cell phone and that I'll lay it out for her."

I broke the connection and used Google to find listings for firms in Stamford, Connecticut, that provided copies of birth certificates. There were dozens of them. I picked out the first in line and called.

A chirpy-voiced woman answered. "Weeks and Company public records."

"I want a copy of a birth certificate, fast. How quickly can you get it to me?"

"Our usual turnaround time is forty-eight hours; however, if—"

"I want it in forty-five minutes. Can you fax it to me in California in that time?"

"Well, we have a man at the town hall now. But I would have to charge you quite a bit on a rush order like this."

"Charge away." I gave her my credit-card number, the fax number at my condo, and promised a dozen roses if the document was faxed to me within the hour.

"You seem quite excited," my mother said, placing on the table a tray with a cup of her foul green tea and a round blob of a muffin studded with dark, unpleasant-looking things.

I stood up and gave her a great big kiss. "Mom, you, Terry, and I are going out to dinner to celebrate very soon. Anyplace you want. You're terrific."

"Yes, I know that," she said modestly. "Try the muffin, dear. I made it myself."

I was so happy, I almost could have taken a bite of the damn thing.

"Gotta go. Talk to you soon." I skidded to a stop as I was heading to the front door. "What was that thing about Clifton Webb?"

"Ah, Mr. Webb. Another gentleman I never got to meet. A true mommy's boy. Legend has it that he didn't stop breast-feeding until he was in his twenties."

"What has that got to do with Ron Maleuw?"

"Oh, the young man they found dead on Vicky's beach. I saw one of Webb's better movies the other night, *The Man Who Never Was*, and it got me thinking. It was supposedly based on a true story that happened in World War Two. Webb, a Royal Navy spy, gets his hands on the corpse of a man who died of natural causes, fills his pockets with false secret documents, and makes sure his body washes up on the shore of some beach in Sicily to make the Nazis think that's where the Allies are going to land. Get it, dear? The body was just put there to confuse people. Do you think that could be true in this case?"

I hugged her and gave her another big kiss, then scorched the Mini's tires on the way to my condo.

While I waited impatiently for the promised fax, I used the Internet to check for crooked little fingers, and damned if I didn't get a hit. The medical term is camptodactyly, a hand malformation characterized by a contracture deformity of the joints of the little fingers. An inherited dominant trait.

I found the copy of Kjeldsen's autopsy that Detective Manner's had given me, and skipped through the legal jargon until I found the results of the X rays. Mentioned at the bottom of one paragraph was a note of broken bones in the minimus fingers of both hands.

The phone rang, but I didn't pick it up. After three rings, the fax machine kicked in with that peculiar tone common to all such machines, followed shortly by a grinding noise as a piece of paper slowly eked its way out.

I snatched up the first page, which was a bill from Weeks and Company. The birth certificate followed: "Name of child: Charles Talbot, Jr., born at 10:45 A.M., March 6, 1972. Father: Charles Talbot, 1111 Bridgecrest Road, Stamford, Connecticut. Mother: Luvina Talbot. Place of birth: 1111 Bridgecrest Road, Stamford, Connecticut. Name of attending physician: Walter Foley, M.D." No hospital affiliation or other information was given for Foley. I guessed it would have looked a little *too* suspicious having a child born at the family home in Stamford, with the attending doctor being someone who practiced medicine in Tijuana.

I sat for a long time staring at the certificate. Junior, supposedly born in Stamford. Vicky giving birth in Tijuana. The phone rang, interrupting my thoughts.

"What the hell is going on, Quint?" Katherine Parkham demanded.

"Has Talbot signed the papers for the sale of the *Bulletin*?"

"Word travels fast, doesn't it? The deal was worked out, over my strong objections. Sir Charles merely has to sign on the dotted line. Now, what's this about a silver bullet?"

"I found out something about Talbot that—"

"He's involved in the murder of that woman in the houseboat, or the guy who stole his painting? And you can prove it?"

"It's a long story, boss. Something we should discuss in private."

"Then get right down to my office. And Quint, this better be good."

Charles Talbot, Jr., Mark Selden, the *Bulletin*'s attorney, and two prosperous-looking middle-aged gentlemen in expensive dark suits were in Parkham's office when I arrived.

Junior gave me a smirk. I didn't smirk back. I somehow felt sorry for him. Selden looked as if he'd just won the lottery.

The Great stood up from behind her desk and said, "Gentlemen, I'd like a word with Mr. Quint. You'll find coffee and food in the reception room. We won't be long."

Junior couldn't resist throwing out a nasty line on the way out. "This is your last day here, punk. Enjoy what's left of it."

Parkham sat back down and glared at me. "Give," she said bluntly.

I told her about my meeting with Vinnie Renzo in Los Angeles.

She asked a lot of questions. I made sure I mentioned the three thousand dollars I'd given to Vinnie Renzo, as well as the cost of the airplane tickets and dinner, in some of my answers.

Mark Selden stuck his pointy nose in the door halfway through and said, "Sir Charles is in the building. He'll be here in a few moments."

"Buy him a cup of coffee," the Great said. "And keep that door closed."

She strode over to her liquor cabinet and poured us both a drink.

"So what have we got here, Quint? Gossip from some old-time chauffeur. You expect me to print this? There's nothing in all of this that connects Sir Charles or anyone else to the two deaths. Sir Charles's son apparently had a mother who was a dishy movie starlet rather than a blue-blood Brit. I need more than that for the paper. This is the *Bulletin,* not the *National Enquirer.*"

"I have absolute documented proof that Vicky Vandamn was the mother of Sir Charles's son, Charles Junior, and I think she was murdered to keep that very fact from coming to light, boss."

Parkham wiggled her fingers in a "Give it to me" gesture.

"I don't think you want to see the proof, boss. Talbot could live with me having it, but not you. Let me show it to him and see what happens."

"I hope you're not bluffing, Quint. Sir Charles plays real down and dirty hardball."

"I'm not bluffing."

"Okay, talk to the man. We've got nothing to lose except the *Bulletin,* and our reputations." She upended her glass of expensive scotch in one gulp. "You're a nastier bastard than I thought you were, Quint."

Twenty-five

*J*unior, Mark Selden, and the dark suits didn't like the idea at all. Sir Charles seemed puzzled, but he agreed to see me, no doubt thinking that I had turned up Vicky's book.

When the door was closed and we were alone, he said, "Where is it?"

"I don't have the book, but you should look at this."

I handed him the birth record from Stamford, Connecticut. Talbot held it close to his glasses and read it slowly.

"So? All this shows is that my son was born at our house in Stamford."

"By the same doctor, Walter Foley, who delivered Vicky's baby in Tijuana? Give me a break."

Talbot rolled the certificate into a ball and threw it. "You bastard!"

"When it comes to being a bastard, Sir Charles, I'm an amateur. You're the pro."

He started toward me, then stumbled a bit, fighting to keep his balance. I wheeled the cracked leather chair to him and he sat down carefully, as if he were afraid he'd break a bone or two. "It still doesn't prove anything. There's no way you can tie Vicky to Charlie."

"Yes, there is. Here's something that absolutely no one else knows. Your son has long, crooked little fingers. It's a condition called camptodactyly—an inherited condition. Vicky's condition was passed down from her father, and from her to Charlie."

"Bullshit. There was nothing wrong with Vicky's fingers."

"She was ashamed of them, and she had them broken, reset, and straightened out before arriving in Hollywood. That surgery is documented on the autopsy report, Sir Charles."

"No one is going to pay any attention to this garbage, Quint."

"Junior will," I said.

Talbot rose from the chair for a second, then settled back on his haunches. "So what do you want, Quint? How much?"

"Not a penny. Just drop the deal for taking over the *Bulletin*."

He laughed, softly at first, and then it turned into a choking gasp. "Get me a drink, damn it," he said when the wheezing had stopped.

I poured him some of the Great's thirty-year-old scotch.

He sniffed the glass. "I used to put away a fifth of this stuff a day. Now I fall asleep after a few. So you don't want a cent. I don't believe it. What's Parkham's idea? Is she going to publish this trash?"

"She hasn't seen any of the material I've shown you, and even if she had, I doubt that she would print it, unless it had something to do with the murders of Vicky Vandamn and Ron Maleuw."

"But you, you'd find a way to get this into print, wouldn't you? If not at the *Bulletin,* somewhere else—another paper, a book. Well, go ahead. You've got me by the short hairs. Start squeezing."

"Tell me why you told Vicky that terrible lie about the child dying. Or did you have Johnny Sands tell her that? Before she disappeared. You told me you were certain that she was dead."

"This was *my* son, and I didn't want the world to know that his mother was a slut, so we told Vicky the kid died. My wife, Luvina, was in a bad way. Addicted to drugs. I spent years trying to cure her. She wanted a child, but she wasn't physically up to it—there were several miscarriages. She was so far out of it that she came to believe that she had given birth to Charlie. Sands and Vicky got along well. They both spoke Italian. I had made . . . financial arrangements for her. Very generous arrangements. She was fed up with Hollywood. She realized she'd never be a star. She was beautiful, but she had no acting talent, and her accent didn't help. She had family in some damn town in Italy. She was going there to live; then Sands told me she was killed in a car crash in Mexico. He made it sound like a suicide, said she was very depressed about the baby's death."

"Did you have Johnny Sands kill Jerome Ramsey, Sir Charles?"

"If I did, I wouldn't be foolish enough to admit it." He sampled the scotch, rolling it around in is mouth before swallowing. "I told Sands to talk to the little faggot, to make sure he kept his mouth shut about Vicky. Maybe Johnny got carried away, or maybe Ramsey did commit suicide, like the police said."

"The police. How convenient. The cop in charge was Freeze Chanan, another man who worked for you."

"Freeze Chanan. The two of you barmcakes are working together, aren't you?"

"No. Chanan's on his own, as far as I'm concerned. Maybe you could do business with him, but not me. I called him to get some background on Vicky. He'd been quoted in Los Angeles newspapers as saying he thought she was dead. 'The kid knew too much about a certain local big shot' was the exact quote, if I remember correctly. Chanan thinks I know where Vicky's book is. He says he has a buyer for it, and for your stolen painting."

Talbot took a handkerchief from his pocket and wiped his face with it. "Chanan came to the house the other day. I wasn't there. George kicked him out. I don't know what the hell he wanted. We've done business now and then. He's a . . . resourceful son of a bitch."

"Who killed Vicky and Ron Maleuw, Sir Charles?"

"I wish I knew, and that's the bloody truth."

"Maleuw was also your son, wasn't he? The adoption by Philip Maleuw, you arranged that. Who was the mother? Another starlet, like Vicky? Or was it Cynthia Maleuw?"

Talbot's face went from red to white and back to red again before he answered.

"Don't be daft, Quint. The Maleuws were good friends. They got the child form an orphanage. Phil was damned good at what he did, and Cynthia was family, a second cousin. Nice woman—flat as a flounder, and she had a face that could have stopped Big Ben. She was a fine painter, and a divvy—she could spot a fake in the blink of an eye. She helped me with my collection—thinned out the garbage and helped me buy some very fine pieces. She also taught Ronnie the business. When she and Philip died, I took care of the lad. And in the end, he betrayed me. I'm going to have a hard time finding someone to replace him. He knew more about my collection than I do."

"Who killed Johnny Sands, Sir Charles? It was soon after his death that Vicky left Italy and moved to Canada."

He nudged his glasses to the edge of his nose and stared at me over the rims. "Canada? What the devil was she doing there?"

"She got married. To Arnold Ramsey, Jerome's brother."

His head jerked and his glasses fell to the floor. I picked them up and handed them to him.

"Jerome's brother, eh?" he said when the glasses were back in place. "Was he a cock jockey, too?"

"Jerome Ramsey was bisexual, Sir Charles. Didn't you know that? Vicky wasn't the only girl he'd accompanied to Dr. Foley's clinic in Tijuana."

I wasn't sure if that was true, but it hit Talbot like a punch to the jaw.

"Ramsey? You're full of crap."

"No. It's true. All those times you and your buddies used Ramsey as a beard, he was probably keeping the girls quite happy."

"Jerome, the little puff," Talbot said bitterly. "He *was* the one who told me about Doc Foley's place. Charlie's my son, laddie. I made damn sure of it, so I don't want you spreading any filthy rumors around. Is that understood?"

I nodded. "What about the *Bulletin*, Sir Charles? Do we have a deal?"

"I've lost my taste for the damn thing. But if any of this turns up in print, I'll make them an offer they can't refuse, and the only thing you'll ever write is your own obituary."

"I don't think your son is going to take this too well."

Talbot made a grunting noise, then said, "Charlie tells me you cheated him out of a big pot in a poker game, then trashed one of my cabanas."

"That's not the way it happened, and I have a hunch you know that."

"Hunch. Whom do you expect me to believe? You or my son?"

"You know him better than I do, sir."

Talbot had some trouble getting out of the chair. I grabbed him by the hand and gave a gentle heave. His grip was wet and slippery. He used the edge of the desk to steady himself, then walked slowly over to the wall where the Great's black-and-white abstract painting hung.

"Ah, Franz Kline. I've got a few of his pieces. Wouldn't mind having this one. Amazing what a man can do with a brush and a piece of white canvas, isn't it? Is this the paper's, or Kate's?"

"It's hers."

"She'd drive too hard a bargain." He turned to face me. "You're young. I've grown to hate the young. They think they know everything, and they don't know squat. No one knows anything until they're in their seventies, and even then, most haven't figured it out."

"Figured what out, Sir Charles?"

"How to end the game. How to finish it up." He mopped his brow with the handkerchief again. "I have to go to London on business. Sell a few things and find a new curator. I'm taking Charlie with me. Find that book, Quint. My offer still stands, a hundred thousand dollars. And if Vicky *was* murdered, I'd bloody well like to know who did it. Maybe I should have treated her a little better, but what's done is done."

He shrugged his shoulders, straightened his tie, and walked to the door. He had his hand on the knob when he turned to give me a final piece of advice. "Watch yourself when you're dealing with Freeze Chanan. He's got balls the size of church bells."

Twenty-six

Sir Charles Talbot had called me a "barmcake," among other unpleasant things; his son had called me several nasty names, and was the frontrunner as to who had tried to land a flowerpot on my head from ten stories above. Talbot's flunky George had used British slang, "F.O.A.D.," telling me to do something obscene, then die. The Great claimed I was a "nastier bastard" than she'd thought I was. Detective Manners of the Sausalito Police Department had told me I was "kind of a prick." Freeze Chanan had called me a "punk" when he wasn't calling me "pally," and Della Rugerio had threatened to send the Knight of Wands after me if I didn't watch myself.

Despite all of that, my back was sore from all the pats I'd gotten during the celebration dinner Katherine Parkham had thrown at the Bix, a stylish 1940s-looking supper club located on Gold Street, in the Financial District of the city. It had the ambience and feel of the kind of spot that Nick and Nora Charles would frequent, leaving their dog, Asta, tied up to a fireplug out front while they quaffed dry martinis and listened to a superb jazz trio.

The Great liked it because it had a cigar bar. She picked up the tab for more than a dozen *Bulletin* employees, which included her secretary, Rosie, Terry Greco, Max Maslin, me, and several editors and reporters. Mark Selden was there, acting delusional, as if the people he was talking to actually liked him.

The word was out that somehow I had held off Sir Charles from taking over the paper. I was pressed for details, but I gave none, playing dumb, which is something I'm very good at, except with Parkham. She had whooshed me into her office after Sir Charles left, demanding to know what had taken place. "Give, Quint. Now."

I gave, and was rewarded with the good news that I was no longer on a forced vacation; however, I was still assigned to the stories on Ulla Kjeldsen and Ron Maleuw, not my beloved movie and play reviews.

"Find out who done it, Quint," Parkham had said, "and then you can go back to that showbiz junk."

It was a hard-drinking crowd, and Max, after a few Cherry Heerings, made a rather lewd suggestion that perhaps I had negotiated the deal with Talbot's sexy wife.

I tried to have a good time, but I couldn't quite get there. Maybe it dated back to my early Catholic grammar school days, when Sister Mary Holy Card had preached to us that when things are going very well, it's a sign from God that very soon they'll get rotten again. The good sister seemed to like the rotten days the most.

I had that tingly feeling in my stomach, in addition to the vodka, wine, and filet mignon squishing around in there. The dreaded old "What if" questions popped up. What if Talbot changed his mind about taking over the *Bulletin*? What if his son threw a hissy fit and came after me armed with more flowerpots? What if Freeze Chanan mucked up the waters by finding out about Junior being Vicky's son, and used a little blackmail on Sir Charles? What if Talbot was a better actor than I gave him credit for, and he *had* been behind Ulla's and Ron Maleuw's deaths? And what if Terry spotted Rosie's hand, liberated by all the booze, dropping onto my lap at dinner?

Selden cornered me on the way to the men's room.

"You've made some enemies, Quint. The attorneys handling the takeover put in a lot of work on this."

"The *Bulletin*'s attorneys, or Talbot's?"

"Both," Selden said. His mouth twitched, which is as close as he could come to a smile. "I'm not among them. I think you've opened a few eyes. Have you spoken to Lady Talbot about that proposition I mentioned the other day?"

"I haven't had the chance, Mark."

"Well, I think Sir Charles's actions today, canceling the deal at the last moment, might possibly point to his being . . . less in charge of his senses than perhaps he should be, and there is the potential that all this could be very promising with regard to the matter we discussed."

Possibly, perhaps, potential, promising—and all in one long, tortured sentence. No wonder its takes three or more years to get through law school.

"If I see Erica again, I'll bring it up," I said, merely to get Selden out of my hair.

The next morning, I was safely ensconced at my desk, staring at my computer screen. The dreaded writer's block. I needed a story to "feed the beast," but nothing came to mind. I called Detective Manners, got her answering machine. I called Freeze Chanan in Palm Springs and got his answering machine.

I dialed Talbot's place in Napa, just to learn if he had indeed taken off for London. The phone was answered by a woman with a lovely Latin voice: Carla, the housekeeper. She remembered me, and told me that George had taken Sir Charles and his son to the airport moments ago. Mrs. Talbot was out riding.

I thanked her, then stared at the blank screen for another ten minutes or so before deciding to get some fresh air. A quick drive to Tiburon to check out Talbot's yacht, the *Sir Charles,* seemed in order. Especially with George and the gang out of the way.

Tiburon. Spanish for shark. Think of a finger pointing out to Angel Island and Tiburon being the fingernail. A well-manicured fingernail. The town's population is around eight thousand, the average per capita income is on a par with that of Beverly Hills, and the crime statistics make Sausalito's look like Beirut's by comparison. Rich, quiet, rich, warm, rich lily-white population, and, oh, did I mention rich?

There is one great saloon restaurant, Sam's Anchor Cafe, on the pier, and from the deck you can look into the docks at the Corinthian Yacht Club.

I enjoyed an early lunch of a hamburger and a Coke while watching tourists take "Kodak moment" photos of the beautiful surroundings.

A rough-looking guy in work-spoiled jeans and a bright orange windbreaker was working on the engine of a small boat on the dock just below me. He had sun-weathered skin and a thick crop of ash-colored hair. I leaned over and offered to buy him a beer.

He gave me a skeptical look. "Why would you do that?"

"Because I'm interested in one of the boats in the yacht club, and you look like a man who would know what's going on around here."

"Which boat would that be, buddy?"

"The *Sir Charles*. It's a catamaran, I'm told."

"You were told true. Make it a Heineken."

I bought two bottles at the bar, then went back outside, leaned over the railing, and dropped one down to him.

"Come aboard," he said.

I walked down to the dock, found the boat, and climbed aboard. It was nothing special—eighteen feet, I guessed, powered by a single outboard motor. Its once–bright red fiberglass was going a more mottled color, and tools and fishing gear were scattered everywhere.

"Name's Joe," he said, toasting me with the Heineken. "Let me make a guess. You write for some magazine that's doing an article on Talbot's boat, right?"

"Something like that, Joe. I hear it's a beauty."

"It's a beast of a beauty. A damn shame the way they treat that boat."

"What do you mean?" I asked, looking for a clean spot to sit down.

He took another swig from the beer. "It's the wrong horse in the wrong race. A twin-hull catamaran doesn't make much sense here. Forty-eight feet in length, and over half of that beam. It's a floating apartment, not a boat. Want to take a look?"

"I do indeed."

Joe wiped his hands on his already-grease-smeared pants, fiddled with the outboard motor, and told me to cast off.

I unhooked the mooring line and we scooted away from the dock, the outboard motor sounding like the magnified buzzing of insects. It was only a hundred yards or so to the rarified waters of the Corinthian Yacht Club. It wasn't hard to pick out the *Sir Charles*. It was the only catamaran in the water: a gleaming vanilla white beauty with a rolled-up royal blue sail at mid-deck.

"They keep it up real good," Joe said. "I've done some work on it myself. I don't want to be quoted on this, buddy."

"You won't be."

"Old man Talbot's kid uses it like it's a Jet Ski, powering it through the straits like he's in some goddamn lake, rather than the bay. The water out by the Golden Gate Bridge is three hundred and sixty feet deep, and we've got some fierce riptides. He's going to get himself, or someone else, killed one of these days. He has no respect for the right-of-way, just plows through, not giving a damn what his wake will do to some little dinghy like mine. The English guy, he knows what he's doing, though. Smart-mouthed bugger, but he knows boats."

English guy. Good old George. Joe maneuvered his boat close to the *Sir Charles*. The center of the boat was a few feet above the waterline. There were built-in steps on the rear deck, so that someone could descend into or climb out of the water. A black wet suit, looking like a crumpled body, was drying on the stern decking.

"How long would it take to sail this over to Sausalito, Joe?"

"By sail? Twenty minutes max. Using power, probably five or ten, depending on the weather."

I watched the people on the yacht club piers walking leisurely to and from their vessels. A body couldn't be dragged down the pier without being noticed, so if Ron Maleuw had been transported to Sausalito via the *Sir Charles*, he would have had to board the boat voluntarily.

"Ain't you going to take pictures?" Joe asked.

"No. I've seen all I need."

Joe took me back to Sam's Anchor Cafe. My cell phone started humming as I was walking back to the Mini. It was Max Maslin.

"Carroll, old buddy. You know your vacation is over, and the Great is making inquiries about tomorrow's edition. Have you got anything I can use?"

"Not right at the moment, Max."

"Well, maybe I can point you in the right direction. That sergeant in Sausalito called for you. She told me to pass this along. Says her hunch about Della Rugerio was probably right. Ulla Kjeldsen had a living trust. The beneficiaries were some priest, Father Carmody, and a guy named Caribbean Joe. Who the hell is he?"

I had to park several blocks from Harbor Point. As I made my way down the pier toward Ulla's houseboat, I passed several people carrying boxes of clothes, pots and pans, and bottles of wine. Two muscular young men were lugging a rowing machine like the one I'd seen in Ulla's workout room.

There were half a dozen people in front of her place. A hand-painted sign slapped on the entrance proclaimed ESTATE SALE. EVERY-THING MUST GO.

I edged my way through the front door. The living room was jammed. Men and women were picking up glasses, lamps, and silverware. One heavyset woman with bubble gum–colored hair was rocking up and down on the gray leather couch.

Della Rugerio was sitting in front of the glass-topped dining room table. The green Tupperware bowl in front of her was half-filled with cash. She had a touch-pad credit-card machine alongside, ready to do business.

She was arguing with a young woman over the value of a crystal vase.

I took the circular staircase to the second floor, brushing by more happy customers clutching blouses, sweaters, and shoes. The fur bedspread was gone; so were several of the exercise machines.

Someone nudged my back and said in a sweet southern accent, "God, don't I just wish I could fit into this."

I turned, to see Mary Tucker holding a lettuce green peignoir in front of her full figure.

"Hi, Mary. How's Bert?"

"He's so happy, he doesn't know whether to die or go bowling. He's finished his book, the mystery, you know. He can't wait to spend the money he's gonna make." She gave me a saucy wink. "Probably gonna get him some new telescopes."

I waved an arm around the room. "I'm surprised by this. I just learned that Ulla had a living trust, and that Rugerio's cat was one of the main beneficiaries."

"Ain't that a bitch," Mary said. "A stupid cat." She dropped the peignoir onto the bed and picked up a lacy black nightgown. "I might be able to squeeze into this one. You gonna buy anything? Nice-looking young man like you gotta have some girlfriend who likes this sexy stuff."

I was tempted to look in the drawer where Ulla had stored her sex toys to see if they were still there. Knowing Rugerio, she probably had fresh batteries to sell with them.

"I'm just looking. Say hi to Bert."

I went downstairs and picked up one of the silver-framed photos of Ulla. In this one, her face was in profile and she was dressed in black. A yellow Post-it stuck to the bottom gave the price: twenty dollars.

I carried it over to Della, who was between sales. No white nurse's uniform this time. She was wearing a too-tight brandy-colored sweater. The bracelets on her wrists looked like gold, and the pearls around her neck and the diamond and ruby rings on her fingers had probably come from Ulla's jewelry chest, too. No need to hide them now. They were hers—or a least her cat's.

"This was a little sudden, wasn't it?"

She tapped her fingers on the table, as if she were playing a piano. "I thought it was best to sell now, before the burglars could come back. Someone broke in here the other night. Did you know that?"

The tone of the question made it clear that she thought the *some-one* had been me.

"How's Caribbean Joe handling his newfound wealth?"

"Joe's just fine. He's three years old. With proper care, cats can live fifteen years, I'm told."

I looked into the cash bowl. "It appears that Joe's going to have very good care. What are you going to do with the properties in British Columbia, Della?"

"How do you know about those?"

"I'm a reporter. This could make a good story. Former starlet leaves her wealth to a priest and a cat." I leaned down close to her. "You've known about the living trust for a long time, haven't you? But you never mentioned it to the police, or to me."

"Why should I?" she countered with a knowing smile. "Ulla talked about it more than once, over a smoke and some wine, but I wasn't sure she'd finalized it. The attorney, Ed Galvin—he's local—was a *friend* of Ulla, if you get my drift. He drew the trust up free of charge."

Ulla screwing an attorney out of a fee. She went up a notch in my book.

"Did you have a smoke and some wine with Ulla the night she died, Della?"

"No," she barked, causing a man wearing a cowboy-style straw hat to drop the bottle of wine he was holding. Luckily, it landed on the rug and didn't break.

Della grabbed the picture frame from my hand. "Do you want this or not?"

"Yes. For my mother."

"Forty dollars."

"The tag says twenty."

She lowered her head and looked like she was about to get to her feet and charge. "Forty dollars. Take it or leave it, newspaperman."

I took out my money clip and peeled off two twenties. "I'll buy it. It'll make a nice ending to my story in tomorrow's paper."

She told me what to do with my story in no uncertain terms, causing Cowboy Hat to drop another bottle of wine.

Twenty-seven

There was the usual array of E-mails waiting for me when I got back in front of the computer at the *Bulletin*: questions about actors, plays; some messages from people who said they missed my daily column, others from those who hoped I was gone for good.

I checked my answering machine. Just one call—from Erica Talbot, asking me to get right back to her.

She was all cuddly and cooing when we were connected.

"Carroll, you were fantastic the other night. I'm dying to see you again. Charles, Junior, and George are in London, and I'm bored. When are you coming up to see me?"

That was good news. Especially about George. "When will they be back?"

"Who knows. A few days, a week. Please come. Tonight?"

"I can't make—"

"Tomorrow, then. Early. We can go riding, then relax."

"All right. When I spoke to your husband yesterday, he mentioned that a man by the name of Willie 'Freeze' Chanan had stopped by. Did you talk to him?"

"No. Charles has so many shady business associates. I try to keep my distance. Make it ten o'clock. I'll have Calico ready and waiting for you."

"Calico?"

"A beautiful spotted saddle horse. She's very gentle. You'll love her."

There was a kissy sound, and she ended the conversation by saying, "Get some rest tonight."

If I was to believe Sir Charles and Erica, George had been the only one at the Napa compound to meet and greet Chanan. Freeze wasn't the kind of man to take a brush-off lightly. I dialed his Palm Springs number, and got his answering machine again.

Terry Greco stopped by my cubicle.

"There's someone you have to meet." She linked her arm around mine and led me to the coffee alcove. "He's Paul Verel, the man Sir Charles obtained the missing Picasso from years ago. I had a tough time getting him to agree to talk to us; the caveat is that everything he says is off the record."

The coffee alcove was a small affair: a few tables and chairs, and a coffee machine that got filled up by whoever was desperate enough to drink the stuff.

A short, neatly dressed man in a charcoal-colored suit was sitting at a table, staring glumly at his coffee cup. He appeared to be in his late sixties and had salt-and-pepper hair that was thin at the front and long at the collar.

"Carroll, this is Paul Verel. We've been talking about the missing Picasso, *Jeune Fille avec Fleur Rouge. Girl with a Red Flower.*"

Ah, finally a title for the painting. Verel stood up and bowed, but he didn't offer his hand.

"How do you do. Miss Greco tells me you are on the hunt for the painting, no?"

He had light gray eyes, gabled by dark brows, and a deeply lined face. The wrinkles were all in the right places, giving him the look of an aging rogue. He had a melodious French accent, a light baritone— think Maurice Chevalier before he was thanking heaven for little girls.

"Sir Charles is anxious to have it returned."

We all sat down, and Verel took a tiny sip of his coffee. "Dear old Charles. I'm wondering what game he is up to this time. He didn't take it very well when I told him that I had seen the painting in London six months ago."

"You're sure?" I asked. "The very same painting he claims is missing?"

"Oh, yes," Verel said. There was a bulletin board on the wall next to the table. It was littered with personal stuff from the paper's employees: cars for sale, garage sales, and one for the sports department's picnic several weeks ago.

"May I use one of these?" Verel asked.

I snatched the outdated picnic post and handed it to him.

"It is a very small painting," he said as he folded the paper. "Exactly seven and three-quarters inches by nine and a half inches." He folded the paper to those approximate dimensions, then took a pen from his coat pocket and began sketching on the blank side.

"It is what we call a 'boxer shorts' painting. Picasso had a habit of sleeping late in the morning, then going to work in whatever he slept in. The whole thing probably took him no more than an hour—two at the most. He had another habit, an afternoon assignation after he was through working. Who knows, it could have been with the woman in the painting he was working on, or the wife or daughter of a friend. He liked to seduce his friends' ladies."

He turned the paper so that it faced Terry and me. On it was a rough sketch of a woman with an odd-shaped head, holding a rather grotesque-looking flower.

"It is not one of the master's best, but absolutely anything of his is worth a fortune now."

"What was the price that Talbot paid you for the painting, Paul?" Terry asked.

Verel gave a Gallic shrug of the shoulders. "This took place a very long time ago. I had some creditors at my throat. Charles paid them off, then provided me a two-year lease on a small building he owned in Montmarte, on the rue Damrémont. A flat upstairs, a gallery below. Unfortunately, I was not in a position to turn the deal down." He sampled the coffee and grimaced. "This is awful." He added a dash of cream.

"What did Talbot say when you told him you'd seen the painting in London?" I asked.

Another shrug. "It was the morning of the museum exhibit. Charles was bragging about how he had 'screwed me over' on the Picasso. I told him about London. He was furious. He sent Ronald Maleuw back to Napa to get the painting." Verel stirred his coffee and watched the cream swirl around. "Charles told me I was a liar, and that he would prove it when I saw his Picasso. Unfortunately, you know what happened then. Monsieur Maleuw was found dead, no?"

"Yes, he was. Did you know Ronald Maleuw?"

"I had met him several times, in Paris and London, either when he was with Charles or when he was scouting around after a painting."

"Do you have any idea as to how *this* painting ended up in London?"

Another sample of the coffee, and final surrender. "Undrinkable," Verel declared. "As to the painting, I was visiting a friend's house in Mayfair. He, fortunately, was away. His wife invited me into the bedroom. There, on the wall, amidst a marvelous collection of very fine paintings, was the *Fleur Rouge.* I thought nothing of it, assuming it had been obtained from Charles. Charles seldom sold anything from his collection, but he was quite happy to make a trade, as long as he thought he was coming out on top."

I rolled the sketch Verel had made into a tight cylinder and slipped it into my jacket pocket.

Terry said, "Paul, are you certain the Picasso in London was the original?"

"I have been in the business all of my life, demoiselle, and I assure you it was."

"Can you give us the name of the current owner?" I asked.

Verel gave a low guttural chuckle. "This gentleman—I will provide no name to you—is well known in the *art noir* world—the black market. He is an avid collector, but he seldom buys through a gallery or an auction. That is not how things work in our world. I have two beautiful galleries, one in London, the other in Paris. They are . . . what you say? Window dressing. I do not lose money on them, but I couldn't afford to live the life I've become accustomed to by selling to the public. The *noir* collectors are all very rich. They have to be, but they are not fools. They do not wish the world, especially the tax collectors of the world, to know how much they have paid for a work of art. There would be questions of how the money had been accumulated; and the seller, he is not anxious to share his windfall with some bureaucrats who will waste it on tanks or a soccer stadium." He thumped his chest lightly with the heel of his hand. "That is where I come in. I'm an arbitrator, a middleman who puts the buyer and seller together."

Verel rose from his chair, but before he could get away, I said, "Talbot told me that he was traveling to London on business. Did you give him the name of the man with the Picasso?"

"*Certainement pas,*" he said, as if I'd insulted him. "If I gave out names, my reputation would be ruined. However, Charles is very shrewd, and there are no more than ten or twelve men in all of London who would have *Fleur Rouge* hanging in their bedrooms. He will no doubt figure it out."

Talbot wasn't the only one who was starting to figure things out. My dear mother's theory, from the old spy movie; a body dressed up and put on the beach to confuse the Germans. Maleuw had certainly been dressed up—he'd been wearing a tuxedo. His body was put there to confuse everyone—to tie his death to Ulla's. If you knock off someone, you don't want to leave his body on *your* doorstep, or anywhere nearby. Where's the best place to leave it? Near where another murder has taken place. Even better if you pick a spot where the police have no expertise when it came to investigating a homicide. Let the cops and dumb reporters waste their time trying to connect the bodies.

Terry and I both thanked Verel for his time, and she offered to walk him out of the building.

I was still sitting at the table when she came back.

"Well, what to we do now, Carroll? Go to the police?"

"Which police? With what? We're not sure that any of this is true. Verel is a charmer, but for all we know, he's just doing this to get back at Talbot for 'screwing him over' on the Picasso."

She leaned both hands on the table. "I believe him. Are we just going to wait for Sir Charles to come back from London? Damn it, someone killed Ronnie. We just can't let them get away with it."

"Terry, there's a good chance that Maleuw was involved in something pretty shady. Talbot's vision isn't that hot anymore; he used Maleuw as his good eye in evaluating paintings. If you believe Verel, then Talbot's collection is tainted, and the Picasso is a forgery. Maleuw should have spotted that. He didn't—for a reason. He knew it was a forgery. He was a talented painter himself. Maybe *he* painted the phony one. Who knows how many more forgeries are in the collection?"

"That's an awful thing to say, Carroll," she said, her voice hard and belligerent. "Ronnie wouldn't have done that. I just know he wouldn't have."

She swiveled around and walked off in a hurry.

"Aren't we having dinner tonight?" I shouted.

She did a quarter turn, made a fist, and then extended her middle finger.

I took that as a no.

Twenty-eight

We've all had bright ideas at one time or another. Something just comes to you and you tell yourself that it's good, really good—be it a better can opener, toaster, computer software, or baby carriage. If you could just patent the idea and get it to market, you'd be rich.

My bright idea came the following morning at Talbot's place in Napa. A foam-rubber saddle—maybe with a thin sheet of leather on top to disguise it. I'd arrived a little after 10:00 A.M., and Erica was waiting, looking very equestrian: polished boots with silver spurs, black stretch riding tights, a ribbed white short-sleeve top, and one of those silly-looking hard plastic riding helmets. I had on old jeans, desert boots, a 49ers sweatshirt, a Giants cap, and my prescription sunglasses, with a cord attached so they could hang around my neck, in case they got knocked off during the trail ride. Not exactly king of the cowboys.

The riding stables were half a mile or so from the big house. We rode there in an open-top Jeep. The road was bordered on both sides by rows and rows of grapevines.

A young woman, eighteen or so, wearing bib overalls and rubber boots, had the horses saddled and ready: Erica's big golden palomino, whom she called Adios, and a smaller spotted horse with sad-looking eyes—Calico.

Adios's saddle was hand-tooled and had decorative silver grommets and a scabbard, out of which stuck the butt of a rifle.

Erica noticed my interest. "There are wild pigs, turkeys, rattlesnakes, and a mountain lion or two in the hills. I had to put down a rabid skunk last week."

I remembered to climb onto Calico from the left side. That was about the extent of my expertise. The Quint family had spent their summer vacations more or less wherever Dad was working: a casino, a cruise ship, or a resort. One summer, we'd spent three weeks at a dude ranch outside of Tucson, Arizona. Mom was smart enough to hang by the pool and cheat the paying guests at bridge. I was thirteen, just starting to lust after girls, and all the girls there rode horses. So I saddled up and did my best, which wasn't very good, either with the horses or the girls.

Erica made clicking sounds with her tongue, and off we trotted. She showed me the winery, a huge barnlike corrugated-steel building, and then we moseyed off toward her bungalow. Along the way, we rode over some rugged terrain with clusters of small ferns and wild manzanita, as well as full-grown cinnamon red–barked madronas, gnarly oaks, and an occasional curtain of pyramid-shaped Douglas fir trees. A good-size hawk rode a thermal on motionless wings directly above us. We stopped at a babbling creek with water so clear, I could see hand-size fish swimming through the rocks. The sun sent luminous shafts through the branches of the overhanging oaks. The horses had a drink and then we hit the trail again.

Calico seemed content to follow behind Adios's haunches, as my own haunches bumped against the hard leather saddle.

We crossed a level area that was scarred with deep gouges in the dry russet-colored earth.

"Fifty years ago, this used to be a rock quarry," Erica said. "There are all kinds of caves in the hills. They dumped all the landfill up here. Erosion and earthquakes have taken their toll. Some of those cracks in the ground go down twenty feet. Charles has plans drawn up to level everything and put in more goddamn grapes."

We rode along a cliff for a while, then turned north and onto a hard-packed dirt road that showed recent tire tracks, and finally approached the bungalow: a two-story log cabin, the logs shellacked to a high gloss. There was a bubble skylight, looking like a giant doorbell, right in the middle of the cedar-shake roof.

I climbed down from Calico with as much dignity as I could muster and tied the reins to a cast-iron hitching post in the shape of a little guy in a jockey's uniform. He had a curling Hercule Poirot–style mustache painted on his face.

I patted him on the head with one hand, rubbed my aching butt with the other, and told him, "I didn't realize what a tough job you had, pal."

Erica smiled wickedly as she tied Adios's reins to the jockey. "Is our little tush sore? I have just the medicine."

The front door was copper, burnished to look like old pennies. It wasn't locked, which seemed odd. There were plenty of marijuana growers who cultivated small plots of land in the Napa and nearby Lake County hills. They were a tough breed, and protected their crops with trip wires and weapons, including AK-47 assault rifles.

"Welcome to my home away from home," Erica said, taking off her riding helmet and hurling it onto a cream-colored suede section couch.

There were low tables of hammered brass, and half a dozen deep burgundy club chairs scattered around the room. The floors were covered with animal hides: zebra, leopard, tiger, bear, some I didn't recognize. A three-foot bronze featuring a cowboy riding a bucking bronco stood on a pedestal next to a knotty-pine cabinet holding a collection of old rifles and six-shooters. The heavy brocade drapes were tied back to let the sun in. I looked out and saw Calico and Adios standing in place, looking bored. I hung my Giants cap on the bucking bronco. "Are the guns loaded?"

"Yes. They're no good empty. What will you have, Carroll? It's too early for a martini. How about champagne?"

"A beer would hit the spot," I said.

She gave me a quizzical look. "Beer? My father used to drink beer in the morning. Of course, after that he drank anything. Go on upstairs and relax. The first door on the right. I'll be right with you."

The staircase had tension-wire balusters and a handrail of thick rope strung through horse head–shaped brass holders.

Thankfully, the door on the right led to a bedroom that was animal-free—if you didn't count Erica.

I took off my sunglasses and let them hang from the cord. The bed was the biggest one I'd ever seen. So big that I had to march off the measurements: twelve feet wide by ten feet long. There was room for a basketball team to camp out. It was open like a fresh envelope, revealing bamboo-colored silk sheets. Eight fluffy pillows stretched across the top of the bed.

The rest of the room paled by comparison: ash-paneled walls, a cedar ceiling, and normal-size chairs and tables.

Erica came in carrying a tray with a bottle of beer, a bottle of her husband's California bubbly, and two glasses.

She set the tray on the table alongside the bed, then flopped down on the mattress.

"Well, what do you think? Like it?"

"What's not to like?" I said, reaching for the beer.

She wiggled around, leaning back, resting on her elbows, her breasts jutting out as she arched her back.

"Pour me a glass of wine, Carroll."

I poured and handed her the glass. She shaped the pillows to her satisfaction, and raised one of her boots to me. "Take them off for me, darling."

I did so carefully, first unsnapping the tabs that held the spurs and removing them before tugging off the boots. They were a tight fit, and it took a lot of tugging.

"Does your husband ever get up here to the bungalow?"

"No. Never. It's too long a ride for Charles now. Besides, a girl has to have some privacy, doesn't she?"

"How about Ron Maleuw. Was he a frequent visitor?"

She drained the wine from her glass and set it noisily back on the tray. "Why all the questions?"

"I'm just trying to tie up some loose ends. I have a theory that

Maleuw was forging paintings from your husband's collection, and selling the originals."

"No. I don't believe it."

"Maleuw had been working for your husband for a long time. He could have copied dozens of paintings. Sir Charles wouldn't have noticed, not with the condition of his eyes. Freeze Chanan told me he'd picked up a few paintings for your husband in the past, and that he'd have no problem finding a buyer for the missing Picasso. Maybe Chanan was working with Maleuw. Maybe that's why Maleuw was murdered."

She bounced to her bare feet. "This Chanan man. I told you I've never met him. And I can't believe Ron would have turned on us like that."

"Maybe he didn't turn. Maybe he was pushed, or gently nudged. He was tired of being your husband's errand boy—he wanted to open his own studio, in London. That takes a lot of money. Chanan said he knew you from when you danced in Las Vegas."

Erica was rising and falling on the balls of her feet, as if to strengthen her calf muscles. "How do you know all of this? Who have you been talking to?"

"Everybody I can. I looked at the *Sir Charles*, Erica. A man who knows tells me it could leave the Corinthian Yacht Club and be in Sausalito, where they found Ron's body, in a few minutes."

"Where are you going with this, Carroll? You're ruining the morning. We're here to have a good time."

"I'm worried about you. I spoke to the man who sold Charles the Picasso—*Girl with Red Flower*. I'm sure Ron Maleuw filled you in on all of this. It's hanging in some gentleman's bedroom in London. Your husband will find it. And then he'll find out how it got there."

She almost lost her temper, but she sank back onto the bed and went back to being a beautiful, inviting temptress.

"I still can't believe that Ron would have done something like that to my husband. Charles treated him like family." She patted the mattress. "Sit, darling. Tell me what else you've found out."

"Maleuw's murder wasn't planned very well. It was sloppy. Mistakes were made."

She started that finger thing again, pulling up my sweatshirt and running a nail along my belt line. "What kinds of mistakes?"

"It was rushed, Erica. Things never go well when they're rushed. Ron's autopsy showed that he was drunk, as well as full of Valium, yet his Jaguar was parked a few blocks from where the body was found."

"Maybe he drove there, then got drunk and took the pills," she said with silky reasonableness.

"And then staggered down to the dock and took a swan dive into the bay? In a tuxedo? That was another mistake. The killers wanted it to look as if Maleuw had been on the way to the museum, with the painting. Dumb move."

Erica pulled her sweater over her head and surfaced like a swimmer breaking water. She wasn't wearing a bra. "Why was that so dumb, darling?"

"Maleuw wasn't going to deliver the Picasso to the museum, Erica, because it was a fake. The former owner would have proved this to your husband, and then there would have been hell to pay. Sir Charles would have screamed bloody murder, and then everyone would have known what was going on."

"What *was* going on, Carroll?"

"There was more than the one Picasso, wasn't there, Erica? How many other of Sir Charles's paintings have been forged and the originals sold on the black market? Or were they put away for a rainy day, like after Sir Charles dies. Now your husband will have them all checked—by experts."

"Well then, it might be a good thing that Ronnie took his own life. I don't think he would have enjoyed going to jail. They say they do all kinds of nasty things to good-looking men there, so you had better be careful."

I had to hand it to her; she was one cool customer. I had to hand it to myself, too. Somehow, I was keeping my eyes above her neck level. "Picking the spot to leave Maleuw's body was another mistake. It might have seemed like a good idea at the time—an alleged suicide, the body found close to where a woman who also knew your husband supposedly took her own life."

"Charles was very upset about that. He thought that somehow his newfound God was punishing him for his past deeds by killing off his friends and lovers." She picked up the wine bottle and dribbled some bubbly over her breasts. "Who was behind all of this, Carroll? Your Mr. Chanan?"

"No. Not that I wouldn't put a murder or two past him. It was someone who saw Maleuw every day, worked with him, encouraged him, someone who was going to be shortchanged when Sir Charles died and all those valuable artworks were given away."

Erica ran a finger across her wet breasts, then put it in her mouth and made sucking sounds.

"Junior," she said after smacking her lips. "He is a contemptible little shit, isn't he?"

"I wouldn't argue with you there, but Junior's no killer. George looks like a man who might enjoy getting a man drunk, then taking him out on a little cruise, jumping in the bay with him, and holding him under water until he died. Depositing the body on the beach. Was that planned, or was Ron just supposed to bob up and down until someone found him? If I was making a movie out of this, I'd have George anchor the *Sir Charles* in Richardson Bay, a few hundred yards from shore, do the dirty deed, then ferry the body to the beach. I'd have George wearing a wet suit, like the one I saw on the stern of the *Sir Charles*. I'd have him wearing a scuba tank and mask, too, so he could drag the body down to the bottom and rough it up against the bay floor. The water's not very deep close to shore, twenty or thirty feet. If a boat came near, all George would have to do would be submerge."

"This is not very interesting, Carroll," Erica complained. "You're making a complete fool of yourself."

"Maybe, but let's continue with my movie plot. George is an ex–Royal Marine, a man who keeps himself in good shape. Still, he's no kid; all of this would tire him out. He'd still have to swim all the way back to the catamaran. So what does he do? Takes Ulla's red kayak for the trip. That's a nice touch. We don't know what happens to it after he's back on the *Sir Charles*. Maybe he puts a hole in it and it sinks to the bottom. Maybe that's what he's hoping, that the police will send out diving teams and they'll find the kayak—another link to Vicky. What I can't quite get into the script is how he would lure Maleuw to the Corinthian Yacht Club. Ron certainly wouldn't make the trip in his tuxedo. It would be there on the boat, waiting for him."

Erica shook her lovely head from side to side and gave me a condescending smile. "I told you that George isn't that clever, Carroll."

"I agree. He had to have had help. From you."

Her eyes shifted over my shoulder. "He is very tough, though, darling."

I started to turn, but I didn't get very far. Something big and hard crashed into the back of my skull. I sank to my knees, then toppled over onto the carpet, my head landing on one of Erica's boots before everything went black.

Twenty-nine

*I*t was the pain that woke me up. When my eyes began to focus, I saw the blurry faces of George Mandan, Erica Talbot, and Freeze Chanan. A trifecta of evil. My glasses were still hanging by the cord around my neck.

George slapped me across the face and Chanan, said, "Wake up, pally. It's time for a drink."

He was wearing one of his light blue puff-sleeve shirts. Erica was still topless.

George gave me another whack—this one jarred me down to the soles of my feet.

"Take it easy," Chanan told him. "We don't want to leave the wrong marks on his kisser."

George backed off a foot or so, and I was able to get my bearings. I couldn't have been out very long, because I was still in Erica's bedroom, sitting up on the bed. The only reason I was sitting was that George had a hold of my hair with one of his hands. He released me and mumbled something I couldn't understand.

"You're such a disappointment, Carroll," Erica said with what seemed like sincerity.

"Send George and Chanan away, and we can discuss this over a martini."

That got me another whack from George.

"Leave him alone," Chanan said. "I want this done right."

"I thought you were in London, George." I slowly raised an arm and patted the back of my head. It was damp with blood. He whacked me across the face with an open hand.

"I told you to leave him alone," Chanan said.

"Fuck you, old man," George responded before sending an extended knuckle into my right ear.

Chanan picked something up from the bed—Erica's white sweater. He moved behind George, and then there was the bark of a gun. Two shots. George straightened up for a moment, like a soldier standing to attention, then toppled to the floor.

Erica screamed, and one of the horses outside made loud whinnying noises.

She ran to the window. "God, you've scared Calico!"

She certainly had her priorities straight. George had to be dead, I figured, but that was nothing compared to spooking a horse.

Chanan waved the bloody sweater at me. "This is the right way to do it, pally. You gotta have something to stop the blood from squirting on you." He showed me his gun, a snub-nosed revolver. "And you should always use a belly gun like this. A silencer is nice, but that can only be used with a semiautomatic, and the damn things jam all the time. Two shots are all you need—through the spine: one at the back of the neck, the other mid-chest, to blow out the heart. The bullets should be wadcutters, so they break apart and don't go right through the guy. Warner Brothers hired me to help them with one of those Clint Eastwood *Dirty Harry* flicks. I tried to set them straight, but they wanted Harry to carry a gun that could blast a hole through a tank and whoever was on the other side of it."

Chanan was talking like someone bragging about his golf game.

"Did you have to kill him?" Erica asked, looking disgustedly at her bloody sweater.

"Sooner or later, baby. George was a problem. I told you that." Chanan dropped the sweater onto the bed. "Drink your beer, pally, and, Erica, go and get him another one. Might as well bring me one, too."

Erica opened a closet door and took out a lavender blouse. "I want to see how the horses are doing."

"The beers first, baby."

She put on her boots, then stomped out of the room.

"Great rack on that broad," Chanan said, "but she's not too swift." He nudged George's body with his foot. "She's strong. The two of you shouldn't have any trouble dragging him downstairs."

I picked up the beer and took a much-needed swallow. "I have to admit, you surprised me, Freeze. How long have you been involved in this scam?"

"Not long, a couple of days. I told you I was going to look into Maleuw. When I found he was a loser, and had access to all those paintings, I put everything together. His body being dumped right by Vicky's place. You were right. That was a dumb move. Erica tells me it was George's idea, but I'm betting it was hers."

"Let me guess what's going to happen. You're going to get me drunk, then drop me off a cliff, or drown me in one of Talbot's swimming pools. Isn't that going to look a little suspicious? Vicky and Maleuw were both full of booze and pills when they died."

"Nah, that's more amateur stuff, Quint. Remember, I'm a real pro."

I learned forward slowly. My head hurt with every movement. "Is that how you killed Johnny Sands? A couple of shots in his back?"

"The Sandman thought he was untouchable. I touched him real good, pally."

"What about Vicky? Did you touch her, too?"

"Not me, but I know who did. I'm going to make that someone cough up a lot of dough, and I'm also going to get my hands on her *Payback* book. I'm going to make a lot of money out of that baby. How's that grab you, pally?"

Erica came back with two bottles of beer. "We had nothing to do with the old lady's death."

"She's right about that," Chanan said. "Did you ever figure it out?"

"No. But you did?"

"Sure. I keep telling you, I'm a professional. It was the phone calls, pally."

"Who killed Vicky?"

Chanan scratched his chin with the butt of the revolver. "Ask her when you see her on the other side. Erica, get a blanket or something and cover up Georgie boy. I don't want him leaking all over the place."

She went to the closet, and came out with an orange blanket, which she draped over the body.

"You did kill Maleuw, didn't you?" I asked her. "You and George."

"George, not me," she said, handing Chanan his beer.

Chanan said, "Your movie scenario was pretty good, Quint. Except from what Erica told me, Georgie boy didn't drown the guy in the bay. He did it right on the old man's yacht. Filled a few buckets with bay water, dumped it in the sink, then put Maleuw's head under. Not bad. I never would have thought of that. But the rest of it was stupid." He turned his head toward Erica. "You should have just taken him on a boat ride and dumped the body, or buried him here; Christ, there's a million places to hide a stiff on this property." He swiveled back to me. "Drink up. I don't want you drunk, but I want the blood count to show that you had a couple of beers."

I stuck the tip of my tongue into the bottle, then pretended I was swallowing. When I pulled my lips away, I said, "I'm curious about one thing, Erica. How did you get Maleuw on board the *Sir Charles*?"

She glanced at Chanan, as if asking permission to speak.

"Go ahead, tell him. We've got a few minutes to kill."

Unfortunately, Chanan was planning on killing more than just a few minutes. Erica folded her arms across her chest and cupped her elbows in her palms. "Ron called that morning. He was in a panic because he'd found out Charles had been told the real Picasso was hanging on the wall of some London flat. He was talking about telling Charles the truth about the other paintings. I told him to meet me at the boat, that I'd bring the Picasso forgery he'd painted. He was hysterical when he arrived. George and I tried to calm him down; we gave him a few drinks. Ron started crying. George slapped him around a bit, made him swallow some pills, then drowned him in the sink."

"Why the tuxedo?"

"It was in Ron's Jaguar. I thought that it would look like he'd been on his way back to the museum with the painting. George drove the Jag over to Sausalito, parked it, and I picked him up. Then we went back to the boat, and I returned to Napa to get ready for the museum party. George took care of Ronnie."

"I still don't get it, Erica. Your husband was bound to find out about the forgeries sooner or later."

"*Later* is the key word, darling. Charles has several years of life ahead of him, according to his doctors, and they are very good doctors. He could divorce me before that. Leave me with nothing. George would do anything I asked him to. He knew about Charles's latest will, which left him with just a small pension. And Ron was fed up with working for small change. He showed me one of Charles's watercolors, a small Monet, that he'd copied. I couldn't tell the difference. He laughed and said neither could Charles. That was the start of it. It was easy, really. Ron was the only one, with the exception of my husband, who knew exactly what was in the collection. He picked which paintings to forge, ones that Charles seldom looked at."

"How many are there?" I asked.

"Twenty-four," Chanan said. "A damn nice collection. I won't have any trouble selling the real paintings."

"What about *Girl with Red Flower*? Why was that sold?"

Chanan rapped me on the head with the butt of the gun. "Drink up. You're running out of time."

I took a long swallow. The bottle was half-empty. That and the full one Erica had brought were all I had left. I was trying to milk it for as long as possible.

Erica had no such problem. She poured herself a glass of the champagne and downed it without her lips leaving the glass.

"The Picasso was Ron's fault," she said. "He needed money, a lot of money. He was a lousy lover, and a worse gambler. He had debts, and then there was this fantasy of opening his own gallery. He traded the painting without my knowledge, exchanged it for a Utrillo of a Paris street scene, and sold that one for two hundred thousand dollars. Cash."

Chanan pointed the revolver at me. "Chugalug, pally."

I finished the beer, and he handed me the full one. "Now, listen to me real good, Quint. Who else knows about your theory on all of this, and who knows you're here?" He stuck a finger up in the air. "You've got one chance, just one. If I find out you've lied to me, I going to send your mother to the Motel Deep Six, and I may have some fun with her before I pull the trigger, get it?"

I got it all right. "No one knows, Freeze. I wasn't sure of it myself; I was just trying to see what I could get Erica to say."

My confession seemed to please him. "Good. This crazy deal is messy enough. Erica, go get some rope. We can bundle George up and bury him out by that quarry. Quint can do the digging, so put a shovel in the Jeep."

Erica looked like she was about to protest, but she changed her mind and hurried out of the room.

"Quit stalling, Quint. Finish the beer."

I took a long pull on the bottle. Funny how good a beer can taste when you think it may be your last one. "No one is going to miss George, Freeze, but if I disappear, people are going to ask questions."

"Let them ask. Accidents happen all the time. While you were out cold, Erica told me that you can barely hang on to a horse. People fall from them and die every day. Put the beer down, and wrap George up nice and tight. I don't want any trail of blood in here."

Chanan read my mind. I had the beer bottle by the neck, ready to throw it at him.

"You try anything funny, and your mother will pay hell for it."

I set the bottle on the floor, then knelt down next to George's body. I pulled up the blanket; he was lying facedown, arms akimbo. I put a hand under his shoulder, figuring I would have to turn him completely

260

over to wrap him in the blanket. My hand touched something sharp and cold. One of Erica's spurs.

I grunted as I made motions to turn the body over. "Hey. He's still alive. He's breathing."

"What? He can't be." Chanan stooped down to take a closer look.

I wrapped my right hand around the spur, put my left hand under George's shoulder, and pulled as hard as I could. The body flipped over, and Freeze stared at George's face for a second. It was all the time I had. I lunged at him. The revolver went off. I had no idea where the bullet ended up, but the silver wheel of the spur hit his face in an upward arc, sending a spray of blood into the air.

Freeze dropped the gun, his hands going to his bloody face. I hit him as hard as I could with an elbow to his chin, and he tumbled backward onto the bed, screaming loudly for Erica.

I scooped up the snub-nosed revolver, got my glasses on, and started for the stairs. Erica was at the bottom level, with a big cowboy gun in her hand. I snapped off a shot at her. She returned fire, and I ran back to the bedroom and over to the open window. I tucked Chanan's gun into my waistband and climbed out onto the roof. It was ten feet to the ground below.

A jump would have been the quick way, but I didn't want to break an ankle. I eased myself over the roof, dangled from my arms, then hit the ground with a thud.

I ran toward the horses. Adios wanted no part of me, backing away every time I tried to get near him, and the rifle in the saddle scabbard.

Freeze had mentioned a Jeep. I knew I had to get to it before Erica and Freeze did. I started to run toward the back of the house, figuring that's where the Jeep would be. I'd gone about ten feet when a gun when off. Erica was at the window, the long-barreled cowboy pistol in hand.

Chanan was next to her, holding a towel to his face. "Kill him! Kill him!" he yelled.

I zigzagged back to the horses, hiding behind Adios's bulk. He started snorting and rearing up on his hind legs. I moved over to

Calico, undid the reins tied to the Hercule Poirot jockey, and climbed into the saddle. Her eyes were no longer sad. They were wide with fear. I jabbed my heels into her side, but she wouldn't move. Another gunshot from the bungalow. I pulled Chanan's gun from my waistband and aimed a shot in the direction of the window.

That was all Calico needed. She started to buck, then took off like a shot. I tucked the gun away and held on to the reins and her mane as tightly as I could. I had no idea where she was heading, probably back to the stable. I'd somehow have to try to steer her to the main house, and my car. I had my cell phone in my jeans, but there was no way I could use it and stay in the saddle.

Trees whizzed by; branches snapped at my face. *Bam, bam, bam,* the saddle was hitting my butt like—you'll excuse the expression—a pile driver.

We galloped very close to the edge of the quarry. I turned in the saddle and saw a Jeep catching up with us. Erica was standing up, a rifle braced against the open window. Chanan was behind the wheel.

They were gaining ground, and the only reason I could think of as to why Erica wasn't blasting away at me was that she didn't want to hit the horse.

We crossed a rocky area, and then Calico headed toward the ravine. The Jeep was within twenty yards of us. I could hear the engine roaring. I tried hunching over, keeping my face almost on Calico's neck.

A shot. The bullet whizzed by us, scaring the hell out of me, and Calico, too. She increased her speed and veered to the right, heading for the rough terrain.

I could see a gully coming up, a span of six or seven feet. If Calico kept up her pace, we'd run into it at full speed. I had a death grip on the reins. I pulled back on them and yelled out the only horse word I knew: "Whoa!"

Calico wasn't paying any attention to me. I took a quick look at the Jeep. It was right behind us. Erica was shouting something at Freeze Chanan.

We went straight for the gully, and Calico jumped. I had my eyes closed. There was a final bang of butt against saddle; then I was flying free in the air. I landed in a clump of low-lying shrubs.

I heard the sound of squealing brakes. The Jeep was coming toward me. The front end hit the edge of gully and careened out of control. The vehicle rolled over several times before coming to a wobbly stop and landing upside down.

Erica had been thrown free. She lay in a fetal position some fifteen feet from the Jeep. I approached cautiously, Chanan's gun in hand. When I was six feet from her body, I knew she was dead. Her head was at an awkward angle and had been squashed almost flat; one of her beautiful long legs had been nearly torn from its socket.

That left Chanan. I crept toward the Jeep. It was resting on its roll bar. The two back wheels were spinning slowly. The engine was still running, and I worried about an explosion.

Freeze Chanan was hanging upside down. His head resting on the ground. There was blood everywhere. I was within a few feet of the Jeep when his head moved toward me. So did his hand. It was holding the cowboy gun.

I pointed the revolver at his face. "Try anything, and I'll blow you to hell, Chanan."

His lips peeled back, revealing blood-coated teeth. "Quint, you stupid amateur. I shot Georgie twice, I missed you with one, you shot at Erica in the house—that's four—then you tried to hit us at the window. That's five, pally, and that's all there is. It's a Smith & Wesson five-shot Chief's Special. So you're holding an empty gun."

I aimed the revolver at his hand. I figured I couldn't miss at this distance. Even after all he'd done, and the threats he'd made about my mother, I just couldn't kill him. But the thought of blowing off his hand didn't bother me a bit. I pulled the trigger. There was a clicking noise.

Chanan started to laugh, a deep chest-gurgling sound. Blood flew from his lips.

I moved in, took the cowboy gun from his hand. "Vicky. You said you know who killed her, Freeze. Who was it?"

"Closer," he whispered, then started hacking up blood again.

"Who?" I said, my face almost nuzzling his.

Then Chanan said his dying words: "Fuck you, pally."

Thirty

The next few days were busy ones. As soon as Freeze Chanan had given me his profane send-off, I'd used the cell phone to call 911. The next call was to Katherine Parkham at the *Bulletin*.

The Great was at her best during a crisis. She dispatched two reporters, Al Doyle, the paper's photographer, three uniformed security guards, and Mark Selden to Talbot's place.

For once, Selden came in handy, because the police weren't too friendly. They had me down as the number-one suspect in the death of George Mandan. The gun was in my possession, and there were powder burns to prove that I'd fired the weapon.

It took a trip to the Napa County jail to sort things out. I spent nearly three hours in a holding cell, listening to my cell mate, Stanley, a burly guy with muttonchops, bloodshot eyes, and a matching shirt. His arms were brocaded with tattoos from his wrists to where they disappeared into the sleeves of his ugly shirt. Once he'd determined that I wasn't a stoolie, he regaled me with information on just how and where to buy the best dope in town.

Stanley seemed impressed about my movie reviewer credentials, and informed me that the best flick ever made, "bar none," was Al Pacino's version of *Scarface*. He drooled into his muttonchops when talking about the way the bad guys used a chain saw on Pacino's buddy. "Pure video poetry," according to Stanley.

Selden brought in reinforcements—Jim Biernat, a top-notch criminal attorney. I'd leave the cell, go to a nearby room full of cops, stenographers, and various members of the district attorney's office, then go back and listen to Stan the Man tell me more about the local dope scene.

By the time Biernat sprang me for good, I was tired, hungry, thirsty, and, truth be told, somewhat in a state of shock. I was worried that I might have suffered a concussion in the fall from Calico. Oh, and if you're wondering, Calico made out just fine. She returned to the barn with nary a scratch, which couldn't be said for me.

The police had dispatched an ambulance; I was given a quick examination and told that nothing was broken. The ambulance crew and two of the cops were much more concerned about Calico than about me.

It reminded me of a story from years ago. I was just a kid at the time. Some IRA terrorists had set off lethal nail bombs near Buckingham Palace during the Changing of the Guard. The bombs injured more than fifty people, killed eleven of the Queen's Calvary, and seven of their horses. It had all been captured on film, and the bloody scenes were shown on TV worldwide. I'd watched it with my father, and made note of the fact that when the TV crews spoke to people on the street, the main reaction was great sympathy for the horses: "I can understand them killing the guards, but why did they have to hurt the horses?"

I asked Dad why anyone would put the lives of horses above those of human beings. He gave me one of his usual blunt answers: "They're morons, son."

I found Katherine the Great waiting for me with a stretch limousine, which had a full bar and goodies she'd ordered from her favorite Napa restaurant, Celadon. I knelt down—sitting was a problem—and gorged myself on calamari, pasta, and Kobe beef. In between bites and sips of wine, I related to Parkham and Rosie, the Great's secretary, what had happened at Talbot's place. The two of them had the story put together by the time we arrived back at the *Bulletin*.

I was treated like a hero—by most. Terry Greco was somewhat heartbroken that Ronald Maleuw had turned out to be a no-goodnik, and my mother's only response was, "That's all well and good, Carroll.

But you still owe me a dinner, and you didn't do what I asked you to—find out who killed Vicky."

She was right. I had no clue. Freeze Chanan had said he'd figured it out from the phone calls. I typed out from memory the names on Vicky's phone bill, which Chanan had shown me, and was satisfied that it was complete. There was nothing suspicious there: liquor store, beauty shop, calls to her neighbors: Della Rugerio, Bert and Mary Tucker. And then there were the ones to St. Agnes. Father James Carmody had inherited half of Vicky's estate, and he'd been given a $100,000 check by Sir Charles. Following the money led straight to him, or Della Rugerio.

I visited Carmody in Sausalito, and he told me that the money from Vicky's estate would follow Talbot's check—directly to the Catholic bishop's office. That left Della. I couldn't get her to come to the door at her place, and telephone calls to her there weren't picked up, even when I used a phony accent and said I was dying for a psychic reading and a Clark Cleansing.

Maybe Chanan had just been putting me on, bragging about his being "a pro" to a man he was about to kill. Maybe Vicky had indeed taken her own life. I was resigned to the fact that I'd never find out.

Three days after the Napa episode, the Great summoned me to her office. She was in a good mood when I arrived. I was rewarded with coffee, cookies, promises of a raise, and the blessed news that I was no longer a crime reporter. "Go back to the showbiz crap, if you want to, Quint."

She had more news. "Sir Charles Talbot was here this morning. He's quite grateful about what you did."

My heart jumped several beats. Grateful. A small Picasso? One of his modern paintings, perhaps a Franz Kline skid mark like the one hanging on the Great's wall? Something I could sell for big bucks, and live happily ever after.

"So grateful that he's offering you a job: entertainment editor of the newspaper he's purchasing, and he says that the offer he made you for Ms. Kjeldsen's manuscript still stands."

"Talbot's buying the *Bulletin*? He promised me that he wouldn't do—"

"Not the *Bulletin*. The *Herald*."

It took a few moments for that to settle in between my ears. The *San Francisco Herald* was our biggest rival.

"As for the job offer, he'll pay you more money than I can," Parkham said. "So there will be no hard feelings if you accept the offer."

"Not a chance, boss. I'm happy right here."

And I was. Back in the saddle, so to speak. I left her office and went to my cubicle, settling my backside gently into the two pillows on my chair. The Calico Kid was still suffering from that long, hard ride.

I was catching up on E-mails, checking invites to screenings, and, all in all, having a good time, when a cheerful voice drawled, "Hi there, Mr. Quint. Y'all are famous now, for sure. We've been readin' all about you."

Mary Tucker was beaming down at me. Her hair was done up nicely, and she was wearing a powder blue pantsuit that looked great on her.

She was holding a shoe box. She handed it to me. "Bert said to give it to you."

I took the box, which had once held New Balance walking shoes, size ten and a half medium.

"There's some pictures in there," Mary explained. "The ones ol' Bert was taking of Ulla. Some of them are kinda risqué, if you know what I mean. He's got one of those little home digital-photo developers. I wouldn't want him takin' those things to the drugstore for prints."

"Thanks, Mary. Where is Bert?"

"Oh, he's with that woman you said would review his book, Terry Greco." Her eyes widened. "I bet Bert wishes *she* lived within telescope range of us."

"I stopped by to talk to Della Rugerio, but she wasn't around."

"Nah. I hear she's moving, buying a house in San Francisco. I think she's afraid someone will kick old Caribbean Joe into the bay and drown him. Can you imagine leaving all that money to a silly cat? Oh, well, I gotta go shopping and spend some of Bert's money. I hear that Bloomingdale's is having a pisser of a sale. See ya."

I made sure Mary was out of hearing range before letting out a loud groan. Bert dumping his manuscript on Terry. She'd been avoiding me of late, and siccing Bert on her wasn't going to help the situation.

I opened the shoe box. There were groups of four-by-six-inch photos rubber-banded together. I began sifting through them.

Most showed Vicky working out in her home gym: she wore shorts and a halter, sometimes just the shorts. There were numerous pics of her naked, just walking around, or holding a cell phone, seemingly looking directly up at Bert's camera.

Then there were the ones where she and a man were having sex—on the gym mat, on her weight bench. The participants were people I'd never seen before: young men, middle-aged men, and a few who had to be Vicky's age. I went through the rest of the batch. There were three that showed her with Father Carmody. Both of them were fully dressed. The next picture showed Vicky and a man with a craggy face and a shock of steel gray hair that flopped over his forehead. Harry Baum, the Realtor and former partner of Vicky's ex-husband, Arnold Ramsey. I recognized his face from the photo on his Web site.

When I'd talked to him on the phone, Baum had told me he didn't know that Vicky had been living in Sausalito. I'd told him who I was, and that I worked for the *San Francisco Bulletin*. I tried to remember what the hell it was he'd said. 'Is she living down there now?' That was it. And he claimed he didn't know she'd changed her name from Vicky Ramsey to Ulla Kjeldsen.

I went through the shoe-box portfolio and found that there was just that one picture of Vicky and Baum. I took a magnifying glass from the desk drawer and studied the photo closely. Bert had caught them both in profile. Baum's face had a stern look on it. Vicky, in her shorts and halter outfit, was holding a piece of paper in one hand, pointing it at Baum. A page from her *Payback* manuscript? It looked like they were having an argument. About what? I wondered. Arnold's estate? Or maybe there was—

A sudden slamming sound made me jump out of the chair. Terry Greco was glaring at me, her hands on her hips, her jaw thrust out.

269

"You told that goofy old man that I was going to read *that*?"

That had to be the thick pile of papers that she'd slammed on my desk. Bert Tucker's manuscript.

"*The Michelangelo Cipher*. Catchy title, Terry."

She looked as if she was about to pick up the manuscript and bat me on the head with it, so I quickly added, "Look, I didn't tell him you'd read it now, but I suggested that you might look at the book if and when it's published, which is never going to happen. Bert's a nice old guy, and he and his wife are helping me on Vicky Vandamn's murder. They live right next door to her houseboat."

Terry tapped her foot on the floor and simmered down a bit. "All right. But you give the damn thing back to him. I'm going out to lunch."

"I'm available," I told her. "And hungry."

She nibbled on her lower lip, and I thought I had scored a date, but she said no, she had some shopping to do, but that maybe we could have a drink after work.

That sounded so good to me, I almost told her about the "pisser of a sale" at Bloomingdale's.

I studied the photo of Vicky and Harry Baum again, my mind reeling with questions. Why had Baum lied to me? How often had he seen Vicky? I explored several possibilities, the juiciest one being that it had been Baum who'd killed her. If so, how could I prove it? And if so, was Baum the one who Freeze Chanan had pegged as Vicky's killer? "It was the phone calls, pally." Chanan had bragged to me that he could get anyone's phone records, even mine. Had he used his contact to pick up Baum's telephone records? The list of numbers from Vicky's cell phone bill had come from his "contact." How had the contact gotten the list to Freeze?

I wandered down to the second floor and into the lair of Josh Hickey, the paper's electronics wizard. Josh's office was bigger than anyone's in the building, with the exception of the Great's. It was jammed with boxes containing computers, television sets, digital cameras, printers, scanners, PlayStaions—in short, every electronic gadget known to man, or at least to a man who got them for free, the donors hoping their products would be reviewed in the *Bulletin.* Josh was too honest to sell the goodies after he'd given them a look-see; however, he was happy to barter them away for whatever was offered. Over the years, I'd picked up a home PC, software, and some phones in exchange for tickets to plays. He had boasted to me that he could crack anyone's E-mail account or answering machine in a few minutes. It was time to put him to the test.

Josh was a self-admitted nerd, but he didn't fit the stereotype. He was six three, had linebacker shoulders, a face that looked like it came from a recruiter's poster for the Hell's Angels, and dark shoulder-length hair, with bangs that reached to his eyebrows.

He greeted me warmly. "Hey, Carroll. Just the man I was looking for. I see that they're bringing a new production of *Chicago* to the Orpheum Theatre. I could use two good seats." He slid past a pile large of boxes, heading for one of the shelves jammed with smaller boxes. "I've got a new cell-phone watch with a high-def camera that will knock you out. And if you're interested in a—"

"I'm interested in cracking somebody's E-mail records, Josh."

Hickey hitched up his pants and said, "That would be, like, illegal."

"But you told me that there are ways to do it."

"Yeah, the software is designed to be used only by law-enforcement agencies."

"Three tickets, opening night, Josh. Way up front."

"Hmmm. I could show you how it's done, purely as an instructional safeguard, only so that your can protect your own mailbox, however." He made a motion with his flattened hand, dropping it between us like a shutter or screen. "Absolutely no one is to know about it, right?"

"Right."

"Do you have physical access to the target's computer?"

"No. Just the E-mail address. Is that a problem?"

"It makes it a little more difficult." He moved to the door, shut it, locked it, then made his way to his desk, which was littered with three phones, four computers, and an assortment of blinking white-and-black-cased boxes of various sizes.

"Give me what you've got, Carroll."

I handed him the business card Chanan had given me that night at Wiley Lee's restaurant.

He looked at the card, on which was printed Chanan's E-mail address: Freeze@cyespace.com.

"What the hell does this guy do? Sell refrigerators?"

"Nope. Private investigator."

Josh's fingers began clicking away at a keyboard. "The first thing we do is access his E-mail provider." He pushed his bangs away from his forehead, did some more clicking, and said, "Okay, we're into the provider. Do you have any clue about what type of password he'd use?"

I thought about that, almost said no, but then came up with "Pally." I spelled it out. "He called everyone 'pally.' "

Josh went back to the keyboard, while telling me things about using a "rat," which was a Trojan virus, and something about an Optix Pro download, which went way over my head. After about five minutes, Josh smiled and leaned back in his chair. "Here we go, Carroll." He made a few final clicks and the computer made sounds like someone riffing a deck of cards very fast.

"Bingo," Josh said. "Write this down." He recited Chanan's password—a bunch of numbers and "pally." "Now, if you want to commit a felony, like getting into his mail, do it on your own computer."

I went back to my cubicle, booted up the computer, and, feeling rather slimy about the whole thing, entered Freeze Chanan's electronic mailbox.

There was just one entry in Chanan's mailbox: from a Lexus dealer in Palm Springs. I checked his junk mail: a stock option offer he shouldn't pass up; a ten-dollar gift certificate from onlineshoes.com; and an announcement from someone named Blondie, offering him an amateur porn video featuring girls "just barely legal."

I fluttered my lips in frustration. I'd broken into Chanan's E-mail, and there was no there there. I was ready to exit, when I saw that there was something in his trash file. I opened it and found a message from BBCBB. "Subject: mabells & cr." The message began with "$2,600."

What followed was an invoice: "Kjeldsen, r—$200, cr—$200, c—$200; Talbot, r—$200, c—$200; Carmody, r—$200; Rugerio, r—$200; Quint, r—$200, c—$200; Baum, r—$200, b—$200, c—$200, cr—$200.

Mabells meant old Ma Bell—phone records. I figured the letter *r* had to stand for residence; *c* for cell phone; and *b* for business. The *cr*—credit card? Chanan had paid his source $2,600 for the information. Eight hundred of that was spent on Harry Baum. Now the trick was to find the records in Chanan's files.

Josh could have probably done it in seconds, but it took me awhile to figure it out. I opened the box to send a message, typed in my E-mail address in the "To" slot and "I hope this works" in the subject slot. Next, I clicked on the attachment file, which offered me the option of attaching pictures, documents, or contact information. I browsed through Chanan's "Documents" file and was shown everything. It had been so damn easy. I vowed to find a way to protect my own files from ruthless, unscrupulous snoops like me when this was all over.

It took some twenty minutes of plundering Chanan's documents before I found the one I wanted: BBCBB: 0.006 megabytes. The Ma Bell mother lode. I attached this document to the E-mail I was composing and hit the send button.

Thirty-one

I thought that I had developed enough information from my Internet sleuthing to nail Harry Baum. You watch those TV cop shows were they have all the latest electronic wonders: Jack Bauer uses them to save his whiny, ungrateful daughter, his latest lover, his best friend, in fact the whole damn world, and all in twenty-four hours. The various CSI and cold-case units solve homicides that took place back when FDR was president—merely by finding a strand of hair, a fingerprint on a buried teacup, or a single drop of blood on a rusty bathroom pipe. Ah, but real life is—as always—so much different.

In nearby Oakland, the police had to handle close to 150 homicides a year—a tough enough assignment, made much tougher due to the fact that, while they still took fingerprints at the scene of the crime, the department's crime lab had been shut down for lack of money and staff. The cops were so fed up, they didn't even bother to submit the prints for departmental analysis! The message was clear: Want to get rid of grouchy Aunt Martha and rich old Uncle Herman? Bring 'em to Oakland for a weekend.

The Sausalito Police Department didn't have such problems, because they didn't tolerate homicides within city limits.

I approached Detective Manners with the photograph of Harry Baum with Vicky, and—from Freeze Chanan's computer—the list of Baum's phone calls to her, Baum's credit-card bill, showing that he'd hopped a flight to SFX the day before Vicky's death and then flown back to Vancouver on the red-eye the morning after.

Manners's response was not the one I was looking for. She was ready to call in the Royal Mounted Police and have them lock *me* up. She moved the documents around on the top of her desk with the eraser end of a pencil, so as not to come into personal contact with them.

"Where did you get this information, Quint? Credit and phone records are off-limits. You could go to jail for this."

"Freeze Chanan gave them to me," I told her, which, in a way, wasn't a *big* lie. "But forget the source. Go with the information. Harry Baum told me he had no idea that Vicky Vandamn had been living in Sausalito, and he acted as if he'd never heard the name Ulla Kjeldsen before, yet he'd spoken to her a dozen times, and flown here to meet with her the day before she died."

Manners flicked the photograph with her pencil. "Did Mr. Chanan happen to tell you when this was taken? It could have been anytime in the last year, for all we know."

I had checked with Bert Tucker. He couldn't remember when he'd taken the picture.

"Detective, Chanan told me that he knew who the killer was and that he was putting the screws to him for money—and Ulla's manuscript."

"Did he tell you *directly* that Harry Baum was the killer?"

"No, but—"

"And isn't Mr. Chanan one of the three people who died in Napa as a direct result of your actions? I spoke to a friend in the Napa County sheriff's department, Quint. They're still not satisfied with their investigation. You'll be talking to them again."

"Harry Baum was here in Sausalito the night Ulla—"

"You can't prove that." She tapped the eraser against the credit-card records. "These records show charges for a round-trip flight from Vancouver to San Francisco and back. He could have been visiting a friend, or been here on business. There's nothing to prove he was in Kjeldsen's houseboat that day."

"Baum had a motive—money. I spoke to Ed Galvin, the attorney who set up Ulla's living trust."

"I know Mr. Galvin. He has a drinking problem. Three DUI charges in the last two years. He works out of his house, which is mortgaged to the hilt. The IRS is looking at him, too. It seems he either works for cash or barters his services for whatever he needs, and doesn't report the income. We're not talking Perry Mason here, Quint."

"There are conflicts regarding the number of properties she inherited from her ex-husband, Arnold Ramsey. Ramsey and Baum were partners, and the real estate they purchased prior to Ulla marrying Ramsey was jointly owned—Ramsey never bothered to have the title of ownership changed. Ulla filed a civil suit in Victoria, claiming that her husband had planned to have his interest in the properties deeded to her upon his death, but he died before he could get it done. Another interesting coincidence, isn't it?"

Manners rose to her feet and ground the heels of her hands together. "Mr. Quint, I haven't got time to argue with you; Ulla Kjeldsen is officially listed as a suicide. Her body was cremated, her houseboat stripped by Della Rugerio. She wasn't shot, strangled, or cut to pieces. She died of a drug overdose. There is absolutely nothing in the documents you've shown me that could induce me to contact a citizen of Canada about this case. I will do you one favor, however. I won't report you for having illegally obtained the phone and credit-card records. I strongly advise you to destroy them. If Mr. Baum finds out you have them, he could initiate criminal and civil charges. Good-bye."

I wasn't giving up that easily. "Detective, I'm telling you that Harry Baum killed Ulla Kjeldsen."

"Good. Get him to confess, and I'll arrest him."

"If we don't act, he'll get away with murder, Detective."

Manners picked up her purse and slipped it over her shoulder. "Unfortunately, it happens all the time, Quint."

"How would you know?" It was a cold, cruel thing to say, but I was feeling cold and cruel.

I headed back to the *Bulletin*. Katherine Parkham was off on a cruise to Mexico.

I ran my theory and evidence past Mark Selden, who backed away as if I were radioactive. His one bit of input was that attorney Ed Galvin was a "sleazeball." Coming from Selden, that was high praise indeed.

Actually, I had met with Galvin before going to see Manners. He'd treated himself to a breakfast on me at the Lighthouse Café in Sausalito. He seemed to be a likable-enough guy. He was in his fifties, overweight, had a fleshy face and a slightly bulbous nose. Think William Shatner, but with a full head of real hair. Even at 9:00 A.M., there'd been a heavy scent of essence de bourbon about him. He'd told me he was in the process of "hooking up with a Canadian barrister to sue the pants off that bastard Baum."

If I was going to get Baum to follow Detective Kay Manners's instructions and confess to Ulla's murder, I was going to have to get *him* to help me. I'd have to bluff Baum into giving me a confession. No doubt Freeze Chanan would have dubbed Baum "an amateur." But so far, Baum had gotten away with murdering one human being, possibly two. He'd been on an emotional roller-coaster ride: the conflicts with Vicky Vandamn, sweating out the trip to Sausalito to meet with her, then killing her. Then I'd called him from the *Bulletin*, suggesting that Vicky might have been murdered. That had to have shaken him up. Then he'd been contacted by Freeze, and Chanan had really put the screws to him. But good luck jumped back on his side when Chanan was killed. I figured Baum must have been monitoring the Bay Area news, and the deaths of Chanan, Erica Talbot, and George had made all the major wire services.

How had he felt then? Elated? Jubilant? It was like winning the lottery, or getting a reprieve from the governor just as the hangman was slipping the rope around his neck. He was home free. But I had a plan to change that. I was banking on Harry Baum being a physical and mental wreck when I met with him. If not, he'd tell me to go to hell, and there wouldn't be a whole lot I could do about it.

It took me a couple of days, another visit to Josh Hickey's electronic gadget emporium, and the logging of a lot of phone hours from the *Bulletin* to Victoria, but I was finally ready. The final touch was an E-mail I sent Baum from Chanan's server.

It read: "As you probably know, my associate, Mr. Chanan, is dead. The deal with you is still on—the same terms and financial arrangements. If you do not respond to this message, the materials will be turned over to the police. I'll be in Victoria tomorrow."

He responded with a terse "Advise place and time."

It was one of those things that you simply *had* to do—like driving over the Golden Gate Bridge on your first visit to San Francisco; viewing the White House; or buying a phony Rolex on the streets of New York City. I'm talking about having high tea at the Empress Hotel in Victoria, British Columbia. The Empress was really spectacular, a restored 460-room, ivy-clad, copper-turreted Edwardian masterpiece. The tea was no less grand: berries in Chantilly cream, those little English cucumber sandwiches, scones, bite-size pastries with chocolate truffles, and all kinds of delicious gooey things, all served on expensive china, not to mention the elegant silver silverware and the crystal glasses for the six different kinds of fruit juices available. The only downer for me was the tea. I didn't like the stuff, but I thought it would be sacrilegious if I asked for coffee.

I was seated at a bay window overlooking the city's beautiful inner harbor. It had been a two-and-a-half-hour flight from SFX to Vancouver, then a ninety-minute ferry ride over to Victoria. I was munching on a shortbread cookie when I spotted Harry Baum wandering around the luxurious main lobby.

He was wearing a dull gray business suit, much like the one in the photograph, and a muted paisley tie. And he was looking nervous as hell.

When I'd arrived in town, I'd sent Baum another E-mail, advising him to be in the lobby of the Empress at two o'clock in the afternoon, and not to worry about looking for me, that I knew exactly what he looked like.

I wasn't really sure exactly how I'd play it. There had been no photographs of me in the *Bulletin* regarding the recent stories of what had taken place in Napa. I had spoken to Baum briefly on the phone that time, and there was a chance he'd recognize my voice, so I'd practiced speaking in front of a mirror, sucking my cheeks tight against my teeth, which gave me a dry, clipped accent, and saying "pally" every other sentence. I figured if Baum somehow did recognize me, I'd just act like a crooked reporter. Needless to say, I'd known more than my share.

I stood up and waved at him. He had a flat-footed, plodding walk. He waited until I was seated before sitting down across from me.

"Glad you made it, Harry."

Baum looked as nervous as I'd hoped he would. He had a beef and bourbon complexion and a rash around his neck where his shirt had scuffed his skin. Flakes of dandruff coated the shoulders of his his suit. He looked beaten, like a man who hadn't had a good night's sleep in a long time.

"What do I call you? I have a hunch it won't be your real name."

"Jake will do just fine." That was the name my father had chosen for me. My life would have been a hell of a lot easier if Mom hadn't overridden him with Carroll.

One of the white-jacketed servers came over and asked if he wanted tea.

"Coffee, black," Baum said. His eyes moved by degrees around the room. "I've lived in this area all my life, but it's been years since I've been inside the Empress."

"I thought it would be the kind of place that Vicky would have loved," I said. "You saw a lot of her, didn't you?"

He shifted uneasily in his chair. "We had some of the same interests: sailing, poker, fine wines, and—"

"Sex."

"Listen, Jake," Baum said, lowering his voice when the server delivered his coffee. "I don't know who the hell you are, or what you want. So spell it out for me."

"I'll do better than that." I slipped the photograph that Bert Tucker had taken of Baum and Vicky onto the snow-white linen tablecloth.

He picked it up and examined it closely, his face going through a series of emotions—none of them happy.

"There are more, Harry. You'll get them when you give me everything I want."

Baum handed the picture back to me and said, "So I saw Vicky once. This doesn't prove that I harmed her in any way."

"The rest of the pictures are pretty graphic, Harry." I reached into my jacket again and laid out the copies of his phone and credit-card records. "Don't act like a virgin. Freeze told you what we have. You're nailed, Harry. There's a detective in the Sausalito Police Department who will have your ass in front of a grand jury if I give her this."

A sheen of sweat swept across his forehead. He scooped up the picture and documents, stashed them in his suit coat, then pushed his chair back. "Let's get out of here."

I paid for tea—sixty bucks!—then followed Baum through the lobby, out the hotel doors, and into a sunlit afternoon. We crossed a boulevard where red double-decker buses and horse-drawn carriages cruised by, then walked down to a walled off promenade skirting the city's inner harbor. Under most circumstances, it would have been a pleasant stroll: magnificent five-ball cast-iron streetlights, baskets of flowers everywhere, a Ronald McDonald–like clown juggler, a dozen or more artists, with their works displayed against the stone walls.

After a few minutes, and numerous looks over his shoulder, Harry Baum stopped at a small table shaded by a yellow canvas umbrella. He sat silently for a couple of minutes, staring out at the harbor. The moored boats were several steps up from the ones at Harbor Point in Sausalito.

"I don't know what to do," Baum said finally.

"It's simple, Harry. Give me what I want, I'll give you what you want, and the two of us sail happily out to a beautiful sunset."

"For all I know, you're a cop and you're recording all of this."

I spread my arms apart. "Pat me down, pally." I put my cell phone, pen, and keys on the tabletop. "I'm not a cop, and I'm not wired. I'm a businessman, just like Freeze Chanan, and we don't do business with the cops, unless we're forced to, so don't force me."

"So you're not a cop. But you'll come back for more." His gaze turned inward like a blind man's. "Your type always does."

"My type doesn't kill defenseless women, pally." I put my things back in their proper places. "And no, I won't be coming back at you. That's an amateur's play. This is a one-shot deal. You have my word."

He straightened up in his chair. "You can't prove I killed Vicky."

"Sure I can, pally. Though I have to hand it to you. You damn near got away with it. You made a major mistake with the Nembutal, though."

"Is that right?" he said, a little stammer in his voice.

"You didn't think that the Sausalito Police Department would check with the cops up here and find out that Arnold Ramsey had taken a potent prescription drug cocktail before he had his seizure? The autopsy showed that he was taking pills for his epilepsy, and for diabetes, all prescribed medicines, but he didn't have a prescription for Nembutal, Harry, that's a no-no for someone with his medical condition. You overdid it. No wonder the poor bastard had a seizure before you shoved him over that cliff near Lake Cowichan. What did you do? Slip it in his morning pancakes or his coffee before you boys went out fishing? Whose Nembutal pills were they? Yours? Your wife's? I could get into your medical records, Harry, but it would be a waste of my time and money. We both know that you did it."

"That still wouldn't prove anything," Baum croaked.

"It's another peg in your coffin. And not only with the cops. Think what it would do to your life up here, pally. Your wife would dump you, and then she'd have control of those properties you were trying to swindle from Arnold Ramsey."

"*Pally*. You perverts even talk alike."

A street musician dressed like a Gypsy strolled by, his fiddle scratching out "Somewhere My Love."

"I never swindled Arnie out of a dime. Years ago, when we first went into business, we started buying houses, fixing them up, turning them over, reinvesting in more property. I did the majority of the work. We moved up to apartments, commercial buildings, and a shopping mall. We were partners; everything was jointly owned. That was the way he wanted it—the way we both wanted it."

"Then he married Vicky. She knew you killed Arnold, before he could change things, didn't she? Freeze thought so. He had it all down, except for how you got Vicky to swallow the pills. I told him you just got her drunk and dissolved the pills in champagne."

Baum took the photo of him and Vicky from his coat and rubbed his thumb across it roughly, as if he was hoping the images would vanish. "How many more are there?"

"The photographer had a thing for Vicky. He has dozens of them. In most of them, she's having sex. She seemed to have had an insatiable libido."

" 'Dancing.' That's what she called making love. 'Let's dance tonight. Arnie's out of town.' 'Let's take the boat out and dance all night.' 'Come over for a quick dance.' She liked to use ecstasy pills. She told me they made her feel like she was young and in love with whoever she was with; that it allowed 'the life force Chi' to flow freely through her body and soul."

"So she thought the Nembutal was ecstasy?"

"Yes." A tear formed in his left eye and trickled down his cheek. "She had no pain. No pain at all." He blinked his eyes rapidly, then blotted them with a handkerchief. "You're right. Vicky knew I'd killed Arnie. I never actually confessed to her, but she knew. Let's get this over, Jake. I have your money at my office."

"And the manuscript? Freeze wanted to get a look at it. So do I."

"I destroyed the relevant parts. You're welcome to the rest."

"By 'relevant parts,' you mean the ones that concern your killing Arnold Ramsey?"

"Vicky showed the book to me. There was all of this Hollywood garbage, and just a few pages about her coming to Victoria and marrying Arnie. She threatened to go into details about us. And about the other men she went 'dancing' with. It would have ruined a lot of marriages, that's for sure." He let out a sobbing laugh. "We used to talk about it, about Arnie dying, then me divorcing Betty and the two of us getting married. I thought she'd be happy when he was gone. As it turned out, she never loved me. I was just another dancer." He got to his feet slowly, gripping the back of the chair he'd been occupying, his knuckles white. For a moment, I thought he'd fall to the ground.

"You don't look too good, Harry. Tell me: Why did you save Vicky's manuscript?"

"I . . . I thought that if things . . . that if I ever got into trouble, I could use the material in the book for what you're doing to me now. For what Freeze Chanan was going to do."

"Blackmail."

He straightened up a bit, and his eyes gained new life. "I could say that she mailed me the damn book, that she wanted me to help her get it published. There are some dynamite things in there. Maybe we could make a deal, Jake. Truthfully, I'm having trouble coming up with the money. I've only got a few thousand." He was talking in a rush, as if he couldn't get the words out fast enough. "You could make more off of these people than you ever could from me."

"You're probably right, Harry. Let's take a look."

It was only a four-block walk to his office, but it didn't look like Harry was going to make it. I had to steady him several times. It was a nice location for a Realtor, on the ground floor of a stone-front three-story building. A tall, mature woman in a pinstriped pantsuit greeted Harry warmly and told him that there had been no calls for him. He ignored her and led me to his private office. The first thing he did after closing the door was to put the photo and credit-card and phone records through a shredder.

Baum then swung a painting of a Paris street scene away from the wall, revealing a built-in safe. He hunched his shoulders, shielding me from watching him spin the safe's dials. It opened with a loud click.

He reached in and withdrew a mailing envelope lined with bubble wrap. "This is Vicky's *Payback,* on a disc. I shredded the manuscript.

I never believed Vicky could be so vindictive. The things she says in there, if true, are awful."

"What about the money, Harry?"

He compressed his bloodless lips and looked as if he was about to cry. "I told Mr. Chanan the money was a problem." He opened a desk drawer and took out another envelope, much thicker than the first one.

"There's twenty-five thousand dollars there, Jake. I swear to you, it's all I can come up with right now."

It was enough for me. More than enough, in fact. But I didn't want Baum to know that.

"I'll take it, Harry. And if *Payback* is all you say it is, you won't hear from me again."

"The pictures," he pleaded. "What about the rest of the pictures of Vicky and me?"

"I'll put them in the shredder, Harry," I promised. I was becoming a damn good liar.

Thirty-two

My father always liked to end his show with a Johnny Mercer tune. That night, he used "You're Just Too Marvelous for Words," and directed the lyrics right at my mother. We were in a booth in the Bellagio, Mom, Terry Greco, and I. I had finally paid my mother off on the dinner I owed her.

The three of us had flown to Vegas and checked into a beautiful two-bedroom penthouse suite, compliments of the management—actually, compliments of my father. One of the perks given to the hotel's performers was the occasional room for friends. We'd had dinner right in the hotel—at Circo, an upscale Italian place with a window that looked out at the Busby Berkeley chorus line of soaring fountains in front of the Bellagio. Mom was beaming from ear to ear as Dad made his way through the tables of well-wishers. It was his last night in Vegas, and he looked fantastic in his midnight blue tuxedo, not to mention his desert suntan.

Terry rubbed her knee against mine. "His voice is so . . . romantic."

My mother had come up with numerous descriptions of my father's charms; her favorite was "Jiffy Lube," because women became moist when listening to him.

I had had more than my share of scotch, and Chianti, but it was one of those times that no matter how much you drank, you just couldn't seem to get the buzz. I was sober as a judge, except for those of the Ninth Circuit Court of Appeals, a group of scholarly legal pontiffs who held the record for having decisions overturned by the Supreme Court. Maybe that was because they worked out of San Francisco. The city did strange things to normally rational people.

Or maybe I just hadn't come down from the emotional high of finally nailing Harry Baum. After I'd left him in his office, I'd found a FedEx desk at a Kinko's right in downtown Victoria, had Vicky Vandamn's *Payback* manuscript printed, and read it on the ferry back to Vancouver, and then on the flight back to San Francisco. Four hundred and twelve pages, starting with fifty-three pages covering her early childhood in Denmark, then on to New York City and her time in Hollywood.

That's where it got interesting, and outright nasty. According to Vicky, Charles Talbot was fond of providing people he wanted to impress with the drug of their choice and pretty women, such as Vicky: "For a long time, he didn't care who I slept with, as long as I was there when he wanted me," she wrote. Talbot had put her into the beds of numerous actors, actresses, gangsters, union officials, several senators, and an unsuccessful presidential candidate. Several of the involved parties are still alive; you'd know their names, and you'd be disappointed in their behavior—as would their families and friends, and Mom definitely wouldn't approve of Vicky's behavior.

If there was a blessing in the mess, it was that Mom's name never appeared.

Payback was a soap opera, with Vicky the one covered in dirty bubbles. All that bed hopping changed after she and Talbot started seeing each other exclusively. "Was it love?" Vicky asked the reader. "I think so. Charles was having so much trouble with his drug-crazy wife, Luvina. And when I became pregnant and refused to have an abortion, he began treating me like a princess."

Willie "Freeze" Chanan made an appearance in the book. There were a couple of rooms in Talbot's Beverly Hills mansion with two-way windows, and he was fond of watching his guests in action. According to Vicky, Chanan liked threesomes: Chanan himself, a woman, and another man. All that homophobic talk from Freeze was to cover up his real lifestyle. It made me wonder about Jerome Ramsey's death. Had Jerome filmed Chanan during one of his orgies? Or had he been the other man in those twisted threesomes? I'd never know, and, truth be told, I didn't want to know. Harry Baum must have read that chapter. When I'd called him "pally," he'd said, "You perverts even talk alike."

There was a full chapter on the birth and death of her child. Vicky had gone to the grave without knowing the boy had lived. She broke down into literary tears when describing what her life was like after the baby died: "Charles wanted me out of his life—out of America. He made arrangements for me to go to Italy. I can't say he wasn't generous, but I received only half of the money. Johnny Sands, who I thought was a friend, threatened to kill me if I didn't turn over half of it to him— and I believed Johnny." There were several paragraphs about Sands and the types of errands he did for Talbot: beatings, arm breaking, and an arson fire at a competing studio. "Johnny flew me to Italy. He told me he had friends there and that if I ever left, he'd know about it, and he'd kill me. Again, I believed him."

The next chapter went into excruciating detail about her life in Italy, a major comedown from her Hollywood days. She'd lived in the town of Tarvisio. "I wasn't cut out for the dull life of an Italian house-wife, but Donello was good to me." Donello, I learned, owned a small factory that turned out window shutters.

"When I heard of Johnny Sands's death, it was as if a stone had been lifted from my heart, and I came back to America, to Hollywood, only to find that there was no real Hollywood anymore."

More sob-saga pages, then the remaining pages told of her decision to go to Victoria and see Arnold Ramsey: "My true love's brother. Arnold was no Jerome, but he was rich and sweet."

The rest of her rocky voyage through life had gone into Harry Baum's shredder.

Once I'd gotten back to San Francisco, I'd had to make a decision about the book. As tasteless and badly written as it was, Sir Charles Tal-bot would still probably pay me the promised $100,000 for it. But then he would know that I'd read it and, in doing so, knew his dirty little secrets. He wouldn't like that, and a man like Talbot wouldn't have a hard time finding a modern-day Johnny Sands to silence me. And then there was a worry about just how much of everything Vicky had written was true. Her life on the page painted a much different picture than the one my mother had given me of her. She seemed to become more bitter with the turning of each page. Certainly no legitimate publisher would touch the thing—if it saw the light of day, it would have to be through a vanity press, like the one Vicky had contacted. After a great debate with myself, and the legal advice from a few Jack Daniel's, the printout had gone into the shredder and I'd destroyed the disc.

I'd recorded my conversation with Harry Baum on one of Josh Hinkley's gadgets, a digital recorder and MP3 player with 128 MB of internal memory (whatever that means), all housed in an ordinary-appearing ballpoint pen. Fifteen years ago, James Bond could have used the damn thing in one of his flicks and the audience would have oohed and aahed. Now, according to Josh, you could order them online for twenty bucks, and the damn things write just fine, too.

Before meeting with Detective Manners, I'd made contact with Katherine Parkham. She'd been impressed enough to fly back to the city and discuss everything in detail with Mark Selden and me.

Selden had gone through his usual one foot to the other foot legal gyrations, but he'd finally determined that the *Bulletin* was not in any "litigation posture from Quint's juvenile behavior."

There'd been a lot of discussion about the *Payback* disc. I had given Parkham a brief description of the contents prior to the meeting.

"The police will never believe that you destroyed it," Selden had predicted.

"So what?" Parkham had countered. "We're handing them Harry Baum on a silver platter. They'll get a killer, and we'll have a hell of a story. We can spread this one out for a month." She'd given me one of her frozen glares. "You *did* destroy it, right, Quint?"

So the pen recorder and the money from Baum had been presented to Detective Manners. You'd think she'd have been happy, but no way.

There'd been meetings with the Sausalito city attorney, the Marin County district attorney's office, and Lieutenant Candella of the Marin County sheriff's department. Candella was the guy Manners had had a turf battle with the night Ronald Maleuw's body was found on the beach.

Candella had turned out to be the pick of the litter. While the others were inventing new ways to cover their butts, he'd put everything in perspective: "This jerk Baum killed someone in our territory. Let's fry him."

The possibility of Harry Baum actually frying was pretty remote, since there was no death penalty in Canada and there was a problem regarding extradition, but Baum had been officially charged with a homicide, and the Canadians were looking into his legal shenanigans and the death of Arnold Ramsey. All of this attention had hit Baum pretty hard. He'd suffered a heart attack, and was in intensive care at a Victoria hospital. So maybe he would fry, when he got to Motel Eternity, as Mr. Chanan might have said.

"You ladies look beautiful," Dad said when he slid into the booth after the show. He was right. Mom was wearing a shimmering red sequined outfit, and Terry had on one of those little black dresses with a plunging neckline. Las Vegas had an odd dress code nowadays. About a third of the women in the lounge were dolled up like Mom and Terry; the rest looked like they'd purchased their clothes at a Wal-Mart warehouse sale; and the majority of the men in the audience were decked out in sports jerseys and gimme caps.

Dad wedged his way between Mom and Terry and passed out hugs and kisses.

"You were wonderful," Terry purred enthusiastically

"Thanks. Anyone feel like a little barhopping? I want to stop at Steve Winn's place—they want to book me later in the year—and I know some downtown jazz joints that are really good."

The idea seemed to perk Mom up. Then I felt two feet kicking at my knees, and she said, "I bet you youngsters have other plans."

Both feet made contact with me again. "Yeah, I'm kind of tired, and Terry wanted to do a little gambling."

291

"No problem. Come on, Karen, we'll do the Strip first."

We walked through the casino together, and my dad pulled me aside. "Is your suite all right?"

"Fine, Pop."

"All the food and booze is comp here at the Bellagio, so just sign for it, and enjoy yourself." He looked anxiously over at the ladies, then swiveled around so that he blocked their view of me. "Ah, I'm a little short on cash right now. I'll get paid tomorrow, but can you duke me a few hundred for cab fare until we get back home?"

I took out my money clip and gave him most of what was there. He pocketed the money and patted my shoulder in appreciation. "This is a tough town to work in, son. Stay away from the tables."

Terry watched the two of them walk off arm in arm. "They're so *right* together. Do you think that they might ever get back . . ."

Her voice trailed off as she saw a drop-dead-gorgeous red-haired woman with showgirl legs race up to my father and whisper something in his ear.

Dad broke away from the redhead in the wispy blue dress, said something that made her frown, then grabbed Mom by the elbow and steered her toward the main exit.

"Was that you kicking me under the table with *both* your feet, Terry?"

"No, just one. The other must have belonged to your mother. She made it obvious to me in the powder room that when the show was finished, we should go our separate ways."

"Let's separate up to our suite."

"I want to do some gambling first," she protested. "Let's try the roulette table. I've got a system."

"A system? Why didn't you tell me that earlier? These places send private jets for people with systems, Terry."

"Don't be a dork," she said, pouting prettily. "Just a hundred dollars, and if we lose that, we'll quit."

The hundred dollars went very fast, and then we were playing with plastic—my credit card. That money went, too.

"Exactly where did you get this roulette system of yours?" I asked her as we took the elevator back to our suite with all of that free food, booze, and a Jacuzzi built for two.

"I knew a blackjack dealer in Reno."

"*Knew?* As in dated?"

The elevator stopped at our floor. We headed down the hallway hand in hand. Be careful what you do in those hallways. They're all monitored twenty-four hours a day. Thankfully, the video surveillance ends once you're in your room. Or so they say.

"He was an old man," Terry said. "His wife had run away with all of his money. He'd lost a lung from so much smoking, one leg was shorter than the other, the result of a car crash, and he was blind in one eye. But he was a really sweet guy."

Her eyes were twinkling, so I was ready with the punch line as I slipped the plastic key card into the door of the suite. "Really? Let me guess. His name was Lucky."

Terry slapped me lightly on my chin as she edged by me. "Wise guy. That's a name no one's going to be calling you in the morning."

She ran through the living area, heading toward the room with the Jacuzzi. She was wrong. I was feeling very lucky.